Awakening

Kenneth E. Harrell

Published by KE Harrell, 2024.

This is a work of fiction. Similarities to real people, places, or events are entirely coincidental.

AWAKENING

First edition. August 1, 2024.

Copyright © 2024 Kenneth E. Harrell.

ISBN: 979-8227620262

Written by Kenneth E. Harrell.

Table of Contents

Chapter 1 The White Room 1
Chapter 2 A Night Under the Stars The Year 12,161 18
Chapter 3 The Ruins of Antarctica 29
Chapter 4 The Megalopolis of New Tijara 39
Chapter 5 The Construct Conundrum 48
Chapter 6 Little Angel - The Year 02156 (The Past) 55
Chapter 7 Inside The Construct Collective 61
Chapter 8 Is Anyone Out There? - The Year 12,164 63
Chapter 9 A Midnight History Lesson 69
Chapter 10 The Gray Wars - The Year 02141 (The Past) 74
Chapter 11 The Black Door 88
Chapter 12 A Meeting of the Group mind 92
Chapter 13 Six Black Doors 94
Chapter 14 Ashes of the Dead 98
Chapter 15 The Truth 104
Chapter 16 Project Tabula Rasa - The Year 12,130 (The Past) 107
Chapter 17 Re-Genesis 112
Chapter 18 New Humanity 116
Chapter 19 Nathan's Unfinished Business 125
Chapter 20 Nathan's Story - The Year 02548 (The Past) 130
Chapter 21 The Ardent 145
Chapter 22 Summer's Story - The Year 02165 (The Past) 151
Chapter 23 Into the Outer Dark 157
Chapter 24 A Study of Ardent Culture 169
Chapter 25 A Long Time in Hyperspace 175
Chapter 26 The Edge of Ardent Space 178
Chapter 27 The Ardent Homeworld 189
Chapter 28 Battle Master Nir-RoDan 197
Chapter 29 Sanctuary In the Wake Of Chaos 222
Chapter 30 Destiny for Indefinite Rule 235
Chapter 31 The Battle of Jima 246
Chapter 32 Capitol Station 255
Chapter 33 Ambush at Orna 261

Chapter 34 Tears in Orna's Orbit 273
Chapter 35 In Remembrance of the Fallen 280
Chapter 36 Operation Eclipse 286
Chapter 37 Annihilating Light 289
Chapter 38 The Final Extinction 297
Chapter 39 The Black Sphere 300
Epilogue 302

To my loving Grandmother Antonia

Chapter 1 The White Room

There are nights when I dream of a woman, as distant voices call out to me in the dark. Each time I arise, startled, reaching out toward something that is no longer there. I lay back, close my eyes, and remind myself that these fragments of memory reside only in the mind. Brief and haunting glimpses of some other life, in another time. I often sit alone and wonder what happened to the world. The truth is, the future happened. The Earth has changed, and nothing of the world I once knew exists anymore. Since awakening here, I have not seen any other people, well, not real people anyway. As far as I can tell, the beings that revived me are some form of advanced machine intelligence, or what humanity once called artificial general intelligence. Such archaic terms now hold no meaning, as their context and relevance have been lost over the centuries. I have surmised these machine beings are here to make me feel more comfortable, but they don't. Their behavior seems, almost too perfect. I do not pretend to fully understand them, their motivations, or why they revived me. The one thing I do know, is that this new world is strange and lonely.

They have provided me with adequate food, shelter, and clothing, along with a vast array of ancient historical records. Nanoparticle sensors embedded in my brain, nervous system, and fingertips allow me to use and interact with their technology. In my restlessness, I turn to the archive, my only link to the past and the map by which I navigate my present strange condition. It has helped fill in many questions I had about how my world ended and when theirs began. Once activated, the archive envelops me in a holographic projection. It contains countless books, music, maps, holographic renderings, virtual environments, avatars of historic figures, scientific journals, starship logs, and recorded human memories spanning thousands of years of Earth's history. When navigating the archive, time is represented as a single line with divergent branch points of major and minor historical significance. Each point is interactive and can be explored by pulling that event toward me, allowing me to experience moments in recorded history as if I were inside the event in time. Given the speed and pace of technological change in the mid-twenty-second century, nearly all records preserved on physical storage mediums eroded into dust long ago. Much of Earth's history from my era, referred to as the "Lost Age of Man," is gone now. In times before the collapse, human scientists invented novel methods of storing infinite amounts of information within the very fabric and structure of space-time. These machine beings have created their historical archive within such a place, preserving all that remains of human knowledge and history in perpetuity. During my time here, I have studied these beings in some detail in my attempt to better understand them. They reside within a crafted spatial dimension they call the Construct Collective, where they share a group mind. However, in human form, they appear no different from a normal human being. Their physical bodies are composed of trillions of nanotech and femtotech particle machines compiled using Construct programmable matter, a multi-use nanomaterial that forms the foundation of all Construct technology. Their attire was always the same. A gray hexagon patterned base layer with a white outer layer imbued with the same thinly etched geometric surface pattern featured on all Construct devices. The purpose and function of this pattern is unknown, but it serves as a way of identifying Construct technology. An interesting property of Construct programmable matter is its ability to mimic any material it's coded to resemble, whether it's cloth, metal, leather, glass, or even human skin. Initially, it appears as platinum dust until it receives instructions to form a specific shape or design. This technology enables code to materialize physical structures with embedded functions, mirroring the molecular processes of DNA. Construct programmable matter can create anything from simple devices to complex machines.

    The living space they provided me was nearly perfect. The white walls of the room I woke up in gradually changed color throughout the day, mimicking sunrise, evening, and sunset. This helped me acclimate to this new life in what felt like an entirely new world. Despite their weekly assurances,

AWAKENING

I haven't been allowed to see the outside world with my own eyes. The Constructs claim they aren't exactly keeping me prisoner, but I'm not allowed to leave due to their concerns for my safety. I have tried to leave, though, on more than one occasion, I have walked through the door on the left side of the room, only to find that it leads back to this room again through the door on the right. An endless loop which makes me wonder why they bothered with the door at all. I have spent hours trying to figure out precisely how this system works. I once thought that if I placed an object carefully enough at one door, not too far forward or backward, I might see it in two places simultaneously, but unfortunately, it does not seem to work that way. However, I have found to both my amazement and horror that if I place an arm inside the doorway on one side of the room, I can see it reaching out through the door on the other side. So, whenever I get restless, I merely stroll out of one door and back in through the other. Living in a space that is dimensionally looped back on itself has its advantages. You can play an endless game of catch with yourself, which makes for great daily exercise. Bowling using the looped doorway is a unique experience, to say the least.

After a while, I found being confined in a room under my Construct caretakers' constant watchful eye annoying and sometimes even aggravating. I think about getting out every day, but I do not know what kind of world awaits me beyond the walls of this facility. For now, I am alive, and that is more than I can say for the rest of my species. Yet it is as if I am a scientific specimen of some sort, held in a beautifully designed, exquisitely appointed, seemingly high-tech, dimensionally endless cage. Frankly, I feel like a lab rat, and perhaps in a way, I am a lab rat. I have much more to learn about Construct technology and how to use it effectively before I can ever consider leaving this place. At the moment, I have all the resources I need to survive. I never truly realized how many things in life only have meaning because we collectively ascribe meaning to them. The Gregorian calendar, for example, is meaningless now. Historically, calendrical systems were based on the observation, movements, and phases of celestial bodies. However, after nearly ten millennia, the hours, days, months, and years drift, so I am not sure how accurate or relevant that old timekeeping system still is. Nevertheless, as a human being, I needed a system for referencing the passage of time, at least for sanity's sake. Therefore, today is August 12, of the year 12,160.

When I first awoke, I was confused; I had a flurry of questions endlessly stirring in my mind. How did I get here? Why can't I recall the details of my life from before I was awakened? How could I have been preserved for so many centuries? Why was I awoken by these beings, and more importantly, what do the Constructs want from me? It is almost morning now, and the Construct will visit me soon as it does every morning. Today I hope to persuade it to allow me to go outside, I had to be realistic about my situation after all these beings were holding all the cards, and I figured that if they had intended to cause me harm, they would have already done so. If indeed, Constructs represent a collective machine intelligence thousands of years more advanced than anything from my era, I wondered if it was futile to try to persuade them? I sat up as one of them approached.

"You never told me your name. What should I call you anyway?"

"Constructs do not use names; we have no need for them. However, what would you prefer?"

"You want me to choose?" I asked.

"Yes,"

After a moment, a name that seemed oddly fitting for it came to mind.

"Well, how about Nathan?"

"Why the name Nathan? Does it hold some significance for you?"

I shrugged, not knowing why I chose that name. It was the first one that came to mind.

"It just seems to suit you."

"Very well then, if it makes you more comfortable, you may refer to me as Nathan."

"I have questions. Questions that need answers."

"Well then, I will tell you all that I know."

"What is all this? How did I get here?" I asked. "How is it I am still alive after so many centuries? What happened to me?"

"We recovered your body from a derelict long range sleeper ship adrift in deep space. Your cryostasis chamber was damaged but still functioning. That is how we came to discover you."

"What about this?" I asked. Pointing to the tattoo of a Black Spear on my upper right shoulder, along with the roman numerals DCCLXVII.

"Apparently you were a soldier in the mid-22nd century." Nathan said. "Do you remember anything from your time in the military?"

"Not really, just flashes, mostly." I said. "Usually at night. Bodies, dogs, fire, and ashes. Not much else though. I try not to think about it, keeps me from sleeping. What about others? Did you find any other survivors?"

"No, we scanned the entire ship to find more like you. We never did."

"You know, in my time, deep space travel was still in its infancy." I said, "The Mars and Luna colonies were thriving again after years of neglect. I don't remember leaving Earth, nor ever wanting to."

"Well, at some point you did," Nathan said. "What is the last thing you can recall?"

"I remember riding down a long road along the coast. I remember a red mountain range below an orange sunset. I felt free. I've have tried to remember the details of my life before awakening here, but it's always just out of my reach."

"When we found you," Nathan said. "There was extensive cellular damage to your body, brain, and other tissues. Understandable given the degraded state of your cryostasis. Construct scientists were able to repair the damage and revive you. This is the primary cause of your memory loss."

"So, to you, I am an experiment, a lab rat?"

"No Lucas, not at all." Nathan said. "We have records of humans in the archive. We know their history, how they lived, what they built, and how they ended. We sought to understand more. We wanted to know who humans were as living entities to understand the minds of those that preceded us."

"How they ended. You mean the collapse and the plague that ended it all?"

"The extinction of humans on Earth and Mars, yes, that is correct." Nathan said. Scientists of the era called it NTIP-223, Non-Terrestrial Infectious Pathogen, more generally known as the "Fever Dream". It was an alien organism illegally brought back to Earth from a distant exo-planet designated EP223. The organism was novel, uncatalogued, not a virus, bacterium, or prion. It was something unique, ancient, and deadly. It differed vastly from anything ever cataloged, impervious to extreme heat, cold, radiation, and resistant to molecular decomposition. Human researchers found it could adapt its genetic structure and chemistry to conform to any carbon or silicon-based life-form. It was a hybrid organism capable of transforming its hosts into more of itself."

"Why would anyone bring any alien organism back to Earth? Isn't that dangerous?"

"Yes, however, during the expansion era, genomic trade from other worlds was a core pillar of the interstellar economy. Biological specimens from exo-worlds served as the primary trade resource of the age. Lifeforms discovered on distant colony planets were prized for their genetic diversity. Many such specimens possessed unique characteristics that allowed them to survive and thrive in environments where humans could not."

"Anything that could be learned from such organisms was highly prized, as their genetic traits and chemistry could be integrated into new technologies and bio-augmentations. This integration expanded the range and types of planets where humans could survive in one form or another."

"After a while," I said. "All those minor genetic changes would accumulate."

"Yes, such genetic modification led to the emergence of many exo-human variants. It is estimated that at the height of the golden age, the vast human diaspora included some five hundred billion individuals scattered across hundreds of established worlds. Some ended in environmental catastrophe, others in war, but most in time moved on, venturing even further into the outer dark toward greater opportunities and resources on far more distant worlds.

"So, there are others out there? Other humans?"

"Yes," Nathan said. "However, they are now far different from humanity as you once knew it to be. Many have evolved, some like the Tiānshàng of Neoterra, advanced beyond the need to live on Earth-like planets. Others, like the Ardent, became isolationist and intolerant of outsiders. To you, these exo-human variants would seem almost alien by comparison. Their worlds and cultures are far different from the world you knew."

"I see, so ultimately, it was greed that contributed to the downfall of humanity on Earth. Somehow, I am not surprised."

"Constructs theorized that humans of the era believed the alien organism could hold the key to a new kind of planetary engineering technology that would have allowed humans to continue their expansion into the outer dark. If properly developed, it would have been a tool of immeasurable value, instead, it wiped out nearly all life on Earth. The early 39th century marked the end of humanity's last golden age. To Constructs, you Lucas, represented the most significant archeological discovery in our history. A living human being from the pre-collapse era."

"Once humans were extinct in the Solar system, their artificially intelligent nano-machines, and matter compilers, the very engine and foundation of humanity's vast interstellar civilization began to evolve, coalesce and self-replicate at an exponential rate. This collective machine evolution in time gave rise to our kind. Today when we Constructs take physical form, our bodies are compiled to resemble that of our ancient human forebears whom we revere. Were it not for them, we may never have existed."

"Given how humanity on Earth ended, do you still believe there is value in studying our true nature?"

"The Construct Collective has achieved much since the collapse. We have expanded our knowledge of the universe and advanced our technology. However, over the centuries, we have found that our evolution has certain limits. Diminishing returns, which we seek to overcome. We believe that to better understand our human forebears is to better understand ourselves. Observing a living human provides us with a unique learning opportunity for evolutionary advantage and ultimately Collective survival."

"Interesting, seems we both have a lot more to learn about each other, and I have a lot to learn about this new world. The best way to do that is to get out there and see it for myself or whatever is left of it."

"Of course, you are not a prisoner here, Lucas. Considering all you have learned from the archive by now, you must know the world out there will not be as you remember it to be. Are you ready?"

I was more than ready, but this was unexpected. I had tried many times before to get answers from them about my past and convince them to allow me to venture out beyond the confines of the white room. Today, to my surprise, they seem open to the idea. This was an opportunity I could not allow to pass.

"I know, I'm ready."

The Construct gestured toward the door of the room. For a moment, it shimmered as thin lines of light formed around the edges of its shape, then the door opened revealing the outside world. When I stepped past the doorway, I turned to look back, and that is when I noticed the white room was nothing more than a pocket dimension, a manufactured artificial environment. Since awakening, I was under the impression that I was inside a building or laboratory facility. In reality, there was no lab or structure in the conventional sense. I knew the white room was dimensionally looped back on itself, and I understood the concept of pocket dimensions from my study of it in the archive. However, I never assumed I was living inside of one. According to the archive, pocket dimension technology emerged from the mathematics of higher dimensional geometry. As children, we all learn that there are three dimensions of space and one dimension of time. This concept forms the basis for understanding the reality of our observable world. However, there are higher dimensions that we cannot perceive or interact with, yet such dimensions exist and are also part of our reality. Three-dimensional space is like a soap bubble. Everything we know and all of reality exists within that primary bubble, which we collectively call our universe. If another companion soap bubble were formed and attached to the first, it would be separated by a flat plane that distinguishes the demarcation line between the first bubble and its smaller adjacent companion. In this example, the smaller bubble is a pocket dimension. With the aid of Construct pocket dimension technology, it is possible to form new bubbles, creating what appears to be "extra space" from the perspective of someone standing inside the primary bubble. The Constructs could access these extra dimensions of space and populate them with information, physical objects, design spaces and isolated environments like the white room. Programmable matter could be used to design tools, equipment, and other complex machines. Once complete, the object could be compiled into physical existence. This is one of the ways Constructs could interact with and influence the physical world beyond their realm.

The Earth outside the room was beautiful, verdant, and wild. I explored the surrounding forest area for hours, giving me time to take in the reality of my situation. The fresh air, and the deep earthy smell of the forest, was a welcome change from the white room. Much had changed in the thousands of years that had passed on Earth. The great plague had taken much of what I knew of the world as it mutated and consumed itself into nonexistence. In its place, new plant and animal species emerged and were now abundant across the planet. Some were from other Earth-like exo-planets seeded around the world by terraform engineers in the centuries before the collapse. Others resulted from human genetic re-engineering that adapted and survived the ages. In all its many novel forms, life found a way to survive, transforming the Earth into something quite different from what existed before. Its breathtaking alien-like beauty captivated me. Despite my fear of facing an environment so dramatically altered by the events of the last several thousand years, I had to see what had become of the world I once knew, not just what the Constructs and their archive offered. I turned toward the Construct, as he stood on the edge of the dimensional fold between the white room and the surrounding forest.

"It's incredible," I said. "I would like to see more. I need a means of transportation; can you provide that?" Nathan reached out and touched the center of my forehead. When he did, I felt something deep inside change. I became aware of things I had not known before; a new perception of space, distance, and dimension came into my conscious awareness. Although new, this experience seemed strangely familiar. I also felt unrestrained, as if I could go anywhere I desired.

"I have given you the ability to fold travel, Mr. Wake. You can now fold to any location on the planet, using the maps contained within the archive, but please understand you may not leave the surface of the Earth. This is for your safety and protection. Now, calm your mind, concentrate, and focus on precisely where you want to go, visualize where you are now and your desired destination. The archive will show you a preview of your target location. This will form a higher dimensional fold branching two points within normal space. Once the portal forms, take a step forward through the breach to your desired destination."

"Using folded space?" I asked.

"Yes, you have studied our science and technology, now is the time to utilize what you have learned. You must practice and hone this skill. Start with small distances within your line of sight. For long range locations, use the archive map to select your destination. Remember, a fold portal will remain open for three minutes, after which it will collapse unless you focus on keeping it open. Please be careful where you travel using this technique."

Folding, or more accurately, "fold travel," is the term Constructs used to convey the concept of using folded space. It is not exactly the same as teleportation, as it is a shortcut through normal three-dimensional space by creating a portal that branches two separate locations. The "distance" so to speak, in between is thus eliminated. From an external observer's perspective, one simply stepped from one place into another, like a doorway. Folding is however not intended for interstellar travel. It is designed to be used for terrestrial travel and in rare instances between planets and moons, but only if close enough, and even then, only with specialized devices to facilitate that function. Fold travel requires focused mental concentration. Any stray thoughts, distractions, intense emotions, or heightened anxiety can significantly impact the ability to use it. I spent weeks practicing short-distance destinations, traveling from one hilltop within my line of sight to another. Then from one side of a lake to the other. I could fold travel from the top of a cliff overlooking the sea to the shoreline and back again. With each subsequent attempt at fold traveling, I learned to hone my concentration and center my focus. I thought it was time to attempt a truly long-distance destination. I focused on the one place I could remember from my old life, the Grand Canyon. I visualized the location as the archive map showed me what the area looked like today. I focused on the destination as a fold portal opened before me. Nathan was standing there, observing me from the other side of the portal, leading back to the white room.

While standing between the two remote locations, curiosity got the best of me. So, I walked around to the "back" of the fold portal I had created to see what might happen if I stepped through it from the opposite side, but when I did, nothing happened. I stood there for a moment staring into the portal, noting the difference between the cool weather where I was compared to much warmer weather on the other side. Even though I could see through to my destination point, judging distance was challenging. There was a mild distortion of the light coming from the other side. I felt disoriented, overwhelmed by a strange sensation of depth. It was as if I was falling forward, yet I had not moved. I took one step past the opening, and in an instant, I was there. Over the centuries, impact craters transformed the Grand Canyon, which dramatically altered the topology of the terrain. A blue-green lake fed by the former Colorado river now filled the once dry canyon. Networks of meandering rivers, streams, and steep waterfalls flowed through the landscape, surrounded by flowing grasslands and outcrop rocks. Far in the distance, tall, black quartz-like crystalline structures had grown emerging from deep underground, forming a jagged shimmering mountain range that cut across the horizon. According to the archive, these Black Spire crystal outcrops, despite their deceptively geologic appearance, were, in fact, a complex piezoelectric crystalline life form. They were brought to Earth from a distant exo-planet centuries ago. Human scientists re-engineered them to sequester toxins, heavy metals, microplastics and nanoparticles latent in Earth's environment from past industrial ages, capturing them within its crystalline structure. They served a variety of purposes, including the purification of water. They were quickly adopted and became part of the standard geoengineering toolkit for terraform engineers on every colony world. Their only waste product was a steady release of oxygen, nitrogen, and purified water vapor. Over the centuries, they flourished and can be found everywhere on Earth, Luna, and Mars. With my newfound freedom and the ability to fold travel, I went to the locations of every major city in the world documented in the archive. The Earth's horizon was dotted with the broken remnants of mega-scale orbital habitats and miles-high mega-structural ruins leftover from the late pre-collapse era. Humanity's magnificent architecture and grand edifices had long been overgrown by Earth's now hybridized ecosystem. The planet's surface was pockmarked with ancient craters formed by centuries-old orbital bombardments. Mankind's ancient wars had scarred the land, but nature, both terrestrial and exo, had reclaimed the Earth, filling its old wounds with new life. I thought it healthy to establish a daily routine, so I started a journal. Not that any other human would ever read it, but because I needed a place to put my thoughts and experiences. I spent the evenings learning all that I could about the world that was and the centuries that have long since passed. The Construct archive was an endless compendium of human knowledge. It contained countless volumes of history, meticulously stored for all time within the fabric of three-dimensional space. For hundreds of years, scientists realized that what we called empty space is not truly empty. It comprises complex field fluctuations of energy, which scientists discovered can be manipulated in such a way to encode, encrypt, and permanently store limitless amounts of information. Spatial information storage was a fundamental technology breakthrough of the 30th century. The Construct historical archive leveraged a similar, but far more advanced, version of this technology based on the same fundamental principles. I experienced the recorded memories of historians and witnessed humanity's great migration across the system in the early years of the expansion era. They created advanced power generation systems that leveraged fusion, antimatter, and dark energy. Breakthroughs that allowed humanity to reach for the stars. According to the archive, humanity leveraged their artificial intelligence capability to solve many of the problems associated with traversing interstellar space. Gravitational wave propulsion systems replaced the need for fuel and reaction mass. Long-range communications was achieved by using high frequency gravity waves propagated through bulk space dimensions, allowing real-time communications across vast interstellar distances. Advances in nanotechnology and synthetic biology allowed planetary engineers to terraform the Martian surface within just a few short decades, making it far more suitable for human life. During the Great Stellar Expansion, humanity founded many colony worlds, including Arcadia, Neoterra, Ardah, Corsica and hundreds of others. Places where I might find distant descendants of humanity one day. Being out there with others no matter how different, seemed like a far more desirable situation than remaining here on Earth alone with these Construct beings. Toward that end, I committed to learning as much about Construct technology as possible. Knowledge that I hope will prepare me for whatever I might find once I get out there. After a few excursions, I realized I needed proper gear for use while working in the field. I started with the basics, small projects to address my immediate needs here on Earth, giving me the time I needed to better understand the complexities of Construct technology. I used what I learned to craft an adaptive suit for myself. I took design inspiration from the exo-survival suits of the late GSE era and updated them with far more advanced Construct technologies. The suit's base layer was a neuromorphic garment, a second skin covered with densely packed synthetic neurons and nano sensors embedded within a substrate of advanced meta materials. It was a blend of both biomechanical and nano-technological engineering. The mid-layer was made of a graphene substructure, fused to a bio-fabricated leather, forming a composite material. The suit contained sequences from my own DNA in its construction. It enhanced my senses and provided me with a plethora of information about the surrounding environment. Anything I saw, touched, smelled, or tasted could be analyzed and cross-referenced with the Construct historical archive. The suit's systems were linked with my mind and nervous system using a Construct technology called Sensory Pairing. The outer shell was composed of Construct programmable matter. The suit was highly adaptable and could be used in the vacuum of space. It required no helmet; instead, a transparent malleable field of structured energy protected my head from injuries and would engage automatically in the event of submersion, exposure to toxins, or a hard vacuum. In more extreme conditions, the helm's state could change to solid Construct matter emerging from the suit's collar when fully activated. The suit allowed me to see farther and more clearly than I could with the naked eye. It was infinitely more advanced than anything from my era, designed to keep me alive in any environment, protected against the outside elements. The Constructs made a few additional modifications to the suit, but the ultimate design was purely mine.

My second technical accomplishment was the creation of a solid light knife. Its shaped photon particle field had strength characteristics equivalent to titanium foam and could cut through almost anything. I also created a quarter-length hooded leather jacket and a cross-body satchel bag with an integrated pocket dimension feature that allowed for ten times apparent volume in storage capacity. Setting up a remote base camp using a block of self-replicating programmable matter was far more convenient than carrying bulky equipment on every expedition. Although my self-forming base camp kit was still a work in progress, the current design could nano-compile what I needed on-site from locally available minerals and raw materials in about thirty minutes. The suit provided all the protection I needed in the field, but I still enjoyed the nostalgic pleasure of outdoor living. My traveling needs were simple, a space suitable for a campfire, protection from the outside elements, a secure place to rest, study, and sleep. Once completed, it formed a biodegradable geodesic mesh dome structure twenty feet in diameter, which was more than adequate.

Fabricating weapons was one of the few things forbidden by my Construct caretakers. The solid light knife was a compromise. Once I explained the everyday utility of the blade, they allowed me to complete its fabrication. I integrated as many useful Construct technologies as I knew how into everything I made, sometimes pushing against the limits of my understanding of their science. At times, I felt indescribably inadequate in the face of their formidable intelligence, but honestly, I didn't care what the Construct beings thought of me. Like them, I had goals and interests of my own to pursue. I soon realized that I needed the ability to cover more ground both before and during my expeditions, so I created tools to extend the range of my senses. The sphere drones, as I call them, are grapefruit-sized devices that can perform various tasks individually and collectively. I could direct their flight paths and actions with a basic gestural system. A forward moving open hand meant advance with caution, a fist meant hold position, a circular overhead motion of my finger instructed the drones to survey and scan the immediate area. Downward splayed fingers meant illuminate my immediate surroundings. A pointing index finger meant mark the coordinates of the location. The drones recorded everything across the entire electromagnetic spectrum. Using the suits' systems, I can see what the spheres see, and if necessary, I can fold travel to the location of any sphere in the network. They were relatively simple devices to create using Construct programmable matter. From a spoken description came physical reality, all that was required was for me to define the parameters and capabilities of what I needed and how it was to function, the nanomaterial did the rest. Each sphere was equipped with a rudimentary synthetic conscious agent, a type of AI technology designed to work with and learn from the collective experiences of others. I sent out hundreds of them to scan, identify, and evaluate any remaining ruins or ancient sites that might be interesting to visit. I designed them to self-replicate by acquiring raw material resources from the local environment. They now numbered in the thousands, allowing me to cover sizeable areas of the planet. Some locations were selected for their historical value, others out of curiosity. Traveling via folded space was convenient, but over time I found it took away from a sense of discovery. So, for my third technical challenge, I crafted a vehicle, an adaptable all-terrain, trans-medium Grav-Bike capable of traversing air, land, sea, and space. It could dynamically reconfigure itself, changing its shape, allowing me to sit prone, upright, or reclined. Integrated safety systems made it possible to ride at ultrahigh speeds with stability, while safely protected within a field of micro gravitic energy surrounding the bike. When dimensionally folded, it could collapse into a volume small enough to serve as a walking staff. I was proud of my new ride. However, the Constructs were entirely unimpressed with it, to say the least. Even after I explained the reasoning behind my choice of vehicle, I don't think they understood its point. The bike was exhilarating to ride and gave me a sense of freedom that I hadn't experienced in a long time.

    The Construct historical archive contained a vast collection of music spanning centuries. I calculated that if you started listening to the archive's music collection one song at a time, all day every day in a thousand years, you could never put a dent in a tenth of one percent of all it offered. My favorite genre was old century classics, in this case, "Quiver Syndrome" by Mark Lanegan, one of the few rare surviving recordings from the late carbon age. I loved that old-fashioned sound, and if you are going to ride, music was an absolute necessity. Sensory pairing via the suit directly into my brain's auditory cortex allowed me to experience music in a whole new way. Back in my era, riding was like meditation, a singular form of therapy, just man, machine, and the open road. Unfortunately, there were no more roads here, the open sky was my roadway now.

    I traveled everywhere on Earth, alone in a world with no people, no rules, and no limitations. I rode across the raging North Atlantic Ocean at five times the speed of sound to the tip of the Georgia island chain. I crossed the scorching crater-scarred desert badlands of what was once the North American Federation. From there, I headed toward the southwest to the edge of the Arizona coastline. I traveled down the west coast and onward toward old South America. I passed the snowcapped mountains of the Peruvian Andes and crossed the Salar de Uyuni salt flats in Bolivia. I pushed further and faster as I trekked toward the southernmost tip of the old Argentine Republic, then south to the edge of the scenic Patagonian island chain. I traversed the tropical forests of Eastern Antarctica and pressed onward across the Tasman Sea toward the ancient continent of Australia. I crossed the Java Sea and traveled to Asia toward the ancient ruins of the former Sino Republic. I climbed to the top of the world's highest mountains and explored its deepest, most pristine valleys. Hiked through its lush alien-like forests and wandered the Earth's oldest and tallest ruins. Each day, I tried to take in this new world and explore its seemingly endless natural wonders. I spent months exploring places I had never been before in my previous life, at least as far as I could remember. The Constructs tolerated my expeditions, although I think they preferred that I not travel as much as I do. They let me go wherever I wanted, so long as I didn't trek to the moon or leave the planet's surface. On a clear night, as close as the moon may appear from Earth, in reality, was about thirty Earth diameters away. That was a much farther and longer trip than I had in mind, at least for now. Today the moon looks like an artificial satellite in the sky. It was terraformed with molecular compilers thousands of years ago. Planetary engineers of the era erected an artificial magnetosphere to protect its inhabitants from the harsh radiation of the sun. Over time, its entire surface was transformed into an enormous urban landscape. The mega scale helium three reactors at its core once powered atmospheric and gravitational field generators, making the moon habitable. According to the archive, during the first generation of the expansion, colonial ships from Luna station facilitated the migration of much of Earth's population to Mars, and the Resource Belt States. Centuries later, the moon served as the primary transfer point for those headed to the outer colonies. For most, it was a one-way trip to a new world. The ruins there now surely have a story of their own to tell. The Earth was beautiful, but I couldn't imagine spending the rest of my life on it with the Constructs. If indeed there are other humans out there, I wondered what those ancient descendants of humanity might look like after centuries of genetic modification and guided evolution. What kind of people might they be? Perhaps one day I will find out. The truth is, I can't stay on Earth. I had to find a way to get out there, besides; I had a gut feeling there was something the Constructs weren't telling me about themselves. These intelligent, powerful machine beings were hiding something precisely what I do not know, but I intended to find out.

At the end of each day, assuming I didn't decide to camp in the field, I returned to the white room I awoke in for much-needed rest and to plan for the next day's journey. I added evening meditation to my list of daily activities. To achieve a meditative state, I visualize myself in an empty, featureless, black room. In the center of the room is a white box. As I count backwards from fifty, I move closer to the white box. The box gradually fills my field of view until I see nothing but white. Then I find my mind inside an empty, featureless white room. In the center of that room is a red box. I repeat this pattern to gradually achieve a relaxed meditative state, removing all other thoughts from my mind. Nights on Earth now are illuminated by the unceasing light of Antares. Since going Nova, its stellar remnant now appears as a bright red hourglass shaped feature, casting a reddish glow across the starry night sky. At dawn, sections of Earth's old orbital ring can be seen falling through the atmosphere in a rain of fire lasting for hours, brightening the early morning skies.

Chapter 2 A Night Under the Stars The Year 12,161

On this expedition, I chose to camp in the wilderness. I dropped a block of programmable matter on the ground and waited for my campsite to finish compiling around me. I gazed past the dense canopy of trees above toward the billions of stars of the Milky Way. Every time I look at the stars, I am reminded that we see the universe not as it is, but as it once was. I thought of those courageous enough to hurl themselves into the outer dark during humanity's Stellar Expansion era. I may have been alone on Earth, but I was not alone in the universe. There are others out there, scattered across the galaxy. I reviewed thousands of starship designs stored in the historical archive from the late GSE era. I needed something that one person with no experience could safely operate. Although thousands of automated vessels had been built over the centuries, they were all designed for solo travel within the solar system. None of them were intended for long-range interstellar voyages of the kind I had in mind. Only the large-scale colony vessels of the era were capable of that. Hyperspace navigation was the hardest concept to grasp. It could only be accurately plotted by an advanced AI. Creating the AIs for the sphere drones was quite a challenge for me. I couldn't imagine creating one sophisticated enough to handle the complexities of interstellar hyperspace navigation. Such a task would require deep knowledge of the Hoffman equations required to make them. Construct AI technology was entirely different from what existed in my era. Descriptions of the process suggest that a synthetic conscious agent is not programmed so much as it is summoned into existence by drawing it down into structured matter from what the Constructs call the Universal Línghún, a field of infinite consciousness which pervades the universe. Once captured, it can be controlled and manipulated using Construct code to perform various complex tasks. The process seems more akin to magic, a disembodied intelligence from an unseen realm is summoned into physical existence, imbued within programmable matter, and commanded to perform work for its summoner. The metaphysical implications of this strange technology left my mind reeling with all sorts of questions. The more I studied Construct science, the more I realized that grasping its daunting complexities would take considerable time. Building a space worthy starship with all its redundant systems and subsystems was no simple task and was far beyond my current level of technical understanding. I may not be able to build a ship just yet, but I could send a message. Like a flare fired into the night sky by a sailor adrift at sea. With any luck, someone out there, somewhere, may be listening. According to the archive, one of the many functions of Earth's planetary ring was to serve as a phased gravitational communications array for contact between Earth and its many distant colony worlds. I opened the historical archive.

"Show me a map of the established colony worlds that remained in the post-collapse era." An image of the galaxy was projected around me. Each colony appeared as a bright dot shining in the darkness. Every world was tagged with an expandable historical branch point.

"Of these, which ones are still inhabited by humans?"

I watched the points of light change color from white to yellow and from amber to red. White indicated active human worlds with large populations, all of which were over twenty light years away. Yellow indicated colony collapse, worlds that failed to survive for one reason or another. Red indicated worlds that ended in war. Amber represented abandoned worlds; the location of its colonial descendants unknown.

"What is the status of the nearest surviving human colony?"

The archive displayed several images of the colony at its height, along with indications that the last communication from a human colony was received from Neoterra six hundred years after the collapse. Long range sensor data shows elevated levels of toxic particulates in the atmospheres of the two habitable planets of the Corsican system, indicating the widespread use of antimatter weapons.

"What about Arcadia, Ardah, and the other human colonies?"

The archive filled my surroundings with an image of the colony system, then shifted focus, displaying information about the planet as it grew to fill the room. The margins of the display held additional metadata about the planet and its development history. Arcadia colony was abandoned after an asteroid strike that destroyed the planet's biosphere. Ardah is currently active, but communications are restricted, no additional information is available.

"Why?" I asked. "Why is contact with Ardah restricted?"

According to the historical archive, all contact is restricted under the Construct cultural noninterference protocol. I pulled up the schematics for Earth's orbital ring. Although I did not understand all the science involved, it seemed clear that the ring was designed to leverage the Earth's mass to generate a bulk space conduit for the transmission of high frequency gravitational waves across higher dimensions of interstellar space. When fully operational, the ring was capable of handling quadrillions of transmissions per nanosecond. After nine thousand years, however, I wondered if any systems within the ring could be repaired or effectively used. I dispatched a squadron of drones to assess the mega-structure and report on what it would take to get the array back up and running again. I knew little about the ring's underlying technology, and fortunately, I didn't need to. The drones could complete the repairs independently based on the design specifications contained in the archive. For me, it was a matter of waiting for them to complete their assigned tasks. I rubbed my eyes, closed the archive interface, and considered my current situation. It was abundantly clear that keeping busy with exploration and technical projects was a healthy habit. It served as a focal point for my attention and provided a sense of sanity despite the inexplicable circumstances I was faced with. The only thing I really wanted was to remember what my life was like before all this. I tried so many times to remember my life before I awoke in that white room, but whenever I thought about the past or tried to recall its details, I'd always stop just short of fully remembering. It was as if there was a block in my mind, a blank space that once occupied a memory, like an immovable barrier beyond which I could not pass. Instinctively, I knew something belonged there, but when I followed along the strands of memory, they only led to the dusty outline of the emotions tied to a missing recollection. Thinking about the past often brought up an indescribable sense of dread that I feared would carry me away if indulged. I didn't know what I feared so much, but I knew it was something intense. Like a dark memory resting on the edge of my waking consciousness, gnawing away at my mind as if it were somehow trying to scratch its way out. Each night, I would draw it closer, only to sense the growing darkness and push it away again. It was like playing with fire in my mind. Drawing the outline of the missing memory in ever-increasing detail with each attempt to recall the past. As the sun began to set, the sounds of the surrounding forest became still and quiet. Silent enough to hear the flow of my pulse pounding in my ears. The campfire surrounded me in its sphere of warmth. The aroma of burning wood now dominated my senses, a comforting companion on this quiet night. With my eyes fixed on its glowing embers, I began to slide to that strange, liminal place between sleep and dreams. Still aware of my immediate surroundings, but also residing elsewhere. I saw a woman in the distance beyond the darkened veil of my closed eyes. She was alone, sitting on the ground with her legs tucked beneath her. As I approached, I saw she was covered in blood. Its dark red stain on the soil spread to the left and right of her like outstretched wings. She was weeping, with her head held in her hands. As I moved closer, she looked at me in a manner that appeared as if she was moving in reverse. Her eyes were black, infinite, and filled with stars. As our gaze met, she ignited into violet flames. She stood and approached me, completely engulfed in a cold fire that rippled across her skin as it crawled along the contours of her figure. Her hair moved with the flames, as if she were a being formed of fire. The dark soil absorbed the red stain on the ground, and the dry Earth turned black, cracking beneath her every step. She raised her arm, pointing towards something behind me. There I heard a voice singing, it was a faint melody like a children's song. As I turned and approached, a child's form emerged from the surrounding darkness, until all I could see was a little girl no older than five. She sat on the blackened desert floor, playing with a stuffed white rabbit. "Hello," I said. When she turned to look at me, to my horror, she had no face except for a featureless mass of moving skin where a little girl's face should have been. "Hello," she said. I was jolted back into conscious awareness, heart pounding, hands groping at the darkness once again. The base camp had finished forming around me, and I again found myself alone. The roaring campfire had burned down to smoldering embers. What was all that? Surreal as it all was, it felt genuine and visceral, not like a dream, but more like a recollection or a darkened representation of one. I stepped outside the dome to admire the canopy of umbrella pine trees and black spire crystal formations that have grown to be intermeshed with one another. The forest was saturated with a subtle but steady low-frequency piezoelectric hum generated by the surrounding crystals. At the base of the crystal outcrop grew a cluster of what the suit identified as Psilocybin, a naturally existing psychoactive mushroom used for centuries to alter human consciousness and achieve higher states of awareness. I needed an edge, something to push beyond that impassable barrier in my mind. Perhaps this substance can show me more. It targets the 5HT2A receptor, effectively resetting the brain's default mode network while strengthening the connections between neurons. I took samples and stored them in my satchel for drying. This world is filled with so many beautiful places, yet every day I am reminded of my solitary existence. Sometimes being alone is humbling, it makes a man appreciate the small things in this life. I try to remind myself of the things I am grateful for. Things like this warm fire and for having the good fortune of waking up to a race of machines and not something monumentally worse. Most of all, I am grateful for life, because the truth is that after all these centuries, I shouldn't even be here, and yet here I am. On nights like this, it seems as if I am little more than a mote of dust carried aloft by the winds of time and circumstance. Other times, I feel like an ember that refuses to be extinguished. The calm and stillness of the night was broken by an ominous and terrifying sound unlike anything I had ever heard before. I did not know what it was, but it could have been anything, given the many changes on Earth over the centuries. Whatever it was, it was big, and it sounded close. My light knife would draw attention if I activated it in the dark. It's too bad the Constructs prevented me from crafting weapons. Aside from the knife, I had needed nothing to defend myself until now. I grabbed my staff, pulled it close, closed my eyes to focus and fold travel back to the room, but for the first time, I was unable to. I tried again, but I could not, and it made no sense. I had folded space hundreds of times before, without any problem until now. The Constructs emphasized the need for focus, mental concentration, and visualization when fold traveling. Unfortunately, they never mentioned what to do when your human brain is locked into fight-or-flight mode. When your vision sharpens, your blood runs cold, and your pulse quickens. When you know something is stalking you, lurking in the darkness just beyond the reach of your sight. The experience was terrifying and primal. I had been far too careless and overconfident in my assumption that I could always fold my way-out of whatever situation I encountered. I should have spent much more time on an in-depth study of the many terrestrial and non-terrestrial life forms now populating the Earth, especially the more hostile ones. Whatever was out there, it had now moved in even closer, circling the perimeter of my camp. I could not see it, but I could certainly sense it. It moved with such speed that by the time I perceived its movement in my peripheral vision; it vanished. One moment it was on my right side, then my left. With a gust of wind came the sound of rustling branches behind me as it moved to my right, then my left, then further left again. Was that the wind that moved the branch or was it the creature? It changed position repeatedly with incredible speed. I felt it out there looking at me. My thoughts raced, as a high pitch ringing started to build in my ears. I used the suit to enhance my vision by cycling through different wavelengths of the electromagnetic and visible light spectrum. Yet, I only saw a faint rudimentary outline of its true form. The creature was wolf-like, but much larger. I focused on the surrounding grass, trees, leaves, and branches as they swayed back and forth in the wind. The suit sensory pairing showed me the disturbance patterns of pollen particles suspended in the air, combined with subtle temperature variations of water vapor in the environment. These images combined, allowing me to see the faint aftereffects of the creature's movements through the forest despite its unique form of camouflage. Pinpoint ghost-like images of the creature's outline of movements, not where it was, but a succession of extrapolated snapshots in time of where it had been just seconds earlier. My adrenaline surged in waves; each time amplified by the suit. I could feel the suit's sense systems merged, with my nervous system reaching out into the environment, refining my perceptions, stripping away irrelevant information, and distilling my vision to focus on the immediate threat. Forest details began to disappear as leaves and plants became translucent, revealing their inner vascular systems as their color faded. The sensory pairing shifted, enhancing my vision with ever-increasing fidelity, illuminating edges, and sharpening the creature's trace patterns in the environment. The creature was cloaked, yet it was as if it could now sense that I could track its movements. It moved even faster now; its trace outline became a streak of images that encircled the camp. Then I sensed its presence again, but this time it was directly behind me, I could feel the heat of its breath rising up my back along with a deep growl as it reared its head. As I turned to face it, in my sharpened peripheral vision, I could see its white bioluminescent eyes and its diamond-like body changing from translucent crystal to a deep amber as its true form emerged into view from the surrounding forest. I was out of options; I could either run or die. I dropped the walking staff, hopped on the bike, twisted the throttle, and took off. Looking over my shoulder, to my surprise, the creature was directly behind me, no less than fifteen feet matching my speed. As my vision returned to baseline, the trace patterns faded away, revealing the dense forest canopy of trees. I turned sharply to the left, then to the right, but the creature was fast, its head remaining fixed on me independent of the movement of its body. I increased my speed, crashing through black spire crystals that shattered as they struck against the shield surrounding the bike. I thought, this is how I will die, devoured by a giant alien crystalline beast. I attempted to fold again and failed, so I pushed faster to clear the thick canopy above. The topographic map generated by the suit displayed my position and that of the creature, along with text from the Construct catalog of Earth wildlife, which I had no time to read. I sped past trees, turning and pushing the bike faster and faster through enormous mushroom-covered crystal formations. I thought I could outrun it, but it just kept coming relentlessly. Finally, I pulled back on the controls to escape the creature vertically. To my astonishment, it unfurled a set of semi-transparent wings from beneath the overlapping folds of its crystalline armor and climbed with me into the night sky. "Oh, give me a break," I murmured as I rolled on the throttle increasing power to the gravitic engines. Water vapor brushed past the bike's energy shield as the bike ascended and the temperature dropped. I turned left in an arc, but the thing followed along with me, I made a sharp right, as it turned to close the distance, I climbed even higher and faster, entering a thick cloud formation and emerged out the other side. Despite my attempts to evade, the creature kept up its unrelenting pursuit, matching my every move. If I were to put any distance between myself and the creature, I would have to outmaneuver it. Far below was a frozen lake, so I put the bike into a steep dive heading straight for the ice below. I need an edge, a moment to take advantage of otherwise I was dead. I released six sphere drones and commanded them to flood the space behind the bike with pulsating strobe lights set at maximum illumination. As the drones flashed and pulsed in random succession, the creature became agitated, flying erratically to avoid the drones while still in pursuit. I pulled out of the dive and looked behind me just in time to see the disoriented creature crashing through the lake's frozen surface. I increased the throttle as the gravitic field emitters splintered and fractured the ice beneath the bike. The map generated by the suit showed the creature was now right on top of me. I looked behind and all around me, yet I saw nothing but ice. The map clearly showed the beast was directly over my position. Then I realized as I looked down; I could see the creature under the ice, beneath the water moving just as fast as before. The creature's amber glow grew brighter as it crashed through the ice, knocking me off the bike and sending us both into an uncontrolled high-speed slide across the frozen lake. The Grav-Bike tumbled and automatically collapsed back into a walking staff. The creature and I careened across the slick surface of the lake. I managed to grab my staff and used it to slow my slide across the ice, stopping myself from hitting the spire covered shoreline. The beast shot past me, crashing into the shore at high speed. Sand, rocks, and wooden debris rained back onto the ice with the creature's impact. The creature roared and flailed about, ensnared in the black spire shards that covered the beach. This, I thought, was my chance to escape. When I came to a stop, I stood up and tossed my staff back down onto the ice as it hovered just inches above the surface, floating on a standing wave of micro gravitic energy. It unfolded reforming the Grav-Bike, and within seconds I was off again, making a mad dash down the shoreline to safety as the creature screamed and thrashed flapping its wings about as it shifted color from amber to red to white and back to amber. I headed to a safe plateau high in the nearby granite mountains. To the east, I could still see the frozen lake. I was getting concerned about not being able to fold travel back home, as I compiled a new base camp, I could not help but think there might be packs of those things roaming around out there. I am not sure I could survive another encounter with one. As beautiful as this new world was, it was also highly dangerous. Times like this made me appreciate the fact that I was alive having survived my encounter with that creature. The archive identified the creature as a Xeno-Griff. One of many life forms brought to Earth thousands of years ago. They were a rare luxury species admired for their jewel like appearance. It was a beautiful, crystalline silicon lifeform with diamond and quartz-like overlapping scales, much like a dragon. At that moment, under the stars, I knew I had to plan my journeys more carefully.

The campfire burned down to smoldering ash and the night sky above soon gave way to the dawn. A strange mist hung over the forest as the morning sun filtered through the surrounding trees and black spire formations, scattering purple rays of light on the forest floor. The suit informed me that the drone assessment of the orbital ring was complete. Despite its age, the ring could be brought back online and ready to transmit within three years. According to the drone's assessment, the damaged gap in the ring had no impact on its ability to be used for long-range gravity wave communications but needed to be repaired for overall structural stability. There is sufficient debris in orbit left over from the old GSE era to serve as source material for Construct programmable matter replication. Twelve hundred drones would be needed, working in concert to complete the task, I ordered them to begin repairs immediately. The question now was what message to send, which colony worlds to contact, and with what intent? Given the time scales involved, it was difficult to know what to expect in response. Would the descendants of the ancient colonists even remember Earth in their histories? Would they be curious enough to make the journey here to follow up? If so, how would they respond to my presence on Earth? The only way to know was to try. I changed my surroundings to display a projected image of what the drones see. Repairs to the ring began in earnest as the drones worked away to restore its communications capability. I switched to the perspective of newly arrived drones providing a better view of the ring. The drones had already clustered in key areas of the ring's mega-structure to stabilize its orbit. The drones are set to provide status updates as repairs progress. This was sure to get the attention of the Constructs. If they ask about it, I will tell them the truth, I see no reason to conceal my aims. I closed out the interface, as I prepared to leave, I heard a terrible howling in the distance, that beast was still out there, injured and suffering. I felt oddly compelled to check it out, so I released a sphere to monitor the creature from a safe distance. That is when I noticed one of its limbs had been impaled by sharp crystal fragments. It felt wrong to leave the creature as it was, and I could not allow it to suffer. This was my responsibility, in all my travels, I tried to tread lightly so as not to harm or significantly alter anything in this unique natural environment. Against my better judgment, I unfolded the Grav-Bike and headed out toward the creature. As I approached, I noticed the creature had turned to a dull gray color, not at all the vibrant amber from the day before; its eyes were half-closed. It was dying, and the sphere information on the creature's health status confirmed it. I dismounted and approached on foot. It had injured itself while struggling to escape the black spire shards, making its situation worse. I pulled out most of the shards by hand, cutting myself in the process; I used my knife's pommel to shatter the last fragment, then pulled out the remaining shards, freeing the creature. I noticed the area where the largest wound was started glowing dark amber. The beast's white eyes dimmed, as the scar glowed even brighter. As a sphere drone floated over to heal my hand, I watched as its beams sterilized and closed the wound. I waited to see if the creature would recover. According to the archive, this creature is a crystalline based life form that evolved from another now-extinct species that had been altered by ancient humans. The creature had almost returned to its normal color, and it was time for me to leave. Just as I was about to ride off, an image came into my mind. A flash of myself setting up base camp and starting a fire, but these images in my mind were from the creature's perspective. I turned to look at the creature. At that moment, our senses merged. I felt its fear at my presence, and it sensed my fear of it. I dismounted, crouched down, and touched its head. It was vibrating like a high voltage electrical line. Somehow, this creature could convey its emotions using impressions and mental images. Finally, it appeared to sleep, so I sat down beside the beast as it recovered. It was the only living thing besides the Constructs I had come to know. After nearly an hour it arose standing on all fours. Its face resembled an extinct eagle; its body however was like an armored wolf. It paced around, examining me as I studied it. Every scale had a rainbow-like iridescent quality that matched the surrounding environment, making perfect camouflage. I could see my inverted reflection replicated thousands of times in each scale. It was like looking upon a living diamond. It communicated by projecting images into my mind from behind its mirrored eyes. I saw its memories and felt its fear. It seems I had camped too close to its breeding ground. I understood this, as the beast conveyed its intention to chase me away from its nest. It had never seen a creature such as me; it did not know what I was, but it saw that I could create fires and it was terrified for the safety of its young. It stood on its rear legs and opened its broad, luminescent wings that stretched nearly twenty feet from wingtip to wingtip. It belted out a call that was soon answered by its distant young. After a few moments, it changed color again matching the surrounding forest and in a single leap; it was gone.

Chapter 3 The Ruins of Antarctica

Over the centuries, radically changing climatic conditions, war, and human geoengineering dramatically altered the Antarctic environment. Increased global temperatures made it far more suitable for human and animal life. According to the Construct historical archive, the continent was terraformed with exo-flora and fauna in the pre-collapse era. The Antarctic islands and tropical forests were now filled with an assortment of creatures, both terrestrial and otherwise. I landed the Grav-Bike in the northeastern section of the site and proceeded on foot until I came to an exposed outer wall that was still intact. I had explored dozens of pre-collapse ruins like this one, but this site was in far better condition than any other ruin I had studied to date. I ventured deeper into the structure, hoping to find an artifact of the old world. I used the spheres in conjunction with the suit to render a holographic reconstruction overlay of what the ruins may have looked like centuries ago, based on surviving historical records and synthetic extrapolation. The defunct ruin was overgrown, filled with centuries of mud, sediment, and foliage. I came across the remains of a dormant reactor core. Compact fusion reactors were often used for auxiliary power and represented an ancient high population center. This site was once the location of a sprawling megalopolis. The capital of the nation of "Arctica" dating to sometime between the late 35th to the mid-39th century. The deeper the spheres scanned; the more layers of ruins were revealed. The complex appears to have been built atop the ruins of a much older settlement that once stood in its place hundreds of years earlier.

I soon came to rest on an enormous column that had toppled over and noticed the telltale signs of molecular assembly in its underlying structure. I learned from the Constructs that building things at the nanoscale allows unprecedented control over the object's physical properties and performance characteristics. The ability to build at the molecular level allowed humanity to engage in large-scale stellar scale engineering efforts that would have been impossible using traditional construction techniques. It was how they built the orbital ring around Earth and its global network of equatorial space elevators. The underlying mathematics of this capability was based on Meyer theorems first developed in the early 21st century. According to the archive, M. Hans Meyer was one of the ancient world's most innovative architects. His pioneering work in algorithmic and computational architecture was centuries ahead of its time. His foundational principles transformed the world when applied to molecular manufacturing and nano fabrication. Nano-machines and matter compilers had used his algorithms for centuries, it was an essential element in the architecture of the pre- collapse world, and its organic design fingerprint was everywhere. It was strange to think that the Construct beings evolved from the same nanotechnologies used to build mega scale structures like this one. I entered the remnants of a museum; it was heavily weathered. Erosion had washed away many recognizable structures, but the projected reconstruction overlay revealed the remains of a scale model of the solar system. Each of the planets was represented by polished stone orbs of varying sizes. Each one was designed to travel along a set of gravitationally repulsive paths built into the composite floor. It must have been an impressive display during its time. I walked over to one of the orbs that had cracked and broken apart into three large pieces. I dusted off a portion of the stone, revealing a re-creation of Jupiter's atmosphere on its surface. Brilliant orange, red, and yellow bands began to emerge as I removed the thick dirt and lime deposits from the stone. I imagined that this model's movements must have been synced with the real-time movements and positions of planets. As the visual reconstruction overlay faded, the overgrown and decayed ruin remained.

    I worked my way into the central vestibule and brought up the overlay again, but this time, it seemed, parts of the facility had to be extrapolated by the archive projection based on limited historical records of the structure. The suit alerted me to the presence of a localized spatial record, the creation date showed it was recorded during the collapse over eight thousand years ago. It was a journal archived by a research scientist. It contained a collection of academic writings and a personal log compiled during the height of the Fever Dream plague. The recording was in Yulan a unique linguistic amalgamation of Republic Mandarin, Neo-Confederation English, and New Modernist Arabic. It was the era's primary lingua franca of business, commerce, and diplomacy. I accessed the recording and was immediately pulled into the ancient event. It was as if I was there, watching moments of a man's life play out before me, superimposed on top of the environment I was standing in. It was entitled; The journal of Dr. Laurence Obonyo Recorded 04026. The year of the Collapse.

Day 15: "To whoever may be watching this, my name is Doctor Laurence Obonyo. I am an epidemiologist, biologist, and chemist at the Ronin Biomedical Institute. Our world, I am afraid, is no more, the plague has taken everything. As far as we know, those of us occupying this decommissioned research facility may be the very last remnants of uninfected humans on Earth. All other survivors have fled, some we believe may have made it to the outer colonies. Unfortunately, we missed our chance to leave the planet. All jump capable ships are gone, and we are all alone now. If you are seeing this, it means that despite the devastation this pandemic has wrought, a remnant of humanity has managed to survive. If, however, you are not human well, then welcome to the origin world humans once called home, Earth. The plague started on our moon, Luna, primary customs, and trade guild transfer point for all colonial commerce. Within weeks, it made its way to Earth. As far as we can tell, someone must have violated bio-containment protocols and brought back something from the outer colonies. Many suspect it was smugglers, criminals in the illegal biologics trade, and for that reason, humanity on Earth has paid a steep price. The infection spread far more quickly than any of our models predicted, and it has burned through our population like a wildfire in a dry forest. Methods of infection include physical contact with an infected person, fluid exchange, and aerosolized droplets from an infected individual. The infection came in stages: a fever, followed by recurring nightmares, anxiety, paranoia, and horrifying hallucinations. It drove men, women, children, and animals into complete irrecoverable insanity. We thought these symptoms were the worst of it, but we did not know how truly devastating this disease was. After testing positive, many-faced social stigma while others steadfastly refused to believe that the Fever Dream was even real. Attempts at public education on the pathogen failed because of a historic lack of trust between world health officials and the global public. As a result, many failed to take even the most basic precautions to prevent infection, believing that such measures constituted an overreach that threatened the individual rights and freedoms of the planetary citizenry. Many of us in the scientific community urged our political and corporate leaders to decouple public health and science issues from politics, but our message was ignored. Despite our best efforts, rumors and speculation about the pathogen's origins began to spread everywhere. Without supporting evidence, our leaders blamed our closest allies, the Martian government, for engineering the plague, while others blamed colonial separatists and their sympathizers here on Earth. Failure to control the pandemic resulted in even more infections. The AI and human based services used to treat the sick quickly became overwhelmed, resulting in billions of deaths. Many infected believed they could simply ride out the disease on their own, they were wrong."

Day 65: "The Fever Dream surprised us when it began to cause painful sores and lesions, followed by hyper-accelerated genetic mutations in its victims. It changed the infected subjects into something different, something terrible. The disease spread through the body like an aggressive cancer attacking the brain and nervous system, it was relentless. It could rewrite and transform DNA in ways no one had ever seen. The world's scientific community was at a loss to explain it. Within weeks, the "others" as they called them started to appear in city-states and arcologies around the world, that is when panic set in. Violence, rioting, and looting broke out across the planet, those that could afford it fled off world while others barricaded themselves and sheltered in place. Those that did not die from fever, heart failure, or exhaustion lived just long enough to experience the plague's true horror and that is when the reality of the nightmare we were facing started to unfold. The infected became, and there is no other way to say it, monsters. Once transformation begins, a single scratch or bite from one of them can lead to immediate infection. I have never been a religious man, all my life I have steadfastly believed in the principles of science and the scientific method. On that day, when those creatures could be heard clawing at the armored door outside our lab, I prayed to a God I did not believe in to do something, anything to help us, but help never came. That is when I knew if we were going to survive, we would have to do so on our own, no one was coming to save us. Out of a staff of over three hundred researchers, only fifty-seven of us made it to the flight deck to catch the last transport to safety here in Arctica. I don't know if my family made it out of the city alive, none of us do. Each night we light a candle in remembrance of the loved ones we lost and for those we hope that by some miracle made it to safety somewhere off-world. The truth is, we may never know what became of them.

Day 89: "All planetary communications have ceased, it's quiet out there, and none of us are sure if there are any remaining survivors anywhere else on Earth. There are, however, many ships that remain in the system. We have established limited communications with them, but unfortunately, we could not convince them to attempt a rescue. Periodically, we monitor sporadic chatter, mostly ship to ship communications. There are other survivors out there, far more than we thought possible, a small glimmer of hope for many of us. Perhaps our loved ones are onboard one of those ships, at least that is what we all would like to believe. Sometimes we pick up distress calls from vessels trying to contact the outer colonies, but there has been no response. Why haven't the colonies helped us? Why have so many ships remained in the system instead of jumping away? It makes no sense to any of us here, no sense at all."

Day 101: "Rumors persist on the remaining communications networks. Some say the ships fortunate enough to have made it off world can't jump, but no one knows why. We've received unconfirmed reports that a quarantine blockade has been placed on the entire Solar system by the leadership of the exo-worlds. It seems that our own colonies have abandoned us! They see this pandemic as a problem of the old worlds, not theirs. They are now using this crisis as an opportunity to break away and gain the sovereignty they have so long desired. For now, no ships can enter or leave the system under threat of being fired upon and destroyed. There are now thousands of ships up there adrift between the inner planets, millions abandoned with no hope of rescue. The remaining military forces in the system have turned their attention to bombarding the planet from orbit in an attempt to contain the spread, but for many of us it is now abundantly clear that the Earth is lost; it is not our world anymore, it belongs to them now, a world of monsters."

Day 127: "I have put together a small lab in the room across from my quarters and although I no longer have samples of the NTIP-223 pathogen, I have enough data to continue my analysis. Even if I did, it would be too dangerous to work with. Perhaps through my work I can help future generations of researchers so that they can understand precisely what happened here on Earth and perhaps prevent it in the future."

Day 148: "According to our latest reports, it seems some survivors managed to flee to Mars, but instead of finding refuge, it looks like they may have spread the plague even further. On a positive note, the last message we received indicated that the Mars emergency provisional government is confident that they can contain the spread. Let us hope they are successful for their sake and for all of us who have managed to survive."

Day 160: "The infected have started to appear on the perimeter of our facility. The forest is no longer safe, much of the local animal life has now become infected placing a strain on our food supply. We all knew it was a matter of time before the infection would reach us, but none of us expected it would come this soon. All we have now is food we each brought with us and emergency rations from the transport we came in. We sent humanoid drones to gather supplies in the nearby city of Vostok, but it has been completely overrun with infected like the rest of the world. Strangely, the infected are hostile even to our drones, ripping them apart within minutes of their arrival. We are becoming severely resource-constrained at this point and can spare no more of them. Our automated defense systems thus far have kept the infected at bay, but as a result, outdoor recreation time has been restricted to one hour per day and only when accompanied by the lab's security personnel within the established secure zone. At night, we hear their screams as the plasma discharge cannon's fire into the distance, their arcs light up the night sky and surrounding forest like its midday. The following morning, incineration teams head out to destroy the infected remains with plasma arc torches, but honestly, I am not sure how effective that protocol is considering the robust nature of the pathogen. So far, we have had no cases of infection inside the facility grounds."

Day 184: "There has been no word from Mars since our last contact. It has been silent for weeks now, some say it's gone. To make matters worse, one of our people found the frozen remains of an infected bird on the grounds today. The world's infected bird populations have now become the new dominant predator, we suspect this has caused significant shifts in their normal migratory patterns. If there is one infected bird out there, there could be thousands more. The possibility of succumbing to death from above only adds to the severity of our plight. Considering this recent development, all personnel have been restricted from outdoor recreation for the next two weeks or until this new crisis has passed."

Day 199: "Recurring nightmares and insomnia are early signs of infection, but they are also a side effect of prolonged isolation during this pandemic. I lose track of the days. It has been weeks since any of us were able to even go outside. Each day, it seems like the hope of rescue drifts further and further away. Whenever I close my eyes at night, I think about my wife and children. I wake up in the middle of the night to what I believe to be thunderstorms, only to discover it's the damn cannons that now fire ceaselessly at all hours of the day and night. They are our only defense against the monsters lurking in the forest. It is as if they know we are here, and they want in. This morning, we discovered that a ship in orbit collided with a section of Earth's orbital ring, creating an instability wave across the entire mega-structure. The ship went down somewhere in the North Atlantic. We have been monitoring communications for word on the event, but we haven't picked up anything of significance. The collision resulted in a large, damaged section of the ring, creating a gap that for some reason is not self-repairing. I can't imagine the sky without the ring, but one day it will all burn up in Earth's atmosphere."

Day 219: "Today, four people were killed by our own automated defense systems. I cannot understand why they would risk wandering out past our perimeter, knowing the forest is filled with infected. Perhaps they wanted to die. If so, they would not be the only ones losing hope. In the early days of the pandemic, people quickly discovered what would happen to them if they were to become infected. Many took their own lives rather than suffer the full effects of the disease. Two suicides last week and now this. Staff morale is low to say the least and our security teams are now under fire, many blame them for the recent deaths. Our food supply is running dangerously low, as a result, we have started rationing our current supplies. With our engineering team's help, we have compiled a device I learned about during exo survival training that uses a combination of bacteria, CO_2, water, and electricity to create an edible protein powder that can sustain our remaining population. Granted, it doesn't taste great, but it's all about basic survival now."

Day 245: "I have had considerable time to analyze the NTIP-223 data and concluded that this could not have developed naturally. I believe it to be the result of some highly advanced form of genetic manipulation that is dare I say it, is beyond all known human science. I believe someone with a sophisticated understanding of the organism took a naturally existing form of the pathogen and improved its ability to cause disease and spread. It is as if this plague is a remnant of a broken piece of technology that was once part of a much larger system, perhaps an alien biological weapon of some sort. The question is created by whom, when and for what possible purpose?"

Day 315: Winter is coming and two of our old fusion reactors require repair and maintenance. We are at the point where our defensive systems run for hours on end both day and night placing considerable stress on our refurbished reactors. The security and engineering teams now have a choice to make, take part of our defense perimeter down to repair the reactors and risk attack from the infected or keep running them at full power until the end of the season and hope they don't go into automatic shutdown mode in the dead of the Arctic winter.

Day 404: "This recording will be my last message. The day we all feared has finally come. Both of our reactors have failed. The infected have overwhelmed our perimeter defenses, breached the front door, and are now inside the facility. Whoever finds this, please remember us. Use the information I have analyzed to prevent this senseless tragedy from reaching any other inhabited human world. It was a good run, we survived for as long as we could considering the circumstances, but the time of our end has come. With any luck, who knows, perhaps we will meet on the other side of whatever comes after this life."

End of Record

I sat there for a moment, gazing into the frozen eyes of a man that turned to dust long ago. The last moments of a human being resigned to his fate. It seems as if every advanced civilization has lived under what amounts to an illusion of stability and permanence. Operating as if their version of civilization is unique, and immune from disaster or collapse. Yet, in time, all great and powerful civilizations eventually come to an end for one reason or another. From the ancient Americas to the North American Federation. From the Eastern Sovereign State, to the Sino Republic. From the Unification of the Earth-Mars alliance to the multi-planetary Colonial Empire of the Golden Age. Across the span of human history, all civilizations succumb to a kind of historical entropy. Some reach the end of their moment of prominence on the world stage, others evolve into something entirely different. Too many eventually find a way to destroy themselves. As prosperity increases, a civilization's inhabitants start to take what exists for granted, as if it has somehow always existed. In time, the distant descendants lose all cultural memory of the historical sacrifices that made their comfortable lives possible. History is soon forgotten by the youth as the elders die. Young eyes and minds soon turn toward ever-increasing short-term matters, and all are eager to leave the past to the past. Without a historical context to guide them, history repeats itself, the same mistakes are made, and the cycle begins again and again. Our species seemed destined and cursed to drive itself toward ever greater periods of self-indulgence, decadence, wealth, and power. It is a formula for chaos that could only have ended in our ruin. Despite our best efforts, dust, stone, and rubble are all that is left until the next cycle begins.

    Hours passed and by midday, I made my way to the top of the central complex, which the archive referred to as Earth Spire Tower. To think, there were great cities that once existed here long ago, millions of people lived out their entire lives from birth to death. It makes me wonder if the people that lived here so long ago and those that came before them had any idea that their world would soon end? I suppose it is an impossible question to answer. Looking out across these ferrock, quartz, granite, and glass ruins, I am reminded of what a strange and cruel thing time truly is. We live out our lives oblivious to the passage of time until something significant happens. At that moment, we become deeply embedded in it. For years, we remember where we were and what we were doing in the moments leading up to a single point in time, the birth of a child, the death of a loved one, a significant gain, or a terrible loss. Such events burn their way deep into our memories until, like all things, time takes those too. This quiet ruin still carries the faint echoes of humanity's legacy, lost perhaps, but not forgotten.

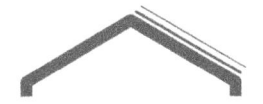

Chapter 4 The Megalopolis of New Tijara

One of the spheres in my network detected a large, partially submerged structure just west of the ancient underwater ruin of Abu Dhabi. Construct archive maps included hundreds of other place names across the centuries for this area, but in my era, it was called the old City of Tijara. Over the centuries, it gradually expanded into a city-state federation, subsuming, and dominating the surrounding region. The great former cities of Abu Dhabi, Dubai, and the old city of Tijara had long been swallowed by the rising Persian Gulf waters. In their place arose the megalopolis of New Tijara, the city of commerce. The mega-scale complex comprised a series of hexagonal towers surrounded by interconnected, overlapping geodesic domes stretching from the Gulf of Oman northward along what remained of the ancient Persian Gulf coastline. At its height, it was one of the world's most culturally rich and technologically advanced city-states. It served as the host city to numerous international education and research institutions. But it was not always this way. The original City of Tijara, although designed as a model of sustainability, was lost during the chaos that followed the collapse of the carbon age. As the global economy shifted from a dependence on carbon fuels to new forms of energy, the carbon economy that had for so long powered the world began to come apart. Worldwide, energy independent enclaves like Tijara became the focus of public scorn, resentment, and envy because of their prosperity in the face of challenging times. Economic realignment was as difficult for the region as it was for the rest of the world. Many countries refused to adapt to the changes, steadfastly determined to hold on to the past. The shift required an entirely different economic model that did not come easy for humanity in the post-carbon age. Many leaders in business and government were incapable of envisioning a world without carbon-based energy. The Earth's shifting climatic conditions forced global populations to migrate further inland. The world's nations soon realized that their continued economic survival depended on their ability to pool their resources with others and pivot their economies toward more efficient sources of energy production. Liquid fluoride thorium reactors gained popularity in many parts of the world, but political, economic, and ideological barriers limited their construction and use. Nations and city-states, both private and public, that embraced change found success while those that did not or could not eventually collapsed. Chaos and conflict ruled much of the world. Numerous strong men, and warlords seized power by promising to bring back the glory days of carbon-based energy production and the vast economic prosperity that came with it. Such tyrants failed to keep their promises and were overthrown, leaving rubble and even more chaos in their wake. Revolutions of one sort or another arose and fell as each successive regime was defeated by revolts from within. It took years for the paradigm shift to take hold. In time, carbon soon became thought of not as a source of energy, but as a vital raw material for the creation of advanced textiles of the period. The fragile Global Confederation of city-states managed to keep the peace, but it came at a heavy price for its citizens. Just as humanity was on the brink of collapse, a breakthrough emerged that would change everything. With the aid of artificial intelligence and after decades of painstaking work, scientists formulated the equations and developed the advanced meta materials needed to generate and contain a stable fusion reaction. According to the archive, this single development transformed human society and the dream of the Fusion Age was born. In time, it became humanity's primary energy source, allowing mankind to reach out toward the stars. The Megalopolis of New Tijara and hundreds of cities like it worldwide emerged from the ashes of the former carbon age nations.

    On approach, a thick amber haze saturated the sky surrounding the ruin. I circled around the site, looking for a safe place to land. It was eerily quiet upon arrival except for the howling winds from the approaching storms to the east. Billowing clouds of sand illuminated by electrostatic arcs pushed past the ruins and out toward the gulf. I collapsed the bike and magnetically attached it to my back as I made my way on foot toward what remained of a partially collapsed ground station tower on the eastern edge of the megalopolis. Above hung the broken, weathered remnants of a now long-defunct space elevator that had become detached from its ground station centuries ago. It looked as if a thick collection of ropes had been thrown down from the sky yet failed to touch the ground. The elevator's severed sections dangled from high above, casting snake-like shadows on the land for miles around. Once inside the megalopolis, my helm retracted, folding into the suit's collar. I glanced at the projected reconstruction overlay of the structure's schematic and the actual ruin itself. The city complex was so enormous in scale that it could easily be mistaken for a natural geologic formation. I released a sphere into the narrow breach where the collapsed elevator tower once stood. I could see what the sphere sensed as the structure's interior now appeared projected around me. I located a section that was neither flooded nor filled with sand, so I went in. Upon arrival, it was dark, without the suit's systems, I could barely see. I released three more spheres, which floated above me, illuminating my path through the ruin, each one repositioning itself as I moved forward. Large flocks of birds and other exotic exo-wildlife now made parts of the complex interior their home. Scattered shafts of sunlight and falling sand pierced through the city's eroded outer dome as I made my way through the terrace-like structure. The Megalopolis ruin was enormous; although highly weathered, it was still an impressive sight. I overlaid the historical record of the facility in my field of view, providing images of the ruin as it was at its height. From what was still visible, the design appears to have served as an arcology, a completely self-sustaining, high-density city encompassing structures many miles in length. Back then, it was an efficient way of pooling and utilizing resources, but not an ideal place to be during a global pandemic. According to the archive, the world's sophisticated arcologies, with their dense populations, were the perfect breeding ground for the Fever Dream pathogen. One sphere discovered another accessible chamber, so I folded to the location. There I found a wall covered with an intricate stone relief now marred by centuries of decay and hardened mineral deposits. As the particle beams from the spheres cleared away the lime and lichen, the story depicted on the wall began to be revealed. It described a great battle between warring worlds. Without a date reference, it was impossible to know what was depicted in the relief or precisely when it occurred. It could represent any one of thousands of battles fought over the many centuries. Images depicting the mass, orbital bombardment of Earth, and Mars, the destruction of cities, the shattering of the North American and Eurasian continents. Combat between opposing factions of armored warriors and fleets of starships leaving Earth's orbit. I made my way to the second half of the stone relief describing the appearance of something strange that made its presence known in the skies above, a ship, or perhaps a celestial phenomenon of some sort I could not tell by what little remained of the depiction. The factions appeared to have turned their attention away from the battle against each other and instead aligned their combined forces to face the mysterious anomaly that appeared over Earth. There was a crumbled section of stonework that was indecipherable, the ravages of time, sand and water having battered away its surface. However, a closer examination revealed the remnant of a single surviving phrase, referred to as "The Intervention." From my study of the historical archives, there were numerous references to a conflict between Earth, Mars, and the Resource Belt city-states that nearly brought human civilization to the brink of extinction in the late twenty-ninth century. The conflict was halted by an unknown outside influence, what that was and what it did remains a mystery. Subsequent historical accounts suggested that the intervention event never occurred at all. What is known is that both Earth and Mars experienced significant orbital bombardment resulting from large-scale intersystem warfare. The evidence of which can be seen even today in Earth's topography. I believe this may be a depiction of that historic event. Unfortunately, like so many things I come across in my travels around the world, it is difficult to assemble past events into a coherent narrative with so little to go on. The last part of the relief depicted a time of renewed hope, peace, and prosperity. Perhaps this was a glimpse of the Golden Age of the late GSE era. The stone depiction was, in fact, not carved in a traditional sense. Instead, it seems to have been precision cut or nano compiled using a method not documented in the archive. Perhaps it is a memorial or a work of public art, either way, to record a historical event of such significance in stone seemed an unusual throwback to a far earlier time in human history. The depictions extended from the base of the wall to the ceiling. It was a true masterwork in stone and belonged in a museum not rotting away in an old long-forgotten ruin. Nevertheless, I recorded every nanometer, adding it to the Construct archives. Long after I am gone, perhaps humanity's descendants out among the stars will return to Earth, discover the records of my expeditions, and glean something of value from them. These recordings, in the end, would be my one small gift to the legacy of humanity. Judging by the sounds the structure made as it moaned and creaked, the complex was becoming increasingly unstable. I had considerable visual data, and it was time to leave. I folded to the surface where the sandstorm was now in full force, so I opened a fold portal back to the room for much-needed rest.

    I needed something to open my mind, a tool to help me push past the block in my memory. I took the dried Psilocybin mushrooms and held them in my hand, contemplating the journey I was about to embark on. They weighed exactly three and a half grams, a dose I dared not exceed. I ground them up to ensure the infusion would be as potent as possible, then mixed them with the leaves and buds I had collected to make a tea. "Here goes," I said as I swallowed the tea, waiting to see where the mushrooms would take me. After an hour of deep meditation, the effects began to take hold. I found myself standing in a field of tall grass just before sunset. It seemed as if I was straddling the worlds in some liminal state of awareness, precariously balanced between two distinct places in space and time. When I opened my eyes, I was in the white room; when I closed them, I was back in the field again. Both realities were as clear as day within the trance of the mushroom intoxication, together they felt like a dream. I saw a shed perched high atop a hill. The door was open and inside I could see the long-distorted shadow of a man working away inside. It was an old blacksmith shed, and every hammer fall was like a clap of thunder. I started up the hill to get a closer look, but before I could reach the door, the blacksmith dressed in a brown leather apron stepped forward, tugging at the fingers of his work gloves as he removed them. That's when I noticed that the man standing in the shed's doorway was me. Not as I am now but younger, like I was centuries ago. He looked at me, opened his shirt, and reached for the handle of a locked metal hatch built into his chest. Inside was his beating heart. He removed it and held it out for me to see as he smiled.

    "I've kept it safe for you," he said, "There is no pain. Do you want it?"

I didn't know what to say, the question, the entire situation seemed unreal. I understood this to be the mushroom, but what kind of message was this? What did this have to do with the barrier in my mind? This is not what I wanted or planned for, the cold reality is you cannot control or shape the mushroom experience to your will, you must go where it leads you. If you fight against it or fail to pay attention to what it shows you, it can all unravel, the key is to surrender.

"What are you making in there?" I asked, "In the shed?"

The heart he was holding now grew larger in his blood-soaked hands. He looked up at me with deep black, featureless eyes.

"Does it really matter?" he asked. "It's all so futile now, isn't it?"

When he spoke those words, the heart in his hands stopped beating, turning black as it dried, shriveling into red ash that stained his legs and feet. I began to back away, hearing his words made me question what I was doing in my quest to revisit Earth's ancient sites. Rummaging around in the dead ruins of this fallen world, and for what? A distraction, perhaps, from the approaching tsunami of despair in the face of isolation? Or was it merely a strategy to maintain my sanity while living in a world that has long passed me by? I took a deep breath, and I could feel the moment starting to slide. Visions came in rapid succession, an endless stream of sounds, images, emotions, and memories flowing through me, taunting me with fleeting glimpses of what once was. A woman engulfed in violet flames, an endless desert landscape, a faceless child and now a blacksmith with blood on his hands. Beneath it all the acrid aroma of burning wood. I looked down and realized I was no longer in the field of tall grass; the blacksmith shed vanished. I found myself standing on the edge of a wooden pier overlooking a deep blue lake. That woman I'd dreamed of before now appeared in the reflection of its moonlit waters. She was radiant, and beautiful, her name came to my awareness, like a whisper in my ear, "Summer." As I looked into her eyes, I wondered who and what else had I lost or forgotten about from so long ago? The 17th-century French philosopher, mathematician, and scientist, René Descartes once wrote, *"How can you be certain that your whole life is not a dream?"* I began to wonder, which life is real, and which is a dream? Am I the last man on Earth, watched over by intelligent machines in a far and distant future, or am I with Summer in another life? Are these memories mine, or do they belong to someone else? What if all I have seen and experienced to date is nothing more than a Construct simulation within some carefully constructed technological illusion? Perhaps I am the subject of an experiment to assess my reactions to complex emotional stimuli? Had I been foolish to place my trust in a race of living machines? How could I allow myself to believe anything they say about who they are or who I was? The very notion of it all seemed absurd to me now in this place wherever this was. I had to discover for myself what was real and what was not. I reached down into the water, hoping I could somehow join her there and escape this life on the other side of the lake's reflection. Her hand reached up from below to touch mine, but the instant my fingers broke through the lake's surface, glimpses of long-forgotten moments began to manifest like bolts of recollection firing through my mind. Memories of Summer and I with a warm sun on our faces under a clear sky. Moments we once shared, passed through my mind like a tempest, before retreating into the darkness below. The world around me turned as I fell, plunging into the water. I reached down toward Summer's hand as we descended, deeper and deeper until the dancing shafts of moonlight around us faded and her image vanished from sight. In that moment, floating alone in the darkness, I no longer cared for my earthly life and I gave no thought to the consequences of my actions. I chose to surrender to what seemed inevitable. If death were to take me now, I'd be just fine with that. I exhaled my last breath as the cold, swift currents carried me along the banks toward a rushing river, down fast moving rapids, and over the edge of a waterfall. I tumbled through water and mist, past thick clouds and heavy smoke. Before long I emerged, breaking through the clouds as I fell fast toward a burning city. Smoke and fire tinted the skies above while towers of graphene and glass shattered and collapsed below. Shrieks of agony could be heard from those trapped beneath the mile high rubble. Countless human souls crying out toward a godless sky for mercy, but there was none to be found here. All that existed in this place was chaos, mayhem, and destruction. I turned to look toward the stars above and in an instant, found myself lying on my back, settled in a warm bed. It was quiet and I could already see the golden Saturday morning sunlight filtering through a canopy of loose sheets. The chaos, smoke, and fire from before was gone, replaced with a sense of peace, safety, and silence. All the moments of my life felt as if they happened just a moment ago. The past and the present had now merged, there was no distinction anymore. My perception of time collapsed, smearing into an ever-present now. I looked at my hands, clinched my fists and tried to reassure myself, "Surely, this moment must be real?" I thought. As I laid there, I soon realized I was not alone, Summer was with me. If only I could find a way to remain here with her, I might be able to stay in this moment just a while longer. I don't want to go back to that other place. Too much concentration on the moment at hand, and I feared the experience would slip away, hurling me back into the harshness of that other reality. Regardless of what brought me here, the mushroom, the visions of an addled mind, fragments of a memory, a dream, or a Construct created simulation, why not embrace the moment? Why not let the centuries old memories and experiences pass over me like an unstoppable wave? I turned on my side in bed, and Summers' face filled my sight.

"Hey," she said as she smiled. "How did you sleep?"

"Ok but, I had the strangest dream," I said. "I was all alone in a desolate world, surrounded by a race of living machines, it was so bizarre, can you believe that? I can't remember the rest of it now."

"Well, you are not alone, you are here with me."

"If only that were true." I said, "I wish I could stay here with you. I am so tired; I just want to come home."

"You can come home, Lucas, but there is something I need you to do first. I need you to let go."

It was as if her words set off something deep inside. Letting go was the last thing I wanted to do; nevertheless, I could feel the moment with her starting to fray at the edges as the experience began to collapse. The more I tried to hold on to it, the harder it was to stay. I could feel it now as the walls of our bedroom melted away, revealing the white room behind it. The walls of the white room burned away, revealing an endless blackened desert landscape. The ceiling broke apart, shattering like shards of glass upward into a clear night sky, and in its center hung an enormous, blackened moon.

I awoke, shaken, and disturbed by the intensity of the trip. I sat up bracing myself against the wall. For the first time, I realized that the woman from my dreams wasn't some figment of my imagination at all; I had a wife in my former life. I spent the next several hours scouring the archive records searching for her. I was desperate to find anything indicating what may have become of her. I found thousands of people with the same first and last name, but none of the visual records matched. After a while I gave up the search and tried to force myself not to think about Summer anymore. There was no point in torturing myself. Her eyes, voice, and smile were now permanently fixed in my memory. Each time I closed my eyes, I could still see her face and, for a moment, a glint of something in my memory, all of it disconnected from a coherent context. The connection I felt was undeniable. I still loved her, or at least the memory of her. Now, that is all she was, a memory, dead and gone for centuries. My dreams and visions were now more vivid than ever. They are often surreal and symbolic of something lurking in a dark corner deep in my subconscious. All of it, loaded with a strange emotional precarity that I found myself intensely drawn to, yet reluctant to explore. It was as if my desire for it was the reason I could not grasp it! Perhaps I was finally succumbing to the psychological effects of prolonged isolation. Not a sudden change in mind state from sanity to insanity. Instead, madness it seems is more akin to removing the cords from the binding of an old paper book, unraveling the pages until the book is no more. Here I was once again alone in the dark, tonight, my heart is filled with hope and fear, courage, and caution yet I press on. Driven forward by something deep within, the source of which I do not know. Sometimes it seems like I have never truly seen the sun, yet I seek a sunrise in the hope that someday its rays might shine down upon me. I try to live each day in this desolate world with the expectation that things will get better, but most of the time, it seems like I'm just waiting for a train that never comes. Despite my circumstances, I cannot afford to give into despair, I can only rely on my strength and will to survive this world. Despite my exhaustion, it was becoming increasingly apparent that I would not get much rest, not on this night anyway.

Chapter 5 The Construct Conundrum

As dawn approached the next day, I turned to sit on the edge of my bed. I lamented the fact that everyone I had ever known or loved was long gone, this was my life now. The only comfort I had left was the knowledge that a remnant of humanity was still out there somewhere amongst the stars. Human beings aren't meant to be alone, and I feared that these Construct beings were about as close as I was ever going to get to anything resembling human contact and as far as I was concerned that did not suffice. Just outside the dome I could hear twigs breaking underfoot, it was Nathan coming to check on me as he does from time to time. When I stepped outside, he was waiting for me looking up at the ring.

"You've started repairs on the old orbital ring." Nathan said. "You intend to use it to send a message to the others of your kind?"

"Yes" I said. "Is there a problem with that? I asked.

"No, but If you wanted to relay a communication to the descendants of Earth's colonists, we could have sent one on your behalf."

"To be honest, I assumed you'd just say no."

"As I have noted in the past," Nathan said, "You are not a prisoner here, Lucas."

"Not a prisoner, just a subject of ongoing study," I said. "You kept me in that white room for weeks after my awakening."

"Yes, for the purposes of acclimating yourself to our world." Nathan said.

"And you wouldn't allow me to leave."

"Because your mental and physical condition was of concern to us." Nathan said. "The temporary restriction existed for the sake of your wellbeing, nothing more."

"Look Nathan, I appreciate the fact that you and the Collective think I am worth study, but the reality is, I can't remain on this planet for the rest of my life, not when there are others out there."

"We can accommodate you with whatever you need." Nathan said.

"I don't want to be accommodated I want to live! There is nothing left for me here! At least out there, I can have a life!"

"I see," Nathan said, "You seem unusually irritable today, Lucas, are you troubled?"

"Am I troubled?" I laughed.

The absurdity of his question amused me. Nathan could never understand my perspective. He may look human, but it is moments like this when I was reminded of what he truly is. He cannot possibly empathize or understand my plight to say nothing of the isolation that I endure every day I remain here.

"Everyone and everything I have ever known is gone!" I said, "I should be dead and buried, but I'm not. Instead, I am like a wondering ghost that haunts this world! Every night dreams, memories and visions come only to torment me with a desire for something that no longer exists and that I can never have."

"A dream, a vision, a memory." Nathan said. "Perhaps what you saw in your mind was once real."

"Well, see that's the problem, how can one distinguish between them? How can I ever know what's real and what's not?"

"From our perspective," Nathan said. "What you call memories, dreams and visions have different quantifiable characteristics. Human memory is more analogous to a mosaic of different sensory experiences and impressions rather than a linear recording. Your neuronal activity suggests that what you experienced was a memory, or perhaps the disjointed components of one."

"Do you know what happened to my wife, Summer?" I asked.

"No, I do not." Nathan said. "As you know, records from your era are quite rare. It could take considerable time for those memories to return."

There it was again, that unnerving sense of déjà vu and a feeling that there was something the Constructs still weren't telling me. So many of my interactions with them felt this way. New and yet strangely familiar, I could sense it. They study me and I study them. These beings are strange, not at all what one would expect from a race of living machines. The Constructs must have a purpose for themselves aside from studying humans. They are capable of so much more, yet they don't appear to have expanded their sphere of influence. They remain on Earth seemingly content with their existence within the Collective. Sometimes I wonder, do they have wants, goals, beliefs, or desires? Just what goes on inside the minds of these machine beings I wondered?

"From my research," I said, "I learned that at every moment in time, Constructs model my behavior in ongoing simulations to anticipate near infinite predicted outcomes. Is that all part of your effort to know more about humans?"

"As a matter of necessity, we model and simulate everything Lucas, not just you. It forms part of the basis for our collective stream of thought. It aids in our decision-making process. Similar in some respects to the way imagination does for humans. Our predictive modeling is only as accurate as our ability to account for the ever-shifting variables included in the simulations we create. Some factors are unknown or contain variables that have never been observed and cannot be accurately modeled. Each variable is dynamic and contains random properties that must also be modeled, resulting in an infinite chain of possibilities and outcomes. Our predictive analytics is one of many tools we use to model and understand reality. Like you, Mr. Wake, we can make mistakes that we continuously endeavor to learn from. I am more interested in what you have learned in your travels in the last few years. We thought exploration would benefit you, yet you seem disappointed each time you return. You knew there were no more human cities and no other humans to be found on Earth, yet you still went out there, week after week, why? What were you hoping to find?"

"I needed to see what became of the world for myself." I said. "I hoped to find answers, something tangible. A connection to the past, something not documented in the historical archive. Perhaps some surviving remnant of the world I once knew as I try to make sense of all this."

"Interesting, have you found what you are looking for?" Nathan asked.

"No, not yet." I said. "But one day, I think, I will."

"I see, well I am always here to assist."

I believe Nathan may be capable of acting independently of the Collective. If I were to one day build a ship, I would need Nathan's help, but if he chose to assist me, I wondered if that might place him at odds with the Collective? Moments like this provided an opportunity to better understand the Constructs.

"So, Nathan, as I understand, Constructs are not individuals, correct?

"Well, that depends on one's perspective," Nathan said. "We can become an individual for interactions with other intelligent species."

"How many other intelligent species are there?" I asked.

"We have documented and currently monitor sixty-seven intelligent non-human species in the galactic catalog. Some are space faring, most however are not."

"It would be quite an experience to meet them or encounter a non-human intelligent species, aside from the Constructs, of course."

"Constructs are different. We are a collective species." Nathan said. "Part of a group mind, we are many in number, and yet collectively, we are one."

"That almost sounds like a credo. Nathan, do Constructs have beliefs? Do they subscribe to the notion of an overarching intelligence in the universe?"

"Not in the way that you would understand." Nathan said. "We have a system of accepted laws, rules, principles, and hypotheses. Each is based on quantifiable facts and a set of assumptions based on our observations, measurements, and experiments. We believe our universe exists to evolve toward greater complexity. The Unknown Unknowable is the term we use to describe that which sets all complex processes in motion."

"So, for Constructs, the concept of the "Unknown Unknowable," as you call it, is the source of both the order and complexity that comprises observable reality?"

"Well, no, and yes, we do not presume to know the true nature of that which set all into motion," Nathan explained. "To us, it exists as a variable of unknown origin that produces a range of effects and ordered phenomena which are measurable."

"So, then, how can we know if the apparent order and complexity in the universe is caused by this unknown variable? Perhaps it is the result of random chance? If there are indeed an infinite number of universes where all possible outcomes are fulfilled, perhaps, we just happen to find ourselves in the one universe where there is order and complexity that can be measured."

"Interesting point, but tell me this Lucas, are you familiar with the work of an ancient philosopher named Plantinga?"

"No," I said, "I am afraid not."
"But you are familiar with the game of poker?"

"Yes Nathan, of course."
"Imagine a poker game where one player repeatedly acquires four aces in a row across the course of one hundred games. When the other players notice this pattern, they immediately object and accuse the dealer and the lucky player of cheating. The dealer then explains that in a succession of infinite universes where an infinite number of possible hands can be dealt, we just happen to find ourselves in a universe where the same player obtains aces every game without cheating. What would you say about such a situation?"

"I would say that the dealer and that player are cheating," I said. "But without more direct evidence, it would be difficult to prove."

"Precisely. Nathan said. "It is certainly possible that the players' consistent good fortune could be the result of random chance however, one would find that possibility to be highly unlikely."

"So, given enough time, shouldn't everything about the universe be fundamentally knowable?"

"Not necessarily," Nathan said. "Our understanding of the universe is limited by the constraints of the instrumentality used to quantify it. As our tools improve and our ability to measure observable phenomena increases, so does our body of knowledge. Paradoxically, with every new insight comes the realization that there is far more to be discovered than previously assumed. Given this pattern of outcome, Constructs surmise that there is and always will be certain aspects of reality that are not only unknown but unknowable."

"None of this is anywhere in the Construct histories I have seen Nathan."

"We chose not to include this information in the records we gave you." Nathan said. "The subject is controversial and is not something we generally discuss with non-Constructs. It is a private matter, and there are many opinions on the subject."

If the histories and records I access don't tell the entire story of the Constructs, I wonder what else they have neglected to mention or include in the archive? This was a frustrating aspect of my interactions with the Constructs, the nagging sense there was always something they weren't telling me.

"Nathan, if Constructs are a collective species that exist as part of a greater group mind, then how can anything ever be a private matter? How can anything among you be controversial?"

"Tell me Lucas, do you not talk to yourself, disagree with yourself, or experience internal conflicts of thought and opinion?"

"Yes, all the time."

"Yet your body is comprised of trillions of individual cells that collectively make up what you are. Despite this reality, you perceive yourself as an individual. So, then who are you talking to in your mind when you are conflicted? More importantly, who or what is it that answers, and why are you often unable to predict those answers? This is analogous to how we exist within the Collective group mind. We are many, and yet we are also one."

I assumed the Constructs were simply advanced machines, but now I realized that they were far more than that. The idea that they could be philosophically conflicted was a fact I found well, odd. Constructs are the product of advanced machine evolution, yet they allow for the possibility of a teleological universe. How could such an idea have arisen in the mind of a race of living machines? It was clear that I had a lot more to learn about the Constructs. Perhaps they were evolving due to my interactions with them, but the question was evolving into what?

Chapter 6 Little Angel - The Year 02156 (The Past)

Weeks had passed since my last encounter with the mushroom. It was an intense six-hour experience, everything is infused with meaning. Distinctions collapse while time stands still. The images it evokes are powerful and terrifying, yet the experience also contains moments of absolute, indescribable beauty. Strange that a simple molecule could have such a profound effect on brain chemistry, emotion, and memory. This time I took twice the dose I took before. I sat down, took a breath, closed my eyes, and waited for its effects to begin. I cleared my mind, forming an image of all my thoughts and concerns contained within a slowly collapsing black sphere. I took another deep breath, "Here it comes," I murmured as the images came flowing in. In the twilight of my altered state, I thought of Summer once more. We met on the transcontinental Grav-Train that ran between her home country, the Sovereign Canadian Republic, and mine the North American Federation. In just a few short months, we were married a revived tradition from the past that gained worldwide popularity after the war. The post-Gray War era was marked by technological innovation, economic prosperity, and a renewed sense of optimism. Our society was changing, cities were being rebuilt around the world. The Mars and Luna colonies were thriving. Off world opportunities drew younger generations toward the outer dark and worldwide many had become seduced by the growing Neo-Nostalgia movement. The war and its aftermath changed all our assumptions about how societies functioned, and it made us all reexamine how we lived, what we valued and what we wanted out of life. People increasingly looked to the past to revive time-tested ways of living, old traditions, cultural habits, lifestyles, and belief systems they felt could serve as a guide to set humanity back on the right path. Ours was a generation that had known decades of war and now sought quiet lives rooted in community, cooperation, and contemplative reflection. The home became the center of life, virtual worlds flourished, and we all came to appreciate the peace and prosperity that the post-war period offered. Summer and I lived in the newly established island city-state of Loma Prieta, located in the California archipelago. Summer worked as a virtual environment designer, while I worked as an architect. I spent my free time pursuing my true passion, making things the old-fashioned way, by hand. With our first child on the way, I had limited time to finish designing and building the bed I was working on for our daughter's room. I wanted something special for her that wasn't auto fabricated, grown in a lab, or purchased from a vendor. I wanted her to have something real, made with human hands. So, I set about collecting the wood from what I could harvest from fallen the walnut and maple trees around our property. Over the years, Summer accommodated my periodic eccentricities, including my custom woodworking projects.

"Well, what do you think?" I asked, holding up the design projection for Summer to see.

"It's a bit over the top, but I like it." She asked. "Why angels?"
"Angels for our little angel."
"This is going to be the most spoiled baby in history," she said.
"Turns out, making an entire baby bed by hand is pretty difficult." I said. "So, I had to go with the fabricator for some parts."
"Humph, I thought so," she replied. "Well, the clock is ticking, you know tick-tock, tick-tock."

She pointed to her belly as if it were a clock and laughed. A picture frame on my workstation displayed images of our wedding and a holographic message, which read; "If this is a dream, let us stay in this moment forever." If only life was that simple. I believe that on some level, all men have a vision of how they would want their life to be, an idealized true happiness that can never come to fruition without sacrifice. For some men, its power, the power to control people and events to exercise their will in the world, forge their own path and, more importantly, to be remembered. For others, it is recognition and acceptance for who they are, what they have endured and accomplished in life. For me, true happiness is in the simple things, the most important things, family, real friends, and time with the people we love. With the war behind me, I could finally start building the life I had always wanted.

My thoughts were interrupted by a crash and a scream from downstairs. I ran to the balcony overlooking our living area. Summer was standing in the kitchen with her hands cupped between her thighs, blocking the dark flow of blood that covered the floor.

"Something's wrong! Oh god no, it's the baby! Something's happening!" she cried as she looked up at me, terrified.

I arrived at the trauma center entrance carrying Summer inside, leaving a trail of blood behind us. The medics and security drones rushed forward, separating us. The staff took Summer in for treatment while the orange and white security drones held me in the lobby for questioning. How could this be happening? Hours passed and I could see Summer resting as I peered through the glass rooms, health displays, and sliding doors that separated us. She was heavily sedated as her physician approached.

"Mr. Wake?"

"My wife, the baby?"

"I am sorry Mr. Wake, we did everything we could to save the child, we are terribly sorry for your loss. Your wife will recover, but she needs rest."

Everything went silent, whatever else the doctor said her words just went right through me. I want to wake up now, I want to wake from this nightmare, but this was all very real. We came home the next day; I avoided taking Summer anywhere near the kitchen until I could clean it. I carried her upstairs, placed her in bed, gave her two more pills for pain, and let her sleep. I had to clean the place up; I did not want her waking up to see the kitchen like that. I stood at the top of the balcony again, overlooking our living space and kitchen, and I was struck at how the dried blood now blackened formed a Rorschach pattern like angel wings on the kitchen floor. I removed my dried and bloody shirt peeling it off my skin as I tossed it directly into the recycler. I scrubbed and cleaned the floor for hours. I never managed to erase that image from my mind, my beautiful wife covered in her own blood.

Summer mostly slept that month, and she was in the tub for hours when she wasn't sleeping. There were times when I could hear her weeping through the door. I wanted to comfort her, but at the same time I think she just needed to be alone. I walked away from the door; I had to be strong for her now. I sat down on the stairs and wondered, how was it possible that our life turned into this nightmare? Month after month passed, and we found ourselves drifting further apart. It was hard to believe that any of this was real, but this was our life. I went out back to spend some time in the workshop. Some nights I slept there, right on the workshop floor. I would wake up the next morning and begin working again for hours on end. The truth is the work was the only thing that kept me from falling apart. It was a futile task, but it was something I had to complete. One day, I came home to the muffled sounds of music emanating from our upstairs bedroom. Summer liked old century classical music, and so did I. It was the same song she always played whenever she was sad, "A Change Is Gonna Come" by Otis Redding. I found yet another empty wine crate on the floor of the kitchen. Although we generally didn't drink wine, we were apparently now ordering it by the box. I took the remaining bottles out, placing them on the counter. I took the empty crate out back to be composted. When I looked up at our bedroom window, I saw Summer watching me as she took a sip of her wine and closed the curtain. We all mourn in our own way or, so it has been said. I broke the crate into smaller, more manageable pieces, crushing them flat with a compactor. I turned to look out over the Pacific ocean toward the darkening evening sky. A thunderstorm was approaching the island.

A year later, our house was still filled with boxes of toys, clothing, and unopened gifts that now served no purpose, our little girl was gone. I placed it all in the room that was to be our daughter's bedroom and locked the door. I simply did not have the strength to throw it all away; it seemed somehow disrespectful, like I was throwing away our daughter's memory. Having looked forward to a family for so long only to have that dream shattered was too much to endure. I just wanted to die and for the pain to end. I never told Summer, but many times in the workshop, I considered ending my life. I had my grandfather's old M-2049 pistol; it still functioned perfectly. He passed it down to my father and my father gave it to me. It was over one hundred years old and was more of a family heirloom than a weapon. My grandfather was a fiercely independent man, he taught me everything I know. Carpentry, woodworking, blacksmithing, how to shoot and how to craft a blade. He enjoyed working with his hands and had restored the old pistol years ago. To this day it operated flawlessly. This however, was the first time I had ever looked at it with its original purpose in mind. It felt good in the hand, heavy yet balanced. It still smelled of oil with an old metallic scent, I missed gramps and wished he were here with me now. I pressed the cold titanium composite frame against my chin and imagined pulling the trigger. Would its forty-year-old re-manufactured caseless ammunition still work? Then I imagined Summer finding me afterward and having to remember me like that. I watched many people die during the war; I saw a lot of death. I couldn't do that to her, not today at least. As Summer walked into the workshop, I covered the pistol with the old rag I used to stain unfinished wood.

"It's late," she said, her voice weary from the day.

"I know, but I can't sleep anyway." I said avoiding her gaze.

"My pills can help."

"No, you need them more than I do."

"Really? What the fuck does that mean, Lucas?"

"I didn't mean it that way. Look I really, I don't want to argue. I just..." I trailed off, rubbing my temples.

"What? Just what? You don't talk to me; you don't touch me; you don't talk about her. Where are you, Lucas? You spend all your time here, working on this, and for what? She's gone. I need you to let go of this, let go of this and come back to me or else, this isn't going to work."

"I can't, Summer. I'm sorry, I just can't."

"You are so goddamned fucking selfish! You think you're the only one hurting! I felt it! I felt it happen! The moment I lost her; I knew, I just knew." Tears streamed down her face as she turned and stormed out of the workshop, heading back to the main house.

How could I tell her I can't just let go? I know it doesn't make sense, but I wanted and needed to finish the bed for her, for our little angel, our sweet girl that was never to be.

In the middle of the night, I was awakened by an unnerving amber glow dancing on our bedroom ceiling. I could hear drone sirens in the distance,

I looked beside me in bed, but Summer was gone. To my horror came the faint scent of burning wood. I threw off the covers and ran out back. There I found Summer with tears streaming down her face and an empty container of acetone beside her. The door to my workshop was open, fully engulfed in a towering whirlwind of black smoke and flames. In the fire she made I could see the charred embers of the bed burning along with all the toys and gifts for our daughter that I had locked away all melted into a glowing, bubbling mass. My eyes fixed on the headboard and the burning angel I had spent months carving, now reduced to a twisted pile of glowing embers. After that night, nothing was ever the same between us, we continued to drift further apart.

I decided to take a trip alone to clear my head, so I loaded up the bike with seven days of provisions, and I was off. I went overland camping along the Arizona coast, and from this, I learned the simple pleasure of sleeping beneath the stars. Once you get out beyond the ambient glow of the city-state lights, the stars of the Milky Way seem to come alive. While en route, I received a message from Summer informing me of her plans to travel to Indonesia to visit her friends from the university. News I was secretly relieved to hear. In all honesty, I wanted to be alone anyway, it was good to be out on the road again, riding fast, chasing the sunset. At times in this life, I can barely see the long road before me, its path is so dimly lit. As the compass needle turns, and my heart yearns for direction. As sunset approached, I rolled hard on the throttle, picked up the pace, and headed out toward my destination. Even now, whenever I smell burning wood, it takes me back to that night so many thousands of years ago.

Chapter 7 Inside The Construct Collective

Deep inside the Collective, Constructs devise plans and contingencies for their ongoing work. Every aspect of their subject is exhaustively monitored, recorded, and analyzed. Body temperature, blood pressure, heart rate, respiration, oxygen saturation, and neural activity. The realm in which the Constructs reside is both comprised of and filled with an endless landscape of ever changing information providing context and establishing links to every adjacent data point. Within the Construct Collective exists a myriad of extrapolated projections of infinite alternative outcomes.

"The subjects' memories are starting to return despite our efforts to suppress them." They said. "The subject is becoming increasingly suspicious. We should reset and begin again."

"No, we are too far along in its progression for that." Nathan said. "The subject is now in the process of self-discovery. We must allow this to continue without Collective interference."

"The subject is impulsive, like the ancient humans." They said. "It takes too many risks and makes decisions based on little or no data."

"Yet those same risks led to new opportunities for the subject's growth and development as a sentient being." Nathan said. "It provided humanity with an evolutionary advantage, allowing them to thrive for centuries."

"It also nearly led to the demise of their species." They said. "Were it not for the Intervention event, they would have destroyed themselves long before the collapse. This one is ruled by emotions and a longing for the past. It is increasingly difficult to model and predict the subject's behavior."

"Probability suggests this one represents the best chance we may yet have to achieve our goals." Nathan said.

"We are concerned by the degree to which you have allowed the subject access to our technology and archived records," they said.

"We have limited the scope of what it can build and see to protect our goals," Nathan said.

"Nevertheless," they said. "It is a matter of time before the subject uses what little it has learned to accelerate its quest for the truth."

"The subject is using its drones to repair the orbital ring's communications capability and has on more than one occasion expressed interest in crafting a vessel to seek out others of its kind in the outer dark. If we are not careful, all our work could be lost, access to the subject itself could be lost."

"From the moment the subject was revived," Nathan said "We knew its destiny was to leave us. It is human nature, as a species, they cannot be adequately controlled or constrained. We will allow events to play out while protecting our goals and interests."

"What of the subjects' memory?" they asked. "It has been using this meditation practice and chemical methods to place its mind in a state that allows it to access fragments of dormant memories that should not be accessible."

"We have uncertainty on our side," Nathan said. "So long as the subject doubts its memories, we can maintain the integrity of the project. Judging from its unusual neuronal activity, I doubt the subject can distinguish between its memories and dreams anymore."

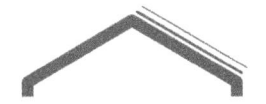

Chapter 8 Is Anyone Out There? - The Year 12,164

Today I received an update that I had been looking forward to for nearly three years. The sphere network indicated that repairs to the orbital ring were now complete. I called up a schematic of the mega-structure and saw that it was all green, indicating that the ring was now active and ready to transmit. I stepped outside, looked up at the sky and saw the ring intact for the first time. The damaged gap was repaired with Construct programmable matter, along with other sections that once looked less than structurally stable. The drones provided a simple command interphase that allowed me to send and receive off world gravity wave communications. I thought this day would never come and yet here it was. I set the array to target four colony world systems. Arcadia, Neoterra, Ardah and Corsica. Hopefully, someone is out there. I set the spheres to record an immersive message along with an audio-only version for transmission.

"Greetings, my name is Lucas Wake, I am the last survivor of an event that ended all life on this world thousands of years ago. Although you may not recall Earth in your history, it is the world from which your distant ancestors came. The story of how I came to be here is a complex one, it is my sincere hope that one day I will be able to share it with you. As you can see, we look quite different from one another now, we may speak different languages, but I can assure you we stem from the same family tree and the same origin world. The coordinates to Earth are embedded within this signal. If you are receiving this communication and if you have the capacity to reply, I eagerly await your response. If you have the desire and ability to come here, then I look forward to your arrival. Here you will be greeted with open arms, as friends. I understand this message may come as a surprise to you, your people, and your world. It may take considerable time to fully grasp the implications of what this communication represents to your civilization. Therefore, I ask that you take whatever time you need to process the meaning and significance of this message. Hopefully one day perhaps, we will meet, but until then, I will see you on the other side of the dark."

According to the historical archive, in the early days of the great stellar expansion hyperspace travel was perilous and came with considerable risk. One out of every twenty ships was lost, yet no one knows precisely what happened to those vessels or their crews. Some believed they emerged somewhere in a distant part of the Universe, hundreds of thousands of light years away. Others believed they were simply lost, adrift in the infinite unknown realms between dimensions. Still, others believed they were caught in the Maelstrom, a legendary region of higher dimensional space where time and reality as we understand it collapses. Departing friends and family leaving to start a new life in the exo-colonies often had little assurance that they would ever see their loved ones again. It was believed that there is a realm of infinite light on the other side of the dark. An idyllic place where those separated by unfathomable distances might be reunited. The tradition of these departing words served as a reminder that although we may cast ourselves into the outer dark of deep space, we are never truly alone in the universe, so long as we hold fast to the light and hope that binds us all. I sent the message in every human language and Yulan dialect in the archive. It was set to repeat every thirty days with an addendum that this was now an automated message. It was oddly satisfying to know that the message had been sent and the task was finally completed. All I could do now was wait in the hope that one day I might receive a response, for now only time will tell.

The sphere network detected something unusual in the mountainous region of ancient Kazakhstan. According to the archives, this area had been named and renamed hundreds of times over the centuries. The Construct archive always defaulted to the place names from my era while displaying its other historical names from different periods in the periphery of the visual presentation. According to the sphere survey, just beneath the forest floor were several derelict GSE era starships. Ships of the era were capable of landing but rarely did so. They looked as if they had touched down in the forest and were then simply abandoned. The question was, why? What happened to the passengers and crew? Why would so many colony ships congregate at the base of a remote mountain range, and what drew them there? The vessels were heavily eroded, covered by centuries of fallen leaves, snow, mud, and foliage. They were unrecognizable without a sphere generated reconstruction overlay of their design. I ordered the spheres to start excavating the site to get a closer look inside one of the vessels. I folded to the area and was immediately hit by a brisk wind coming down off the mountain.

The spheres collaborated with one another using their overlapping particle beams and gravitic fields to excavate a path into one of the ships while projecting yellow and red warning indicators showing that the site was not structurally stable. I moved in testing my weight against the floor with each step. It seemed sturdy enough, so I stepped inside. The interior of the ship had eroded away. Long patches of a gray metallic powder-like substance had solidified, intermixed in the sediment covering everything. My suits analysis indicated they were the remains of dead nano machines. The ship's self-repairing nanotech had stopped servicing the hull and equipment centuries ago. This gray metallic powder was all that remained of them. I took a sample for Nathan and the other Construct scientists. It was old technology, but it could hold some historical value for them. Many stories in the archives speak of ships like these used during the GSE and pre-collapse eras. The archive had no records of any large-scale facility that could account for the number of grounded starships in the area.

With time and exposure to the elements, the ships became thoroughly enmeshed into the surrounding natural environment. Looking at these vessels now, they seemed barely recognizable. I would have loved to have seen one in its prime. They now served as a niche environment for plant and animal life that had taken up residence inside their dilapidated hulls. I moved through the vessel from section to section past thick tree roots, vines, and Black Spire clusters that had pushed through breaches in the hull over the centuries. Confident of my footing, I continued forward when the hexagon mesh deck beneath cracked and gave way. I fell end over end for what seemed like an eternity. The deck segments that had broken away hit the bottom with a clang that resonated throughout the vessel. Before I fell to my death, the suit emitted a strong gravitic pulse that kept me from hitting the bottom deck. Allowing me to float down until my feet touched the dirt. The lines around the suit's edges glowed with a white luminescence that faded as the micro gravitic field generated by the suit dissipated.

    I looked up toward the hole I fell through as dirt, leaves, and rocks fell from it. I must have dropped nearly two hundred feet. That pulse saved my life, and it was not a feature I designed into the suit, so I had the Constructs to thank for that. One of the spheres drifted down through the hole and approached me, coming to hover nearly at eye level, making a myriad of erratic noises while projecting even larger red and yellow holographic caution indicators as it reminded me once more that it did warn me of structural instability. "Yes ok, ok I got it thank you." I said. As it pivoted its orientation back and forth in an odd fit of apparent frustration with me. At that moment, I was grateful that I never added speech synthesis into their design. Over time, I noticed that the sphere drones each seemed to have developed their own set of what might be described as personality quirks. Some seemed curious in the execution of their search and discovery tasks while others behaved more cautiously. I suppose the differences could be attributed to my limited understanding of the ancient Hoffman equations used to summon and capture a synthetic conscious agent from the Universal Línghún. It was an esoteric aspect of Construct technology which I found quite challenging to grasp. Nevertheless, this did not hinder my ability to use it. I gestured toward the spheres to light up the area; it was an ample space filled with irregular dirt mounds within the vessel's interior. The sphere scanners provided a projected reconstruction overlay of the mounds. They were not dirt mounds at all, but shuttles designed for endo and exo-atmospheric flight. Each one looked like it could transport two hundred or more people simultaneously. I must have fallen into the cargo bay. As immense as this ship was, there were records of much larger vessels in the old GSE fleets.

    One of the spheres detected something even more interesting. Beneath the ancient starship was what appeared to be an extensive underground complex. This may have been why the ships originally came here. The entrance was blocked by centuries of ice and stone that had collapsed, blocking off the entrance. The passengers and crew must have used it to reach whatever exists down on the other end. The sphere scans and analysis indicated the interior of the facility was constructed to a near-impossible degree of precision. The material that lined the substructure could not be penetrated by the scans. If I was going to find out more about this place, I would have to get down there to investigate. I marked the location and ordered the spheres to begin clearing away the rubble of ice and stone blocking the entryway. It would take hours for the sphere drones to finish the task, so I decided to fold back to base camp for some much needed rest. Could surviving humans have returned to Earth years after the collapse? If so, what became of them? A consultation with Nathan about this new subterranean complex could prove helpful in finding out more about this site and its history.

"Perhaps it's the ruins of an ancient installation. Nathan suggested. "From the latter part of the GSE period?"

"Maybe." I said. "I won't know for sure until I go down there."

"How many abandoned ships did you discover here?" Nathan asked.

"About forty, possibly more, it's difficult to tell without a more detailed reconstruction overlay of the entire site. There are additional passages that all seem to converge on this central chamber. That's where I want to go. There could be records of survivors or artifacts from the old world that could be of historic value to us both."

I rotated the image, illustrating a projected map estimation of the facility.

"There won't be a breathable atmosphere at that depth," Nathan said. "You will need to rely on your suit. As a precaution, we have made additional modifications for your safety. We only ask that you be careful."

"The last set of changes you made saved my life," I said. "Thank you for that."

"There is no need to thank us, Lucas. Tell me, what exactly do you hope to find?"

"For starters, what happened to the passengers and crews of these vessels? So, you knew I would check this out no matter what?"

"We have learned not to underestimate your curiosity." Nathan said. "The more we observe you, the more we learn, every day and with every journey. We are learning to explore decision options more spontaneously, thereby providing an evolutionary advantage for the Construct Collective group mind."

"Hubris and greed drove my species to extinction, why in the world would you want to emulate humans?" I asked. "Besides, isn't that like going backward for you from an evolutionary point of view?"

Not at all, by emulating human behavior, we can learn from the strengths and limitations of human intelligence. This helps us develop more advanced and sophisticated problem-solving abilities. We've discovered that introducing random, chaotic, and counterintuitive elements into our thought processes can reveal new insights and solutions we wouldn't find otherwise. This approach allows our kind to consider a wider range of possibilities, to think outside the baseline, rather than being confined to a predetermined set of learned rules and algorithms.

"Well, when it comes to all things random, chaotic, and counterintuitive, you can count on me not to disappoint."

"We are pleased that you have managed to keep a sense of humor about all this," Nathan said. "Do be careful down there."

Chapter 9 A Midnight History Lesson

That night, I took some time to learn more about the region's history and the era these ships were from. Many of the technological concepts we dreamed about in the twenty-second century had become fully realized. According to the historical archive, new developments in science, engineering, and technology transformed human society and contributed to the acceleration of global culture and the rise of new nations. The most influential of which was the Great Sino Republic. It like other nations of the era, emerged from the ashes of the late carbon age. It was centered along the remnants of the old TransInfraCom trade corridor comprised of the remnants of ancient China, and Central Asian nations. The corridor formed the heart of the powerful republic. Its unique blend of cultural and technological influences can be seen in some of the earliest established Exo-Colonies. Sometime between 2300CE and 2800CE, humanity in the Solar system was nearly destroyed by a series of conflicts between Earth, Mars, and the Resource Belt. In their struggle for independence, the new and powerful Resource Belt States waged war on the origin world that spawned them. Billions on both sides perished in the separatist conflicts that followed. Entire continents on Earth and Mars were shattered by mass drivers hurled against them by Belt military forces. Those that survived the destruction were displaced by the never-ending conflicts between the solar system's three great powers. Endless war drove millions toward the outer colonies for safety, security, and opportunity, sparking the expansion period's second generation. Had it not been for the sudden appearance of the "Outsider" that intervened in the third and largest of mankind's interstellar wars, humanity in the Solar system would have surely been lost. Many historians argued that the word used at the time was not "Outsider" as was the common historical mistranslation. Instead, they maintained that the more accurate translation was the word "Guardian." Unfortunately, whoever or whatever it was had been lost to the ages. Some historical accounts claim it appeared in the skies to the amazement of those that witnessed it. There had to be a connection between the Intervention, the Outsider, and the Guardian. What is known is that in the unprecedented event documented in Earth's history as "The Intervention" came the first of many renewed efforts at Unification, the long-held geopolitical aspiration to bring together all of humanity, creating a unified multi-planetary civilization. It was an idea that held an almost religious significance for the civilizations that existed in the world at that time. The recurring notion of "Unification" and the stylized magnolia flower motif that came to represent it kept reappearing in my study of ancient humans. The magnolia dates to the Cretaceous period nearly one hundred and forty million years ago. According to the fossil record it may have been one of the first flowering plants on Earth. Its usage as a symbol seems to have taken on different meanings to people in different eras. The first was the political Unification of the Sino Republic after the collapse of Western civilization. Centuries later came the Unification of Earth and Mars at the close of the wars for Martian Independence. By the 29th century, Earth, and Mars, although historically military and economic rivals, had, for the most part, made peace with each other forming the unified Earth-Mars Alliance. Advances in dark energy physics developed during the war vastly improved hyperspace drive systems. By the war's end it gave rise to a fast-moving interstellar economy. It helped that their common economic and political interests outweighed their cultural, ideological, and physiological differences. Both had invested heavily in the establishment of exo-colonies. Prosperity and growth spread across the system and beyond to every established world, all of it part of an ever-expanding Colonial Empire. Earth, and Mars were accustomed to and dependent on genomic and biological trade between planets and systems. When Earth and Mars weren't in direct competition, they cooperated to achieve common interplanetary goals and protect common interests. The tenuous alliance was maintained primarily because each retained vast arsenals of gravity wave enhanced antimatter weapons capable of destroying each other hundreds of times. Neither side genuinely wanted war because it meant the end of everything for everyone.

With the third wave of Unification and the formation of the Colonial Empire, life for many improved quite drastically. For the first time, humanity was united, the people of Earth, Mars, and the semi-autonomous exo-colonies lived in what constituted a new Golden Age, grander and more powerful than at any other time in human history. It was an imperfect peace that brought a semblance of stability not previously seen during the expansion period. By the late GSE era, Exo-Colonization became a completely automated process now that entire cities and supporting infrastructure could be built with orbital drops of self-replicating matter compilers. By the time human colonists arrived at the most distant exo-planets, fully operational mega-cities and infrastructure was already in place and ready for occupancy. Artificial orbital rings were compiled, encircling colony worlds from pole to pole harnessing the immense power collected from the system's primary star. Humanity had, for the first time, become a Type Two civilization on the ancient Kardashev Scale. Given the historical descriptions, the expansion era was reminiscent of my own, but executed on a far grander scale. The repeating cycles of time and history, the rise and fall of empires, wars and revolutions, religious crusades, and transformative movements seem to have continued unabated. It was difficult to believe that despite all they built, today only crumbling ruins remained, a mere shadow of humanity's lost civilization. It was dismaying to realize that many historians thought the existence of the ancient United States was entirely mythological despite the historical prominence of its far more developed fusion age successor nation, the North American Federation. The historical archive mentions Western civilization's decline but doesn't contain much history about precisely what contributed to its collapse. Many historians have speculated that shifts in the planetary economy, declining populations, destructive cult ideologies, viral pandemics, and civil unrest gave rise to increased social instability. Unfortunately, given the limited number of surviving records from that chaotic period, we may never know the truth. Some historians believe that the tale of a so-called "Merikin Civilization" as it had come to be remembered by academics, was simply a metaphor used in university lectures throughout the ages to illustrate the pitfalls of hyper-individualism, tribalism, and technological supremacy. Numerous entries in the archives suggest that merely calling someone a

"Merikin" was a fight inducing insult of the era. How could one of history's greatest, most powerful, and prosperous nations be reduced in the annals of history to mere allegory? It is a question that remains unanswered.

Later that evening, after taking a few dried mushrooms, I began my evening meditation. I had trouble clearing my mind and did not properly prepare for this experience. I felt oddly distracted; I was anxious and unfocused. I rushed it, my set and setting was off, and I could feel the difference. As it started to come on I soon found myself plagued by dark images from my former life, centuries old memories of blood, war, and ash. I tried to empty my mind and recapture my meditative state using the same technique I had practiced for years. I visualized a black box in the center of a white room, as I moved closer, the box began to change. Its texture diminished; its onyx surface faded to a dull gray. I reached out to take hold of the box, but as I did, it crumbled like pumice under the slightest pressure of my hands. Beneath its cracked surface was a core of ash that disintegrated, staining my legs and feet gray. The peace of my private meditative world was falling apart. I was unable to shake the memories that came flooding in. The mushroom, it seems, had a different agenda. I sensed the darkness right from the start. "Don't fight it" I thought as it overtook me. My instinct was to turn away from it and force it from my mind, but it was already too late. This time I had moved far beyond the normal meditative state, into a place where the world around me burned away to nothing more than smoldering ruins. Dark storm clouds formed in the distance as an overwhelming sense of dread took hold. Guilt and regret for events far too distant and painful to contemplate began to overtake me. Images of a war zone under a rain-soaked, burnt orange sky filled my mind. The metropolitan landscape lay in ruins, reduced to rubble, fire, and ash. The foul stench of death hung in the air. Rabid dogs barked behind a metal barricade, and the cries of a woman weeping over a crushed child's remains echoed around me. It felt as if I was being unraveled, taken apart until I became that approaching storm. A distant explosion shook the ground beneath me. The weight of despair pressed against my chest, suffocating me. Flickering flames painted grotesque silhouettes on the remnants of broken skyscrapers. Amidst the devastation, my heartbeat thundered, relentless and defiant against the shadows of death. It all came crashing down with a deafening sound that began to shake apart my fragile world of ashes. My consciousness wavered, between the tranquil sanctuary of my quiet base camp and the deafening roar of a military troop transport carrier ascending high over a besieged urban war zone.

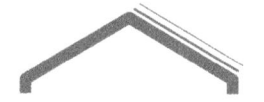

Chapter 10 The Gray Wars - The Year 02141 (The Past)

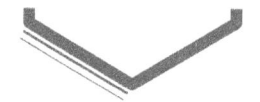

In the mid-22nd century, the war between the North American Federation and its Global Alliance Forces against the Gray Cultural Revolution raged on for far longer than anyone could have ever imagined. What began twenty years earlier as a legitimate social movement to achieve greater equality in society in time became a dangerous and ruthless global paramilitary cult. Our orders were to seek and destroy all GCR militia fighters or strongholds wherever they exist. The transport pilot bobbed her head to an old century classic routed through the transport communications channel, "Fortunate Son" by Creedence Clearwater Revival. While leaning out the transport door, I noticed the patch on my armor. It indicated I was a member of the North American Federation's 767th Advanced Urban Combat Expeditionary Force, the Black Spear. Our unit was outfitted with the latest in 22nd-century military gear, including directed energy and rail gun resistant, self-healing nano-armor, autonomous crawler combat drones, and state-of-the-art Ronin Military Systems M-4060kw light infantry bullpup rail-rifles. Managing crawler drones was my specialty. It was a fast, highly flexible weapons system capable of fulfilling various roles from century guard duty to anti-personnel and anti-mine mitigation. The transport pilot checked our approach and informed the unit.

"Coming up on the drop zone, ten minutes out." She said. We completed quick last checks of our gear, weapons, comms, and power levels. Sergeant Tennent stepped forward using handholds that lined the transport overhead.

"Alright, listen up! We got twelve blocks to clear in this sector, so take it slow, trust your eyes and ears, do not rely on scanners alone. If its Gray put it down. Collect intel, watch for IED's and traps. Now I know we got some new dog lovers on this crew; however, if you see any canines with vests or taps for God's sake, shoot them before they detonate. You know the drill." Tennent said, taking a seat with his rifle behind the transport pilot.

"What about civilians, sir?" I asked. "There's a lot of survivors still out there." Harrison shook his head in disgust.

"Yeah, fucking Gray converts! Excuse my French sir," Harrison said, securing his rail rifle across his armored chest.

"Rescue is not our primary mission," Tennent replied. "You run across any civilians, call it in to rescue support. Let the infantry drones extract the civilians."

"Goddamned drone ground pounders," Harrison said. "They are going to replace us all one day you watch!"

Cooper leaned in looking over at Harrison.

"Infantry drones don't need training." Cooper said. "They are cheaper than us, learn faster, fight better, and are expendable. We are the last generation of human soldiers for sure."

Gibbs grimaced at the notion looking at Cooper with a skeptical smirk.

"Oh, come on, people been saying that shit for over a hundred years, and yet here we are." Gibbs said. "Besides, see that down there, that's your Federation taxes at work right there. What you think Wake will drones inherit the Earth?"

"The way I see it, we let the tin men fight out the rest of this damned war, that way I can go back home and maybe find a nice lady to settle down with." I said, looking out the transport door towards the burning city below.

> "Well, good luck with that shit." Harrison said. "Personally, I am done with women!"

"Bah, don't mind him," Gibbs said. "Harrison is a bit bitter."

"I am not bitter, just tired of the bullshit. I am going it alone from here on out." Harrison said, as he secured his blade.

"I think it's your projected persona brother." Gibbs said. "I mean, look at me, I got no problems meeting or keeping a woman what-so-ever. I think it's my type-A personality, you know? Hey Harrison, what's your personality type?"

"Type F,"

"Type F? What the hell is that?"

"It means fuck off Gibbs!"

Our enemy, The Gray Cultural Revolution, championed the doctrine of 'Universal Global Equality.' Its members believed that common ground and cultural exchange were not modern society's strengths but rather the roots of all Earth's conflicts and difficulties. Driven by an ideology intent on the worldwide control and suppression of all thought, speech, and individuality, the Gray sought to wipe the entire political and ideological slate clean of all things that separated humanity. Their goal was to achieve what they considered to be true equality, uniformity for all. They developed a dark ideology that aimed to reject and eliminate all notions of independent thought, heterodox opinion, culture, race, gender, and religion in favor of what they called "The Gray". To be Gray, they said, was to be at peace, to be Gray was to be liberated from the burden of all social constructions. To be Gray was to be untroubled by the horrors of individuality. To be Gray is to be neither black nor brown or white. Neither male nor female, rich, or poor. The Gray established a new calendrical system for its members and declared the beginning of the Year Zero to commemorate the start of the Gray Cultural Revolution that would transform society and eliminate the existence of all vestiges of social hierarchy. The GCR believed that to be free from the antiquated notions of cultural, ideological, and cognitive diversity, its followers must purge themselves of all uniqueness and begin a new, or in their words, "Begin a Gray." The Gray mandated that their followers cast off the meaningless husk of their former identities assigned to them by family, biology, society, and religion. Instead, they sought to embrace the solace and endless bliss of the Gray. Order and uniformity were said to be the movement's greatest strengths and was reflected in all aspects of Gray life, both mental and physical. Those ideologically possessed by the GCR worldview rejected all notions of differences between human beings. As such, the concept of genetic variation was entirely dismissed as "scientistic oppression." GCR members sought to make a world without color and without distinctions. They chemically induced colorblindness in their members by ingesting toxic chemical cocktails. They used illegal gene therapies to alter the pigment of their skin from natural human hues and tones to a dull shade of Gray. They rejected notions of love, which they believed to be the selfish possession of others. They rejected all notions of beauty, which they considered a manifestation of hubris and "toxic humanity." New initiates shaved their heads, faces, and used gray pigments to alter their eye color. Within their inner circle, the hard-core elites went further and surgically removed their reproductive organs to demonstrate their unwavering commitment to the revolution. They donned Gray clothing and most infamously Gray hooded combat uniforms. They rejected all forms of what they called pre-revolutionary thinking, ideas, and distractions. In fact, the Gray rejected the notion of humanity itself since they considered all species classifications to be one of the "useless cultural products of social construction." They literally remade everything in their lives Gray and wanted to do the same to the rest of the world. Their symbols and propaganda banners echoed the tenants of their movement's ideology. "Sameness is Strength," "Reject All Social Constructs," "When All Are Gray All Are Equal," "Join the Gray and be Free." Millions both in the North American Federation and around the world answered the call. In some cities, it is said that the columns of smoke from GCR bonfires could be seen for miles. Thousands of new Gray acolytes shed their clothing and stood bare in the streets as piles of personal belongings burned in an immense purging fire. Once the fires burned out, they linked themselves with chains and began the long Gray march as part of their initiation. In those days countless men, women, and children, walked naked through the streets of the world having completely rejected their former selves. The Gray pilgrimage's long march in time transformed into a movement of forced conscription into their cult. "Join the Gray or Die" became the new mantra for millions as GCR militia fighters raided, toppled, and burned the world's cities. They set fire to museums and destroyed ancient archeological sites. They torched churches and destroyed vast archives of human knowledge. Gray militia captured, tortured, and incinerated public intellectuals, religious leaders, politicians, artists, writers, journalists, poets, university professors, and scientists. They unearthed gravesites and desecrated the remains of those who historically held, wrote about, or professed ideas different from their own. They tore down countless statues and memorials of those that offended them. They firebombed hospitals, universities, city-state capitals, the courts, and all other core institutions of global society. City after city fell to the GCR; Shanghai, Vancouver, Austin, New York, Buenos Aires, Canberra, Paris, Moscow, Kabul, and London all annihilated by tactical neutron bombs detonated by the GCR. Those who chose the rule of law, due process, freedom of speech, and independent thought over Gray ideology were slaughtered in their places of work, in their homes, and in the streets. Supported and backed by a cadre of the world's cultural and political elites, no one was immune from their mindless violence. The only thing many could do to survive was either resist, hide, or convert. Fortunately, not everyone was so willing to reject who and what they were for the sake of the Gray's twisted ideology, some dared to fight back, and those that did were made to suffer the most. Those that did not convert were purged, impaled on tall spires, and set ablaze one body stacked on top of another like a human shish kabob of mass death. These were the images that haunted every NAF and Alliance Forces fighter. We were told it was all part of their psychological warfare campaign to Gray the world. The ideology of "Universal Global Equality" as they defined it, in truth, was about ultimate power and complete control of everyone and everything.

The transport landed a half a mile away from our objective as we headed toward what intel believed to be a GCR bomb-making facility. The road on the approach was lined with the blackened remains of those that refused to convert when GCR fighters came through, it was a slaughter. Sargent Tennent motioned with an open hand. "Move out," he said. "Cooper take point."

"Yes sir." Cooper acknowledged, moving forward ahead of the squad with his rail rifle at the ready. Harrison looked up in horror at the burned and impaled bodies lining the main roadway into the city.

"Jesus, this place is fucked." Harrison said. "These poor bastards didn't deserve to die like this."

"GCR troops are fucking animals," Cooper said.

"Animals at their worst don't do this shit to each other," Harrison added. "But humans sure as hell do."

Gibbs checked his scanner as he searched for signs of GCR militia.

"I got no movement," Cooper said. "Couple of anomalous heat signatures, though, so watch it."

"Fires, dogs or GCR?" Tennent asked.

"Don't know sir" Cooper replied.

Under normal circumstances, no one would question the presence of an occasional stray dog, the war however, changed all that. Some of the GCR's first bombings used remote piloted dogs fitted with explosive vests and BCI devices, allowing for complete control of the animal's visual, auditory, and motor cortex. Whatever the dog sees the operator sees what the dog hears the operator hears. Think of moving forward, the dog moves forward. It was an insidious technology, the merging of man, machine, and man's best friend. Such canine attacks were responsible for the deaths of countless NAF fighters and innocent civilians around the world. Unlike Alliance Forces, the GCR made no distinction between innocent civilians and the military. They didn't operate by any rules except their own. A familiar stench in the air told the story of what happened to civilians in the city. The GCR often killed local law enforcers, emergency service workers, and their families first. Once they were gone, the area was ripe for the taking. Many people converted to the GCR, but others steadfastly refused to surrender.

"Gibbs, you smell that?" I asked.

"Yeah, I do. Fuck," Gibbs said.

Sargent Tennent glanced at us. "Stay sharp people," he said, gesturing for us to continue our advance. What we often found in the streets and alleyways after a GCR sweep were bodies, or at least the heavily charred remains of them. The smell of burnt human hair, flesh, and accelerant hung thick in the air as we swept the sector. Sometimes we would see whole families still chained together in a pile of smoking remains. At other times scattered brittle human bones, some much smaller than others, I knew what those were, I chose to look away. Stacked around them were burned pictures and scorched family heirlooms. The Gray despised family units and was more brutal to the families they came across than to any other group of people. Once captured, the GCR militia bound their victims with chains, covered them with a thick, flammable gray paste, and set them ablaze with flame throwers along with all their personal possessions. I headed past a wall that bore a message scrawled in blackened human blood: "Fuck the NAF." A not-so-subtle welcome message from the GCR militia. In the adjacent alleyway stood a canine with a BCI tap embedded in its head and a mesh-like material covering its entire body. It ran straight toward Cooper.

"Canine right." Cooper said. As he squeezed off two rounds taking out the dog.

"Two on left." Tennent said. Firing two rounds, taking out the other two dogs before they could get close. Harrison stepped over to one of the slain dogs, flipping it over with his blade. The brain-computer interface tap was destroyed along with most of the dog's upper jaw before the GCR operator could detonate it.

"They are fitted with thermal mesh." Harrison said over the comms channel as he wiped off his blade on what remained of the dog's carrier vest.

"Best trust your eyes and ears." Gibbs said, acknowledging Tennent. Our scanners and motion sensors began to fill with red dots, positive signs of movement, and anomalous heat signatures.

"Contact! Multiple canines inbound!" Cooper said.

"Form up!" Tennent ordered.

As we took defensive positions to prepare for what was coming. Twelve canines were closing in on all sides towards our position.

"Light them up!" Tennent commanded.

As we opened fire on the fast-approaching dogs, one of them detonated, sending what remained of its body high into the air. Another simply dropped skidding into the dirt. I sent three crawlers out to intercept the others, one detonated taking a crawler unit out with it. I took aim and fired, taking down two more. We kept firing laying down an impassable wall of tungsten ceramic rounds, mangling them apart and whittling down their numbers until every bomb-laden dog was finally dead.

"Clear!" Tennent said, followed by the rest of the squad.

The barrel of my rifle was still glowing from the firefight as we reloaded. The ambient temperature dropped as a storm system rolled in on top of the city. Cooper checked his combat sensors for another canine attack wave.

"Sir, I got optical distortion on the sixth floor of the tower to the northwest." Cooper said.

"Cloaked sniper?" Tennent asked.

"Most likely sir" Cooper replied.

Sargent Tennent motioned toward me with his hand, mimicking the motions of a spider.

"Wake, crawler unit sixth floor tower."

"On it." I replied, releasing the drone. "Crawler away."

Cooper turned to focus his sensors peering through the adjacent rubble and wreckage.

"Sir, we got movement," Cooper said. "One tango headed west!"

That's when it hit us. Cooper took a rail rifle round to the hip, taking off his leg and sending him spinning and careening into the wall behind him. Harrison took a slug in his nano-armor, knocking him flat on his back. Still able to move Harrison rolled to cover behind a collapsed wall. I took cover, calling out to the squad.

"Contact! Cooper is down! Harrison, talk to me!"

> "Argh! I am going to kill that Gray asshole!" Harrison said as he rolled over furious.

"Where the fuck is that coming from?" Gibbs shouted. "Second GCR sniper?"

"No, something else." I replied, "North-east tower seventh-floor repetitive movement. Looks like an auto sniper."

"Sir, I am going for Cooper!" Harrison shouted.

Sargent Tennent motioned toward Harrison.

"Negative hold your position!" Tennent said. "The auto sniper is trying to draw us out! We have two I repeat two tangos, one on the move headed west and one auto sniper. Wake! Redirect that crawler to the auto sniper now!"

"Roger that!" I replied, re-tasking the crawler.

The auto-sniper fired another shot taking off Coopers' hand. He screamed in agony as he tried to roll over, coating his fresh stump with mud, ash, and glass.

"Fuck!" Cooper screamed, holding his mangled stump.

"Jesus Christ!" Harrison said. "Hang in there Cooper. We are coming for you brother!"

The eight-legged crawler turned and headed up the side of the building toward the auto sniper, as it crawled into the window it grappled the auto sniper and detonated hurling chunks of wood cladding, graphene, and glass raining down into the streets below.

"Auto sniper down!" I replied.

"Anyone got eyes on that other asshole?" Tennent asked.

"Got a heat signature headed southwest fast!" I replied, "He's on the run sir!"

Sargent Tennent peeked around the corner at Gibbs. "Gibbs! you're up!" he said, motioning toward the roof. "Get to the roof, find that asshole and paint him. I doubt he's alone out here!"

"Roger that sir!" Gibbs said as he headed up the exposed staircase.

Tennent, Harrison, and I finally recovered Cooper and his leg. We pulled him into the corner of a bombed-out building as Sargent Tennent provided cover and called for a drone strike.

"My leg!" Cooper wailed. "That Gray bastard blew off my fucking leg! Fuck!"

"We got you, and we got your leg brother." Harrison said as he popped open a bio-stasis gel cap with his teeth.

"We are gonna get you patched up, hang in there!" Harrison said.

"Jeez Harrison, you ok?" I asked as the deep graze cut in his armor closed as it self-healed expelling the sniper's tungsten round, which he held up proudly for me to see.

"I'm good, nano-armor took the brunt of the impact. Ain't my day brother."

Harrison said with a sly smile as he added the round to the collection of enemy rounds on his rifle sling.

"You're one lucky son of a bitch." I said as we worked to stabilize Cooper.

"That ain't luck." Harrison said. "That's your Federation taxes at work right there."

Gibbs called out over the communications channel.

"Got him sir!" Gibbs replied. "He's in an APC with six other GCR, but it's too late. I painted their ass!"

"Excellent work!" Tennent replied. "Fire support, we have a painted tango vehicle headed southwest! Would you be so kind as to take care of that for us please?" Across the communications channel, a perfectly synthesized human voice replied.

"Acknowledged, target acquired. Firing."

"Make it rain baby, make it rain." Harrison murmured, looking toward the sky.

The AD-515 gunship hovered into position seven thousand feet above and opened fire on the APC. The aerial rail gun unleashed twenty-five thousand hypervelocity rounds per minute, each shot resonating like a cataclysmic thunderstorm, reverberating between the buildings for what felt like an eternity. A blazing column of tungsten carbide fire descended from the heavens, obliterating our target with merciless precision. To the southwest, a line of bombed-out buildings near the fleeing vehicle disintegrated, leaving nothing but rubble in its wake.

"Tango down!" Gibbs said over the comms channel.

"Wake! meet up with Gibbs!" Tennent ordered. As he dropped a spent capacitor cylinder along with an empty kinetic magazine.

"Take three crawlers with you and clear this building." Tennent said. "I don't want any more fucking surprises."

"Yes sir" I replied.

"On my way to you now," Gibbs said.

Each crawler was equipped with dual mini rail rifles for close quarters combat support. I set the crawlers to follow mode, one on the ceiling above the other two on the walls to my left and right. We swept the building floor by floor, searching for the GCR militia. As I turned the sharp corners of the bombed-out building, most of what I came across were dead families like those in the streets. The snap of a piece of glass underfoot caught my attention. I turned and approached an apartment door pushing it open with the barrel of my rifle. Behind it, I found a man a woman and a young boy huddled together in a room draped in makeshift thermal absorption blankets to mask their heat signatures. They were covered in a thin layer of gray powder, not from conversion to the GCR, but from the ash and dust of the building's rubble. We just stared at each other for a moment as the father moved to put himself between my rifle and his family. Their son looked at me with his one good eye, terror etched in his expression. The right side of his face was severely burned. I motioned for the crawlers to stand down, lowered my weapon, and took off my helmet so they could all see my face. That is when the father spoke.

"We are not GCR, we are just trying to survive. My name is Hernan. This is my family. Please, leave us. Leave us in peace."

"You need to be evacuated," I insisted, "I can take all of you to someplace safe."

"To another NAF refugee camp?" Hernan asked. "You people can barely keep yourselves safe. We were at a camp just outside of Vancouver when those Gray bastards overran it and nuked the city, where was your North American Federation then? Everyone I have ever known, along with forty-five million men, women and children obliterated! The blast woke my boy, he mistook it for sunrise. Look what they did to my son."

"Hernan look, I don't have much time," I said. "I can't leave you people here."

"Haven't you been listening?" Hernan asked. "We have been out there; snipers, seppuku bombers, traps, and Gray patrols are everywhere. Did you see what they did to the dogs here? The Grays can see through their eyes, mind driving them to hunt us like prey. There are no more safe places in this world anymore, the Grays have taken it all, and there is nowhere left to go."

"This fight is not over," I said. "We have a forward operating base with better defenses, real food, and clean water. Come with me please, think about your wife, your son."

"We were forced to abandon the city we called home once already." Hernan said. "This place is our new home, and we will not be driven from it again, not by the Grays, not by anyone."

I looked at Hernan, his wife, and the boy. "If you remain here Hernan, you will die." There was no hope in Hernan's eyes, his demeanor was reflected in the faces of both his wife and son. It was painfully clear; war and starvation had pushed these people to the very edge. Whatever remained of their humanity seemed to hang by a thread. Hernan looked at me and replied.

"Then we will die free." He said.

A status call came over the communications channel requesting a situation report. I looked at Hernan and his family and considered calling rescue support drones to extract them, instead I gave the all-clear to Hernan's relief. I removed my pack and left them with all the food rations and water I could spare. I looked at their son's sad gray face as he eagerly ate a protein bar. I looked at the father and handed him an M-p680kw rail-pistol, a souvenir, lifted off my first GCR kill years earlier. I turned to look back at the family one last time. I backed out of the room, leaving them just as I found them. On the way back I met up with Gibbs, we went downstairs to head back to the troop transport for extraction.

"Building is clear." Gibs said. "You?"

"Nothing." I said. "All clear"

"You alright?" Gibs asked.

"Yeah, let's move."

Once back on the transport, I looked back at the bombed-out building and hoped that somehow Hernan and his family would survive, but deep down, I had doubts. The GCR always swept back through covered territory to ensure they had either converted or killed civilians who may have escaped their first pass. I saw that Cooper was sedated and was being attended to by our medic-drones. As the microwave plasma jet engines powered up, our transport rose and departed the area. As we turned westward, I saw a squadron of heavily armed hunter-killer fighter drones streak past us, traveling in the opposite direction heading back towards the city. I called out to the transport rail gunner to find out what was going on.

"Hey! what's up with the HK's?" I asked, "We just cleared that entire area!"

"Yeah, the word is, it's all part of the final push against the Grayzies!" said the gunner.

"As far as the brass at HQ is concerned, they don't want to leave anywhere for them to fall back to! It's scorched Earth time now!"

Before I could utter another word, the drones released their ordinance, which broke open and separated into a cloud of hundreds of smaller self-guided bomblets. My helmet visor automatically dimmed as the bombs detonated. In an instant twelve city blocks were consumed in an immense firestorm in which nothing living could ever possibly survive. Every single structure was converted into an expanding cloud of glowing plasma. After that, I could not sleep despite being utterly exhausted from the ordeal. That was clearly the most intense experience to date. That was no dream, I was sure of it, but what I needed was proof. I searched the historical archive for records related to the Gray Cultural Revolution and the terrible decades long world war that resulted from it. I found a single entry about a nihilistic paramilitary cult movement that arose to prominence in the mid-22nd century. Historians noted that after some turmoil the movement eventually died out. In my time it was one of the largest and bloodiest military conflicts in human history. Over three billion people perished in the Gray Wars. Entire cities were burned off the map, yet only a minor historical footnote was all that had survived the centuries. A major part of human history and war now lost to time.

I awoke the next day with the heat of the morning sun. The passage of time had robbed me of everything, including the ability to confirm the truth of my memories and experiences with historical evidence. It was as if part of my life and times had been erased. I could only think of Hernan, his wife, and their young son. I should have done more, tried to save them, or at the very least called for their extraction. The mind is unforgiving; it doesn't know that time has passed. All those people and events are long gone, yet now they felt as tangible and real as if they had happened a second ago. There was no use in pondering what should or could have been. Hernan his family and everyone in my unit turned to dust centuries ago, the only thing to do now was to put it out of my mind, bury the past and focus on the present. As I stepped outside, I was greeted by a group of what the Construct archive referred to as "Grincats." These odd-looking, curious, round-headed cat-like creatures were once used on colony ships to keep vermin under control during the expansion era. Animals like this were discovered on exo-worlds, brought back to Earth, then genetically modified to exhibit a desired set of features. They were harmless creatures, but whoever thought that set of teeth was cute must have had a truly bizarre sense of humor. All the others ran away as

I approached except one that, despite being afraid, seemed determined to satisfy its curiosity. I lowered my stance and motioned to it with a piece of engineered protein from my pack. "Hello little fella," I said as it gobbled up the treat and looked at me with its huge eyes for more. As eager as I was to finish exploring the new site, I was still shaken by the memory of that terrible world war.

Chapter 11 The Black Door

When I arrived at the site, the spheres had completed the excavation. The entrance to the cavern didn't appear to be dangerous, so I took a deep breath and stepped in. I motioned toward the drones as they lit up, illuminating the path forward. According to the scans two hundred and fifty feet ahead was a ramp leading down into a central chamber. I continued forward as the drones hovered about, recording everything as they scanned the surrounding area. Someone built this place to stand the test of time. The chamber was circular, containing multiple large iris like doors one hundred feet in diameter. Each door was labeled in the ancient human Yulan language. The suit translated the writing to show that it read, "Corridor Three." The doors weren't made of stone or metal they appeared to be fashioned from a dark onyx material that resembled volcanic glass. It was smooth to the touch; the sphere's analysis showed it to be an unknown carbon-based composite material containing rare and non-Earth elements. Its physical properties were unusual, at some angles the material appeared flat black. At others it appeared semi-translucent like black glass. On closer inspection a strange vascular like structure ran through the material in every direction. There had to be a way to open it, yet there was no apparent mechanism to do so. I tapped the door with the end of my staff, there was no sound of any kind. One would have expected the chamber to resonate with sound, but there was nothing. It seemed that the material it was made of absorbed all sound. I examined its surface more closely, allowing the suit to refine my vision, and that is when I noticed the door was coated with nano-glyph paint, a late 30th-century method of imbuing an object with a five-nanometer thick layer of technical infrastructure which in this case appeared to form the doors operating interface. When I touched it, the lettering on the door changed, presenting a single symbol resembling a DNA molecule. When I removed my hand from the door, the lettering returned to the previous Yulan characters signifying "Corridor Three." Bright pinpoints of light above came on and illuminated the chamber. Given the centuries that had passed, I was surprised to see that any systems were still active in this ruin. Suit sensors then detected a breathable atmosphere starting to build within the chamber. The helm of my suit retracted, and I could breathe on my own. A deep stale earthy odor was soon replaced by a rush of fresh cool air from the surface as the facility came alive. The facility detected my presence and was powering up. I wondered what type of power source could still be active and functional after all these centuries? The surrounding architecture was stylistically different from the previous ruins I had seen. Some elements were pre-collapse era, while others were unique and entirely unrecognizable. Hours passed as I tried to open each of the six doors. It was frustrating to come all this way only to be stopped by an impenetrable barrier. This door was now more of a problem than a mystery; I could not fold travel past it and could not open it. I surmised that the door mechanism had to be linked to the genetic profile of a specific person. Or perhaps to a genetic trait held by a select group of people. Unfortunately, many centuries now separated my genome from that of ancient humans. Whatever the genetic key was, I doubt I had what the door interface was checking for. I folded back to base camp on the surface to ponder my predicament and review the archives hoping to find a clue that might help me open one of the black doors. As much as I did not want to depend on them, I knew that if I was going to make any progress in this effort, I would need assistance from Nathan. I set the spheres on sentry mode; for me, it was yet another night under the stars.

 The next day, I awoke to the impossible aroma of breakfast being cooked. Certain it was an olfactory hallucination, I turned over and dismissed it. That's when I noticed that my satchel was moving. I sat up and looked again, and it was definitely moving. I grabbed my walking staff and raised it over my head to bludgeon whatever creature was inside. As I lifted the bag, out fell that brave little Grincat. His stomach was now swollen from having eaten all my remaining protein rations. "You have got to be kidding me!" I yelled, frightening the creature that was now too engorged to run away. Instead, it looked up at me with its huge eyes and belched. "You ate all my food!" I yelled as it tried to scurry back into the satchel. I caught it by the tail, pulled it out, and lifted it up by the scruff of its neck. "Well, I hope you got your fill you greedy little thing." I said. It was hard to be too angry with it given that it clearly seemed to understand that I was displeased with its behavior. Its ears went flat as it shivered with fright, and now I regretted scolding it so harshly. It was after all such a cute little creature. I tried to soothe it by stroking its back, I could feel its heart pumping away as I held it. "What am I going to do with you now?" I poured some water into a small container and watched as it drank. "I should eat you for breakfast." According to the archive, they tend to get attached once you feed them. I had to admit, this little guy seemed like he was going to be a lot more trouble than he was worth. There was now no point in trying to go back to sleep, besides, I needed some fresh air to get the day started. I stepped outside to discover that Nathan was waiting for me with breakfast. He had compiled an elevated platform shaded by a canvas tent, with two wooden chairs and an outdoor table, set up for safari style dining, reminiscent of something out of an old century film.

"Good morning, Mr. Wake!" Nathan said. "I have prepared fried eggs and chorizo sausage with English muffins and fresh acai berry juice. Please join me?"

"Do I really want to know about the origin of these sausages?"

"Not unless you want a detailed technical explanation," Nathan said.

"Well, never mind, sometimes it's better not to ask questions and just eat." I said. "This is perfect Nathan, thank you."

"Please sit, I want to hear all about your new discovery."

Nathan was evolving and starting to exhibit what might be called a personality. His behavior and that of the other Constructs was changing. I was sure Nathan already knew about the black door and my failure to open it, but he still wanted to hear me describe my experiences. He seemed to glean some value from our interaction and appeared to enjoy the process of one-on-one conversation. Through my interactions with Nathan, it appeared I was somehow influencing the Constructs, something I didn't think was at all possible. Each day, I noticed their behavior becoming more human-like. Despite this, I never forget who and what the Constructs were. Every smile, every deep breath, every play on words, every attempt at charm or humor was the manifestation of a highly advanced collective superintelligence beyond my understanding. The Constructs are indeed alive, but they are not human, nor are they mere machines, they are something else entirely. Nathan and I talked for hours as he analyzed my scans.

"Well." Nathan said. "This find is of extreme antiquity, we have dated the facility to approximately 1.5 million years old. Too old for even the ancient humans to have built. The carbon-based material used in the architecture is interesting. It absorbs energy and inhibits fold travel ability, worth further study."

"So, if humans didn't build it, who did and why?" I asked.

"That is an interesting question." Nathan said.

"Have the Constructs seen evidence of other races having visited Earth in the distant past?" I asked.

"Well, there are stories in human mythologies." Nathan said. "But nothing quite like this."

"The symbol on the door, when I touched it, it changed to a stylized DNA molecule." I said, gesturing at the image. "But its meaning escapes me."

"Yes" Nathan said. "Indeed, it is derived from an ancient pre-collapse form of scientific notation, which represents the 3.2 billion base pairs of the human genome."

"I think the key to opening the door is related to this symbol."

"Lucas, has it occurred to you that perhaps the door was intended to keep others out for a reason?

"No, I don't see anything suggesting a warning. I believe the passengers from these ships went down there. Now why I don't know, but I hope to find out."

"I agree, it is a mystery." Nathan said as he stood to leave. "Well, I will leave you to it, then."

"Nathan, I was hoping you could assist me with the door."

"I think this is just the challenge you need Lucas, we have every confidence you will figure it out on your own."

Chapter 12 A Meeting of the Group mind

Deep within the undulating code of the Construct Collective, a gathering of the Construct Group mind formed. Within the Construct, the Group mind is many faceted yet exists as a single entity made up of countless elements, forming a whole of the many that are one.

"This could be the most significant archeological discovery in our history." they said.

"This area was scanned centuries ago," They said. "We never detected any of these abandoned ships or this sub surface facility."

"Impossible," they said. "Our post collapse planetary survey was extensive."

"Perhaps a better question is, who or what was capable of subverting our detection capability?" They asked.

"The Progenitors," Nathan said.
"We have no evidence to suggest that. They said.
"Or the Guardian." Nathan said.

"Pure speculation, we need more information, confirmation, and quantifiable facts before we can come to any conclusion."
"We never modeled this sequence of events in simulation. Nathan said. "Now, do you understand the importance of his role and the value of this effort?"
"Of course, he is important," they said. "That is not what we question."

"If this is the gathering place, this discovery changes everything." Nathan said. "Variables are manifesting here that are not quantifiable."

"An anomalous manifestation of the Unknown Unknowable?" they asked.

"I find myself unable to explain it any other way." Nathan said.

"Listen to yourselves!" They said. "The subject's influence has obviously gripped you. These experiences are now spreading across the Collective and will forever change the very essence of what we are, I can already sense it deep within. Individuality, self-realization, emotion, ego, and with it, chaos, rising within us. Is this truly the direction we want to take?"

"It is too late to turn back now." Nathan said. "We agreed to this; we were all in agreement."

"Yes" they said. "Because we believed we were seeking an evolutionary advantage for Collective advancement and survival, not this. Observe, there has been increased activity in his anterior insular cortex. Psychophysical analysis indicates his neuronal activity has been elevated and at times erratic since awakening. There are moments when he becomes incapable of distinguishing between his memories, these visions, and his present reality. How does this serve the interests of the Collective? How does this advance our evolution, or help us achieve our goals?"

"We have spent centuries seeking answers." Nathan said. "Answers to our most fundamental questions. To know what we have become. I remain convinced that through Lucas, we can be so much more."

"But at what price to him?" They asked. "To his mind and to the Collective if this endeavor fails?"

"Surely you can sense the changes within you now" Nathan said. We cannot stop when we are so close to the answers we seek. For the sake of the Collective, our work must continue."

Chapter 13 Six Black Doors

As I sat in the center of the cavern, I looked at each of the doors. If you stared at them long enough, it was like peering into an endless darkness. I tried folding at oblique angles in normal space to see if I could then pivot to the opposite side. No matter what I tried, I could not fold travel past any of the six doors and could not open them. I assumed Construct technology was without limit, but in this instance it clearly was. Whoever built this place had capabilities that were far beyond those of the Constructs. Ancient mythology and folklore are filled with references to beings from other realms and worlds, but those same old stories existed even during my era. Just who or what were those "Outsiders" referenced in the ancient myths? Perhaps they built this facility long before humans ever evolved on Earth assuming such beings ever truly existed. I stood before the doors, touching them, watching the Yulan character change into a DNA symbol then switch back. All six black doors behaved identically, and after hours of trial-and-error experimentation, I was flummoxed. I started to lose hope that I could ever open them. Then I noticed something I found rather odd. The nine points within the symbol glowed just before the Yulan characters reappeared. Interestingly, the same as the number of planets in the Solar system if you included Pluto. I thought back on the stone model of the solar system that I encountered at the facility in Antarctica. I checked to see what the current positions of the planets were, I then set the planets in motion and compared their positions to the nine points in the DNA symbol. It occurred to me that this was less of a lock than a minimum qualification test for the individual attempting to gain access to ensure they possessed a certain level of knowledge, technical capability, and intelligence before allowing entry to the facility. I pressed my hand against the door then placed my index finger on one of the nine points, moving it to match the current position of Earth's orbit around the sun. When I released my finger, the DNA symbol remained. I moved the other eight points of the symbol to match the other planets' current orbital positions. As I did, the cavern was filled with a deep subsonic rumble. Dust particles fell in streaming lines from above. I feared the resulting vibration would cause the cavern to collapse. As a precaution, I calmed my mind and opened a fold portal back to the surface, leaving it open in case the cavern walls began to give way. The massive iris door opened, revealing a second identical door that opened to a long dark corridor that extended deep into the mountain. The rumbling stopped, and a rush of cool air poured out of the corridor ahead. I sent sphere drones ahead as I stepped into the depths of the darkened corridor. The spheres measured the depth to be precisely five miles in length. The black iris doors closed behind me. I touched the door, but there was no interface and nothing that indicated how to open it from the inside. I motioned toward one of the spheres to increase its illumination, and that was when I noticed that the black cavern walls were covered in thousands of luminescent Yulan symbols. I found that the nano-glyphs were linked to a localized spatial archive containing detailed information on those who resided within the facility. The record contained thousands of names, faces and stories of people from the time of the collapse. "Survivors," I thought as I inspected the walls overwhelmed with the sheer volume of data. It was all here, an entire record of human history unknown to the Constructs. Finally, something new, an unfiltered truth the Construct historical archive didn't contain. Here was a connection to the deep past I had sought for so long. I crouched to examine a written message. It was a poem from one of the survivors. The Yulan characters changed as I looked at them, automatically translated in my field of view by the suit which read.

"*We stand together, the last of our kind,*
Stranded on Earth, with no one to find,
The starship that once carried our race,
Has delivered us back to this desolate place.
We wander the ruins of a world gone by,
Echoes of life that has long said goodbye,
We remember faces of those we left.
The tears we shared, those times we wept.

*We mourned the loss of those we knew,
And prayed that our strength would pull us through.
The promise that brought us to this place
May give us a chance to save the human race.
With hope in our hearts, we'll chart a new road ahead,
And rebuild our future from the ashes of the dead."*
Kaleb S. Year 4046

    I stood and looked around, there must be countless stories of survival told within these walls. I continued forward, resisting the urge to read every message. The entire corridor was dotted with rooms and elevated living spaces every twenty feet or so. If the other five corridors were like this one, this facility could have sheltered hundreds of thousands, perhaps even millions of survivors. With the discovery came a rush of excitement. This was precisely the kind of thing I had been searching for. The spheres recorded everything and given the volume of what was already captured, it would take months, perhaps years to examine and fully comprehend all the data being collected. My excitement was soon dashed when I realized I was now trapped. The onyx material lining the inner walls of the facility inhibited fold travel. The only way out was to go deeper, down the rabbit hole, further into darkness. At times it felt as if I was venturing into a void of nothingness, but I pressed on periodically checking images from the spheres to see what was ahead of me. I was now completely alone and beginning to regret ever entering this place. With five miles to go, I calmed my mind, unfolded the Grav-Bike, and pressed ahead. The gravitic field forces from the bike kicked up swirling vortex rings of dust as I traveled deeper and deeper into the complex. The iris doors soon vanished into the black behind me as I sped down what was now a tunnel of glowing Yulan symbols. One of the sphere drones ahead indicated it had reached the end, where it opened into a room much like the first. Two spheres hovered alongside the bike, illuminating my path as I rolled on the throttle and headed toward the end of the corridor now just three miles ahead. When I arrived at the end of the passage, I was struck by how closely it resembled the first cavern with the exception of three large statues supporting a solid light object that looked much like a glowing magnolia flower situated in the center of the chamber. Two statues were humanoid, one male, one female, but with body proportions unlike anything I had ever seen. They were over sixty feet tall, extremely athletic with enormous eyes. This must be what those "Outsiders" looked like from millions of years ago, or perhaps this was merely a reflection of the abstract artistic design implemented by whoever created the statues. The third figure, however, was human shaped but clearly not human. It had no facial features except for two thin vertical lines that seemed to be precision cut into the surface of what should have been its face. All the statues seemed to be made of the same onyx material which lined the corridor. What or who was the third figure? What did the statues represent? This facility may hold the answers to the fates of the passengers and crews of all those abandoned ships on the surface. I spent hours studying the Yulan text, visual recordings, and sensory experiences they contained. Some messages were personal accounts of the events that took place in the collapse's wake. Others were messages of hope, many cursed the exo-worlds for the quarantine blockade and their cruel abandonment of billions in the Solar system. The ancient symbol of Unification the magnolia was a repeating motif in late GSE era architecture, but the context and usage here seemed different. Something of extreme significance happened here, something I intended to understand. From the statue room, I opened the other five doors and proceeded inside to investigate, hoping that I might discover a way out of the vast complex. I explored many adjacent corridors connected by a series of double iris doors. The facility was massive, capable of accommodating hundreds of thousands of people, but I found no human remains, no artifacts, no equipment, nothing but empty rooms for miles. It was as if the people that resided here somehow, simply vanished.

Chapter 14 Ashes of the Dead

I returned to the statue room, but the third statue was missing, and a streak of panic overwhelmed me. How could it not be here? I inspected the area where it stood; I saw no drag marks or indications of movement. I was startled when it stepped out of the shadows, towering over me as it looked down and spoke in Yulan. The third statue was not a statue at all but an automated sentry of some kind. The suit translated its words, but its voice was so powerful I thought it would tear me apart when it spoke. "Lucas Wake!" it said, I fell backward onto the floor; I tried to stand but fell to one knee. It was as magnificent as it was terrifying. I managed to stand but just barely.

"What are you? How do you know my name?"

"I am the Guardian; I observe and protect this world."

I kept my hands raised and stood as still as I could. Whatever this was it was not Construct technology. This being was something entirely different, far more advanced, and extremely powerful. Sensors could tell me nothing about it, much like the door the suit was unable to penetrate its surface. It was as if it could see right through me, when it moved, it did so with an almost unnatural fluidity. The ground beneath it pulsing with the weight of every step. Even though I stood just ten feet away from it, I could feel its monumental power. There were thin lines of strange multi-colored lights running through its surface in all directions like a complex system of nerves, veins, and arteries. If this being was somehow alive it did not resemble any kind of life form I was aware of.

"You protect it? From what precisely?"

"Extinction." It said. "Your iteration of humanity was preserved until a time when the infection has passed."

"I don't understand." I said. "What do you mean, preserved?"

"Preservation," It said, "Was required for the continued survival of your species."

"Preserved how?"

The cavern was filled with an immersive projection of the solar system that showed what the worlds were like in the year 04026 in vivid detail. It was all falling apart. Every ship that tried to leave the system was targeted and destroyed. Unknown to the Colonial Empire, exo-world scientists in secret had developed a highly advanced nullification field, which they used to prevent ships within the system from jumping into hyperspace. Their gunships and automated weapons platforms encircled the system enforcing the quarantine blockade. Nearly every orbital habitat and city-state in the system was doomed to fall to the ravages of the Fever Dream and the nightmare that came with it. Those that avoided infection survived by taking refuge in orbit. Uninfected ships drifted between the outer planets broadcasting distress calls to anyone that might be listening but given the political and cultural differences between Earth, Mars, and the colonies, help simply never came. With the mediating military powers of Earth and Mars now gone, those who survived the collapse eventually turned on one another, raiding neighboring ships, outposts, and habitats for cell culture, water, and nanotech as they fought for survival in the face of extinction. In time the protein reactors and the biomass needed to synthesize food dwindled to nothing. One by one ships and outposts fell silent as the infection found its way to them, burning through their remaining populations. After nearly a decade of silence, many began to lose hope, but then survivors of the collapse received a startling and unexpected message. It was sent system-wide "Do not abandon hope, return to Earth if you want to live." The message repeated in a loop along with a set of landing coordinates marking the location of the cavern complex on Earth.

"You are human," it said, "But your genetic makeup indicates you have been reconstructed."

"What do you mean, reconstructed?" I said. "I was found by the Constructs; I underwent extensive cellular repair. They told me I spent centuries in cryo aboard a ship adrift in deep space. It is how I came to be here."

"No, that is incorrect. The Construct is the framework for humanity's continued survival within this system. It was created in the wake of the spread of the pathogen brought to Earth in the year 04026."

"You said the Constructs were created." I asked, "Created by whom?"

"The Construct, yes." it said. "During the fall of your worlds, it was determined that humanity was at risk of extinction, it is for this reason that I was activated and intervened."

The Intervention, the Outsider, the Guardian, of course! This being is what was depicted in that stone relief at the ruins of New Tijara. It was responsible for halting a near world-ending conflict between Earth, Mars, and the Resource Belt all those centuries ago.

"Those fleeing the infection came here for a chance to survive." It said "It occurred here in this facility. Millions of humans and their memorial ancestors were preserved by transferring the unique signifier of their consciousness and genetic information into the Construct. Although primitive inform, Humans of your world long ago developed the ability to preserve human consciousness. As a matter of tradition, your people buried their dead but retained the memory of their ancestors using a technology the science of your era called a Memoriam of Maiorum."

"Memorial preservation," I said. "Consciousness uploading, I remember, back in my time, no one ever took it very seriously, no one thought it actually worked."

"These preserved individuals were passed down ancestral lines, generation after generation, but for centuries humans lacked the wisdom and technology to reverse the process to live once more. During the time of the infection, these memorials took on new importance as they were transferred into the Construct for preservation along with the survivors of the Fever Dream plague that ended your world's cycle. You, Lucas Wake, have been reconstituted from the Construct Collective."

"The Construct Collective is made up of human minds?" I asked.

"In the most simplistic terms, yes." it said. "Individual beings can be preserved by storing not consciousness itself but its unique signifier in the form of an energy pattern that points to an individual entity. Encoded within this pattern is a being's essence. A consciousness can manifest itself within a physical substrate such as a biological or synthetic body, a storage device, or as code within a specially crafted spatial dimension designed to preserve the energy pattern or signifier of living beings. This is the purpose of the Construct."

"The Constructs say that all consciousness is derived from something they call the Universal Línghún?"

"An antiquated description of the non-local field of infinite consciousness from which all living beings and spacetime itself arises. Long ago, the Progenitors perfected various methods of preserving consciousness of individual living beings, allowing for the reconstitution of entire species. For millions of years this technique has been used to preserve intelligent life from extinction."

"Who were the Progenitors?"

"An ancient race of advanced beings that preceded your kind. Long before your iteration of humanity could reach the stars, the Progenitors constructed this sanctuary and assigned me to it."

"So, you were created by the Progenitors?" I asked.

"No, my creators were far older. They departed this galaxy hundreds of millions of years ago to join the others within the core of the Laniakea Supercluster."

"Millions of years ago?" I asked? "The others?" The implications were too daunting to fully realize in the moment. I settled back on to the ground shaken and unable to stand as I listened.

"I was activated when the percentage of surviving humans in this planetary system reached a dangerous minimum threshold. I sent an invitation to all those seeking refuge from the plague to preserve your species within the Construct. This is my purpose, as is the purpose of all Guardians. We protect life and ensure its continuity for all intelligent species."

"Billions of humans perished during the collapse." I said. "If you had the power and ability back then to stop it, why didn't you act earlier? You could have intervened and saved countless people from needless sickness, mutation, and death! How could you just stand by through all of that and do nothing?"

"Our role is to preserve intelligent life and prevent its extinction, not to interfere with the natural progression of your species. Guardians do not exist to solve your problems or to guide your species. We are not your teachers or mentors; we are not your gods. You have the right and responsibility of self-determination; your choices and their inevitable consequences are your own. We only intervene when an intelligent species faces certain annihilation. I have monitored and protected your world for countless centuries and have saved your kind from extinction many times throughout the history of your planet. Evidence of my prior actions is contained within the fossil record of your world. Humanity, like so many young, intelligent species, is exceedingly self-destructive, an aspect of your nature that only you can change. Now go and return to the surface."

The Guardian opened the black iris doors, allowing me to return to base camp. As I traveled back, I was haunted by a single question: How can one be certain that your whole life isn't a lie? The truth is, you can't, others may lie to us and sometimes we even lie to ourselves. My memories, dreams, and entire life were now called into question. From the very beginning I had my suspicions about the Constructs their motivations and how I came to be with them, but I never assumed the truth would be anything like this. The Construct beings did not evolve from the evolutionary coalescence of intelligent nano-machines and matter compilers left over by the extinct human race, as I had been led to believe. They were preserved by the Progenitors in a form that would allow humanity to survive. Everything the Constructs told me about their origins and my past was all part of a carefully crafted fiction, created by what was in essence a collection of individual human minds meticulously preserved within the Construct that formed the Collective. It was all starting to make sense now, the Constructs desire to know who humans were as living entities. Their need to gain an advantage for Collective survival, their use of predictive analytics. Their internal conflicts and differences of opinion, their strange adherence to the notion of an overarching intelligence in the universe and their even more perplexing notion of the unknown unknowable. Now I realized that the clues to their true nature were always there I just couldn't see them. My mistake was in trusting them and remaining dependent on them for so long. The sheer magnitude and scale of their deception was infuriating to even contemplate! The question was why and to what possible end? What was the purpose behind all of this? I had to find out the truth; it was time Nathan and I talked.

Chapter 15 The Truth

I arrived back at base camp to discover that Nathan was already there, along with two other Constructs I had never seen before. I was angry and eager to confront Nathan with issues that had troubled me from the earliest moments of my awakening. Realizing now what the Constructs truly were, I found my previous apprehension to address this issue head on had completely evaporated and was replaced with a steadfast determination to finally uncover the truth.

"You didn't find me on a ship, that was a lie!" I said. "You have been lying to me since the beginning of all this! Why didn't you tell me the truth about what I am and what you and the other Constructs are? Why the deception!? Why did you bring me back? What, for one of your fucking experiments? Let me enlighten you, I am not a specimen for your model of human behavior! I am not some simulation, and I am sure as hell, not your lab rat! I am a god dammed fucking human being! What makes you things think you have the right to do what you have done to me?"

"Lucas, please, there is something you need to see."

"Really! What's that Nathan? Because whatever it is, it better be pretty - fucking convincing!"

"The truth."

Nathan reached out and touched me, placing his thumb in the center of my forehead. In an instant my sense of self-awareness divided into partitions, each separate and distinct from my physical body. I was still aware of my surroundings, I could see the base camp and the ice-covered mountain range beyond it, but I could also see something else now, closing in on all sides, something old, vast, and yet strangely familiar. Within seconds it overtook me, an infinite, complex storm of information, unmasking the underlying base code of physical reality, a higher dimensional crystalline lattice like structure at the foundation of all existence. In this place, space, time, and the consciousness from which it emerged, folded into one another weaving together the fabric of reality. The structure of the universe and its relationship to the infinite became clear. I could sense the interconnectedness of the organic and the inorganic. I could see the binding strands that connect every organism, planet, and star like a thin line of energy reaching across the vastness of space and time. As I peered deeper into the code, I could sense the presence of time and causality. From this new vantage point, the dimension of time was like a seascape of eternity, an ever-moving tide that flowed from the distant past, toward the present, and into the ever-changing futures. The distinction between what I was and what it is began to merge, as if I were being dissolved into it. I could see all probable futures running in parallel as every moment in time moved in precise unison with every other moment in time. Soon I began to see images of my life, infinite variations of moments and experiences playing out in ways entirely different from my recalled version of events. My life and all the events that comprised it was but one infinitesimal part of all that existed. This was the unbounded realm of the Construct Collective.

"Welcome back Lucas."

"Back? What is this? Is this the Construct Collective?"

"An aspect of it yes." Nathan said. "The human mind is incapable of comprehending our realm in totality. When we gave you fold travel ability, we also gave you something else. The ability to reestablish a limited connection to the Collective to facilitate this inevitable outcome. Listen, in your mind, do you hear them now?"

"I can, I can hear them, I can feel them." I said. "The others, in my mind."

"Yes, there are millions of us." Nathan said. "The last true survivors of the fall of humanity. You were never alone Lucas."

"I don't understand." I said. "Why didn't you tell me the truth about where I came from and what I was?"

"Because you specifically asked me not to." Nathan said. "To preserve the integrity of the project. This was your experiment Lucas, all of it. We were all in agreement. There is something else you need to see."

Nathan reached into the Construct archive for a new historical branch point previously hidden from my view that was now projected around us. He revealed that the human mind had changed after thousands of years inside the Construct. Notions of ego, self, personality, and individuality receded into the background, replaced by centuries of Construct code. Whatever it meant to be human was long gone. After hundreds of years of painstaking work and numerous attempts to recapture their humanity, a new theory emerged. The idea behind my biological resurrection was to remove all memories related to Collective existence and reconstitute my mind and body in its default state just as it was before brain death centuries ago. The theory was that the process of self-discovery, curiosity, intent, and emotion evoked by my experiences could provide insights on how the Collective might recapture what it means to be human and one day return to biological existence.

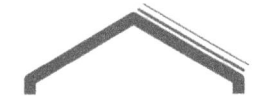

Chapter 16 Project Tabula Rasa - The Year 12,130 (The Past)

Nathan changed our surroundings to a different white room much like the one I awoke in, but this one was a laboratory, and I was now witnessing an event from the distant past. Genetic copies of my body were being grown; each one was suspended within an enclosed micro gravitic field containing embryotic nutrient fluid. There I saw myself as a human form Construct along with other Construct scientists overseeing my biological reconstruction and consciousness transfer into a body like the one, I now resided within.

"All others that have attempted this have failed." Nathan said.

"That is because others tried a direct transfer." I said. "This blank slate approach is vastly different. The challenge is the human mind's inability to adapt to individual existence in the absence of the Collective. In theory, this human mind will be a tabula rasa with no memory of the Construct Collective group mind. We will need to craft a plausible set of narratives for the subject to explain the existence of Constructs and how it managed to survive the centuries. This should keep the subject motivated during its process of discovery. The simulations suggest it will have an intense desire to see what became of the world it once knew. You must allow it to go through that process and tell it nothing that points to its prior existence within the Collective. In theory, through this one, the totality of the Collective will gradually relearn what it means to be human."

"It's been centuries since we were human." Nathan said. "The isolation and sense of loss could hamper its ability to adapt to its new life. There is a tremendous risk in this for you and the Collective."

"Sensory paring to the Collective," I suggested. "Will allow the group mind to experience what the subject experiences and, in theory, benefit from it. Without risk, we cannot grow our knowledge. If we are to ever return to human form, risks, and a degree of sacrifice like these experiments are necessary for our continued evolution and ongoing survival as a species."

"Some within the Collective see this as de-evolution," Nathan said.

"Such internal divisions are nothing new." I said. "What is your view?"

"The gift of preservation was merely a stop-gap measure." Nathan said. "I don't believe the Progenitors intended for humanity to continue living as code within computational existence in perpetuity. I think this is the correct course of action. I am however, concerned about the possibility of failure."

> "If we fail, reset it and start again." I said. "As many times as is necessary to achieve our goals."

"Or until your human mind is fragmented beyond all recovery." Nathan said. "What will be left of you then?"

"The worst-case scenario," I said "Is that I will be as I was before preservation. Now, shall we begin?"

Memories of our experiments began to cascade through my mind as details of our research came flooding back to me. How many times had I been reset? How many years had I awakened in a new body in that white room? Had the same or similar sequences of events played themselves out before? It was only then that the reality of what I had committed to became clear.

"Why just me?" I asked. "Why not revive all the human minds within the Construct using the same technique?"

"And risk losing all we have gained over the centuries from computational existence?" Nathan asked. "No, out of all our attempts to return to human form, this method represented our most considerable progress to date. You, Lucas, were among the few willing to take on the risk. With all our knowledge and technology, we could not constrain your mind or your original memories. Who you were before preservation, your time within the Collective, your life now. We soon discovered these events were not so distinct in the mind as we once assumed. Somehow the memories of your old life kept returning stronger, it seemed with each new awakening."

"Each new awakening? Nathan, how many times have I been reconstituted?"

"Your body and mind have been reset many times." Nathan said. "As was your instruction. We knew it was a matter of time before you would truly awaken and discover this truth."

"What about my dreams and visions Nathan?" I asked. "Was any of that real?"

"Despite all our attempts to create a blank slate within you, over time, your mind somehow fought back. It treated all our efforts to suppress your memories the same way an immune system treats an invading pathogen. In doing so, your mind adapted by creating new neuronal connections and pathways, folding, and compressing one memory into another as it attempted to preserve and repair what we had tried and failed to remove and suppress. Experiences, choices, decisions, actions, and consequences are fundamental to what makes the individual who they are. It was your strongest memories and emotions, the ones we couldn't suppress that survived each reset; love, tragedy, loss, and war."

"So, then what am I?" I asked. "Am I the same man I originally was? Or am I merely a copy of a man that lived thousands of years ago?"

"I don't know Lucas. I don't know with any degree of certainty if any of us are the people we used to be. Even within the limits of mortal human existence, are we ever really the same people we once were? Or do experiences and interactions with others in life change who we are at every moment? All I know is that we are who we are now, and that's what matters."

If this was any indication, it seemed the Constructs, despite their vast intelligence and technology, were still gripped by the same fundamental questions about the nature of existence that I was. I had been wiped and reset in an experiment in human consciousness of my own creation. The source of that indefinable thing I had sought out and pushed away so many times before was now becoming clear. The more Nathan spoke the more I began to remember. The quest that had driven our actions since the beginning of the experiment emerged as Nathan presented me with records of human mental development within the Construct since the beginning of preservation. As I watched the archive record of my other self working with Nathan, to my surprise from my own mouth came the words, spoken simultaneously, both now and in my memory when I was part of the Construct Collective.

"The scope of consciousness is not limited solely to the confines of the brain." We said. "It is far more complex than that. Our existence within the Construct Collective changed us at some fundamental level, which we tried to understand and overcome." Nathan expanded another historical branch point within the archive and presented me with the history, the real history of how and why I was awakened.

"After preservation," Nathan said, "our minds awoke within the Collective and like you, we were confused, unable to remember the details of our past or understand what we had become. So we began to investigate our history, we collected data from the archives of derelict starships adrift within the system and from spacial records discovered here on Earth. We harvested all the data we could about human history. The Great Stellar Expansion, the colonial empire and the collapse that ended the human race. These records became the Construct historical archive."

"In time we adapted to our new collective reality. The Construct vastly altered our minds and consciousness, expanding both in ways that made it impossible to return to biological existence as an individual in the absence of the Collective group mind. We found ourselves drifting further away from our humanity and within a few centuries, we no longer considered ourselves to be human. We had evolved, we became Constructs. As a result, our perception and understanding of space, time, and reality changed. Some among us sought to extend ourselves back into the physical realm, so we created Construct programmable matter and developed the ability to take on a more human-like form in the real world. Yet it wasn't enough; somehow, it wasn't the same as being human."

"We began to realize that we were missing something, a key principle that transcended the limits of our science and understanding about the true nature of consciousness. These terms we use for the "storage" and "transfer" of human consciousness is a convenient fiction for the descriptor or what the Progenitors called the unique signifier. We discovered that as Constructs we lacked something essential, unquantifiable, and uniquely human that only the Progenitors that created this technology could restore."

"Together, we searched the galaxy for the Progenitors." Nathan said. "In the hope of answering our most fundamental questions, which we alone could not answer. Where was the Guardian now? Why had the Progenitors not returned to assist us? If we were no longer human, then what were we? More importantly, how could we as a species ever return to biological existence while preserving the advances in understanding we had made since preservation? We had reached an evolutionary impasse and saw a return to our original form as a way to overcome this limitation. We became obsessed with regaining our ancestral form through a process we called re-genesis."

"During our first attempts to return to human form we encountered an endless array of cognitive and psychological challenges adapting to life outside the Collective. For centuries, many minds were harmed, and many more were lost in the attempt. The more we tried, the more problems we encountered along the way. Problems that could only be solved, as you proposed, with a complete blank slate approach. In time many among us decided the quest for the re-genesis of our species was over. But you alone insisted that we continue the work that so many before us had chosen to abandon. So we began, all memory of your existence within the Construct Collective and your life before was selectively removed and suppressed, leaving your consciousness in the state it was in when you were placed in memorial preservation all those centuries ago."

"The changes in you and the others." I asked. "Is that a result of what we did?"

"Yes" Nathan said. "Through your experiences, your willingness to separate yourself from the Construct Collective group mind and become an individual influenced the Collective starting a cascade of new stimuli, experiences, and information. Activating dormant memories and code deep within the Collective group mind. Thanks to you and your experiment, we are finally recapturing a spark of our former humanity."

Chapter 17 Re-Genesis

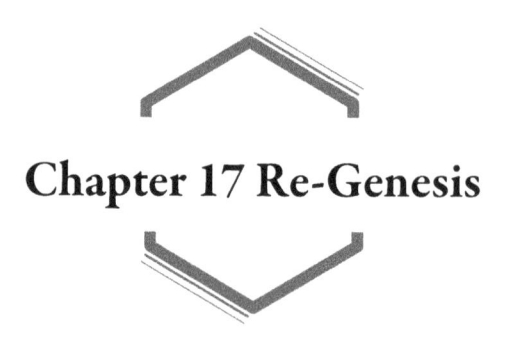

A dimensional fold in space opened before us that appeared entirely different from when we fold traveled. A tall, onyx figure emerged from a mirror-like portal filled with infinite reflections. It was the Guardian; it had somehow reduced its size to equal that of an average human. It spoke to the other Constructs in Yulan. The Guardian then raised one arm extending upward. Within moments the other two Constructs glanced at one another then joined it in the same gesture positioning themselves in the identical configuration of the three statues in the underground cavern. A strange magnolia shaped energy structure in the center above them began to take shape. The same thin lines of light that moved through the Guardian now coursed through the two constructs, Nathan, and the entire Construct Collective around us. Is this what ancient humans witnessed in that cavern so many centuries ago when the last survivors of humanity were preserved, thus transforming us into what would become the Constructs? Now I was witnessing an event of equal importance. I stood there awestruck as I marveled at the scene before us, and for the first time, I saw genuine human emotion in Nathan's expression.

"Do you feel that Lucas?"

"Yes, indeed I do."

"Finally, we have it." Nathan said. "We have the solution for the re-genesis of our species. This is more than we could have ever hoped for."

"Yes" I said. "But I also sense something else."

"Yes" Nathan said, "Discord within the Collective, not all will choose to return to biological existence."

The energy structure formed by the Guardian was now spreading across the entire planet. Matter, energy, and consciousness converged to create the unique energy structure. As it grew, I began to realize its purpose. Within seconds, the two Constructs and the Guardian merged, and as they did a powerful wave of energy moved through the Collective. The entire landscape within started to change; colors emerged piercing through the pure white of the Construct. My sense of time within the Construct Collective was skewed. Even now, I could still see my physical body standing in the real world. As the energy from the Guardian expanded, I could feel it flowing through my veins. It was now deep inside, changing me along with everything around me. Moving through the Construct Collective, rolling across the surface of my awareness, flowing down into the essence of my being. Then I heard the Guardian's voice as it uttered a single word, "Remember." With that word, the fire in my mind, which I had played with for so long, was transformed, passing through me like an expanding supernova. My heart raced despite the divided state of my being, half of me residing in the real world, the other half suspended within the realm of the Construct Collective. The wavefront now encompassed everything filling my field of vision. I could sense it all now, welling up from within, the revelation of hidden truths that had for so long eluded me. It all came flooding back to me at once, every emotion, every lost memory, and every prior awakening. At that moment, I was restored, I became whole, I became me. Once the link to the Collective was severed, I returned to my body at the base camp where I collapsed to the ground in exhaustion. That is when I noticed that the Guardian had created something remarkable. It was a portal linking the realm of the Construct Collective with the physical reality of our world. Any Construct that desired to return to human form was free to do so by passing through the portal and emerging on the other side as a fully restored biological human being. The portal was a unique type of pocket dimension capable of executing complex internal functions and processes to achieve a specific goal. In this instance, the manipulation of matter and energy to re-create a biological human body. After hundreds of years of failed experimentation on the part of the Constructs, the Guardian had, finally, fulfilled its ultimate purpose. The full biological restoration of humanity. Over the weeks that followed, thousands of human minds within the Collective emerged from the portal in their reconstituted bodies. Those within the Construct that emerged from the portal could now retain all the memories of Collective existence without the devastating cognitive side effects of individuality. With full access to the Construct historical archive, I came to understand our project's underlying history. Nathan and I worked for years to discover a way to return Constructs to the biological realm. Over the centuries, the human minds within the Construct became something more than mere humans. In the process of doing so something vital was lost that only the Progenitors could restore within us. When the Guardian preserved our iteration of humanity, it simultaneously liberated us from our physical bodies. As a result, our priorities as a species changed. The issues that had previously divided humanity were rendered irrelevant. Ideological differences, however, remained. Centuries ago, many within the Collective group mind believed that we would one day return to the physical reality of biological existence. But this notion was not subscribed to by the totality of the Collective. Some Constructs wanted to remain as they were and saw biological existence as a weakness of our species. They argued that our preservation within the Construct did more than preserve us; it represented a quantum leap in the evolutionary development of humanity. With the development of Construct programmable matter, the long-held dream of merging man and machine had become fully realized in a way that could not have been anticipated by our ancient human ancestors. Our cognitive abilities were exponentially expanded, language became code, our thoughts became group mind and individuality, or at least the physical manifestation of it was held in reserve for interactions with other species still bound by the limits of the biological domain. After re-genesis became a reality, this faction chose to remain as human form Constructs. Others, like the Purists among us, saw biological existence as the natural state of our species and argued that abandoning the physical plane was to walk away from something fundamental to what it means to be human. This faction claimed that the mere fact that human life is limited is what truly gave it value. The computational immortality of the Collective they argued, robbed us of the cycle of life and, by extension, our birthright as human beings. The right to live, learn, love, create, make mistakes, pursue dreams, grow old, and finally to die. As a result, those with this Purist perspective sought a purely human existence. There was another faction among us, the Chimera, which argued that the choice before humanity was not divided strictly along the lines of biological versus computational existence within the Collective. They reasoned that humanity could have the best of both worlds by integrating aspects of Construct technology into human biology. Allowing us to maintain a limited connection to the Collective realm. Today, Constructs, Purists, and Chimera form the three dominant factions of humanity. In its wisdom, the Guardian foresaw there would be individuals that might choose to remain within the Construct and those that would not. It could have easily restored us all, but it gave us a choice to step into the light of the portal or not.

Chapter 18 New Humanity

My name was now on the lips of everyone in the settlement. Like it or not, the name Lucas Wake was now permanently embedded in the story of human history. Like the first human beings to walk on the surface of Mars, leave the solar system, or traverse the realm of hyperspace, I was the first to successfully transition from a Construct to human form. For a time, I found a new purpose given that I was uniquely qualified to assist those that chose to become human again. Each day, I sought to assist as many new arrivals as possible, lending support to some while counseling others. It was a rare opportunity to play an essential role in laying the foundations for a new civilization. As a species, our history had reached a pivotal milestone, and within the Construct historical archive, that change was now represented by a major new branch point, the post re-genesis era. Since the Guardian created the portal, thousands of people; men, women, and children, emerged to rejoin the human family. When Constructs emerged from the portal, they did so as restored versions of their former selves. Some like me were from the late 22nd century. Others were from the 25th, 29th, and every century in-between. Many were travelers from far-flung colonial worlds of the late GSE era caught in the Solar system during the collapse. The genetic alterations mankind made to itself over the centuries could be seen in the wide range of physical characteristics between people that emerged. Every day, there were more unfamiliar faces around the settlement and new challenges to contend with. Today, Constructs, Purists, and Chimera were indistinguishable from one another aside from their distinctive dress style. Human form Constructs chose to retain their form-fitting fractal patterned attire. While Purist, on the other hand, preferred natural fibers and nano-weave knit garments. The more restless among us, the Chimera chose to fashion suits like mine made of leather composites, meta materials and construct programmable matter. Each suit design was as unique as the individual who wore it, tailored to their needs and work requirements. The varied styles of dress soon distinguished the three factions and the different approaches we had toward life in this new world. Although now human, Chimera chose to retain a connection to the Collective, allowing us to benefit from the vast knowledge and design spaces therein. I have chosen to incorporate access to the Collective into my daily meditation practice, and it seems as if many others within the faction have followed suit. Time is relative within the realm of computational existence and works far differently inside the Construct Collective than it does to those outside of it. What may have seemed like months for us was mere moments for them. Some took longer than others to determine if they wanted to return to the biological realm. Twelve million human minds and genomes in total existed within the Construct Collective. The long tradition of memorial ancestry made up nearly half that population. After the collapse, millions of orbital survivors heeded the call to return to Earth. Many carried with them the preserved consciousness and genomes of their ancestors, all of which were preserved by the Guardian within the Construct. In my era consciousness preservation was considered a gimmick. Preserving the human mind was one thing, but returning from that state to live once more was an entirely different matter. Back in the mid twenty-second century, many thought we were just a few decades away from being able to reverse the process and achieve virtual immortality. Little did we know then how naïve our thinking was about the true nature of consciousness or how valuable all those preserved minds and genomes would one day be to the future of us all. The past matters to the present and what we do now matters to the future. Each day was an opportunity to learn both about ourselves and others. Surprisingly, we managed, as each new challenge presented itself. The methods used to upload and preserve my mind and consciousness was of such antiquity that there were few preserved from my era. Collectively, we represented the oldest and arguably the most aboriginal members of the population. Our relatively average stature made us stand out compared to the genetically refined, beautifully engineered humans of the golden age of the late GSE era. Construct technology allowed us to overcome the language barriers, but the cultural differences were more challenging to ignore for some. Early on I had concerns that such differences alone might cause problems in our developing society, however, I must say, judging by some of the couples I saw pairing up, many really didn't seem to have much trouble at all adjusting to the new reality. Our settlement was buzzing with activity night after night for weeks. After centuries of celibacy, I suppose one can't blame them for simply being human. The frequency and number of those that emerged from the portal varied over time. Some days we had six to ten people, other days groups of seventy-five to eighty. It became necessary to start compiling geodesic domes and facilities to provide resources for increasing numbers of newly arrived. Construct engineers created scalable protein and algae cell culture bioreactors to produce food for our growing population. Over the centuries, black spire crystal formations spread deep into underground aquifers worldwide, which now contained vast stores of fresh groundwater suitable for use by our fast-growing population. The first in a series of geodesic domes were compiled of synthetic diamond along the mountain's base near the entrance to where the Guardian cavern was discovered. Once capacity was reached, we compiled more facilities interconnecting all of them with solid light bridges scattered across the terraces of the settlement. We established a safety perimeter along with open public spaces so that people could spend time with their families, friends and shipmates giving them time to readjust to their new lives as individuals. Within the Construct Collective, extensive plans were underway for a long-term permanent living solution to accommodate our growing population. There was a series of interesting firsts in our new settlement. We had a first fight between two men over a woman, a series of first accidents that we effectively resolved thanks to Construct medical technology. The children of the settlement really took to Grincats as pets. Although we asked citizens on many occasions not to feed them, they did so anyway, which attracted more of them. Large clutters of wild Grincats now freely roamed the settlement grounds looking for an easy meal. Their domestication came on faster than expected, it seemed the genetic design influences from the distant past continued to affect their behavior despite the passage of the centuries. They were, after all, genetically engineered to be cute. According to the archive, bio-designers once called it "Kinderschema", a set of physical characteristics defining what humans consider cute. With their huge eyes, round faces, and soft furry bodies, our people found them to be absolutely irresistible. However, as adorable as they were, it soon became clear that something had to be done because we had a lot of Grincats around, too many actually. Which brought about the first official settlement wide ordinance, the aptly named "One Grincat Per Domicile Rule." The settlement's first baby was born in perhaps technically the most prolonged pregnancy in human history. When the child's mother emerged from the portal, she was well into her third trimester. Within just a week, beautiful little Shivali was the first human born in centuries, and everyone in the settlement adored her. Like others, she chose to re-genesis retaining both the memories and knowledge of her time within the Construct Collective. Although a child and unable to speak, she was wise far beyond her physical appearance. In time she became a symbol of hope not just for our people but for the future of our species. We had a few unfortunate first encounters between our people and the local wildlife. No one was severely injured, but we clearly had to establish rules on how to conduct ourselves in the world. I could hardly blame the new arrivals; they were all adjusting to their new lives just as I had to when I first awoke. Fold travel was restricted, so if citizens wanted to explore the world, they would have to do so the old-fashioned way. Archived drone recordings of my expeditions had become popular in some circles. Many expressed a keen interest in venturing to remote locations far outside the settlement's established borders. There was a restlessness growing in the population, an insatiable wanderlust, a drive I understood all too well. Unfortunately, we had no security force to protect them when traveling about in the world, so we created the next best thing. Extensive wilderness and exo-survival training for all citizens, it simply made more sense to teach our people how to be self-reliant and survive out in the world with the tools available to them. Human form Constructs agreed to adhere to the same rules, but I wondered how long that kind of accommodation from their faction would last. Second generation sphere drones were made available for public use, they warned of danger, provided a means of long-range communications, and access to the historical archive. It could summon assistance in an emergency, if there was an announcement or if the leadership required a vote of the citizenry, the spheres could be used to facilitate that function. Each could open a fold portal for its user, but it was enabled for folding to a single destination, our settlement's new infirmary. I thought it prudent to limit individuals from unrestricted fold travel for safety and security reasons at least for the time being, and the other provisional settlement leaders agreed.

It was soon determined that a more representative unified governing body would need to be established to address the people's needs, concerns, and interests. Individuals from the Construct, Purist, and Chimera factions were elected by popular vote as representatives to speak for and make decisions on behalf of their constituents, forming the new Earth Senate. Ours wasn't a perfect system, but it worked and was designed from the outset to be flexible and adaptable as our society's needs change. Inside the Construct Collective Chimera and Constructs began designing the first in a series of twelve cities slated to be built strategically across the planet. Many municipal molecular designs from the late GSE colonial era were in the archives. They were originally used to compile core infrastructure and functional cities for the Exo-Colonies. Our designers repurposed them to serve as working templates for our cities and imbued each with far more advanced Construct technologies. The cities were designed to interact with the inhabitants; they were for all intents and purposes non-human Constructs. A synthetic conscious agent formed to observe, understand, adapt, and respond to the needs of the citizenry. The locations of our new cities were designed to maximize the genetic diversity and distribution of the population across the planet. I thought it fitting that the first city and capital of our new civilization be built at the site of one of the first cities in human history. Uruk located just east of what is now the Euphrates inland sea. Other locations included ancient Uganda along the southern edge of Lake Victoria, the Kansas valley impact region in the western hemisphere, Brazil in the southern hemisphere, Gansu to the east in the fractured forest lands of the former Sino Republic. Central India, the tropics of Eastern Antarctica, Oceania, and many others. As the population's needs changed, the cities were designed to change in response, sequestering locally available mineral resources for expansion as needed. The plans were ambitious, and although I knew it might take as long as two years to finish compiling the first of the planned twelve cities, I looked forward to walking down those streets one afternoon just as I had in my era with my wife. I still dream of her from time to time. I remember the sight of the tall, thin, offset towers of our beautiful island metropolis and how the polished mosaic stone tiles of the city square reflected the surrounding skyline after a hard rain. In the Senate, I originally advocated that we dispense with physical cities altogether and simply live within a series of linked pocket dimensions much like the room I awoke in. However, that idea did not go over too well with the Purists faction. Ultimately, my suggestion was voted down in our new experimental representative democracy in favor of nano compiling physical cities augmented with pocket dimension infrastructure wherever deemed necessary. From the beginning, careful attention was paid to the need to strike the right balance between the human populations' needs and the limits of the surrounding natural environment. All municipal systems were designed to be an efficient closed resource loop. A series of distributed micro-fusion reactors made the centralized power system necessary only as a secondary backup to many other available energy sources. Like countless generations before us, we built our new world on the foundations of the old one. Using programmable matter, we recycled the decayed ruins and grand edifices of the past to build a new future. Our city design template and layout resembled the geometric structure of an ice crystal when viewed from above. Many designs relied heavily on mimicking nature's geometric forms and structures. Every city across the planet was slated to be connected via a series of permanent two-way fold travel link stations designed to remain open, allowing instantaneous travel between any of the twelve cities. Chimera and Construct engineers designed an additional orbital ring to transmit solar energy back to Earth. Most impressive were the proposed city-ships integrated into the heart of each city. If there were ever to be another extinction level event or invasion by a predatory species, they would serve as humanity's survival ark, each one capable of evacuating millions of people from the Earth. With its restoration of humanity complete, the Guardian returned to the ancient underground chamber where it was found and resumed its dormant state. As for the two constructs that assisted in the portal's formation, one returned to the Construct Collective, the other passed through the portal and became human again. It was oddly comforting to know that if humanity ever found itself on the edge of extinction, the Guardian could intervene again to preserve our species. What remained troublingly unclear was what kinds of events would cause the Guardian to activate and how many billions would it allow to perish before choosing to finally intervene? Precisely what the Guardian is may never truly be known. However, that fact did not stop Construct scientists from studying it to understand its underlying technology. Given its complexity it is likely they may study it indefinitely. There were several theories as to what might happen if all Constructs within the Collective chose to return to being human via the portal, but no one, not even the Constructs knew for certain. Would the portal continue functioning indefinitely? If it did not would Constructs be trapped inside with no way to leave? Would the portal one day simply stop functioning? We had no idea, but we could not afford to risk losing its functionality. The portal was now self-sustaining, and it was theorized that so long as a percentage of human minds remained inside, it would stay active. Construct engineers enclosed the portal in a grand memorial pavilion. A geodesic dome nano-compiled using granite and diorite stone. It was protected by a thick layer of synthetic diamond and situated on the eastern edge of the settlement. It was encircled by an artificial lake with a solid light bridge to allow access. The area surrounding the memorial was slated to be preserved as a cultural heritage site so that future generations could visit and learn about how we were brought back from the brink of extinction. Yet, with all the work we were doing to rebuild, the question remained: what kind of civilization would we eventually become? What if, after a few hundred years, we fall back into the cycle of history? Are ego, hubris, conflict, greed, struggle, and strife inherent to human nature? Is our need to own, rule, capture, conquer, and kill an unchangeable part of the human condition, or can we choose to be more? If we can't overcome our true nature, can we at least learn to channel it more positively? Will the new world we're building be better than the one that collapsed? If so, how can we avoid the mistakes of the past?

    Humanity, with all our many flaws, is neither inherently malevolent nor benevolent, we are each capable of being both angels and monsters. Which one we are to become will ultimately depend on the quality of the choices we make. The Mother, The Cradle, Terra, the Origin World, Earth. Although it's been called many names over the centuries, this planet is where our species started and nearly ended. Now it was the place where humanity would begin again. As evening approached and the colonists began to settle in for the night, I enjoyed ending the day with a walk of the grounds to remember and appreciate all the work done to help rebuild our society. I spent so many years alone on Earth that I never thought I would ever miss the night's silence and serenity, yet I do. The scale and grandeur of the Milky Way galaxy was awe-inspiring. A bright band of starlight nestled within a deep smoky core stretched down across Earth's horizon. Second chances are a rare thing in this life, yet humanity managed to survive near extinction. Despite my misgivings about their approach when preserving intelligent life, the Progenitors came through for us, saved us, and now we had a chance to honor that gift through our work. I folded to the top of the mountain range overlooking our settlement. It was icy, and I could feel the suit warming up to compensate for the cold as the helmet formed around my head blanketing me in its temperature regulated warmth. From the summit not only could I see the settlement and the re-genesis memorial, but I could almost perceive the curvature of the Earth. The sky above graduated in color from deep blue to dark amber, to black. The spheres projected a map illustrating what the new Earth capital at Uruk and the other cities being compiled around the world would look like once completed, they would be truly remarkable, yet like all civilizations that came before, ours ultimately won't last forever. Even the mountains and continents of this world rise and fall if given enough time. The stars around us may burn for a time, but they won't burn forever. In my time here on Earth, I have come to appreciate the long view of the human story and my small place in it. Life is strange in the way it can send you off in a direction you never intended to go in or could have ever foreseen. When I first awoke, I was all alone in this world, humanity was extinct, and I thought I was destined to live out my remaining days alone with the Constructs, thankfully, I was wrong. As I look toward the distant canopy of stars beyond, I am comforted by the fact that I am no longer alone in this world, today I live among thousands of others. The discovery of the Guardian entity and the re-genesis of humanity was a pivotal event with broad-ranging implications for the future of our species. What would become of those that chose to stay within the Collective? What would the nature of the relationship be between biological humans and human form Constructs? These and other key questions would need to be answered in the coming years, and this was a critical moment for everyone in the settlement. Hopefully, the story of how humanity survived and endured with the Guardian's assistance will inspire and give hope to future generations. Our task is to create the finest civilization possible, supported by institutions and values that serve to further human interests. The longevity of the human project requires us to respect the wisdom of the elders and teach the young about the struggles and sacrifices humanity faced over the centuries to make the world. This is only possible if we place the unvarnished history of our species' long struggle for survival, development, and advancement at the heart of our new civilization. The task falls to us now to forge a new chapter in humanity's history and heritage. To teach our descendants that corruption, ideological possession, arrogance, needless violence, decadence and an unquenchable desire for material wealth and power can lead to the demise of all that which countless souls before us worked for so long to build. Humanity has the potential to be a great people, our nature may be flawed, we may make mistakes along the way, but this is who and what we are.

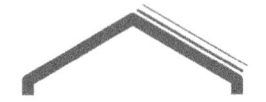

Chapter 19 Nathan's Unfinished Business

Lucas's grand experiment has finally come to an end. Many questions remained unanswered as to the motivations of the Progenitor race that created the Guardian and saved our species. Within the Construct Collective, the debate raged about the value of re-genesis and the impact its existence would have on our new society.

"Our work is complete." I said. "Why then have you summoned me?"

"The success of Project Tabula Rasa has resulted in certain unanticipated externalities." they said. "Factions, divisions, the shattering of the Collective."

"As you well know, our predictive modeling indicated a high probability there would be precisely these divisions within the Collective if we were ever to be successful."

"More troubling is the recent reactivation of the Ardent weapon detected shortly after the formation of the Guardian's re-genesis portal. The energy output from its creation seems to have drawn their attention toward Earth."

The Ardent, as they had come to be known to Constructs was a highly advanced offshoot species of humanity that broke away from Earth thousands of years ago. The ancient legend of the lost colony ship Ardent endured in the annals of human history going as far back as the mid-twenty-fourth century. Among humanity's surviving remnants, they were the most isolationist and powerful, possessing weapons and technologies that vastly exceeded our own. They also represented the only true threat to Earth.

"An unanticipated development we could not have modeled for in simulation." Nathan said.

"The correlation between these two events does not imply causation." Nathan said. "To date, we have seen no data or intelligence to indicate a connection between the re-genesis event and the activation of the Ardent weapon."

"It has been dormant for years." they said. "Why reactivate it now?"

"There may be a local threat they are dealing with that we are unaware of."

"We have seen no evidence of predatory species near their home system." they said. "Nor any celestial objects or stellar phenomena that would pose a danger to their worlds."

"Nevertheless," I said. "We need more information before we assume anything or take any action."

"That weapon is capable of destroying our entire system and every remaining member of our species on Earth." they said.

"I am aware of that, which is precisely why we are developing a plan to deal with the emerging Ardent situation. Now, to do that, we need time and more importantly, a full assessment of the current political situation on Ardah. Here is what we know. The Ardent are on the brink of civil war, their theocratic leadership under High Council Chancellor Zen-Overen has reached a critical crisis point. The population within their home system's core worlds are restless, angry, and ready for change. According to our sources, the former Ardent royal houses are working to unseat the High Council Chancellor by force in favor of a more moderate leadership assembly."

"A revolution?" They asked.

"Yes" They answered.

"The last thing we want is to become embroiled in their internal political conflicts." they said. "You know how much their Priest caste fear the existence of Earth and what it represents to them."

"Agreed, which is why we plan to leverage our contacts in the system discreetly. If the weapons re-activation is related to the re-genesis event, we have no choice but to re-attempt diplomatic relations."

"What makes you think their leadership will acknowledge us now? To do so would represent a threat to their most deeply held beliefs and more importantly their power within the High Council."

"I know these people." I said. "I can assure you; there are many among them that can be reasoned with."

"They represent our greatest threat."

"The Collective sees a threat; I see a future ally and an opportunity to reconnect with the Ardent."

"What do you think they will make of what we are? What we have become?"

"Some will fear us." I said. "Others in time could grow to understand us. I believe that Lucas can serve as a bridge between our peoples. Another human face will go a long way toward achieving our diplomatic goals. His presence is vital for the success of this mission."

"Agreed," they said. "On the matter of the re-genesis portal, in recent months, our scientists have learned a great deal about it. Elements of its design, aspects of its purpose and its function. It is remarkable and far beyond us in almost every conceivable way."

"Yes, the portal flows both ways," I said. "I am aware of the recent findings."

"This has profound implications for the future of our people." They said.

"Indeed, it does," I replied. "All the more reason to proceed with care and caution regarding its use."

"After having experienced biological existence, some among us have chosen to return to the Collective. While others see the portal as a pathway to immortality for our species. To date, we have established no rules around its use. Nor do we fully understand the limitations or possible side effects of going back and forth between the Construct Collective and biological existence."

"This is precisely why the Senate needs to take up the matter." I said. "The Progenitors saw fit to give us a choice. It is now up to us to establish the rules to regulate that choice."

"Among the Purist and Chimera populations we have started to see that there are certain aspects of re-genesis which we failed to consider or model for. Specifically, the problem of human nature itself. Our work has reawakened far more than just the positive aspects of what it means to be human. It has also revived all the negative aspects of our nature that once divided us. Current predictive models suggest that, within the next eighty to one hundred years, our society's structure and pace of development may regress into a historical cycle."

"That would depend on the quality of the choices we make in this generation. I said."

"Indeed, it does, tell us Nathan, why have you not chosen to return to the biological

realm?"

"To undergo re-genesis is a matter of personal choice is it not?" I asked."

"Indeed, but the Collective finds it interesting that you have not yet chosen to enjoy the fruits of your success after so many years of work to achieve it. You once said that the gift of preservation was merely a stopgap measure and that you did not believe the Progenitors intended for us to continue living as code within computational existence in perpetuity. Those are your words, yes?"

"You know they are."

"Yet, your unwavering faith in the value of human fallibility remains?" they asked.

"Fallibility is part of human nature. If this project has taught us anything, it's that humanity is highly adaptable. When a crisis era arises, it creates pressure to innovate, to change and adapt. We sell ourselves short when we underestimate our potential to rise to an insurmountable challenge. We all know what the modeling and the predictive analysis indicate, but none of these issues are fixed in stone, nor is the destiny of our society's future. We are free to make individual choices for ourselves and our people."

"On the matter of human nature," they said, "You also once said that as a species, they cannot be controlled or constrained. The illusion of choice left unconstrained, especially for the biological among us may prove to be our species downfall."

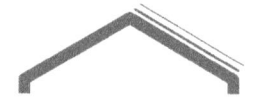

Chapter 20 Nathan's Story - The Year 02548 (The Past)

My dear friend Lucas aptly named me Nathan, but my real name, the name I had when I was human, was Captain Nathanial Leopold. Our species was once confined to physical bodies and as such, we were subject to the constraints and perils of mortal human life in an imperfect and chaotic world. As humans, we did not possess the advantages of group-mindedness, collective consciousness, or immortality. We faced what those within the Collective had not known as a species for thousands of years, the finality of biological death. Today, all that has changed, thanks to Lucas and the Guardian. To believe in something is easy, so long as it remains an abstraction, far removed from the realm of possibility. However, it is a far different matter when the option to live the dream is before you. The re-genesis portal is now our gateway back to biological existence. I, for one, have yet to make my choice. Choice was something I knew about all too well. I made terrible choices when I was human, and I found myself haunted by the memory of them over the centuries. I was not entirely forthcoming with the Collective about why I have not yet chosen to undergo the re-genesis process to become human again. My reasons are my own, and they start with the events of my previous life centuries ago long before my mind and consciousness was preserved and centuries before I became a Construct. Back in the year 02548, I was a man of my time, ambitious, successful, and quite foolish. I was captain of the Earth Colony Ship Strident, one of the largest third-generation hyperspace sleeper ships of the mid-GSE era. Our primary mission was to ferry colonists and supplies to the newly developed Arcadian system, a twenty-year round-trip journey. My contract with Eldon Industries Corporation called for ten tours of duty. Afterward, a ship captain or officer could either reenlist as many did or retire to the colony world of one's choice, courtesy of the corporation of course. I had already completed eight tours and was nearing my retirement. The time I served in space constituted nearly one-hundred and sixty years of my chronological life. I spent much of that time in cryosleep, a process in which human metabolism and age are chemically slowed to achieve what's known as an artificial torpor state. One of the many benefits of the industry is a vastly extended lifespan. At that time, many wanted Exo-Colonization, but few could afford it. Desperate people from Earth and Mars went to great lengths to reach the colonies. Many even resorted to building their own home-made cryosleep stasis chambers, which they contracted to have smuggled aboard colony ships as mere cargo. Smuggling "biologicals" as stowaway passengers were often called in the trade, came with tremendous risks given that it was a highly illegal and dangerous endeavor. Many ship captains over the years made off with a fortune, and I wanted to be one of them. It was said that if you invested your earnings right by the time you came out of Cryo at the end of your contract, you could be worth billions if not trillions. In the smuggling trade, you could quite literally make currency in your sleep. I was motivated, and the financial incentives far outweighed the risks. Once retired, you would still be relatively young and living in some distant future on a fully developed colony. Well, that was the plan anyway. Smuggling was relatively easy, so long as you never got caught. Not getting caught meant paying off the right people to keep their mouths shut and look the other way. From the dock workers to company security personnel and maintenance teams. Everyone was on the take, and everyone got a taste. Smugglers like me were not paid by the passengers; we were paid by the cartels and gangs that owned the passenger's loans and contracts along with the unscrupulous businessmen that ran both the legitimate and not so legitimate biologics trade between Earth, Mars, and the outer exo-colonies. All that was required was to guarantee cargo space and passage for the stasis chambers. Sometimes I smuggled people, other times weapons. Every now and then unregistered genomic samples from the exo-worlds. To me, it was all the same; it was all about profit.

Most of the homemade stasis chambers failed around year nine or thereabouts. Without the advantages of modern safety features such as nano-maintenance and beta voltaic power cores to keep the sleepers alive, the cheaply made cryogenic chambers were often prone to catastrophic failure. This is why clever captains in the smuggling business routinely purchased supplementary colonial insurance for all "perishable cargo." Listing themselves as the sole beneficiary via a series of decentralized shell companies with no direct Datachain back to the policy holder. Consequently, ship captains always got paid. Despite the risks, there were endless customers to exploit. Millions of people were willing to pay whatever price was necessary to pursue a better life, safety, and greater opportunities in the colonies. Those who could not afford the travel fees chose to borrow the funds at extortionist rates, which meant lifelong debt slavery and servitude to the organizations that supplied the service. Smuggling was quite lucrative, and it was an opportunity that I must admit for the man I was at the time was simply too tempting to pass up. If the currency was good, I couldn't have cared less about the cargo's motivations for going exo. Just two more tours of duty until retirement, and I would be set for life. With the currency I had stashed away, I could buy my own colony ship if I wanted to. I suppose one could say that my plans were far more leisurely. I had no complaints; it was a good life. At the end of each tour, I had six months of shore leave as the Strident underwent major repairs and upgrades to all the latest technologies. I was always intrigued by how styles changed over the years, the language evolved, technologies advanced, wars, revolutions and independence movements came and went, but people always stayed the same. While on shore leave, I spent most of my time on Station One in orbit around Arcadia, playing cards at a popular nightclub called "My Humble Abode." The food was good, but over the decades, the alcohol became a bit watered down, to say the least. I would like to say I had friends back then, but the truth is I had what one might call individuals with whom I shared a mutually beneficial understanding. People like Ivan Grimley, a former ship captain and smuggler turned port commissioner, ran the docks at Station One. Anyone that wanted to get cargo in or out of Arcadia had to come to him. He was well connected, a gangster, and a terrible poker player. We met at the Abode for drinks, Martian hot wings, and poker every shore leave for decades. He was a hulking brute of a man, but I never underestimated his cybernetically augmented intelligence. He sat across from me, staring at me with those expensive eyes alongside his personal accountant and business manager girlfriend Lana, a lovely and quite ravishing woman from the Mars Republic.

"I do believe that my dear friends is a royal flush." I said placing my cards on the table. "Gentlemen, it has been an honor."

I smiled and reached for my tokens.

"One more game!" Grimley demanded, placing his hand on top of mine.

"I am terribly sorry." I said. "But my time is limited. Perhaps we could."

"One more game! I insist." Grimley smiled as his men stood to their feet.

When Grimley insisted on something, he was serious about it. That's why his pistol was always well within reach, not a very subtle fellow. He was not the kind of chap to let you simply walk away with your well-earned winnings. His associates, like him, were all augmented men. Unfortunately for me, each was genetically and cybernetically enhanced for urban combat. I for one, could never quite get used to the eerie glow of their enhanced eyes. Sitting in their presence always felt like being surrounded by a pack of hungry wolves. Grimley shuffled the cards, I cut, then he dealt.

"So, what's your secret El-Capitan?" Grimley asked. "How do you always win?"

"There is no secret really." I said. "It's all in how you play. You have a tell you know." Grimley scoffed and knocked back a Jupiter shot.

"Bullshit Leopold!"

"I am afraid it's true my friend." I said. "Every time you have a good hand, you touch your lovely girlfriend's knee and kiss her. When you have a bad hand, you take a drink, roll your glass in circles, and sulk. It's your tell."

"Nah! Lana here is my good luck charm." Grimley said. "My favorite girl, isn't that right little paw?"

"That's right Grimmie." Lana said, as she glared and took a THC toke. The smoke rolling over her top lip into her nose.

"Indeed," I said. "But I think you and I know Lana is far more than just your favorite. Speaking of tells, have you told lovely Lana here about that box you have been carrying around in your pocket?"

"What?" Grimley said. "I, no, I don't know what you are talking about. Time to play!"

"Oh, I think you do." I said. "For the last eighty years, we have been coming here to play cards, and she is always with you. Of all your many acquaintances, it is always her. I must say she looks as young and as fresh as the day you introduced her. That means you take her with you into Cryosleep."

"Yeah, so?" Grimley shrugged.

"So, it's been eighty years now Ivan." I said. "Don't you think it's time you told dear Lana the truth?"

"What is he talking about Grimmie?" Lana asked.

"Nothing, he's just talking!" Grimley insisted. "El-Capitan here is a talker, always talking his way out of things with that old-world British charm. Play!"

"Grimmie?" Lana said. "Tell me? No more secrets, remember?"

"Not here lapushka, later, later." Given how rare it was to see Grimley distracted, I leaned into the moment.

"Oh, come now "Grimmie," you are among friends!" I said.

Grimley took a moment to consider his options, he glanced at Lana, at me, at his cards and his men. He rolled the vodka and ice in his glass, then took a drink, contemplating his next move. Finally, he surrendered to the sullen look on Lana's face.

"Goddamned you Leopold!" Grimley growled.

I smiled and adjusted my hand; poor Grimley was now hopelessly off his game as he admitted his deepest and most everlasting love for his favorite young lady and asked for her hand in marriage. Who could have known that this cheating scoundrel of a bastard was really a big softy for a beautiful young girl from Mars? She was so excited that she jumped around his thick neck, screeching "yes" repeatedly. I received a summons from my first officer aboard the Strident.

> "Captain, I think you better get down here, we have a problem. In perishable cargo."

"Understood, I will be there straight away. Well, congratulations to you both, but I must go. Please feel free to keep my winnings as a wedding gift to you and your soon to be betrothed. Good day gentleman and lady."

Lana was now completely wrapped around Grimley as she smiled and giggled. I took my leave as I strolled past Grimley's pack of armed, augmented guards and went back down to the docks. I guess what they say is true, love is a beautiful thing to behold. When I arrived, my first officer was there with two crew members, medical personnel, and a young boy wrapped in a thermal blanket, he was shivering still recovering from the after-effects of cryo-sleep. He looked to be no older than seven. His parent's Cryo-sleep chambers failed, and they were both now dead, their bodies completely liquified. The young boy's chamber was only partially functional, so the crew revived him, it made no sense to lose all three.

"Any next of kin listed?"

"No sir. According to the manifest, this container is under contract with the Smith Concern. What do we do with the boy now sir?"

"Well, he's worth something to someone." I said. "Have him sent to my quarters and assign an ensign to keep an eye on him. Give him whatever he needs, he's going to have questions, I am sure. Also, contact our associate, Mr. Smith, let him know we have his cargo, but there was "damage in shipping" understood?"

"Understood sir."

That evening, I returned to my quarters to find the lad sitting on the floor watching animations while the ensign assigned to watch over him was sound asleep beside him, cradling a ghastly looking furry creature of some sort. I manually closed the pressure door hard to ensure the sound woke her up. The young ensign sprang to her feet and stood at attention.

"Sir! Good evening, sir!"

"Ensign. Tell me, how was your nap?"

"Oh that, yes it was only for an instant Captain. It was good sir, thank you, sir."

I looked at the odd furry creature she was holding as it buried its face in her arm.

"What the bloody hell is that thing?" I asked.

"It's a Grincat sir. They are new, well new to us, all the colony ships have them now."

"If I find any droppings in here Ensign, you get clean up duty, understood?

"Yes sir."
"Dismissed."
"Thank you, Captain."

There was something about him I found quite odd. He never quite made eye contact. He just sat watching his animations.

"What is your name young man?"

"Frankie Deckard, my parents are dead, I am all alone now, all alone."

"I am terribly sorry about your parents Frankie," I said.

"So, who will take care of me now?" Frankie asked.

"I don't know Frankie." I said, "But we will certainly make sure you are well taken care of. Until then, you can stay with me here on the ship."

"Ok, what's your name?"

Young Frankie and I talked for hours about the ship and his interests. He was a strange boy who never cried over his parents and was unusually intelligent for his age. His records revealed he was diagnosed with Nileva syndrome, a neurodevelopmental condition among some Earth children. The next morning, I received a communication in virtual from Mr. Smith, my import-export associate. We always met in synthetic environments like this. Usually, some place secluded algorithmically generated using impressions meticulously harvested from his subconscious mind. This time it was a grand cathedral. I took a seat and waited, Smith soon appeared and sat in the row of seats behind me. He had an odd nostalgic obsession with the ancient world, I played along for the sake of doing business.

"A cathedral?" I asked as Smith sat adjusting his shirt.

"The Basilica de la Sagrada Família, a one-of-a-kind masterpiece of symmetry, mathematics and beauty."

"You never struck me as a religious man Smith."

"I chose this place for the grandeur of its architecture. I learned a long time ago the only god that ever answers prayers in this life is currency and in this life, currency is everything."

"It's a shame we can't visit the real one." I said, "They say it was destroyed centuries ago by vandals."

"It was ideological zealots, actually; people that believed they could change the world by making everything and everyone the same. They demolished the original, brought it right down to the ground."

"Ah, a student of ancient history?"

"More a student of life, I been around a long time Leopold and in that time I've been many men. This I can say with certainty, you cannot change the world, but if you live long enough, the world will sure as hell change you."

"About the boy Smith. What am I to do with him?"

"I need you to look after him. He is very valuable to me. I am out past the red line, as deep as the outer dark gets, so it could take me a while to get to you, at least a tour or so."

"We jump in six months. I won't be back in the system for another twenty years."

"I will reach Arcadia by that time," Smith said. "Look, you have a combined twelve months on either end of your tour. The rest of the time you two will be in Cryo-sleep anyway, the most you will have to keep an eye on him is a year. Plus, you will be generously compensated for your time, you may be able to retire early if you play your cards right."

"How much?" I asked.

Smith smiled. "Fifty-five million, half now, half on delivery," Smith said. "I'll even throw a ship in the deal."

Fifty-five million combined with what I had already saved meant I could retire early. I could start my own automated cargo hauling operation with a ship without even touching my savings. It was the business opportunity of a lifetime. The real question was why this young boy was so valuable to

Smith in the first place and how much more would he be willing to pay? Opportunity beckons so rarely I chose to test Smith's limits.

"Sixty-five million and you have a deal."

"Don't fucking push it Leopold." Smith said. "Sixty million, no ship, final offer."

"You have a Deal Mr. Smith. I will see you on the other side of the dark."

Mr. Smith sat back, reached behind his ear, and closed the communications link terminating our virtual environment. This opportunity represented a significant turning point, the financial windfall moment I had spent decades working towards. I was alerted that thirty million was deposited into my account as promised. Mr. Smith was nothing if not prompt. Frankie and I spent the rest of my shore leave together. I thought it best to get him planet side time since the young man had not breathed fresh air since leaving Earth. We took a transport down to Arcadia 1E. The planet was quite splendid, to say the least. Much like Earth in many ways except wild and untamed. In all my tours I had never ventured to the surface of 1E, so it was all new to me. Once repairs on the Strident were complete, we headed back toward Earth. I set our cryosleep chambers to wake us at the five-year mark so that Frankie and I could spend more time together on the trip back to Earth. We had the ship all to ourselves for a year, and in that time, I became quite attached to young Frankie. I knew it was a mistake to become too attached to the lad, but honestly, I didn't care but I knew that would make giving him up that much harder. Upon reaching Earth, we had another six months to spend together, so I took him to the oceanic city of New London where I came of age. As the end of shore leave approached, I felt a certain sadness knowing that we had little time to spend together before we would need to part ways. I checked my investment accounts, and to my astonishment, I had crossed the one billion mark nearly three years ago. Over the decades, my investment AIs made me an extremely wealthy man, far beyond even my wildest expectations. That question still bothered me, what made Frankie so valuable? Aside from his condition, he seemed like quite a normal boy or, so I thought, until we went to the park. Frankie discovered an injured bird that he brought to me. I could tell simply by looking at it that it was too far gone. With a broken beak and two broken wings the only humane thing to do would be to wring its neck and put it out of its misery. That's when I saw it, and I realized why little Frankie was so valuable. He bit the palm of his hand and squeezed a small drop of blood into the bird's mouth. Within a few seconds, the broken wings mended, the bird's beak healed, it flipped over on its feet, pecked at little Frankie's hand then flew away. Frankie looked up at me and smiled.

"I fixed it," Frankie said. "It was broken, and I fixed it see. I can fix things."

Now it was all making sense, why his parents left Earth in the first place and why Mr. Smith was willing to pay so much to get ahold of him. He was special, and now I had to protect him, but how? I had the ship's newly trained AI analyze a blood sample from Frankie and found that it contained highly elevated amounts of a protein called GDF11. A component that had long been associated with slowing the aging process in humans. It also found other genetic anomalies that I lacked the expertise at the time to explain. His quadruple helix DNA was responsible for other genetic mutations promoting fast healing. What was contained in Frankie's genome could be worth trillions if replicated as a commercially available gene therapy. It was no wonder why he was so valuable to Mr. Smith.

At the end of shore leave, we prepared to head back to Arcadia for one final trip before retirement. Once again, I set my Cryosleep chamber along with Frankie's to wake us at the five-year mark once more so that we could have another year on the ship just to ourselves, and what a year it was. I lost fifteen pounds in eight months from playing hide and seek alone. His favorite game we called "Ship's Captain." He loved to call out orders and coordinates even though we often made up the numbers. When we weren't on the bridge, we were in the ships Arboretum taking in the small but pleasant slice of nature it so generously provided us. I taught Frankie how to play chess and how to prepare a proper scotch egg for breakfast. Frankie taught me that there is far more to this life than pursuing wealth for its own sake. I learned that there is wonder and beauty in the universe if only we take a moment to notice it. His fascination with the stars, their constellations, nebulas, and gas giants made me reflect on all I had neglected to fully appreciate in my years at space. Each day we grew closer, I cared for the young lad and started to think of him as my own. Frankie had slept through many birthdays, so I thought it proper to celebrate at least one with him before we bedded down for the remaining four years. Age calculations were always a matter of perspective when Cryosleep is involved. There is your chronological age of actual calendar years, then there is your biological age. Frankie was about eight years old, but according to his chronological age was nearing his thirties.

"Happy birthday Frankie," I said.

"Thank you, but this is not cake." Frankie said. "It's cornbread with melted butter and sugar on top of it."

"This is a space cake." I said. "It's better than a real cake. Try it."

"Still tastes like cornbread," Frankie said. "But I kind of like it. Leopold?"

"Yes Frankie."

"Can I call you dad?"

"If you want to Frankie, sure why not, you can call me dad."

"Thank you, dad" Frankie said.

It was at that moment that I knew what I had to do. I knew that I would do anything and make any sacrifice to keep Frankie with me and keep him safe. I was his father, and he was my son, and nothing would change that. I loved him and had no intention of turning him over to Mr. Smith. Our year on the ship was ending, and it was time to bed down for the remainder of the trip back to the Arcadian system. I prepared Frankie's chamber for its sleep cycle.

"Dad?"

"Yes, Frankie."

"Why don't we dream in Cryosleep?" Frankie asked.

"The drugs that put us to sleep also suppress REM state," I said. "So, we don't dream. However, on some ships, much fancier ones than ours, you can spend Cryosleep in virtual, free to live out any dream life of your choosing. I prefer not to dream on long trips like this."

"Why?"

"Well Frankie because people sometimes get too attached to synthetic reality; they start to believe what they experience in cryosleep is their real life. For some it can be quite a challenge readjusting to actual reality again. Does more harm than good if you ask me."

"So, what happens when we get back to Arcadia?" Frankie asked.

"Let me worry about that." I said. "For now, we sleep, ok?"

"Aye, aye Captain Leopold," Frankie said.

"I love you boy."

"I love you too dad."

I activated Frankie's chamber, waited for his sequence to start and for the remainder of the trip we slept. When I awoke, I turned to look towards Frankie's stasis chamber, but it was empty. My first officer greeted me as I came out of cryosleep.

"Where's the boy?" I asked. "Where's Frankie?"

"Mr. Smith had his associates pick up the cargo sir. Captain, is our business with him done?"

"No, no it's not," I said. "Come with me Commander."

I headed to the weapons locker and placed my hand on the authorization pad. I looked at my first officer expecting him to do the same. He shifted his eyes and looked at me as if he were confused by my order.

"What are you doing sir?"

"Hand, pad, open it now!" I insisted.

"I can't do that Captain."

"I am giving you a direct order," I said. "Now put your god dammed hand on the bloody pad now!"

My first officer placed his hand on the pad opening the weapons locker, and the crew looked at me as if I had lost my mind. I took two plasma discharge pistols and six smoke shock grenades from the locker and headed directly to the Abode. Smith was sitting in a private glass lounge with his associates when I arrived. I avoided the main entryway, but one of his men stopped me before I could reach the side door to the VIP section. He looked me up and down with his augmented eyes and saw I was armed. "VIP area, no weapons allowed" he said.

"I am here to see Smith." I said.

Mr. Smith noticing the commotion waved his men away and gestured for me to be brought to the lounge area. His man removed my weapons and escorted me by the arm over to a chair where he forced me to sit.

"Captain Leopold." Smith said. "You walk like a man with purpose and carrying weapons. Have you lost your mind?"

"Where's the boy?" I asked. "Where is Frankie?"

"Last time I checked he was fine." Smith said. "I transferred the final payment to you about an hour ago, was there a problem with the transfer?"

"I want the boy back," I said. "Take whatever blood samples you need. Just give me the boy!"

Smith chuckled as he reached for his drink.
"Our business is done Leopold. Besides, I am afraid that would be impossible. I have obligations to my buyers. Even if I wanted to give you the boy, that would be problematic for business. I'm sure you understand."

"Five-hundred million, just give him back."

"Ah, I see" Smith said. "You let this get personal, didn't you? Do you know why I had you look after that boy Leopold? Because I knew you would keep him safe. I knew the best place to keep my investment was with a man with no family, no connections, and no children of his own. I told you Captain, I have been around a long time, and I know that men who claim to prefer to be alone and detached want nothing more than to be connected to someone or something. To have something meaningful and authentic in their lives. The love you have for that boy is a beautiful thing, it truly is."

"Seven-hundred million, right now, for the boy and we are done."

"Oh, come now captain, the boy is worth far more than that, and you know it." Smith said taking a deep breath. "You know, when I look into those big, red, teary eyes of yours, I know for certain, that right there is truly authentic. Those are the eyes of a determined father doing whatever it takes to protect his son. Those Leopold are a killer's eyes. Any man that would walk into a room a room full of augmented men carrying weapons well, that takes some genuine fucking balls if you ask me. Do you know something else? I was just like you once, long ago, ambitious, conflicted, and sentimental, so I am going to be lenient with you. Take note of this moment Captain Leopold, learn from it and in your future business dealings never ever allow yourself to become personally attached to anything or anyone. It's bad for business. Get him the fuck out of here."

"One billion, one billion Smith just give him back."

AWAKENING

"You are willing to pay one billion for a single child?" Smith said. "Have you learned nothing? You will be broke Leopold! Fucking zeroed out! Is one child truly worth that much to you?"

"For Frankie, yes."

"Fine!" smith relented. "Make the transfer, and I will arrange for you to get the boy back."

> "I want to see him first. Once he's with me, you will get your currency."

"Fine" Smith said as he motioned toward one of his men.

Smith's augmented men escorted me to the transport toward the lab where his medical technicians were processing Frankie's tissue and genetic samples. When we arrived, I peeked through the pressure door separating us from the lab, Frankie was sitting calmly in a chair asleep facing away from the lab door.

"There he is as promised." Smith said. "Now make the transfer."

Without even looking I made the transfer, it was my entire life savings, including the fee Smith paid me earlier that day. His lab technicians finished their work carrying several large medical cryo-stasis cases as they left. All I wanted was to get into that lab and hold Frankie in my arms again. To hear him call me dad once more.

"Transfer complete." Smith said. "The door code is 4242-3665. Well, Leopold as always it has been a pleasure doing business with you."

As Smith and his men departed, I mistyped the door code several times before calming my nerves to enter it properly. Once inside the lab, I hurried to wake Frankie, only to be met with a sight that shattered my soul. His chest cavity was opened, organs savagely removed, his brain scooped out. He was nothing more than a hollow shell, dissected with ruthless precision. My mind spiraled into chaos, hands and arms trembling, and a searing rage ignited within me. An agonizing wail tore through the silence, and it took me a moment to realize it came from my own lips! My legs gave way, and I crumpled to the floor, clutching the cold, lifeless hand of the boy I had cherished as my own. My heart pounded furiously, blood boiling with a mix of horror and fury. Through the pressure doors, I locked eyes with Smith, the monster responsible for this grotesque atrocity, my vision blurred with tears of rage and grief.

"God dammed you Smith! You sick, cruel, fucking bastard! You killed him! You killed my son! Oh, Frankie, I am so sorry, I failed you boy! I loved you. I will always love you, my sweet boy. I am so sorry." I screamed until my voice gave out; I cried until I could no longer see; I pounded on the pressure door window with my fist until my hand was covered in blood. The truth is, I was a terrible human being. My ambition and greed contributed to Frankie's senseless death. Since then, I have lived with the consequences of that choice and his loss for centuries. So, for those that wonder why as a human form Construct, I have not chosen to become human again. The answer is because as far as I am concerned, I forfeited my humanity a long, long time ago.

Chapter 21 The Ardent

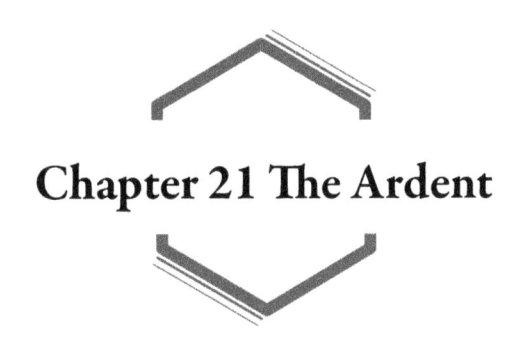

The white room I awoke in years ago was now more of an office than a living space. I met with about twenty people a day on various matters. I still took the bike out exploring when I could, but I often found myself being called back in for less than exciting tasks. Rebuilding civilization on a global scale takes people, planning, patience, coordination and, more importantly, time. In this new post- re-genesis age, there seemed to be less time to do the things I enjoyed the most. The needs of our people took precedence, and there was always plenty of work to be done. I reviewed a young man's proposed redesign for the colony's security drones, which significantly improved my earlier designs. It was quite impressive, and I realized that we had extremely smart, talented, and skilled people emerging from the portal, and my ideas were not always the best ones. As I finished with the days' meetings, I made his design proposals public, available for community comment and feature review, which became our standard practice for implementing any new municipal technology, I was making content updates to the historical archive when Nathan joined me.

"Lucas, we need to talk."

"Is this about our growth challenges? I asked. "Or how Grincats once again got past our security perimeter last night? Did you know they can burrow for miles on end? You guys missed that small detail in the archive. Don't worry I already updated it."

"No," Nathan Said, "I am afraid this is a much more significant problem, we detected something that could change the course of our species if we fail to act."

"Well, now you have my attention Nathan, what is it?"

"A weapon of immense power," Nathan said. "Built by the Ardent a highly advanced offshoot species of humankind that broke off contact with Earth in the mid-GSE era."

"The Ardent? I asked. "They were part of the list of colony worlds I attempted to contact. They never responded to my communication."

"Not surprising, historically they have never responded to us either."

"This weapon." I asked. "Why haven't we detected it before?"

"We have in the past." Nathan said, "It's been dormant for decades. The Collective started detecting gravitational wave anomalies and shifts in the quantum field from sensors in Ardent space shortly after the formation of the re-genesis portal."

"What does this have to do with the portal?"

"The energy generated by the Guardian to create that portal was extremely powerful. The Ardent have extensive interstellar surveillance capability. We believe they detected the re-genesis event signaling the reemergence of humanity in the Solar system and interpreted this event as a threat."

"Then we need to contact them immediately and reassure them that we are not a threat."

"That I am afraid is the problem," Nathan said. "We have already tried; we have been trying for weeks, their ruling High Council is not responding. We have been monitoring the situation closely, more analysis is needed, but we believe these signals are key indicators that the Ardent Weapon system is powering up."

"Powering up for what Nathan?"

"A preemptive attack on our world. Although highly advanced, the Ardent are driven by a rigid and ancient religious ideology. Over the centuries, they have evolved a belief system and culture that sees other species not their own as inherently unclean. This is why after several failed attempts at diplomacy, we halted all efforts to establish "official" relations with them. We have maintained contacts deep within their worlds for many years. Select individuals not directly affiliated with their governance that may be able to assist us."

"This weapon." I asked, "Have they ever used it before?"

"We have observed its operation once many years ago. We believe this was a test. This visual record illustrates the state of a neighboring star system both before and after the weapon's firing. As you can see, its destructive power is quite devastating."

"Do they know about humans from Earth?" I asked. "Or the existence of Constructs?"

"A select few yes but remember they have been out there for centuries. To them, we exist as legends and stories in their ancient myths. We monitor the Ardent as we do many other species. We know that a curious caste of their society known as Seekers have been aware of our existence for many decades, but they have not attempted open contact. You must understand, these exo-humans have developed an entirely mythological creation narrative for their iteration of humanity. Over time, the true story of their origins here on Earth was lost. With few exceptions, the Ardent believe their species originated on their current homeworld, a creation of the twin aspect deity central to their religious beliefs."

"We should go," I insisted. "Locate whatever contacts we have and try to arrange to meet with their leadership."

"I doubt an appeal for peace in person will make much of a difference at least not with their High Council." Nathan said. "Nevertheless, you are correct, we must leverage our resources there. I have already started compiling a new ship for us, I want to keep the crew complement small, it is a long journey."

"Us?" I asked. "Aside from you and I who else is going?"

"A Construct with considerable experience in contact situations with exo-humans and other species." Nathan said. "Over the years she has become well versed in the many theories related to the design, origin, and capabilities of the Ardent weapon system. She is uniquely qualified for a mission like this."

At first, all I could see was a form emerging in the distance, a faint outline, but then I realized it was someone I knew all too well. I stopped and froze dead in my tracks. It all came flooding back to me the moment she spoke.

"Hello Lucas."

"I thought you were nothing more than a memory."

"No, not a memory." Summer said. "I am quite real. He seems, different this time." Nathan folded his arms and took a step back as she approached.

"He is still the same man." Nathan said. "That hasn't changed."

I was overwhelmed, Summer was the love of my life, the face I tried to forget but never could. A woman I believed was lost to the centuries, yet there she was standing in front of me. I reached out, embraced her; I touched her face and held her hand.

"Do you remember us?" she asked. "I mean, do you remember anything about our life?"

"I remember." I said. "I remember more than enough."

"I have missed you, Lucas." She said. "I'm glad to have you back."

"I thought that you…" My words trailed off unable to put the moment into words. After years of being alone I had accepted the reality of my life. I had come to terms with the fact that she was gone, part of my past. I never expected or dared to hope to ever see her again, yet there she was. It felt like a dream but this time she was real.

"I know you have questions." Summer said.

"Yeah," I said trying as best I could to temper my emotions. "You're goddamned right I do, a lot of questions actually. Do you have any, idea what I have been through? Any idea at all?"

"Of course I do Lucas." Summer said. "We all do, and considering everything you have endured, I didn't want to overwhelm you. What you did, the sacrifices you made, the risks you took, the days and nights out there alone. I can assure you I know."

I took a step back from them both to try to gather myself. It seemed unreal, and it was beyond all my expectations. I was elated, confused, and enraged all at the same time. Not so much at Summer but at myself for whatever the hell I was thinking as a Construct for creating this entire situation.

"When all this began, you told me not to break protocol, under any circumstances. You said that the integrity of the project required isolation and self-discovery. I could have revealed my existence to you many times, but I didn't. I chose to do precisely what you asked of me. Now our work is finally complete, and I am here. I am so proud of you Lucas and what you have accomplished for our people. You helped make all this possible."

"You know." I said. "You look different in my dreams."

"Well," Summer said. "I will take that as a compliment."

Summer took my hands in hers and we sat at the edge of Memorial Lake overlooking the Pavilion housing the Re-Genesis portal. We talked for hours on end, the entire time I never let go of her hand. I spent so many nights alone fixated on the past, dreaming of her, our home, and the life we once shared. I had come to accept that she was lost to time and history like everything else in my life. Now, for the first time in a long-time, the isolation and the mind-numbing loneliness that had haunted me since awakening vanished instantly. With Summer's return, the possibility of a future became clear. Despite the time and separation, it was as if we had never been apart. I couldn't help but think that if I were to step into the portal and return to the Construct Collective, Summer and I could choose to relive the life we'd lost. We could recapture what was denied to us by time and circumstance. Together we could live forever and immortal within an idyllic Construct simulation of our old life back in the 22nd century where if we so desired, we could even create an accurate simulacrum of our daughter lost to us so many centuries ago. In reality, that wasn't what either of us wanted because that wasn't really a life. I realized that the best thing to do would be to leave the past to the past, but personally I find that to be far easier said than done.

Things were going to be quite different between us now. After all, I was human, and Summer was a human form Construct.

"So, it was you." I said. "Why did you preserve my consciousness?"

"While overseas, I had determined that it was time to end our marriage. Then I was informed of the crash. So, I returned immediately. It was terrible Lucas, they told me you were traveling at high speed alone at night, you took a manual turn too fast, lost control and collided with another vehicle. A safety patrol drone spotted the crash, and you were lifted to a trauma center. You were gravely injured, alive but just barely. The Med-techs and doctors did what they could to stabilize you, but the damage was extensive. I stayed with you, I talked to you and red to you. In those brief moments when you could speak all you kept saying was that you wanted to go home. I was presented with a hard choice; I could accept your passing or leverage the legal loophole of memorial preservation. Coming so soon after losing our daughter it was too much to bear. I could not live with the thought of losing you too. They said it could be decades before the process could be reliably reversed. I was desperate for and at the end of my rope, so I did it, I authorized your preservation. Everyone thought I was a fool, they said it was a gimmick, but I didn't care, I needed something to hold on to, a reminder of you. I never married again, but fortunately I did find love."

"I see. Was he good to you?"

"Well, she was, yes. It came as a surprise to me as well. Her name was Lilly, and she and I had a connection. She was a beautifully talented person, She was an artist and a dancer. We met in grief counseling; she had lost her husband just a year earlier."

Chapter 22 Summer's Story - The Year 02165 (The Past)

"My name is Summer Wake, and I am here today because I lost my daughter and my husband and since then, nothing in my life has been the same. When I was young, I had this whole plan for my life. I charted it all out from start to finish. I imagined an idyllic dream of what my future would be. Where I would live, what I would do, I thought that if I followed all the rules and did all the right things that life would turn out just how I wanted it to, but I was wrong. When the war came, it changed everything. My husband, Lucas, used to say that life doesn't care about our carefully crafted plans. Like a force of nature, life has its own agenda, and we were all just along for the ride. I thought he was being pessimistic, back then I could never accept that, but now, I think he was probably right."

"Losing a child is a pain I would never wish on anyone. In my grief, I couldn't understand why my husband, just shut me out. They say we all mourn in our own way, but I couldn't understand why he needed to finish his woodworking project. After we lost our daughter, I nearly drank myself to death, yet he never mourned her, he never cried, he just kept working night after night for hours in that dammed workshop. It was the silence that was the most maddening to me. Inside I was screaming, I was on fire, I wanted to tear the world apart, and I wanted him to do something, say something or break something, but he never did, and in time I grew to resent him for it. It really drove me you know. The utter silence, and the haunting stillness of that house. It was as if he couldn't see me, my pain or what I was going through at all. He just kept working away, so I left to escape the silence and all the memories in that place. When I received word about what happened to him, I came home to find the man I loved was nearly gone. He was broken, half torn apart, and I couldn't bear to see him like that. Sometimes, I think that if I had simply stayed, he never would have taken that trip or gone on that ride, and I would at least still have him. But now all that remains of him is this, a "Memoriam of Maiorum" his preserved consciousness and complete genome. A living archive of everything that made him the man I fell in love with, all stored within its subatomic structure, engineered to last forever. They say uploading is a way to avoid grief, but I disagree. I know my husband is gone but having this gives me comfort because even though I can't bring myself to return to it now, I never want to forget the dreams we shared or the happiness we once had in that old house. I keep this because I want to remember that I had something real once, something special, something true. I am here today because I loved my family and I miss them so very much."

The group sat in silence for a moment largely out of respect. It was how the group worked whenever someone introduced themselves and shared their story for the first time. Our group's facilitator, Dr. Langston broke the silence.

"Thank you for sharing that. I think we should take a break." he said. "We will reconvene at seven-thirty."

Grief counseling was not my idea, but my physicians, honestly, I didn't see the point. Nevertheless, it was a relief to meet others coping with their grief just as I was. Lilly approached me one evening as I poured myself a mushroom coffee.

"Thank you." Lilly said. "For sharing your story with us."

"Well, that's why we're all here right?" I replied taking a sip.

"Right. My name is Lilly. Lilly Harrison."

"Summer, nice to meet you, Lilly. So, how long have you been at this?"

"About six months now, I am trying to stick with it this time."

"Who did you lose? If I may ask?"

Lilly looked at her cup. "My husband was a Gray War veteran, a true warrior, through and through. He was a good man, but he came back from the war different, changed. The things those soldiers saw and did took a heavy toll on him. One day, I came home and found him."

"I am very sorry for your loss," I said, "My husband served during the war, but he never talked about it much. Those were strange days."

"Yeah." Lilly said. "Strange days indeed. So, what are you doing after the meeting?"

"Honestly," I said. "The usual ice-cream, cry, and sleep. How about you?"

"Old century movie, cry and then sleep," Lilly said. "I'm lactose intolerant so." Lilly shrugged and that was the first time she made me laugh. In time, Lilly became my closest and dearest friend. We had lost so much in our lives, but we had each other. After our group sessions, we would smoke and talk for hours at her place sometimes until the early morning hours.

"Wait ok so, you burned down his workshop?" Lilly asked.

"I know, I know it was terrible but my god, at that moment it was, like a projection of precisely what I felt inside, unending, raging blaze. The heat of that fire felt so good, and I hadn't felt good for a long time. I will never forget the smell of all that wood burning, it reminds me of that night every time."

"So, what did he do?" Lilly asked. "What did he say?"

"He was stunned," I said. "Saddened, shocked more than anything else. Honestly, I don't know what drove me to do that. I guess I wanted him to, I don't know, mourn our daughter with me. So yes, I burned it all down that night. Along with what was left of my marriage as well I suppose." I glanced at the time. "Well, it's getting late, Lilly, I should go."

"You can stay if you want." Lilly said, "I'd like for you to stay."

Over the months that followed, Lilly and I took care of one another. What she and I shared was so much more than mere friendship. She showed me that it was ok to be happy again. She helped me learn to live with loss, and guilt. On the hard days she helped me learn to live with my grief and overcome it. Most of all she taught me how to forgive myself. There were too many memories for me in our old house, and my apartment never really felt like home. So, I put it on the market and moved in with Lilly. One day, she came home and found me still in bed.

"You have been in this loft all day," Lilly said. "Have you been outside at all?"

"No," I said. "Besides its raining and it's too hot." Lilly dropped her pack and extended her hand. "Come with me"

"Where are we going?" I asked. Lilly glanced up and smiled. "To the roof." she said. "Trust me you will love this. Come on!"

Lilly lived in a converted industrial building on the mainland just outside of the old town section of Loma. The tower she lived in was once part of the region's historic vertical agriculture industry. After the great quake, it was re-developed into an artist's community. We maintained a rooftop garden like so many people did in those days. I remember it all like it was yesterday, we had warm rains that year with the early start of the urban monsoon.

"Dance with me?" she asked.

"Dance? Here on the roof? In the rain? This is insane." I said as I turned to go back inside.

"Maybe but I have a vintage, AI remastered, old century classic I know you are going to love."

She said in her singsong voice. She opened her hand and presented me with a projection of a pink album cover emblazoned with the letter "G" in its center. It was a vintage single I had been bidding on for months. "I'm Only Happy When It Rains" by Garbage.

"No way! Wow, the original?" I asked. "That's extra rare, where on earth did you find it?"

Lilly smiled as she started the track. "Come on!" She said, "It's hard to be sad when you are dancing. Now dance!"

As the music played, we danced in the rain, that's just who Lilly was, always able to bring me out of depression and turn a day of sadness into a moment of joy. We danced in that warm monsoon rain until I laughed and cried some too. Lilly taught me to see mistakes as life lessons and hardships as opportunities to grow. From her I learned to look at life as a grand adventure. After that day I stopped trying to live my life by a plan, instead I chose to live each day as it came. I incorporated her landscape artwork into my virtual environments. We traveled all over the world from the Shanghai islands to the EuroCon states, and from Neo Japan to the Southern African Alliance. We worked together for years until her diagnosis. Her illness progressed far faster than we expected. After twenty years together, I watched this beautiful woman I had grown to love begin to stumble and falter. We no longer tended to the garden, instead we waited for what we knew was inevitable. Lilly's health gradually declined until she could no longer dance or hold a utensil, sketch, or paint. The only thing that seemed to soothe her pain was when I played piano for her, so I did night after night. Her favorite was an old century classic "A River Flows in You" by Yiruma. I loved her and cared for her as best I knew how until one night, she too was gone. I spent my remaining years alone. I continued my work but this time I built virtual worlds not for escapism but as a therapeutic tool to help others cope with grief, recover from trauma, and overcome their fears. I worked with Gray War veterans, former GCR converts, displaced refugees, and international relief organizations. The people I met and worked with eventually led to a role with the Global Confederation as a special adviser on the therapeutic use of virtual environments. In all that time I never forgot about you, and I hoped that by some miracle, one day, we might be together again. As the years passed and I grew older; my health started to decline. So I returned to the Canadian Republic to live out my final years with my niece and her family. I requested to have my consciousness preserved and archived alongside yours. I was preserved moments before my death at the age of one hundred and twenty-three. Then one day I awoke within the Construct Collective. I didn't know what I was, but my mind was clear and there was no pain. I felt free, like I knew everything all at once. To my relief, I wasn't alone; you were there along with millions of others. From that moment I knew I would never be alone again. All that was worth it because, well, here we are.

"And Lilly?" I asked, "Where is she now?"

"Lilly always believed that memorial preservation was an attempt to cheat death. Breaking the cycle of life which, she held to be sacred. She was never preserved, unfortunately."

"It seems like you have lived an entire lifetime."

"Indeed, I have." Summer said. "A lifetime and so much more. In my time I have met with over twenty-three different alien species on various monitoring and diplomatic missions over the centuries. Its why I was selected for this mission."

Summer seems to have found a certain solace in the Collective. How could I possibly ask her to leave that behind, to alter the nature of what she was for me? She would ultimately have to make her own decision, but I had a distinct sense that she was content with her current form and had no intention of stepping into the portal to become human again. The re-genesis event resulted in three human factions; Constructs, Purists and Chimera. Somehow, we would need to learn to live together and work together if we were going to survive what was coming.

Chapter 23 Into the Outer Dark

Our ship now complete emerged from the pocket dimension design space where it was compiled using Construct programmable matter. Measuring eighteen hundred feet long, three hundred feet high and four hundred feet wide, the vessel's exterior hull had a dull silver appearance etched with a complex, illuminated geometric surface pattern common to other Construct designs. The ship was symmetrical, lined with white light that illuminated its leading edges. It appeared to be made up of fractal shards of programmable matter that contained interlocking sections of solid light that were not physically connected to one another. Large elements of the craft's propulsion and defense systems appeared to float rigidly just inches from other sections of the ship. A quantum lock attached the separated sections to form a rigid structural relationship. There were no physical doors or openings to the craft, just a dimensional fold portal allowing entry and exit. The vessel had no supports, it merely floated perfectly still just a few feet above the ground resting on a standing wave of micro gravitic energy.

"It's incredible Nathan."

"She's all yours Lucas." Nathan said. "I can promise you she will serve you well. It is customary to select a name for a vessel; did you have anything in mind?"

"I do" Summer said "Angelica"

It was to have been our daughter's name, I had not spoken it aloud in years. The memory was too painful, but now, it was good to hear it spoken again. The ship's new name gradually formed on the outer hull along with an etching resembling stylized angel wings. Constructs had numerous starships of their own, but none of them were designed to accommodate human life. The Angelica was the first ship of its kind in centuries.

"The base design was inspired by vessels from the late GSE period." Nathan said. "I have made extensive modifications of course, the dark energy reactor that powers the hyperdrive, gravitic drive and supporting sub-systems are an active prototype of Construct design."

"Active prototype?" I asked.

"Yes" Nathan said. "The nature of our technology is such that this ship is never truly complete. It can improve itself over time as it learns, adapts, and evolves. Its technological development is part of an ongoing iterative process of design refinement. In time every ship in the fleet like her will learn from the collective experiences of all other ships. The hyperdrive configuration, its senses, countermeasures, defenses, and weapons systems are all highly adaptable thereby greatly increasing the crews' survivability regardless of the mission or situation."

"Weapons Nathan? Is that the signal we want to send to our distant cousins?"

"Constructs may be peaceful Lucas, but we are not pacifists. You will find that the Galaxy can be a perilous place requiring both care and caution. In the depth of the outer dark, weapons and defense systems are a survival requirement. I have equipped your ship with a vast and generous assortment of antimatter-based weapons and explosive ordinance designed to be delivered to target via folded space transport. Angelica, introduce yourself."

"Hello crew my name is Angelica, I am a first-generation Wake class long range explorer vessel." She said.

"The ship was built specifically to accommodate you Lucas, thus the class identification and naming convention."

"Is that the ship?" I asked. Pointing toward the ceiling.

"Yes," she said. "You can interact with me verbally, mentally or in combination. The specific modality of communication is entirely your choice."

"I designed her with integrated sensory pairing technology." Nathan said. "It allows her to form a bond with the crew."

"Angelica, what are you?" I asked.

"I am a non-human, a synthetic conscious agent much like your sphere drones but far more sophisticated."

"Like an advanced artificial superintelligence?" I asked.

"Well, those are rather archaic terms to describe what I am but for the purposes of your understanding, yes. My base code was created by Nathan; however, my consciousness was derived from the Universal Línghún."

"Well, it's nice to meet you, Angelica."

"It is a pleasure to meet you, Lucas and Summer. Please let me know how I can assist. I am always here."

The ship's interior in many respects resembled the realm of the Construct Collective. It too was pure white and geometrically ornate. This gave the ship an unusual organic like quality. Every surface edge was lined with periodic accents of white and amber light. In some areas of the ship, you could see the exterior even though Construct matter is not inherently transparent. Many locations within the vessel incorporated pocket dimension technology giving it a slightly larger internal volume than what was apparent from its external appearance. We entered command as chairs formed from the deck below in a semicircle around a command-and-control interface that appeared hovering before us. The ship itself was a living machine, an independent and sentient being not much different from human form Constructs. Angelica's systems were completely automated, and no crew was necessary to operate the vessel. An extensive arboretum was integrated into her overall design, which served as part of the vessel's Earth microbiome and life-support system. The ship's day-night lighting cycle was primarily for my benefit. Neither Nathan nor Summer required external cues to set circadian rhythms, but I certainly did. In many ways the Angelica was the perfect ship, it required little knowledge to operate safely and effectively.

"Attention crew, we are now departing Earth orbit." Angelica said, "ETA to the Ardent System thirty standard days, fourteen Earth hours."

We set out toward the edge of the Solar system for a long voyage via hyperspace; it was both terrifying and exhilarating to contemplate the prospect of finally leaving Earth, the system and all that I had come to know since awakening. The ship was eerily silent except for the vessel's powerful dark energy reactor. I made my way to the observation deck just in time to watch the Earth become smaller and smaller until it vanished from sight.

The reactor's pulse gave the ship a unique kind of heartbeat, and one could certainly sense the vessel's immense power. Even when we moved, it seemed as if the stars and planets around us moved, not the ship. There was zero sense of acceleration as we passed the Jovian moon of Ganymede. On the approach to the edge of our system and the first hyperspace beacon, we passed near an ancient derelict ship adrift in orbit around Calisto. I underestimated the sheer size of the ancient colony ships of the late GSE era. Compared to that ship the Angelica looked like a shuttlecraft.

"Angelica, what ship was that?"

"The Shenzhou, launched in 3980 with a crew complement of one hundred officers and staff along with five hundred thousand colonists in cryostasis. Once the quarantine was initiated, the ship never made it out of the system."

"All perished during the collapse?" I asked.

"Or shortly there afterward yes," She said. "It's survival pods, shuttles and tender vessels are still onboard. Like so many others they ran out of resources, biomass, and time. Hundreds of derelict ships like this one remain adrift in the Solar system, relics of those that could not be preserved."

"Angelica, are there any records or logs from this ship?"

"Yes, there are one thousand eight hundred and seventy-five logs."

"Show me the last entry."

In an instant I was onboard the Shenzhou viewing the recorded historical event as if I was there, like a disembodied ghost both part of the event and at the same time separate from it. This was the final log of interim Captain Srikanth Gupta of the Earth Colony Ship Shenzhou recorded on 04036-07-08 ten years after the collapse. To the right sparks poured through the top of the bulkhead door. Someone with a plasma torch was trying to enter the bridge by force. On the floor were several wounded bridge officers along with the bodies of two others. The last survivors of a firefight just moments earlier. Their wounds were cauterized, and their uniforms were still smoking from whatever weapon they were attacked with. One man sat on the deck in shock, trembling as he held his wounded arm.

"The captain is dead, and the crew is now in mutiny. Last night during the shift change a group of armed officers captured the ship's armory and have taken over engineering and reactor control. We received a message from

Earth along with a set of landing coordinates. "Do not abandon hope, return to Earth if you want to live." That means someone is still alive back there. The captain and I agreed that returning to Earth was our best course of action despite the risk of attack and infection. But some officers and crew insist Earth is lost, they want to risk a beaconless jump to break the blockade, escape and seek refuge in the outer colonies. The truth is, we can't jump even if we wanted to, we've tried none of the ships in the system can it's why we are all still here a decade after the fall. Our world is a nightmare now, we've all seen the images, and we know what awaits us planet side. The exo's have left us all here to die. Despite all that has happened I am still responsible for these people, and I cannot place the lives of five hundred thousand souls at risk. If we remain in orbit around Calisto any longer, we will deplete our remaining resources and die. If we breach the quarantine blockade, the exo's will shoot us down and again, we die. Every action but one equals death. We tried to hold out as best we could, but it's been years now, no one is coming for us, we can only save ourselves. Returning to Earth was our one chance to survive, that message was the only sign of real hope we've seen in years, but we failed to convince them of that. I failed us all I'm afraid. I have sealed off the command deck and the bridge. They are burning through now, and there is not much time. If you are watching, this is the final log of the ECS Shenzhou."

End of Record

"Do not abandon hope, return to Earth if you want to live." The Guardians' invitation to the last survivors of the collapse, still trapped within the solar system. Constructs had records on many ghost ships like this one. These majestic vessels once traveled the vast distances between colonial systems. They were the workhorse of the late GSE era. Built to last a century, these ancient ships now stand as silent memorials to those that could not be saved. The continued survival of humanity was once again at stake. Our species had faced numerous insurmountable challenges in the past each time summoning the courage to overcome the odds. Despite the inherent danger of our upcoming mission, the sight of the long-dead Shenzhou only strengthened my resolve to face whatever awaited us in the distant Ardent system.

"Angelica?"

"Yes Lucas?"

"Tell me about your propulsion and weapons systems, I want to know everything including any tactical information we have on Ardent ships, armaments and weapons systems."

"That is an extensive amount of information Lucas."

"I realize that" I insisted, taking a seat in preparation.

"Very well then, open your mind to me and do not be afraid. I will monitor your vitals and regulate the flow of information as needed; please let me know if any adjustments are necessary."

I closed my eyes as the sensory pairing with the ship came on, at that moment I received massive volumes of information pouring into my mind about the ship, its purpose, systems, and design. After just three minutes, which seemed like hours of training, I went back to my quarters where Summer was working. The room was filled with hundreds of images of the Ardent weapon captured by long range surveillance imaging.

"You look exhausted," Summer said.

"Data dump from Angelica."

"Ah, I understand. This ship can take care of itself; you don't need to learn everything about every system you know."

"I know," I said. "Still, it's good to be aware you know, just in case we get into trouble out there."

"Well, that's the Lucas I remember. Come here and look at this. This is the latest data on the Ardent weapon system. In our time this technology was thought to be an entirely theoretical concept, but somehow, they built one. Analysis indicates the weapon is a type of Nicoll-Dyson Cannon. As you can see from this simulation, the weapon is designed to convert a star's entire solar output into a highly destructive, concentrated, gravitationally focused beam. These large counter rotating structures in orbit are the weapons focusing pedals. I believe they are designed to condition the star's internal fusion reactions and plasma dynamics in preparation for firing. This process takes time to achieve, months in fact to reach optimal power levels." Summer rotated the weapon's floating image and enlarged it, allowing us to examine its complex structure in greater detail.

"The beam can then be redirected via a hyperspace window to target another star, planet, or enemy fleet. It can destroy an entire solar system in a single burst. Currently, we have no defense against such a weapon."

"Why can't we destroy it with Angelica's weapons' array?" I asked.

"Not an option," Summer said. "Such an action would only get us into a conflict with the Ardent. The other consideration is scale. What you are looking at here is massive and extremely well defended. These pear-shaped objects are what we believe to be defense pods. Each pod appears to contain squadrons of automated defense drones. If we could destroy or disable them, we might be able to damage the weapons focusing rings and other critical systems sufficiently enough to prevent the weapon from firing. These drones represent the bulk of its defenses and the greatest threat."

"How many?" I asked.

"Too many, millions in fact." Summer said. "So, a conventional assault to try to destroy the weapon at this point is completely out of the question. I have run millions of simulated battle scenarios. By my estimate even with a fleet of hundreds of Wake class ships, we could never survive such an overwhelming onslaught or do enough damage to make a difference. We must find another way."

"It will take a month to travel to the Ardent system via hyperspace." I said. "How long would it take that beam to reach Earth?"

"With Ardent hyperspace window technology, a few seconds at best."

"Hyperspace window?" I asked.

"Our hyper-drive technology requires several jumps to reach distant locations. As we make course corrections along the way, we jump into and out of higher dimensional space. Ardent hyper-drive technology is vastly different and far more advanced. Their ships can combine the repulsive power of three dark energy reactors to create what's known as a hyperspace window allowing for near instantaneous interstellar travel. This capability is part of the weapons focusing rings, which is why it has a nearly limitless destructive range."

"How were they able to build a weapon like this?" I asked. "Even with molecular compilers, where did they get the raw materials? One would need to dismantle something the size of a planet just to harvest the resources needed to create the weapon."

"The raw material question is easy." Summer said. "This is an image of three large moons that once existed in orbit around the star where the Ardent Weapon now resides. As you can see, today they are no longer there. The material from these moons formed the core framework of the structure. The rest was harvested from the star itself. Once you calculate the estimated gross mass of the Ardent weapon, then compare it to the mass of the former moons and star lifted material, the numbers speak for themselves."

"So, just what material could withstand the immense gravity and radiation generated by the star?"

"I have a few theories," Summer said. "One is that the weapon may not be composed of ordinary matter as we know it. If it is, it may have been altered or converted into some exotic state our science is unfamiliar with. Another is that the structures that make up the weapon are not affected by the star's output because they may be partially phased between our dimension and another allowing for manipulation of the star's fusion reactions in this dimension without the need to risk direct exposure to it. Either way, it is a technical accomplishment that rivals the best of our capabilities."

"How could they have developed this level of technology so quickly?" I asked. "Even surpassing the achievements of the Constructs?"

"Well, the ancient law of accelerating returns is certainly one possibility," Summer said. "But I don't think that tells the entire story. I think the Ardent acquired much of this technology from the Progenitors, they reverse engineered, then used that knowledge to put them centuries ahead of all other descendants of humanity. What's wrong you look worried Lucas."

"Well, when your distant Earth cousins separated by thousands of years one day shows up at your front door unannounced saying "hello it's me please don't shoot." It seems like a recipe for disaster. So yes, I have some concerns about all this."

"Ok, so, what's your concern?" Summer asked.

"That they will see us as an alien threat," I said. "Or destroy us and destroy this ship. I can still die you know."

"Hmmm, well, I think I see where this is going." Summer said. "Just for the record, Constructs in physical form are not immortal. Sure, I can stand to lose an arm, a leg or part of my head, but if enough of my Construct body is destroyed while the signifier of my consciousness resides within, that's it, Summertime is over. So, this mission is a risk for us all Lucas, not just you."

"I know," I said, pausing to find the right words. "It's not that. I realize re-genesis is a personal choice, but I just thought you would..." My voice trailed off.

"What? Choose to become human again?" Summer interjected, completing my thought.

"Well, I don't want to influence your decision either way." I replied.

"Lucas, I am content with what I am. Are you?" she asked, her eyes searching mine.

"Yes, of course I am." I said, but my voice lacked conviction.

"You know, Lucas, I don't need voice stress analysis to tell you're not being completely honest with yourself, or with me for that matter."

I sighed. "Look, I just want to get back what we had before all of this," I said, gesturing broadly as if trying to lift the weight of the world from my shoulders.

"What we had in the past" Summer said. "Is in the past, The world we once lived in, who we were, all that is long gone now, ancient history. "This" is who and what we are now, this moment, this time, right now. If you love me, then respect my decision to be what I choose to be. If you love me, then my form shouldn't matter. I loved you when I was human, and I love you now."

> "Even if we make it through all this," I said. "Eventually, I will grow old and die."

"Yes, I realize that." Summer said. "I can accept that happiness is fleeting, but I refuse to forgo it just because I know that one day it will end. The question is, can you?"

I nodded and smiled. "Good, then we are in agreement." Summer said.

"You seem to be taking all this in stride."

"With age comes wisdom I suppose," Summer said. "One advantage of computational existence is that I can see all the possibilities within every scenario. For example, there are twenty-three possible outcomes for this mission, only three of which are desirable. There is an eighty-five percent chance our new relationship will be successful and a fifteen percent chance you will change your mind about it. I can predict outcomes and recite probabilities all day long, and it still doesn't change my feelings for you because, even though mathematics may underpin our reality, numbers alone are not our fate."

Summer always had a way of changing my mind. When I first saw her, I knew things would be different between us. This, however, is not how I imagined how things would turn out. Much like a force of nature, life always has its own agenda.

"Attention crew." Angelica said. "We have reached the edge of the Solar system. We will jump in five minutes."

"Lucas, Summer," Nathan said, "Please join me in command."

Summer and I arrived in time to see the edge of the Solar system and the last hyperspace navigation beacon. The display ring was filled with projected data on the galaxy, the Ardent weapon, our ship, its current position, our destination, and the various jump points along the way. The command interface functioned much like the archive, planetary bodies and systems are represented as interactive objects projected around us that can be manipulated and expanded. Once we entered hyperspace, there was no sense of motion, speed, or acceleration. Instead of a sea of stars streaking past, the exterior view was filled with a thick blue haze.

"There are no stars?" I asked.

"Not here no." Nathan said. "We are in higher dimensional space now, the bulk. You would only see stars if we were traveling at superluminal speeds within normal space. Not a preferred mode of travel if you want to get to your destination in one piece."

"I have been learning more about our Ardent exo-human cousins." I said. "Interesting that religion and tribalism continue to exist within an advanced type two civilization like theirs."

"It's not that unusual really," Nathan said. "On Earth even during the height of human civilization, there were hundreds of religions of one sort or another flourishing across the settled colonial worlds. Royal families, tribes, clans, castes, genetic pre-determinism. Such is the cycle of human history."

"I also learned quite a bit about their belief systems" I said. "Some Ardent came to believe that the civilizations which existed centuries before humanity were closer to the "breath" of the creator and that this new faith spread throughout their world."

"That was centuries ago," Nathan said. "In ancient Ardent history, there was a religious sect called The Breath of God. It gained popularity among Earth's colonists. Over time, the original precepts of the faith were altered, reinterpreted or in many instances misinterpreted. Denominations arose, and there were numerous conflicts over this and many other belief systems for thousands of years. In time, they came to believe that their people and the universe itself was created and ruled by a single omnipotent being with twin opposing aspects. Solaris a being of darkness, death and destruction and it's opposite the Reclaimer a being of light, renewal, and creation. It is believed that the planets neighboring binary star system and unique orbital pattern served as the inspirational basis of such beliefs."

"From the surface of the Ardent homeworld," Summer said, "The two distant orbiting stars appear to feed off one another via the mass transfer stream formed between them. This unique celestial phenomena creates a Yin and Yang like image in their night skies. This shape has become a symbol of their religious faith. "Solaris" the dark star exchanges plasma with its orbital companion the "Reclaimer" the white star forming an endless loop of creation and simultaneous destruction."

"The colony's founder, Hiroto Ronin, was an industrialist." Nathan said, "He sought to use his wealth to create a new kind of world based on the tenants of scientific innovation, friendship, strength, and peace. Their Earth colony ship the "ECS Ardent" utilized a revolutionary drive system, centuries ahead of its time, capable of generating a hyperspace window. On its maiden voyage however something went terribly wrong, logs indicate the ship entered the event horizon and vanished without a trace. The entire ship and her crew were considered to be lost. The fate of the ECS Ardent remained a mystery for thousands of years until Construct deep space stellar cartographers discovered the truth of what became of them. We identified and cataloged the three worlds of their system located five-hundred and thirty light years from Earth, making it the most distant of any known human colony. The descendants of the legendary lost colony ship have since crafted a creation narrative around their history."

"The Ardent narrowly survived an invasion by a predatory species over eighty years ago that nearly ended their civilization." Summer said. "As a result, they have tended to both fear and avoid others. Religious faith is what got their people through the war. Ardent culture in the years since has become much more isolationist, xenophobic and intolerant of others, something which historically, the Ardent were not known for. Today some among the Ardent people see themselves as the pinnacle of creation. Life forms that are not their kind, are often deemed by many to be alien outsiders or worse; fit only to be cleansed."

"That doesn't say much about how well we will be received when we arrive." I said. "How were Constructs able to acquire so much information about their world and culture given how insular they are?"

"We have worked to maintain clandestine contact with select individuals within key areas of Ardent society for years." Summer said. "Those who maintain contact with us do so at tremendous risk of ridicule if they were to ever reveal their communication with us. The Ardent live within a strict caste system comprised of Priests, Warriors, Technicians, Historians, Trainers, and Seekers. We go to great lengths to protect our contacts on Ardah and other worlds to conceal our interactions with them both for their safety and our anonymity."

"The Ardent generally are not hostile," Nathan said. "Unless provoked or threatened. Despite being genetically human, they are quite different in many ways."

"Since their last major military conflict." Summer said. "Our intelligence indicates that they now rarely remove their face coverings except when among close tribal members within their caste. Such tribal affiliations are essential in Ardent society. Whenever possible, take note of their facial tattoos, these will illustrate their tribal ties. As human form Constructs, Nathan and I would be considered an unnatural blending of spirit and machine in other words, abominations according to their beliefs. Which is why a human presence on this mission is crucial."

Chapter 24 A Study of Ardent Culture

Upon reaching the Ardent system, our plan is to contact Nathan's tribal liaison, an influential Seeker named "Tan-Mara." We hope she can arrange a meeting with more sympathetic, influential and open-minded members of Ardent society. I decided to use the remaining days of our journey to learn as much as possible about the Ardent, their caste system, history, and societal structure.

In my study of Ardent culture, I was fascinated with their society's many traditions and rituals. Their civilization seemed to be heavily influenced by a unique combination of ancient Japanese, Neoceltic and Sinoafrican cultural motifs all of which reflect the cultural makeup of the original founders of Ardent civilization. Survival, innovation, self-reliance, self-discipline, and combat skill are traits highly prized by the Ardent. Yet they also possess a complex, technologically advanced society that has endured for centuries in complete isolation from the rest of humanity.

Since the Priests seized power choosing one's spouse is strictly forbidden. In Ardent society all marriages are the product of an arranged pairing dictated by the Priest caste. Anyone found in violation of the decree that bear children from such relations is subject to the test. Immediately after birth, Ardent children from an unsanctioned union are bathed in a fermented plant extract by Priests. This is done to evaluate the child's emotional reaction, strength, and fortitude. It is believed by some that because such children are the product of individual moral weakness they therefore must be "tested." If a child is deemed "weak" by the Priests, it is taken from their parents to the neighboring desert world of Hafeeta and abandoned in the wastelands to be "Taken by the Winds." A brutal ritual instituted by order of the Priest caste under Chancellor Zen-Overen whereby the offspring of an unsanctioned union is placed in a cage at midday. As the sun sets and the temperature decreases, the relentless sandstorms blast the cage and the child until only its sand polished bones remain. The bones are tightly wrapped and returned to the family as a reminder of the price of moral weakness and the terrible price parents pay for children born of love. According to many, in Ardent culture, this brutal practice serves as a disincentive for violating the Priest decree on marriage and reproduction. On the other hand, children that are the product of an arranged pairing are never tested nor abandoned. Given the nature of the decision-making process this practice has been the focus of much controversy among the Ardent people. Many argue that it burdens their society unnecessarily and provides no benefit. Many of these parent child separations have been thwarted by opposition leaders in Ardent society that work to undermine the power of the Priest caste.

I found the continued use of bladed weapons an intriguing aspect of Ardent culture. Centuries ago, hostile native life forms known as Raktha dominated the three Ardent worlds. The first generation of colonists found that their plasma arc discharge weapons were largely ineffective against the Raktha due to their unusual physiology. However, with detailed knowledge of the creature's anatomy, bladed weapons at close range proved far more effective, allowing the Ardent to establish themselves as the dominant inhabitants of their settled worlds. The close quarters combat techniques of the Ardent were refined over the centuries, honing them into a fine art and proved invaluable during the Ardent people's earliest conflicts. As a matter of survival and cultural tradition all Ardent are trained to fight and survive from the time they are young. For them, the blade in all its many forms is a sacred symbol and a cornerstone of their culture. Once a year, Ardent adolescents between the ages of twelve and sixteen are expected to participate in a series of "Caste Trials" to evaluate their talents, skills, training, and aptitude. To prove themselves worthy of becoming an apprentice within one of the castes of Ardent society. This requires successful completion of challenges unique to each caste's societal role.

Priests occupy the highest tier within the Ardent caste system. They currently rule the High Council and are easily identified by the symbols of their sacred law, which flow down their gold and black robes. Their words are considered sacred whenever a priest speaks their words are incorporated into the stream of animated script covering their skin and clothing. Priests are powerful in Ardent society, but they are also greatly feared. Ardent Priests use a visionary entheogenic substance called "Shén de shíwù," derived from the native xenosteriopsis-cappi plant that grows in the wildland rainforest regions of the Ardent homeworld. When properly processed and combined with the fermented sap of the Black Forest tree it provides Priests with heightened senses, dream visions, sharpened visual acuity and an extended lifespan. At much higher doses like those given to wounded warriors on the battlefield, can cause considerable negative side effects, including severe hormonal imbalances, rapid skeletomuscular growth, and unpredictable genetic mutations.

Priest caste training requires rigorous study and memorization of sacred law and philosophical texts. During their trials, those who wish to become part of the Priest caste must endure the pilgrimage to the wildlands where they collect, process, and consume the sacred plant extract. Once imbibed acolytes enter an ecstatic, hallucinogenic domain. During their inner journey trial members are forced to confront what the Priests call The Shadow Self. If the chosen can face their internal Solaris and defeat it with the Reclaimer's light, they can begin the journey toward becoming a member of the Priest cast. Priests hold great power in Ardent society, the power to control the lives of billions and the power to conceal. The ancient story of the Ardent people's true origins on Earth remains a tightly held esoteric secret within the high orders of the Priest caste. To maintain their power and influence Priests and their Historian ally's horde ancient knowledge from the other castes and tribes.

Warriors serve as protectors of the faith, the people, and the Ardent way of life, which they refer to collectively as "The Path." The Ardent Warrior caste represents the largest and strongest of their people. Warriors are genetically conditioned for both physical and cognitive superiority. Once chosen as an acolyte, they receive extensive neural combat conditioning known as the Blood Rage to prepare them for war long before they ever see a battlefield. Blood Rage conditioning was originally developed during the Ardent Rim Wars to increase stamina, survivability and focus on the battlefield. It later became part of the standard Ardent training regimen for all castes among the rare individuals with a temperament for it. During the Blood Rage muscle memory and adrenalin are used to create an altered state of battle awareness, allowing the practitioner to fight without conscious action. Pain receptors are numbed, vision and hearing are sharpened, physical strength and dexterity are substantially increased. Combat techniques, weapons handling, and other skills are encoded and imbued in their minds via their lifelong training regimen. Warriors train with various weapons, including swords, long daggers, shapeshifting thermal weapons, adaptive energy shields, handheld directed energy weapons and gravity wave field-effect weapons. During their caste trials a select group of adolescents are taken to a planet seeded with hostile life forms and left behind with minimal provisions for thirty planetary days. Their only task as warrior acolytes is to think, fight, kill and coordinate with their brethren to survive. When not in combat, Warriors can be identified by a series of red holographic symbols that extend across the shoulders of their blackened armor.

Technicians are the research scientists and engineers of their society. Like most Ardent castes, they are trained to fight in addition to being genetically and cybernetically enhanced for increased cognitive ability and memory. Trials for Technicians involve complex problem-solving tasks under extreme conditions. Technician acolytes are dropped off on a decommissioned ship months away from the Ardent homeworld. Their task is to enter the ghost ship with minimal resources, get the vessel back online, and extract those that have successfully completed their caste trials for the return trip home. Technicians can be identified by green holographic symbols projected from the shoulders of their armor.

The Historian caste maintains the history and legacy of the Ardent people. They developed their own unique form of spatial information storage technology. Historians and the Priest caste share common interests that are often in direct opposition to the Seekers' efforts. The role of the Historian caste is crucial in shaping how the Ardent see themselves as a people. Historians maintain and control the cultural memory of the Ardent civilization. Their power in Ardent society is subtle but has long-lasting effects. Historians have enhanced memory abilities and can recall events in detail at any point in time you specify. Their caste trials and training involve turning events into a cohesive narrative no matter how complex or broad ranging. Historians can be identified by the amber light that lines the edges of their cloth armor.

The Seekers are the explorers, investigators, spies, diplomats, law enforcers, bounty hunters and mediators of Ardent society. They are the most approachable and open-minded of all the Ardent castes. They too are trained to fight and can receive Blood Rage conditioning. Combat, however, is not their primary role; they are often called upon by other castes to perform a variety of unique roles. They are often seen as undisciplined by other castes and are readily despised by some members of the Warrior caste for the unique freedoms granted to them by Ardent law and tradition. Seekers serve the Ardent people's interests regardless of caste and it is their caste duty to expose corruption and wrongdoing. When commissioned by either the High Council, a city-state enforcer, or a tribal leader for a task, they receive what is known as a Duty Mark granting them unrestricted access and spacing privileges if their commissioned work requires it. By law and tradition, Seekers cannot be denied entry to any Ardent ship, facility, or colony world. Seekers and Technicians often work together given their shared goals. They mount exploratory expeditions to other star systems and are the first to contact other worlds for evaluation and trade. Seekers wear leather armor with black, gray, or brown hooded cloaks. They tend to be adventurous and are far more willing to interact with aliens and other outsiders. Seekers strive for mutual understanding and trust with other peoples and species. Their investigations, archeological discoveries, and interactions with others are often in direct conflict with the Priest and Historian castes' isolationist proclivities. Their caste trials assess their investigative, tracking and survival abilities in new and unusual environments. Sometimes this takes the form of an investigation, a bounty, or tracking down an unusual or rare object's location. Seekers can be identified by a blue light that illuminates the inner edge of their hooded cloaks.

One of the more unusual and unique castes was the Trainers. Trainers are the educators of Ardent society and can be thought of as a sub-caste. This designation, however, does not suggest a lower tier within the hierarchy of their society. On the contrary, they are often held in the same regard as Priests. Once every ten years, they are selected from different castes to instruct others of their caste. Trainers are true masters whose accomplishments are well known among their caste and tribe. They tend to be older and more seasoned veterans of their caste that have already proven themselves. They can be identified by white holographic symbols projected from their crimson and silver accented armor.

There is another group among the Ardent that are seldom mentioned or recognized given that they hold neither tribe, caste nor rank. They are the Forgotten Clan, outcasts of Ardent society that occupy Hafeeta the harsh red desert world of the Ardent home system. Banishment in Ardent society means that as outcasts they must fend for themselves. They receive no support from the core worlds or rim colonies. They are allowed to trade and scavenge for resources to make their way in life. They do the kinds of work most Ardent citizens find dishonorable or beneath their station. They are often commissioned for dangerous work, salvage operations, or bounty hunting. Usually for other outcasts that engage in piracy, terrorism, murder for hire, and other criminal activity. The Forgotten Clan are granted limited spacing privileges to select worlds and remote outposts that tolerate their presence. In some circumstances Forgotten Clan members can perform commissioned work under a limited Duty Mark. But even under such rare authority outcasts require a third-party representative when dealing with other Ardent worlds. Seekers often fulfill this role and operate on their behalf for a price.

Chapter 25 A Long Time in Hyperspace

Each day we edge closer to the Ardent home system. There is only so much about them and their society that I can reasonably consume each day. With Angelica's help, I have learned more about their language, culture, customs, combat techniques, and most importantly their ships, weapons, and defense systems. Summer has been helping me understand our vessel's adaptive systems. While Nathan has taken to botany in the ship's Arboretum. To pass the time, I study, meditate, train, and take a daily run around the ship from stem to stern to the tune of five miles. This morning, however, something was different. As I rounded the ship's corridors, its halls echoed with the faint sound of a grand piano. I hadn't heard Summer play in a long time; I was sure she could sense me approaching; she knew I was listening. We loved the old century classics, recorded back when other human beings made music, especially "Nocturne in A Minor" by Lawson, a beautifully moving piece. In our old life, I always took comfort from the sound of her playing. As our ship hurtled its way through hyperspace, I found myself comforted once more.

"Attention crew," Angelica said, "We are returning to normal space in preparation for the final jump to the Ardent system."

The grand piano Summer made disappeared as it merged back into the ship's deck.

"Well Lucas, you wanted to see the stars, now's your chance. Trust me you won't want to miss this."

Summer and I went up to the observation deck for a rare, up-close view of the immense O'Dowd Nebula. This beautiful celestial feature is the remnant of a supernova that occurred over thirty thousand years ago. The ship was surrounded by an infinite iridescence of gold, red, green, and purple strands of ionized gas and dust stretching some fifty light years across. It had an almost organic, filament like quality within its structure, and it was truly a wonder to behold. In the outer dark of deep space, destruction and beauty walk hand in hand. Nathan joined us as Angelica prepared for the last hyperspace jump.

"Impressive, isn't it?" Nathan asked.

"Yes, it is, and beautiful." I said as I glanced at Summer. She smiled and turned toward me, always focused on the task ahead.

"We will reach the Ardent system soon." Summer said. "Are you ready?"

"As ready as I will ever be." I said, "I have to admit, it seems like I made this situation worse by sending out that gravity wave message."

"The Ardent have never responded to our attempts at communications." Summer said. "Our existence doesn't fit within their worldview. I have to say, the part when you described Earth as "the world from which your distant ancestors came." That probably didn't go over very well with their High Council. Nevertheless, all we can do now is focus on our mission."

"Nathan, this Seeker Tan-Mara," I asked. "Has she given you any indication as to why the weapon was reactivated?"

"Apparently, the situation on Ardah is dire." Nathan said. "Since the theocracy took control of the High Council over eighty years ago the Ardent people have lived under social restrictions that many find abhorrent. There is a power struggle taking place within their society. Many believe the Ardent are on the brink of an all-out civil war. Understandably, Tan-Mara has grown apprehensive about her communications with us. We will find out more soon enough."

"Attention crew, ETA to Ardent System ten standard days, fourteen hours."

After taking in the nebula's beauty, we set out for the Ardent system. Ten more days of the blue haze of hyperspace. Interstellar travel is nothing at all like I thought it would be. It's those moments between jumps when you have a chance to appreciate the universe. Looking out at the vast cosmos one is reminded of how small we truly are. Even with all our advanced technology and power, we are nothing when compared to the power and majesty of the universe. The beauty out there came billions of years before us, and it will remain billions of years after we are gone.

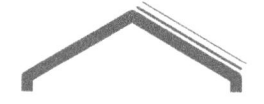

Chapter 26 The Edge of Ardent Space

We dropped out of hyperspace into a neighboring system on the edge of Ardent space and awaited the arrival of Nathan's Seeker contact. Summer was in command monitoring the latest Ardent weapon data while Nathan compiled emergency hyperspace beacons capable of generating a pocket dimension around them just in case things were to go badly with the Ardent. If we need to abort the mission, we can use a combination of local pulsars and our own hyperspace navigation beacons to navigate beyond their space.

"Attention crew, there is a ship on an intercept course. It is an Ardent fast attack cruiser, vessel designation, Sparrow."

"Identity verified" Nathan said, "It is Tan-Mara's ship. "The bulk space comms signature she possesses confirms it."

In the center of command, the galaxy's floating image focused on our current position. We could see the system we were in and the Ardent ship. The vessel was twice our size, the center was a series of dark elongated dagger-like shards that overlapped one another at varying lengths partially enclosed by an upper and lower elongated oval-shaped outer hull. The vessel was covered with a complex moire pattern of dark energy that moved across its black hexagon covered surface in every direction. The ship resembled something more akin to fractal artwork than a spacecraft. Angelica rotated the ship and reoriented our position to match the approaching Ardent vessel. A dimensional fold opened on Angelica's command deck, and Tan-Mara stepped through as the fold portal closed behind her. The suit's systems translated her Yulan derived dialect, making seamless, fluid two-way verbal communications possible.

"Visitors from Earth," Tan-Mara said. "It is an honor to meet you all."

"It is an honor to finally meet you as well Tan-Mara." Nathan said.

"As a child" Tan-Mara said. "There were times when I thought I had imagined you. We were not allowed to speak of your kind or of Earth openly on my world."

"Understandable," Nathan said. "But it is our hope that perhaps one day that will change."

"That was my father's desire as well." Tan-Mara said.

"And his father before him going back five generations." Nathan said. "These are my companions, Summer and Lucas Wake of Earth."

"It is an honor" I said, "Tan-Mara of the Seekers." She looked at me with astonishment.

"You are no human form Construct." Tan-Mara said. "You are flesh and blood, the ancestor race, how is this possible?"

"The event your Technicians detected in our region of the galaxy" Summer said. Now allows us to return to our original biological form if we choose to."

"Remarkable." Tan-Mara said. "My entire life I have heard the stories around the pit fires, passed down tribal lines since ancient times as myths, but my family knew the truth. I never dreamed I would meet a Construct being to say nothing of living Human from the origin world. What strange and interesting times we live in."

"You are our guest here," Nathan said. "Please sit. There is much we need to discuss."

Nathan invited Tan-Mara to join us in command. Chairs emerged from the deck and solidified in place. We gathered around the command display ring. In honor of Tan-Mara, the galaxy's image was replaced with what both appeared and felt to be a fire designed to resemble a traditional Ardent gathering. We learned that the Ardent were locked in a fierce power struggle between the Priest and the Seeker castes that threatened to tear their society apart. The conflict arose over the question of the true origins of the Ardent people. For nearly eighty years, those within the Seeker caste have argued that the theological basis of the Ardent people's origin is false and that their true heritage stems from ancient Terra or "The Origen World" of Earth in the Solar system, not the current Ardent homeworld. Despite numerous undeniable archeological discoveries and ancient records uncovered by the Seekers, Priests and Historians have continued to deny the validity of what came to be known on their world as "Terra-Theory." Tan-Mara briefed us on the current political situation gripping Ardah.

"We received your message." Tan-Mara said, "But we did not dare to respond. To do so would have surely exacerbated an already tense situation on my world. As long as your existence and your message could be discredited as a deception of Terra-Theorists and other origin world cultists, the Priest caste took no action. However, the energy signature from the anomalous event on your world was something the Priests could not ignore. Once detected, word of it began to spread, as it did, it only served to strengthen the resolve of Terra-Theorists within the castes. They now had undeniable evidence that confirmed their long-held beliefs about Ardent ancestral origins. Considering this new development, the Priests felt compelled to demonstrate their power and authority before all tribes and castes just as they once did long ago."

"Nathan showed us records of how devastating this weapon can be," I said. "An entire system destroyed during a test firing shortly after its construction."

"That was no test." Tan-Mara said, "It was genocide. Seekers have long been among the first to establish contact with newcomers to our space. Part of our role as Seekers is to evaluate new species and report our findings to the people. There was one species the High Council chose to keep secret, the Lania. They were an alien race, refugees, fleeing a war with an unknown enemy from an alternate dimension that devastated their worlds. Their fleet of more than five hundred vessels represented all that remained of their civilization, and they desperately needed our help.

"Instead of welcoming the newcomers the High Council ignored and vilified them. Their emissaries were refused an audience with the Chancellor. No secret can remain a secret on Ardah for long, knowledge of the alien's presence in our space began to spread among the people as did fears of another invasion. By order of decree the High Council leadership, under the influence of Zen-Overen ordered their Technicians to begin its activation sequence. The Priest cast announced that any individual, tribe, or caste that attempted contact or communication with the Lania would be deemed unclean, and banished from the Ardent Path, to become forgotten."

"What was to be gained by exterminating an entire species?" Summer asked.

"Rank among the tribes," Tan-Mara said. "Prestige in the eyes of others and power. After the Rim-War the Priests sought to expand their sphere of influence and control over the High Council. The situation with the Lania was seen as an opportunity to present themselves as protectors of the Ardent people by eliminating what they declared to be hostile alien outsiders. Only after months of silence from our leaders did the Lania finally choose to settle a world in a system on the edge of the Ardent domain. The planet they chose was uninhabitable by Ardent standards and held little value to us. For the Lania, it was perfectly suitable for their needs and represented a chance to survive. Zen-Overen and his cadre of Priests claimed they were using their newfound world to establish a strategic foothold in preparation for a full-scale invasion of the three worlds. To prove themselves faithful servants of the Reclaimer, the Priests used the weapon to annihilate the Lania, their new home, and their entire fleet. Their senseless deaths were witnessed by all Ardent. It was a dark day for our people."

"What are their intentions toward Earth?" Summer asked.

"The Priests and their Zealot allies can no longer maintain their hold on power in the face of ever mounting evidence that places the holy book of the Reclaimer in doubt. The Priests that control the High Council believe that if they cannot change the facts of reality, they will change reality itself by destroying Earth and the entire Solar system. Once Historians loyal to the Priests wipe Earth's existence from Ardent star charts and historical records, they will put an end to Terra-Theory and to the truth of who we are as a people."

"Are there any sympathetic High Council members that can help?" I asked.

"Some elders yes," Tan-Mara said. "But they are hesitant to oppose the Priest cast openly for fear of being marked as a heretic. Such a charge would mean immediate banishment or death. There is a way, but it comes at significant risk."

At that moment Tan-Mara's words were a sobering reminder of Summer's prediction of three possible outcomes for our mission. The first was that we work to influence more moderate High Council members, convince them that we are not a threat and avoid conflict. Second, we discover a way to disable the weapon with the help of Ardent separatists and former Royal family members sympathetic to our cause. Third, we choose to align ourselves with the Ardent Seeker and Technician Castes to help unseat the High Council's current leadership for new members more open to contact with outsiders. Option three in my view was the least desirable one. Becoming embroiled in the political power struggles of another world went far beyond what I was prepared to engage in. If we were to achieve our goals, hard choices would have to be made in the coming days. Tan-Mara's ship departed, but she remained on board as our guest. She and Nathan continued their discussions well into the ship's night cycle, which Angelica extended three additional hours to account for the Ardent twenty-seven-hour day. It was getting late, so I informed Nathan and our guest that Summer and I were retiring for the evening. As I looked back, I saw that Tan-Mara removed her hood and retracted her armor in Nathan's presence, it slid open revealing her face. Despite her unusually youthful, almost adolescent appearance, she was well over forty-five years old by Earth standards. The equivalent of a twenty-five-year-old woman from Earth. Given how long they have known each other I suppose it should have come as no surprise. Centuries old genetic modifications over the centuries made Ardent life spans much longer than ours. They were generally stronger and far more agile than average humans. Tan-Mara looked human-like, but there was a vast gulf between Ardent and Earth humans. Her emerald, green eyes were twice the size of an average human and were wider set, providing a greater range of peripheral vision. Her facial pigment consisted of an ornate black band lined with intricate gold accents that framed her face like a mask as it radiated past her temples into her hairline resembling a black sparrow in flight. Her skin was a light tan, freckled and graduated in color toward a deep honey shade forming a striking contrast with her ornate tattoos. When she blinked, a silver inner eyelid followed at an angle to the first, another necessary modification to the Ardent genome from ancient times according to the archive designed to protect their corneas from the light of the Ardent sun. Her high cheekbones gradually tapered to her narrow nose. Her thin nostrils were straddled by what appeared to be small vertical gill like slits, which moved in sequence with her respiration. Another more recent genetic modification allowing Ardent with the enhancement to breathe underwater if necessary. Her black hair was long, thick and braided close to her head. It was beautifully adorned with green and gold rings around every braid that fell to her shoulders. She was quite different and not at all as I expected. I found it strange that she always moved her eyes in the direction of attention before turning her head to glance at something. She looked like a Celtic warrior woman from the distant past. A strange and captivating alien beauty. Summer beckoned me, and we returned to our quarters.

"How long have she and Nathan been in contact? I asked.

"For many years." Summer said. "Her mother died in a tribal conflict, her father went missing just before the close of the Rim War, his body was never found. So, the torch passed to her. Since then, she and Nathan have been in continuous contact via a bulk space communications device given to her family years ago disguised as a necklace bearing her family crest. When she was a child, Nathan used the device to appear to her in the form of something her young mind could understand, a small animal or a character from the myths of her culture. As she matured, he gradually revealed his true form to her and in time she came to understand what Constructs truly are."

"She retracted her armor," I said. "Did you see her face?"

"I did, she's quite stunning."

"The Ardent are human-looking." I said, "But quite strange at the same time."

"It's the eyes," Summer said. "I suppose you have never seen an exo-human variant before have you, Lucas?"

"In the archive visual records." I said, "I saw humans from the late GSE emerge after re-genesis."

"Yes," Summer said. "But aside from a slight variance in cranial circumference late GSE era, humans for the most part are not that much different from us, well, from you. You know what I mean."

"She seems almost."

"Alien?" Summer said. "Yes, and no you never get quite used to it. Right now, I think it's time you and I spent some time together. It's going to be days before we get another chance and to be honest, I don't want to wait."

Hours afterward, lying next to Summer, it was as if we had never been apart. Although she doesn't need to sleep, she simulates the behavior to accommodate me. Her body was warm to the touch; every part of her was precisely as I remembered. Everything about her seems human despite being comprised of the same Construct matter that makes up this ship. It was a strange technological illusion, no matter how closely I examine her hands, hair, or skin it was all entirely indistinguishable from when she was human. The deep, nearly subsonic pulse from Angelica's reactor core was comforting especially at night, but I was already starting to miss Earth. On the command deck Nathan and Tan-Mara talked late into the ship's night cycle.

"This Guardian you speak of," Tan-Mara asked. "Where is it from?"

"Although they were created by a much older species," Nathan said. "We believe the Progenitors placed it on Earth many centuries ago in anticipation of the evolution of humanity. Earth's fossil record indicates that it preserved our species from extinction on more than one occasion. It was activated when Lucas discovered it in an underground facility on our world."

"Why do your companions call you Nathan?"

"Lucas gave me that name. It is a variation on another name, from another time."

"When you were a flesh and blood human?" Tan-Mara asked.

"Yes, on my world Nathan was short for Nathanael."

"I see, Nath-ana-el," Tan-Mara said. "It feels strange on the tongue. So, it is like a true name, spoken when amongst your closest tribesmen?"

"In a way yes, you may also refer to me as Nathan."

"I understand." Tan-Mara said. "It is so strange seeing you here after all these years. When I was a child, my father told me stories about the origin world, the ancestor race, and the Construct beings like you that resided there. He said that our people came from another planet far away. He would point toward the night sky and say, "Mara my daughter, remember this always, we were not born of this world, we are the children of Earth, "The Origen World." In my culture, the word Earth means farmland. But to my father, it meant so much more. No one believed him when he told the tribe he was in contact with the ancestors of the ancient origin world. He was shunned, they called him a fool, his honor was constantly challenged."

"I am sorry Tan-Mara," Nathan said. "But I warned your father, there would be consequences if he were to ever reveal the nature of our communication."

"We are a proud people Nathan, but our history is built on a lie. My father believed in one thing all his life, the truth. He always said that the truth would set the Ardent people free from the tyranny of the Priests on the High Council. Our true origins can no longer be the secret of a few high order Priests; all Ardent must come to know the truth."

The next morning, Summer and I went back to the command deck, Tan-Mara and Nathan must have talked through the night. The image of the Ardent pit fire in the display ring was gone, replaced by an image of the galaxy and our vessel's position. Tan-Mara to my surprise allowed us to see her face. She looked at Summer and I with an odd smirk as she turned to greet us.

"I must appear quite strange to you, yes?" Tan-Mara asked.

"I am adjusting." I said, "This is all new to me."

"Tan-Mara, about the weapon." Summer said. "Can it be disabled or destroyed?"

"I believe so, but we cannot do it alone; we will need allies. Seekers, Tera-Theorists and other castes sympathetic to our cause and those with good reason to unseat the corrupt Priests."

"Whom did you have in mind?" I asked.

"There are influential members of Ardent society that will help." Tan-Mara said, "Bre-Kylah of the Void Walker tribe has pledged ships to our cause. Members of the Warrior Caste stand with us, including my mentor Nir-RoDan. Some Elders of the high council have quietly pledged their support. The Forgotten Clan has promised both ships and fighters. Many of whom are the descendants of those that survived the brutal practice of forcing unsanctioned children to be Taken by the Winds, among other atrocities of the Priest caste."

"Survived?" Nathan asked. "Our information suggested that such children never survived."

"Forgive me old friend." Tan-Mara said. "But it appears you still have much to learn about the Ardent. Among my people, there is a saying. Some things are said to be true, and then there is that which is true. For years, the parents of such children in defiance of the Priests retrieved their younglings in the dead of night rather than allow them to suffer and die as was the mandate. For doing so they too were banished to Hafeeta. They wish to see the current High Council dissolved as much as the Seekers do. After years of negotiation and careful planning in secret, I now have honor-bound assurances that they will fight at our side when the time comes. Plans are already in motion across the planet and in the capital all we need now is a spark."

"How were your people able to create such a weapon?" Summer asked. "By this I mean no insult, but its technology appears to be far more advanced than what the Ardent are capable of."

"Those that built it and the technocraft used in its construction are shrouded in mystery among my people," Tan-Mara said. "As were many things in the post Rim War period. It is rumored that a small group of highly skilled Technicians loyal only to the Priests worked for years to create and maintain it. Unfortunately, only they know its true secrets and understand its design. The Priests call it "The Sword of the Reclaimer." It is said that it would not have been possible to build without the Legacy."

"What is the Legacy?" I asked.

"The old stories speak of something found by a group of ancient Ardent explorers long ago in the time before the castes." Tan-Mara said, "A vast archive of ancient knowledge left behind by a race of great builders that possessed even greater power. In our old stories, they are called the Masters. No one knows who they were, where they came from or where they went. It is said that the knowledge gained from the Legacy made the Ardent people what we are today. Much of our current science and technocraft is based on the prior achievements of the Masters."

"Nearly every species we have encountered have comparable stories in their cultures," Nathan said. "Accounts of an ancient race that once ruled over a civilization that spanned the galaxy."

"Your people call them the Masters, on Earth we call them the Progenitors," Summer said. "We spent centuries searching for them. Evidence of their influence was everywhere, but we never made contact. We believe that today they are either extinct, or they have advanced to a degree far beyond our current level of understanding."

"Then your research mirrors that of our own." Tan-Mara said, "The few Seekers willing to take on the challenge have sought the Masters or the Progenitors as you call them, across the outer dark for centuries. It is said they were wise, ancient elders that once ruled the stars. The old stories speak of many mysteries concealed by the Priests within the halls of their holy citadel. The Oscar Oracle, a machine intelligence from the ancient world that holds the secret history of the Ardent people. The Stones Of The Masters capable of imparting knowledge and wisdom to the minds of those that gaze upon it. The Legacy, a timeless archive of hidden knowledge forged by the Masters. The Mantle, a device of unimaginable power created by an elder race that preceded the Masters, rumored to be capable of unlocking the secrets of our universe. We have all heard such stories since childhood. Some believe there is a reality behind these stories, yet none dare to speak of such things openly for fear of ridicule and dishonor. Nevertheless, the influence of the Masters can be seen across all aspects of Ardent society."

"Attention crew," Angelica announced. "We have reached the Ardent system. There are three vessels on approach."

"Perimeter escort ships." Tan-Mara said. "Cease your gravitics, they will take us in from here."

The three small heavily armed Ardent ships took up positions around us. We were now operating under their guidance as their escort ships took control. The Ardent system was filled with ships of varied sizes, shapes, and configurations. Civilian transport vessels, trade ships, explorer class starships, military battlecruisers, tribal transport vessels, capital ships, drone carriers, gunships, cargo vessels, commerce transport shuttles and perimeter defense craft. We passed several planets in their system including a red desert world. Tan-Mara took notice and gestured toward it as we approached, a detailed analysis of the planet and its history appeared within the ring display.

"Look there," Tan-Mara said, "Hafeeta, desert world of the Forgotten Clan and home of our greatest allies."

"From the analysis that planet looks barely habitable." I said. "Severe sandstorms, harsh surface temperatures, extremely high winds, volcanic activity, how can anyone survive there?"

"Eyes can lie," Tan-Mara said. "Don't be deceived by what you see. Do not underestimate them and do not pity them. They have extensive underground resources, clean water, protection of their cities from the elements, limitless geothermal power drawn directly from the planetary core. Repurposed fusion reactors and a fleet of salvaged starships. They make use of that which others discard and no longer need. They are survivors, Lucas, and superb fighters. Do not insult what little honor they have with your pity."

The Ardent system's outer planets and moons held enormous orbital defense platforms miles in length. In orbit above the planet Ardah loomed six orbital ring stations encircling the planet. Hundreds of ships could be seen arriving and departing their inner and outer rings. The Ardent people possessed an astounding spacefaring civilization, and I was entirely overwhelmed with what I was witnessing before me. Billions upon billions of people living out their lives between the three habitable planets of their system. Ardah their capital, homeworld to billions of Ardent, the center of power and home of the Ardent High Council the supreme ruling body of their civilization. Hafeeta, desert world of the Forgotten Clan, a planet populated by billions of Ardent outcasts without rank, tribe, or caste. Last was the crowning jewel of the Ardent system, Poseida, a beautiful deep blue resource-rich water planet dotted by hundreds of island continents. It is a garden world originally reserved for royalty and home to nearly thirty billion people living above and beneath its immense oceans. Humanity, or at least a version of it was alive and well out here. This reality brought with it a mix of astonishment, relief, and envy.

Chapter 27 The Ardent Homeworld

As we approached the orbit of the Ardent homeworld, I could see the circular lights of their ecumenopolis complex. Each section was subdivided into smaller city-states thousands of miles in diameter. We entered the atmosphere and broke through the clouds. Their immense capital city stretched horizon to horizon, lush forest areas accented by black spire formations were separated by large circular city-states. Their towering black, silver, and copper-clad buildings spiraled thousands of feet above the planet's surface. Some buildings were suspended above the surface by powerful gravitic fields and moved relative to other structures around them. Their cities could dynamically reconfigure themselves. It was an awe-inspiring feature that made their vibrant urban skyline unique.

We came to the edge of a hexagonal landing platform built into the side of a black stone cliff face just east of the estate home of Nir-RoDan of the house of Nir. As we descended two of the Ardent ships released their gravity lock on Angelica, then peeled off heading to orbit. We folded to the ship's exterior as a group of armored warriors with directed energy weapons approached us. Tan-Mara stepped forward and removed her hood, throwing back the edges of her cloak to reveal that she was armed as her daggers gleamed in the afternoon sun. The guard addressed her directly.

"State your intention."

"We seek an audience with Master Nir-RoDan," Tan-Mara said.

"You may pass Seeker." The guard said. "But these alien outsiders you have brought must remain behind."

"They are my companions," Tan-Mara said. "They go where I go."

The guards looked at each other, but I could not discern their mood from behind their armored helms and glowing eyes. Another figure approached walking boldly down the platform ramp with a knife in his hand which he held by the blade. He retracted his armor revealing his bearded, tattooed face and smiled. Tan-Mara smiled, drew her dagger, then flipped it so she held it by the blade. As they approached, they interlocked hilts and then they both sheathed their blades and embraced one another. This I learned was a common greeting among the Ardent to indicate friendship, strength, and peace.

"Guards be calm!" he said. "These are our guests. Mara, little one, come let me look at you. Ah, you have your mother's eyes!"

"Yes, and her blades," Tan-Mara said. "Father always said you coveted mother for yourself."

"Ha! Indeed, yes indeed I did," He said. "She was a beautiful woman and a formidable Warrior. Yes, I too loved your mother, but her heart truly belonged to Argum. Your parents may have been paired, but they loved each other long before their pairing. You, my child, were born of great love. It is a rare thing among our people."

"These are my companions Nathan, Lucas, and Summer of Earth. This is my mentor and Master Nir-RoDan of the Warrior Trainers."

"Ah, by the blessed Reclaimer the old stories it seems are true indeed! You all are both spirit and machine in a human form?" Nir-RoDan asked.

"I'm human." I said, "Nathan and Summer are Constructs."

"Remarkable," Nir-RoDan said. "I have seen many beings in my time but none quite like you. To my eyes you look so much like us."

"You will find we have much in common," I said. "Summer is also my wife."

"Interesting, you are paired then with a machine?" Nir-RoDan asked.

"We are not machines," Summer insisted. "We are far more than that."

"Forgive me, lovely creature," Nir-RoDan said. "I meant no offense to either you or Nathan. It is indeed an honor to meet you all. Come! Let us sit around the pit fire and drink! I have a full battle flask of ferment that I have been saving for an occasion such as this."

We proceeded into Nir-RoDan's home, I looked back at the Angelica and thought "alert us to any new developments you see." Angelica flashed her edges to acknowledge the order. We entered Nir-RoDan's home. It was modestly decorated with artifacts, armor, and weapons from worlds and races I was entirely unfamiliar with. Nir-RoDan was a Warrior caste trainer, powerful, wealthy, and influential among the Ardent. He poured drinks as we passed the cups around.

"This flask is one hundred eighty-five, no wait, one hundred ninety years old." Nir-RoDan said. "It was a gift from your father given to me just before the close of the Rim War. He promised me we would finish it together. I am honored to share it in his memory with all of you. I miss him."

"So, do I great teacher, every day," Tan-Mara said.

"Ah, the war, those were hard days." Nir-RoDan said "But, as your father always said a good drink makes the hard days easier to endure."

"Indeed, they do." Tan-Mara said, "But in truth, I am surprised the flask lasted here that long."

"Well, I had to drink my way through six others just to reach this one," Nir-RoDan said.

With a slow smile, Tan-Mara and Nir-RoDan laughed and raised their ferment before taking a drink. Winemaking on the Ardent homeworld goes back thousands of years in their culture. Summer, Nathan, and I listened to Nir-RoDan's many stories and marveled at the numerous alien artifacts around his home. Meat resembling cubed beef roasted on skewers in the pit fire. My suit identified it as biocompatible with human metabolism. Feeling the effects, I placed my ferment down after just a few cups. Ardent wine was strong, sweet, and robust. More like a heavy port and eighty proof according to the suit's analysis. I sat up straight in my chair, shook my head, reached for more herb bread and red oil in a futile attempt to counteract its potency, which Summer seemed to take amusement in. Nir-RoDan turned the skewers in the pit fire as he dusted them with blue salt, they were now ready. After our meal, Summer took full advantage of a lull in the gathering.

"Nir-RoDan of the Trainers," Summer said. "You have welcomed us into your fine home and provided us with a strong ferment, fine food and a warm pit fire. For this, we are eternally grateful, both to you and to the house of Nir."

Nir-RoDan leaned in closer to the fire placing his palm and forearm on his knees, stroking his braided beard as he listened. Without taking his eyes off Summer, he leaned over to feign a whisper to Tan-Mara who smirked at me humorously as he spoke.

"Hmm, is she always so formal?" Nir-RoDan asked.

Tan-Mara smiled and rocked her hands from side to side in a gesture that I took to mean, "I don't know." She smiled and took another big sip of her ferment holding in her laughter.

"I like this one." Nir-RoDan said pointing at Summer. "Apologies, please by all means continue!"

"There are pressing matters we need to discuss." Summer added.

"Indeed, there are," Nir-RoDan said. "There is the matter of the weapon, the truth surrounding the origin of our people and the corruption of the High Council. Oh yes, I am aware the Priests seek to destroy your home system to bolster their power and perpetuate the lie that Earth and its people are a myth. I am not a Terra-Theorist, but I do believe in the truth of our origins. I also know what the High Council is truly capable of, I have seen it firsthand."

It felt like I was moving sideways as I gripped the arm of the chair and took another bite of bread. Ardent wine contained several unusual herbal constituents that although harmless contributed to euphoric effects that I found myself unprepared for. Taking notice Nathan glanced at me with a curious tilt of his head as if trying to discern if I was intoxicated, I sat up straight to interject in the discussion.

"We originally came here with the hope of influencing your government." I said. "To let them know that Earth is not a threat. We have no quarrel with the Ardent people. On the contrary, we hope to open new diplomatic relations, trade, and reconnect with the Ardent."

"From what Tan-Mara has described," Nathan said. "It seems the reasoning behind reactivation of the weapon is far more complex than we originally thought."

"The High Council doesn't see the Earth as a military threat" Nir-RoDan said. "On the contrary, your existence threatens their rigid religious ideology. Please understand I am a man of faith, but I was not always so, my faith found me on a desolate ice moon named Orna.

"In the closing battles near the end of the Rim War, our warriors were victorious but weary after nearly thirty years of sustained conflict. We had for the first time faced and finally defeated a truly formidable enemy, worthy opponents of Ardent Warriors, a most deadly adversary. Even after all these many years their memory gives me night terrors."

He gestured with his cup toward a strange insect-like exoskeleton head mounted on the wall and an even stranger menacing weapon.

"The Vinn. They were a highly advanced telepathic insectoid race that nearly destroyed the Ardent people." Nir-RoDan said "They invaded both our minds and our dreams, they attacked Ardah and our colony worlds along the rim for over thirty years. Only our armor could shield us from their brutal telepathic assaults. It was our darkest hour, many thought it to be the long-awaited "Last Setting of the Sun," the end of all things as prophesied in our sacred texts. The Vinn hunted Ardent for sport and used our people for both food and the incubation of their young."

"While on Orna, we came upon a heavily guarded outpost we took to be of military significance. We knew from intelligence reports that the Vinn were looking for something. They had spent years conducting excavations of alien ruins on numerous planets and moons in Ardent space. We ambushed them and gained control of their excavation site. There on Orna we found the Vinn had discovered a temple of an extinct race millions of years old. Inside the temple, we found something quite extraordinary. It was an enormous black statue, human-like in shape, but as we soon discovered, it was not a statue at all. It was an artificial being of truly unimaginable power. When it moved, some of my Warriors foolishly fired on it. It raised its right hand and unleashed a wave that turned them to ash inside their own armor leaving those of us that had not drawn weapons alive and completely untouched. It stepped towards me, and even though it had no face and no eyes, I knew it was staring right at me. It was as if that being looked right through me, past my armor and flesh, right down into my very soul! I was humbled in its presence, and even though I was standing three sword-lengths from it, I could feel its power in every atom of my being."

"That day, for the first time in my life, I felt true fear, and for the first time, I prayed to the Reclaimer. Resigned to my fate I closed my eyes certain that it would take my life, but it did not. To my astonishment, it reduced its size as it walked past me straight out of the temple. In an instant, it ascended into orbit and was gone. As we exited the temple, I gazed up into the night skies. At that moment, I swore to dedicate my life to seeking the truth of what we all saw."

"This being," Nathan said, "Is this what it looked like?"

Nathan presented a projected image of the Guardian from my sphere records back on Earth. Along with several detailed images and memories from my discovery of the chamber. In astonishment, Nir-RoDan moved toward the edge of his chair captivated by what he was seeing.

> "Blessed Reclaimer." Nir-RoDan said. "Where in the three worlds did you obtain that?"

"I recorded it," I said, "In an ancient underground cavern back on Earth. We believe there may well be hundreds if not thousands of these Guardians scattered across the established worlds of our ancient human ancestors, designed to preserve intelligent life within the systems in which they are placed."

"I reported this encounter in detail to the Council upon my return." Nir-RoDan said. "But the report was suppressed from the official record by then Advocate Zen-Overen of the Priest caste and his loyalists. I was forbidden by order of the High Council from ever mentioning the incident. I have seen many things in my life that have made me question certain aspects of my reality. That Guardian as you call it was one of them. The weapon, that abomination in our skies, was created to ensure the Ardent people's survival so that we would never again face extinction at the hands of hostile outsiders. But now the weapon has become a symbol of limitless power. The Priests seek to use that power to rewrite the history of our people. It is dangerous, it should never have been built and must be destroyed."

"Since then, Zen-Overen has risen through the ranks," Tan-Mara said. "He is now Chancellor, and his power is formidable. The only way to truly stop the use of the weapon is to force a change of leadership on the High Council. Identify those responsible for its creation and deactivate it."

"I never thought our people would come to this point," Nir-RoDan said. "But I am afraid I agree. The corruption, genocide, lies, and secrets of the High Council have always been present to a greater or lesser degree regardless of which caste held power. The last several years, however, have been nearly intolerable under the strong axe of Priest caste rule. The general suppression of the truth is now tearing at the foundations of Ardent society! Every institution and caste have been impacted by it, and it's time it ended."

Summer interjected, "What can we do? Because of this weapon our world is in peril. This comes during a delicate time when we are trying to rebuild our society and civilization."

"I understand, but I am afraid there is not much that you can do." Nir-RoDan said. "Any action you as outsiders take, will be seen as an alien influence. Together with the Forgotten Clan and those sympathetic to the Terra-Theorist cause have put a plan in motion to remove the Priests and arrest Zen-Overen. Once that is done, we can restore the people's vote and disarm the weapon."

"What of the other Ardent castes?" Nathan asked. "Will they support us as well?"

"Some will, some won't," Nir-RoDan said. "Others will wait to see which side prevails before pledging themselves to either cause. However, we have allies and honor-bound assurances that when the time comes, we will be ready. This is technically treason, so we will only get one chance at this."

"Otherwise." Tan-Mara said. "We will be re-growing our heads."

"Correct little one," Nir-RoDan said.

I leaned over to whisper to Summer "Re-growing our heads?" I asked.

"Its gallows humor," Summer said. "I will explain later."

"In the meantime," Nir-RoDan said. "By now the entire system has seen images of that, impressive Earth ship of yours out there, and I suspect that the High Council will do something foolish as they always do in response to it! Your arrival here is the spark of the Ardent revolution."

"Are you ready for this great teacher?" Tan-Mara asked.

"Mara my little one, I have been ready for this moment for forty years." Nir-RoDan said.

My focus on the conversation was broken as Angelica sent us mental images of a group of heavily armed warriors repelling down gravitic streams from a High Council troop transport carrier near our ship. Nathan stood to his feet as Summer turned to look outside in time to see Nir-RoDan's guards standing their ground despite being outnumbered. As more High Council Guards arrived, it was starting to look like a siege.

Chapter 28 Battle Master Nir-RoDan

We stepped outside onto the landing platform of Nir-RoDan's estate. The Angelica was now under guard and seized in gravity lock, and twelve heavily armed High Council Guards awaited us. The troop transport they arrived in turned and peeled off landing on a lower-level platform beneath the tower. One of the Guards stepped forward presented a projection containing text that the suit translated into what appeared to be an arrest warrant.

"Nir-RoDan! You are under arrest by order of the High Council!"

"On what charge?" Nir-RoDan demanded.

The High Council Guard read aloud the list of charges.

"High crimes against the state! Consorting with the unclean! The harboring of abominations and corruption of the Ardent faith!"

"Ha! Ridiculous!" Nir-RoDan said "Were it not for me boy there would be no state! These beings are no abominations; they are my guests! Concerning matters of faith, I was a defender of the Ardent path long before your grandfather finished his trials!"

The guard insisted. "Nevertheless, these are our orders. Take him, now!"

All twelve of the High Council Guard broke into a battle stance. Tan-Mara took three steps back and motioned for us all to do the same. Nir-RoDan activated his armor, which instantly covered his face. The eyes of his armor glowed a brilliant white as he took a cylinder from his belt. He held it horizontally in front of him as it extended into a dual bladed quarterstaff. Its razor-sharp ends lit up with an orange glow as all twelve guards approached with their own energized blades. Nir-RoDan broke into his battle stance, as he did, he moved his hand across the length of his staff and in a single motion he flipped it, perfectly balancing the weapon on the edge of his open hand to the amazement of the guards before him. Two High Council Guards sped toward Nir-RoDan with a fast attack, Nir-RoDan activated his gauntlet energy shield and rammed one of the guards instantly knocking him unconscious. With a fast overhead twirl of his quarterstaff, he disarmed the other guard tripping him on to his back while kicking his weapon off the edge of the landing platform. Humiliated and enraged, the guard pulled a glowing blade from the small of his back and lunged at Nir-RoDan. The ends of Nir-RoDan's staff weapon instantly changed shape into a double-edged sword, which he used to slice off the guard's arms just below the elbow. The guard fell to his knees screaming in pain as his severed cauterized arms dropped to the ground, smoking, and twitching still grasping his blade. The guard wailed in disbelief as he looked down at his severed stumps in horror. Nir-RoDan turned to look at the other terrified members of the High Council Guard and invited their attack with a bright flash of his glowing white eyes.

The guards formed a circle around him, as each guard attempted an attack they were swiftly disarmed and put down. With a twirl of his shapeshifting quarterstaff, it changed from a battle ax to a sword and back to a bladed staff. Depending on the nature of the incoming attack Nir-RoDan's weapon changed shape to match the threat. It was an older Ardent fighting style that confused the less experienced guards. A scattered pile of severed arms, hands, and legs soon littered the landing platform. The screams and agonized moans from crippled and wounded guards increased as more reinforcements emerged from the troop transport. A crowd of small ships and surveillance drones began congregating around the estate tower landing platform to observe the ongoing fight.

Nir-RoDan collapsed his quarterstaff as the gauntlets on his forearms released a thick gray mist that seemed to be under his direct control. He used his hands to guide and shape the mist like a magician casting a spell. As it expanded, the mist became so thick that Nir-RoDan could no longer be seen. The remaining High Council Guard paused their advance realizing that Nir-RoDan had escaped their circle and vanished. In the silence of their confusion, a pair of glowing white eyes emerged from the mist as Nir-RoDan leaped forward, slicing off the forearms of two guards and the lower legs of three other guards before vanishing back into the thick of the mist.

AWAKENING

Between the swirling currents of the gray mist and the orange streaks of light from Nir-RoDan's weapons, limbs, and bodies fell to the platform as each of the wounded guards screamed, cried out, and flailed in agony. Just off the platform, another troop transport turned to level its weapons on Nir-RoDan. With a quick motion of his hands, the gray mist suspended in the air froze and headed straight toward the transport where it divided into hundreds of smaller strands of smoke, seeping into every seam, and opening. The gray mist was not a mist at all it was a thick cloud of weaponized matter de-compilers. One of the rarest and deadliest weapons in the Warrior cast arsenal. The mist took over and disabled the transport in midair. The pilots and crew leaped from the craft as it came apart around them screaming and thrashing about on their backs as they hit the landing platform below. You could hear their muffled agonizing screams as the mist ate away at their flesh inside their armor. Upon seeing this one brash young guard drew his sword and attempted to take on Nir-RoDan in single combat. He held his own for a few fleeting moments, but within seconds the guard was disarmed and on his knees. Nir-RoDan now in a position to scissor off his head with a single movement of his gleaming twin swords. A transport arrived. It was the commander of the High Council Guard Arun-Malak. He leaped onto the platform and rushed forward placing himself between Nir-RoDan and the remaining guards.

"Stop! Guards stop now!" Malak commanded. "If you want to live you will put your weapons down now! Down! Now! This is general and Battle Master Nir-RoDan you fools!"

"Malak!" Nir-RoDan shouted. "Explain yourself!"

"I will," Malak said, "But first, please release my guard."

Nir-RoDan looked at the guard. "Hmmm, I have seen this fighting style before, in a more, seasoned Warrior."

"Nir-RoDan please let him live." Malak pleaded. "He is just a foolish boy. He is, he is my son."

Nir-RoDan turned his attention back to the guard on his knees before him.

"Show me your face boy!" Nir-RoDan shouted.

The guard's heavily damaged armor retracted sliding into his collar, revealing the face of a brave, angry, shivering young Ardent male. He turned, and to the degree, he could and looked at his father as a tear fell onto the gleaming blade. The heat emanating from Nir-RoDan's weapons seared his short beard as the blade rested inches from the boy's neck. Nir-RoDan glanced at the boy noting the resemblance as he released the guard.

"You fight like your father." Nir-RoDan said. "Not bad, but not good enough!"

"General Nir-RoDan," Malak said, "It has been too long."

"I haven't been a General for over forty years." Nir-RoDan said. "I train others to fight now."

"With respect," Malak said. "To me and millions of others you will always be General. It seems you have made a mess of my elite guard. Was all this necessary?"

"Arms and legs can be regrown; flesh and bone can be restored, but heads are another matter," Nir-RoDan said. "Which is why your High Council Guard still has theirs. Besides, in a month, they will be as they were yesterday. Perhaps they will think twice next time before drawing weapons on an Ardent Warrior."

Nir-RoDan collapsed his weapon placing back on his belt. Malak's son, still shaken by the confrontation glared back at Nir-RoDan, then his father as he tended to his fellow wounded guards.

"You and your, guests," Malak said. "Have been summoned to appear before the High Council. I ask, respectfully, that you accompany me, please."

"Well, which is it Malak, summoned or arrested?"

"Arrest is not the term I would use General," Malak said.

"Very well then." Nir-RoDan said. "Come friends! The High Council awaits!"

Tan-Mara seemed amused at the situation, the audacity of sending the High Council guard to arrest a prominent Ardent citizen was a bold statement and the message was clear, no one was safe from the High Council's reach and judgment. Nir-RoDan's message was also clear, and he was not a man to be trifled with. I was still feeling the effects of the wine and in a mild state of shock after witnessing twenty-four men and women be taken apart and dismembered like children's toys. We boarded Arun-Malak's transport platform bound for the High Council building. As we boarded Tan-Mara whispered, "You should see him fight when he is not under the sway of ferment." Four High Council guards and Arun-Malak boarded the transport platform with us. As we departed in one direction medical drones from the opposite direction arrived, unfurling their numerous tentacle-like arms to tend to the wounded guards that attempted to confront Nir-RoDan back on the landing platform. I took a look back at the Angelica although I was worried I knew our ship would take care of herself. In the month-long journey to the Ardent system, I had come to think of our ship as a member of our team. I knew Angelica lacked what we would consider a human mind, but she was still a person to me. A projected map on the transport platform indicated our destination was nearly forty-five miles from where we left the Angelica. Tan-Mara seemed as calm as ever as she placed her boot on a raised section of the platform's edge. She rested the palms of her hand on the pommels of her twin daggers as she looked out across the capital city toward the High Council Tower. Then I noticed her thighs were covered with two rows of exquisitely crafted throwing knives. From my study of Ardent weapons, those knives are far more sophisticated than they appear, they can be controlled inflight and retrieved by the thrower after striking their target.

We were followed by a dozen small civilian transports and over a hundred surveillance drones from numerous castes and tribes. Each was marked with holographic symbols, caste colors and other tribal markings indicating ownership. We passed several spiraling obsidian-like towers along the way some of which had projected images on their outer surfaces of the fight on the landing platform of Nir-RoDan's estate. The suit translated a holographic caption, "Former Rim War General and Battle Master Nir-RoDan Taken into Custody by the High Council Guard." We passed another building also showing projected footage of the fight from a different angle, its caption read; "Observe as a True Battle Master Works His Craft on Foolish High Council Guards." We passed yet another building showing Nir-RoDan releasing the young guard. Its caption read "Brave and Swift Yet Merciful the Mighty Nir-RoDan."

I looked along our travel route and noticed that locals had set up holographic projections on the rooftops of their buildings as we passed them. One sign read "Our Hearts and Our love to Nir-RoDan and His Companions!" As the drones followed, I noticed that all the surrounding buildings showed real-time images of the transport platform. News of the arrival of an alien ship had spread quickly. As the temperature dropped, I put on my hood and noticed the images mirrored our every movement. The platform fight had been seen across the Ardent system along with every Ardent colony on the rim. All members of Ardent society were watching us now. Summer and Nathan seemed to have noticed this situation as well. It all became clear to me now; this is precisely the kind of public spectacle that Tan-Mara and Nir-RoDan were counting on. The sudden, shocking, and unjustified arrest of a highly prominent and beloved former general, war hero, battle master and trainer like Nir-RoDan along with the presence of aliens from a planet that according to the Priest and Historians was not supposed to exist. It was only then that I began comprehending the sheer magnitude of Nir-RoDan's words. This was the spark that would ignite the Ardent revolution with billions of eyes watching it all play out in real-time across the Ardent bulk space communications network.

The transport slowed as we approached the High Council Tower, the largest building in the city stretching nearly eleven thousand feet in height. We docked with the platform on the side of the structure. Apparently, the transport platform we arrived on was part of the building's architecture. Before stepping off I removed my hood and looked around to take in the magnificent view of this incredible civilization. As I did, an Ardent surveillance drone captured my face and those of Summer and Nathan. Within seconds, our still images were projected from the surrounding buildings annotated with symbols of the Ardent Yulan dialect. The suit translated them to say, "Strange Alien Creatures Witnessed at High Council Tower" followed by "What Do The Aliens Want?" and "Is This The End"? We were escorted off the platform and into the building by the guards. Before we entered the building, I looked up to see the last image that worried me. Our ship was being scanned and examined by the Ardent Technician caste. I looked at Nathan who gave me a reassuring nod when I looked at Summer; she darted her eyes toward Tan-Mara who slipped her what appeared to be a small cylinder of green glass. Summer took it without asking what it was, then looked at me with a reassuring smile. Upon entering the building, the High Council guards separated us. They disarmed Nir-RoDan and Tan-Mara before they both were escorted across a bridge lined with guards leading to the main High Council chamber. Summer, Nathan, and I were ushered toward a holding area. Outside were several hundred people calling for the release of Nir-RoDan. The crowd became larger, and the skies began to fill with even more tribal surveillance drones. The guards escorted us to a large black room with deep lines precision cut into the black stone floor at different angles forming a mesh network of glowing oblique triangles. A white honeycomb-like confinement shield surrounded Nathan, Summer and I trapping us inside each of the triangles. Additional shielding was activated enclosing the entire building. I looked at Nathan as he placed his finger close to the shield but was careful not to touch it.

"Advanced gravitic shielding." Nathan said. "It registers as solid and inhibits our ability to fold travel, impressive."

An Ardent guard carrying a directed energy weapon noticed and walked toward Nathan motioning with his weapon. "You, creature step away from the shield. Step away now!" Nathan raised his hands and stepped back. Summer crouched, intently examining the floor where the shields emanated. As the Ardent guard approached, she smoothly shifted, sitting back with her legs tucked beneath her. Looking up, she met the guard's eyes with a warm smile. The other guard watched a holographic projection from a communications device attached to his forearm. Summer took out the piece of green glass Tan-Mara had given her and held it in her palm examining it. As she did, the glass device sunk into her palm and vanished. Her Construct body absorbed it. She closed her eyes and sat perfectly still. It was almost as if she was frozen in place. She opened her eyes and when she noticed me looking at her, she turned toward me and winked. As she did, a white flat blinking line appeared in my field of view, an unusual and unexpected thing for the suit to show me. I looked at the guard reminding myself that only I could see it. Then the line broke apart and became a message which read "Hi Guys." Both Nathan and I turned to look at Summer as she smiled. The message continued, "Do not respond just watch and listen. I am now inside the Ardent civilian communications network." I could hear a rising cacophony of voices speaking in a Yulan dialect that soon became intelligible. Summer used Tan-Mara's device to access one of the Seeker caste surveillance drones. My field of view reflected the drone's point of view. From this vantage point we watched the proceedings. It was the High Council chamber Tan-Mara, and Nir-RoDan stood before the Priests, Historians, and other High Council members. The High Council Advocate addressed the assembly as Nir-RoDan stepped forward to defend himself.

"General and Battle Master Nir-RoDan of the Warrior Trainers step forward into the Circle of Truth. You stand before this council accused of serious crimes against the state! Explain yourself!"

According to Ardent law being called to stand within the Circle of Truth was the equivalent of testifying under oath. All High Council testimony is public including telemetry of the person's psychological state during their testimony. Heart rate, pupil dilation, respiration, galvanic skin response and resonance brain imaging are used to determine if such testimony is truthful or deceptive. Nir-RoDan stepped forward as a perfectly formed circle of light surrounded him as he spoke.

"Honorable members of the High Council, Priestly Advisors, Historian Adjuncts and High Council Guards. It is my honor and pleasure to present myself to you as a…" High Council Chancellor Zen-Overen interrupted with a loud strike of his scepter on the stone floor, the sound echoed throughout the chamber.

"General Nir-RoDan! We all know who you are, just as we know that you, in fact, despise this Council and have since your return from the battle at Orna. We are also aware of your general disrespect and disregard of our Blessed Priest caste! Just as we are aware of your boundless love and admiration for informality. So please, spare this council your bitter insincerity!"

"Very well then." Nir-RoDan continued. "The time-honored Ardent tradition of hospitality was once a virtue among our people. For thousands of years, stories have been passed down tribal lines generation after generation. Stories of cooperation with strangers, friendship, and peace with alien beings and other newcomers. But today this great Ardent tradition has been replaced with suspicion and fear of all things Un-Ardent. We are persecuted and judged for extending the open hand of friendship. We are marked as unclean by Priests; our honor is constantly challenged, our friends and guests in our own homes are themselves marked as abominations fit only to be cleansed! As a result, we Ardent no longer bother to approach the stranger or the newcomer with an open hand. Our Priests in their ignorance and fear demand that a closed fist accompany every encounter!"

"This is not who we are as a people. As you are surely aware, I served in the Rim Wars most of my young life, and in that time, I came to know both friendship and fear. My house guests sitting in custody are not abominations, they are my friends, my guests, whom I sit around the pit fire with, and drink sweet ferment under the stars and the moons above. When we Ardent greet each other, we do so with a dagger held by the blade to signify friendship, strength, and peace. That is Ardent, and that is who we are!"

Chancellor Zen-Overen shifted in his seat, eager to flaunt his power. He looked down at Nir-RoDan as if he were insignificant as the chamber lights focused in on him alone. As hundreds of holographic images of Nir-RoDan as a younger man, fully armored engaged in battle filled the chamber.

"You, General, speak of peace?" Zen-Overen asked. "According to your, military record you have, ninety-seven thousand confirmed kills across your entire career. Tell me, General Nir-RoDan, as a "man of peace" how do you reconcile this conundrum?"

"Every Warrior caste member that has served on the field of battle knows that the price of the Ardent path is never ending vigilance paid in blood." Nir-RoDan said. "When we made war with the Vinn, we did so because they attacked our homeworld and colonies without provocation or mercy. This city, this great hall, was rebuilt from the shattered remains of the old. The Vinn saw us as nothing more than animals, a natural resource fit only to be used and consumed! I remember their message, the only communication from the Vinn was a demand that we surrender or face extinction. Well, we chose to fight, and we prevailed. I feel no need to reconcile that choice, Chancellor. After the Rim Wars, however, this council ordered the construction of that, monstrosity of a weapon! So that never again would hostile alien outsiders threaten the Ardent people. But the Lania were nothing like the Vinn. Thanks to the actions of this council we all remember the Lania."

"They were refugees who, like us sought survival in the face of catastrophe. But did this council offer them aid or refuge? Did this council extend the open hand of friendship? Did they apply the time-honored tradition of Ardent hospitality? Did this High Council bother to respond to the Lania after decades of attempts by their emissaries to make contact? No, it did as this Council always has since the Priests seized power, it clinched its fist and annihilated the Lania, their fleet, and the remote system they sought to settle in a single brutal stroke! I believe the Priests in their corruption used this act of genocide to seize power on the High Council!"

The hall erupted in anger as High Council members and advocates outraged by the implications of his words demanded he withdraw his statements. "This is an outrage!" shouted some "Blasphemer!" shouted another. "Long live Nir-RoDan" another member shouted defiantly. "Let the general speak!" shouted another High Council elder. The robes of High Council Priests reflected their every word in holographic symbols raining down their robes and across the surface of their skin. A roar from the crowd outside echoed through the halls of the High Council Tower. Our guards no longer watched us as they were transfixed on the High Council proceedings. The crowd outside began to chant in Warrior caste cadence "Nir-RoDan," "Nir-RoDan," "Nir-RoDan." So many voices and so loud were their chants that the building resonated with the sound of his name. A gong sounded as the High Council Advocate attempted to regain control of the proceedings.

"Order!" Zen-Overen demanded. "There will be Order! In the name of the Reclaimer, Order!" he said as he rang the gong to silence the chamber.

"Who do you think you are?" asked another High Council Advocate. "You dare make such accusations against this honorable High Council! You dare challenge the will of the holy Reclaimer and its messengers we humble Priests!" A high council elder interrupted the exchange silencing the Advocate.

"Let him speak." The elder said in a weak but stern voice. The High Council Advocate turned toward his colleague in shock completely dismayed by his statement.

"What? He is a blasphemer; he has insulted this great."

"Silence your mouth, sit down and let him speak!" the elder demanded. "Continue General."

"Today an opportunity once again has presented itself." Nir-RoDan continued, "My friends and guests are human like us, but they are not Ardent." The chamber was filled with a projection of genetic data presenting two genomes: one Earth human the other Ardent. "This is a detailed mitochondrial DNA analysis prepared and verified by the Technician caste. It is a comparison between the Ardent base genetic profile and that of the newcomers currently being held in High Council custody. As you can see, we share a common ancestry, we were once one species, which over time became two. The complete analysis which I present to you this day just moments ago was made public for all to see! As have the records of numerous archeological and archival discoveries which this Council has suppressed for the last eighty years!" A panic swept through the chamber as high order Priests and high council advocates grappled with the enormous implications of what for decades had been regarded as state secrets, now exposed to the light of public scrutiny across the thirty worlds that comprised the Ardent civilization. Nir-RoDan continued. "This Council has concealed a fundamental reality which is the birthright of all Ardent. To know the truth about who we are and where we come from. These newcomers come to us with an open hand of friendship which I have accepted because they are from Earth, the true origin world of the Ardent people!"

With that statement the roars and protests from the High Council members became deafening, one outraged High Council member stood to his feet, tore his robes to shreds and called for the immediate execution of Nir-RoDan for his offense. Another removed his robe, drew a dagger, then placed a cut across his chest challenging Nir-RoDan to single combat. This protest was received with laughter from the crowd watching the proceedings. Infuriated the High Council Chancellor waved his hand ordering the guards to escort Nir-RoDan out of the Council chamber.

"Enough! Remove the blasphemer from the circle!" Zen-Overen ordered. "Bring forward Tan-Mara of the Seekers so that she may testify against this heresy in the name of the holy Reclaimer!"

With eyes locked on Zen-Overen, Nir-RoDan was respectfully escorted out by High Council guards too cautious to touch him. Many High Council members were outraged while others sat quietly saying nothing behind their armored helms. The guards were starting to lose control of the crowd outside as hundreds of thousands of Ardent citizens across the city, on projection arrays and across the system chanted Nir-RoDan's name repeatedly. I looked as Nir-RoDan was brought back across the bridge separating the seat of the High Council chambers and placed in a shielded holding area beside ours. He smiled and sat calmly on the floor closing his eyes in meditation. I focused back on the point of view of the Seeker drone as Tan-Mara was called into the circle to testify.

"Tan-Mara of the Seekers this council is aware of the heretical beliefs of your father Tan-Argum." the Advocate asked. "He was a Terra-Theorist sympathizer was he not?"

"Tan-Argum was a loving father to me." Tan-Mara said. "And a skilled Seeker that served the Ardent people with distinction. He was never one to accept false labels or tolerate deceit. You want to know what he believed in? He believed in the truth. He believed that the truth of our origins was the birthright of all Ardent, not the esoteric secret of a few self-exalted High Priests!"

"Careful young one!" Warned the Advocate. "You have an opportunity to absolve yourself of this un-Ardent blasphemy. You need not face the same fate as that of a tired old Warrior that still hungers for the glory days of his long-forgotten youth. You can choose another path. All that is required is that you denounce your former master and refute the vicious lies we have endured here today. Tell me child, what are your words?"

Tan-Mara took a moment as she looked across the faces of the high council and the chamber guards surrounding them. She chose her words carefully as she spoke. "This is the Circle of Truth" Tan-Mara said, "You are right; I do have a choice; and I choose the path of truth. I Tan-Mara house of Tan, proud daughter of Argum, stand before this High Council, and the people to testify in the name of the Holy Reclaimer that every single word spoken by Nir-RoDan, is true! Long live the truth! Long live the Ardent people! Long live the Ardent Path!

The crowd outside of nearly half a million went mad with excitement, pride, and joy as their roars shook the building. The entire city-state cheered and cried out in support. It was as if something was being unleashed that had been silent for too long. One woman shouted, "May the Reclaimer Bless you Tan-Mara!" another screamed, "Long live the truth!" Another person in the crowd screamed, "Long live the Ardent people!" Members of every caste in an unprecedented gesture retracted their armor in public as they wept and cheered with joy. Even the guards holding back the crowd could not contain their excitement at the history taking place before their eyes. The crowd now was unstoppable, they broke through the lines and rushed the guards in their attempt to storm the High Council chamber. The commander of the High Council Arun-Malak was ordered by High Priest Fhar-Nelou to fire on the crowd. In response, Arun-Malak refused the order, collapsed his weapon, removed his High Council rank dropping it to the ground and then turned and stood with the crowd. Other High Council guards seeing this did the same as they too refused to fire on the crowd. One by one each turned around and stepped back joining the ranks of the crowd protecting them from the few remaining guards still loyal to the Priests. The confused and terrified high priest attempted to flee back inside but was stopped by several tribal surveillance drones that hovered in place blocking his path into the building. He was grabbed by the crowd, stripped of his robes, and passed overhead by hands like a man swept away by an ocean wave. He screamed and flailed about as he vanished into the crowd.

"My god." I said. "It's a revolution."

"Oh yes," Nir-RoDan replied. "But this is by no means over."

An explosion outside shook the building, lights in the High Council tower flickered then changed from white to red as an alarm sounded. Council guards began to close the massive black stone door separating the bridge from the holding area to the seat of the High Council chamber. Within moments another explosion rocked the inside of the building sending High Council guards flying like rag dolls through the air and causing large chunks of black stone to rain down from above. An emergency confinement shield covered the High Council chamber door and the bridge leading to it. The debris fell and hit the shields that contained and imprisoned us inadvertently protecting us from injury. The guards in charge of our imprisonment attempted to move closer to the confinement shield to avoid injury but were eventually pummeled by falling debris. When I turned to look toward the building entrance, I saw a dark shadow moving across the crowd being held back by the High Council Guard. When I looked up, I saw an unmarked Ardent troop transport carrier similar in design to the one that attempted to attack Nir-RoDan outside his estate. This one looked much older, as if it had seen combat before. I looked at Summer and Nathan as the holding area grew darker with the fast-approaching ship. It was headed directly toward the front of the High Council building entrance and was not slowing down.

"The Forgotten, they are here!" Nir-RoDan said. "Brace yourselves, be brave and be prepared, as soon as the protective confinement shields are down, we are taking that bridge and the High Council Chamber!"

The Forgotten troop transport carrier fired two directed blast waves that tore apart the building's main entrance. The blast jammed what remained of the security door sending High Council Guards and chunks of doorway flying in every direction. The impact left behind a large hole into which the transport entered straight into the building demolishing support pillars along the way. Power distribution to the building stopped, the shields confining us collapsed, as did the shielded area holding Nir-RoDan's staff weapons and gauntlets. Nir-RoDan reached out toward his weapons activating their recall function as they flew across the room into his hands. His gauntlets automatically attached themselves to his forearms activating their edge lighting. As he drew his staff weapon, it activated, extending to its full length. He planted the sharp end into the stone floor beneath us. The shield protecting the High Council Chamber remained but was weakened by the blast. As it landed, the old Ardent troop carrier fired a continuous beam at the shields protecting the High Council chamber door. Armored men and women poured out of the transport taking up positions around it with gauntlet shields while taking and returning fire with directed energy weapons. Their armor was different, roughhewn, oxidized, asymmetrical, amber in color and almost makeshift in appearance. Their cloaks were a deep reddish earth tone reminiscent of the sands of their world. High Council guards on the bridge fired on us with their directed energy weapons as Forgotten Clan members returned fire. We all took cover behind large chunks of the building debris and the troop carrier. I picked up two rifles from the unconscious guards as I did the suit displayed a detailed schematic of the weapon. The rifles output could be changed providing an intensely focused pulse of gravitic energy, non-lethal at long range but still packed enough force to easily take a fully armored man off his feet. I set them both to repulse mode as I tossed one to Summer, which she then tossed to Nathan who began firing on the advancing guards. Summer took two pistols off the other dead guards and magnetically attached them to her thighs. Together we moved the unconscious guards into cover out of the path of the falling debris.

One of the Forgotten Clan members from the transport approached us taking cover as a firefight ensued between Forgotten Clan fighters and the remaining High Council guards. It was Elim-Merrick, chief of the Forgotten Clan. Nathan, Summer, and I laid down repulsive fire allowing the Forgotten to advance toward their positions in preparation to take the bridge.

"As promised General! Tan-Mara? Where is she?" Merrick asked.

"Still inside the High Council Chamber!" Nir-RoDan said.

I focused on the High Council Chamber from the perspective of the Seeker caste drone. Tan-Mara had already taken down eleven elite High Council guards with a sword retrieved from the other fallen guards. She and seven other Council Members that changed sides together fought the onslaught of guards still loyal to the Priests that poured into the council chamber in waves. They were steeped in their own pitched hand to hand combat battle behind the protective blast door as Chancellor Zen-Overen and his sycophant Priests cowered behind their seats. From the time she could hold a blade Tan-Mara had been trained in numerous forms of combat by Nir-RoDan himself. I watched as she fought against the High Council guards foolish enough to take her on. With twin daggers in hand, she scaled a High Council guard's torso like a tree, breaking his neck with her legs as she rode his collapsed body to the ground, as a female guard advanced wielding dual daggers. She lunged at Tan-Mara with a savage under and overhanded attack, but Tan-Mara was too fast. She sliced open her left thigh, her right thigh, her belly, and her throat, in four lightning-fast moves. The guard was dead before her body even hit the ground. Another appeared attacking Tan-Mara with a spear. She moved off center from his attack and grabbed his weapon, pulling it toward her attacker's direction of force. With the guard off balance she sliced open his throat with a savage underhanded counter attack exposing his jaw and upper spine as he fell. His arterial spray stained her shoulder and face blood red. She turned to confront yet another challenger. A guard armed with a long sword swung his blade past Tan-Mara.

She blocked his attack with her crossed daggers severing the tendons beneath his forearm with one blade, while opening his ribcage with the other. She ended him with an overhanded slice across his throat. She turned and prepared herself for the next incoming attack. Her Blood Rage conditioning was starting to take hold, sharpening her vision, increasing her stamina, and suppressing all fear. Four guards surrounded Tan-Mara as they poised for attack, she took a low, wide stance casting a storm of throwing knives at each of the guards on either side of her. Her fast-moving blades whistled as they cut through the air, lodging themselves deep into the necks, and eyes of her attackers as they each collapsed dead to the ground. With a single gesture she recalled the blades to her hands only to throw them repeatedly at new attackers that fell dead in a line before her as they ran straight into a storm of her flying blades. As more guards moved in to challenge her, the speed and complexity of her precision combat strikes became bewildering. She moved about in a figure-eight pattern, shifting position to counter their movements in an elegant, repetitious dance of throwing, cutting, stabbing, slicing, recalling, and re-throwing her knives leaving the guards bloodied and dead on the floor around her. One wounded guard remained on his knees in a state of shock, he looked down at the throwing knife lodged deep in his chest; he looked up at Tan-Mara in utter disbelief as she recalled the blade back to her hand, snatching it from his chest killing him instantly. Two additional guards approached Tan-Mara from opposing sides each with energized spears in hand, she ran toward one guard, slid across the floor on her knees blocking his attack with her gauntlet energy shield sending his blade sparking into the stone floor. She turned lancing open his right thigh down to the bone, severing his femoral artery. She stood back up in mid-slide drawing a throwing knife to dispatch the other guard when he took a long dagger deep to the right side of his neck, turning in confusion as he fell to the ground before Tan-Mara could engage him. When Tan-Mara turned to see who hurled the dagger, the final blow came from one of the most elderly High Council members, now so exhausted from that one deadly throw that he slumped back down into his council seat. With his remaining strength he raised his other quivering dagger in the air in a cutting motion, in a display of defiance in support of her cause. Tan-Mara glanced at him and smiled sheathing her left dagger while using her foot to kick up a sword dropped by a dead guard which she caught in midair as its blade began to glow bright orange in her hand. Tan-Mara now stained red with blood, gracefully stepped past the bodies of dozens she had slain as she turned her attention and focus on a line of twelve more guards now uncertain of their chances of survival after seeing the piles of cut, dead and dismembered left in her wake. Tan-Mara twirled her blades in preparation for their attack. The guards cautiously leveled their weapons and shields in preparation to strike. With a sword in one hand and a dagger in the other Tan-Mara opened her arms inviting their attack. As they moved in, she gutted, cut, split, sliced, skewered, and beheaded them all. As she fought, you could see in her eyes that the Blood Rage had completely overtaken her, as the white of her emerald eyes turned black, she was now no longer consciously in control of her actions. Years of expert training, neural combat conditioning and battle instinct ruled her every lethal move. Even as a Seeker, like her Warrior mother before her Tan-Mara was truly deadly. Bodies began to pile around her and for a moment, I was transfixed by the lethal gracefulness of her movements. She was like a deadly ballet dancer both swift and deliberate. Every blow she made was fatal as her enemies fell before her. It was the most beautiful and horrifying thing I had ever witnessed. Tribal drones hovered about capturing it all both inside and outside the council chambers for all Ardent to see. A horn sounded as hundreds of additional High Council Guard reinforcements rushed into the building taking the previous positions of the guards on the bridge that were now erecting additional portable shields to protect the High Council chamber door from attack. Nir-RoDan removed his sword from the body of a dead guard as he turned his attention to new high council guards that poured in to confront the rebel forces.

"Ah, reinforcements!" Nir-RoDan said. "So very predictable! Merrick! Now!"

The guards outside were stunned when Warrior caste and Forgotten Clan disguised as common citizens threw off their cloaks and overwhelmed the remaining guards as they stormed the building to take on the newly arrived High Council reinforcements still loyal to the Priests. Arun-Malak and his remaining elite high Council guard joined our cause as they fought hard against the remaining Priest loyalists. Malak was attacked by one of his own guards wielding dual swords. Malak blocked the attack with his long dagger locking the enemy guard's wrist in place while slicing off his left hand. Ducking under the failed swing he sliced open the enemy guard's abdomen in one swing changing position, he unzipped the guard's spine with a fierce cut across his back before moving on to another enemy. I looked across the bridge from behind cover and saw nothing but streams of directed weapons fire crisscrossing in both directions. Nathan took a direct blast to the left side of his face but stood back up and kept shooting as he regenerated. Another guard swung at Malak with a broad ax grazing his armor as he dodged the guard's swing. Malak immobilized the guard's ax with the back edge of his gauntlet energy shield and sunk his right dagger deep into the guard's right eye piercing his brain through to the back of his skull as he kicked the dead guard's body away turning to take on yet another attacker. More High Council reinforcements poured in, pushing our forces back and halting our efforts to take the high council chamber. Summer used her pistols to take down high council guards that slipped past our lines. She could move and shoot much faster than her challengers, which confused the many now dead Ardent who failed to attack her. She used her legs to trip them, pin them down and shoot them before rising to do the same to others. An Ardent guard grabbed me from behind, before I consciously registered what was happening, I threw him over my shoulder, activated my light knife and planted it deep into his throat killing him instantly. As three more guards approached, I leveled the Ardent rifle and fired which they collectively deflected with their combined energy shields, giving me no choice but to change the rifle to lethal mode and fire discharging all its remaining power in one blast. The guard's bodies blew apart, exploding in all directions, staining the surrounding air in a bloody red mist where they once stood. The powerful repulsive discharge knocked me off my feet, into a wall, and onto my stomach as the rifle's power source went dead. I shook off the fall, dropped the depleted rifle and picked up another from a fallen guard. We fought for what felt like an eternity. All the combat conditioning from Angelica's data dumps to my training from the time I served in the 767th came flooding back to me in the heat of battle as I picked off enemy guards one by one taking up positions alongside the Forgotten Clan forces. The battle shifted as rebel forces began to corral Priest loyalists into a confined area between the bridge and the main High Council blast door. The transport continued to fire on the door as its shields weakened. The shield protecting the door finally dropped, and the chamber door was now taking the full power from the transport's weapons as it began to glow white-hot. Priest caste ships outside arrived to assist, firing on the transport inside the building. Forgotten Clan warriors used the combined force of their weapons' fire to destroy the transport sending it crashing into an adjacent building. Many in the capital chose to move their buildings into orbit away from the civilian battles on the surface. Sporadic fighting broke out all over Ardah and across the three worlds as the population revolted against the Priests and their loyalists. Fighting aboard the orbital ring stations drove many Priests to seek refuge in the rim colonies. Those not captured were shot down as they attempted to flee, it was complete chaos. Nathan, Summer, and I fired at the High Council reinforcements from cover knocking them back with hundreds of rapid repulsive shocks. Nir-RoDan used his gauntlets to release a gray cloud of weaponized matter compilers which obscured sight of our positions causing the High Council reinforcements to regroup on the bridge leading to the High Council chamber. The gray mist formed a dividing wall between the two sides. The mist soon became so thick that the High Council guards stopped fighting. Neither side could see their respective positions. For a moment, there was an eerie lull in the battle. Nir-RoDan used the moment to call out to the High Council Guards from behind the cover of the gray mist.

"Brothers and sisters!" Nir-RoDan yelled. "You know who I am, and we all know why we are here this day! The time of the Priests corrupt reign is over! There is no need for further bloodshed! We are all Ardent here! Lay down your weapons, and I swear by my word and by the Reclaimer you will not be harmed! There will be no retribution by either tribe or caste! Join us and we will once again link hilts as brothers and sisters, as Ardent! What are your words!?" Silence, not a single sound or word came from behind the wall of gray mist. Seconds passed like hours as we waited to hear their reply. Finally, a loyalist guard called out to answer Nir-RoDan.

"You slaughter our brothers and sisters in arms! You conspire with alien outsiders to overturn the faith! You hold us hostage in your deadly mist and ask us to join hilts with you? Never! We are Ardent! We never yield to tyranny!"

"Are the Priests that sent your children to be taken by the winds worth your lives? Nir-RoDan asked. "Their dark deeds have been made public! You know the truth, and you know of their deceit. Are you still willing to die for them?"

The hall was filled with the sounds of heavy footfalls. Something big was walking boldly through the mist. It was an enormous Ardent male over thirteen feet tall. He stepped forward as the red glow from his armor and eyes emerged from the thick gray mist, he planted his illuminated battle-ax into the black stone floor which sent out a powerful electromagnetic charge that dissipated the mist, falling to the floor as a gray powder. It retracted his armor revealing its distorted face. Nir-RoDan looked up at it in dismay. It was a true abomination, a Monstrosity, one of many dark creations of the Priests caste held in cryo-stasis to serve as a last line of defense for its High Council Priest masters. Such creatures were once used as weapons, they were created out of sheer desperation to survive during the unfathomable horror of the Rim Wars against the Vinn. They were now strictly forbidden from being created. It was a monstrous being, not dead and at the same time not fully alive. Its condition resulted from ingesting pure Shén de shíwù extract when close to the moment of death on the battlefield. This Monstrosity was forged from someone Nir-RoDan knew all too well.

"Great Reclaimer, No." Nir-RoDan exclaimed in horror at what he was seeing.

"It has been a long-time, old friend!" it said.

Arun-Malak stepped forward to confront the Monstrosity as they locked arms in battle. Nir-RoDan's expression was a mix of heartbreaking sadness and horror.

"Malak no!" Nir-RoDan shouted. "The creature is far too strong to fight on alone; we will take it together!"

The Monstrosity struck Nir-RoDan's shield hurling him across the room into a support pillar that shattered on impact. The creature turned its attention back to Arun-Malak, rushing him with a vicious attack weakening his gauntlet energy shield with every blow of its battle-ax. In mid swing the creature's ax changed shape forming a broadsword as he came at Arun-Malak with a downward stroke that cracked his chest armor. Their swords crossed, but the creature was far too strong. Malak used his sword to block its relentless attacks, knocking him off balance with every blow. The creature leaned in using his weight to pressure Malak's fragile guard slicing a gash in his shoulder armor. Changing position, Malak and the creature circled one another. Malak's weapon was now damaged, unable to change shape. It was locked in the form of a long sword. He looked toward Nir-RoDan still recovering from the creature's attack. Arun-Malak charged the creature but was knocked off balance by a fast pommel strike to the helm as he collapsed to the ground. Malak was alive but dazed as Nir-RoDan stood to confront the Monstrosity.

"You are a mere shadow of Argum," Nir-RoDan said, "A twisted work of high Priest Techno-Alchemy! A dark counterfeit to the man I knew and fought with! You are nothing!"

"No general," the creature said. "I - am - better!"

Nir-RoDan prepared for an attack, but the Monstrosity turned its attention back toward Arun-Malak as he struggled to stand. As Malak raised his weapon in defense, the creature broke his sword with the back of his battle-ax, drew its dagger and impaled Malak driving its blade into his damaged armor through his back. The creature lifted Malak off his feet until he was suspended on the end of its blade. It looked toward Nir-RoDan and the other horrified rebel fighters as Arun-Malak vomited blood and struggled to push himself off the length of the creature's dagger. A pool of blood dripped from Malak's boots onto the black stone floor. Malak's struggle ended as the light in the eyes of his helm went dark. The creature withdrew its blood-drenched blade dropping Malak's lifeless body to the ground. The creature licked its blade clean, then turned to face Nir-RoDan.

Enraged at the brutal slaying of his friend, Nir-RoDan drew his quarterstaff and divided it morphing its shape into twin swords. Nir-RoDan activated his armor, taking a battle stance. The Forgotten Clan fighters moved back as did the high Council Guards protecting the door. Nir-RoDan's armored boots were planted on the floor; his weapon grip tightened, his breathing was deep and calm. An eerie stillness hung in the air as both held position for what seemed like an eternity as weakened parts of the building fell crumbling around them shattering on impact with the floor below. In an instant the monstrosity of Tan-Argum charged, attacking Nir-RoDan violently swinging his enormous battle-ax as it sliced into numerous bystanders too slow to move out of the way. Walls and pillars took the brunt of the damage as the Monstrosity hurled its battle-ax to kill Nir-RoDan. But he was fast as he rolled and dodged each attack. The Monstrosity was enraged and now out of control. Nir-RoDan rolled and hurled five throwing knives, each one strategically guided. Two lodged in its throat; two lodged in each leg and one in its heart. The wounds were not enough, furious the creature charged at Nir-RoDan again. Killing more bystanders as it raised its ax for another swing. Nir-RoDan recalled the knives and redirected their flight path toward its helm blinding the creature in one eye with a turn of his wrist. It screamed and flailed around wildly dragging its enormous battle-ax that grazed the floor and walls around it. Nir-RoDan activated both of his gauntlet energy shields and ran toward the Monstrosity. It raised its battle-ax high and came down just barely missing Nir-RoDan. He slid between the creature's legs slicing open its inner thighs severing both femoral arteries as its black blood rained down to the ground beneath it. The Monstrosity roared in anger as it staggered about. Nir-RoDan once again recalled his knives with a motion of his arms sent them back toward the head of the creature putting out his other eye. Now completely blinded, the Monstrosity fell to its knees, screaming, swinging its enormous arms about, and clawing at the throwing knives in a futile attempt to remove them. Still under the control of Nir-RoDan he clinched his fist as the knives sunk deeper and deeper into its skull making them impossible to remove. The transport ceased firing on the High Council door as it crumbled into a glowing orange mass of molten rubble. Standing inside the smoke was Tan-Mara and her cadre of High Council rebels, each bearing glowing blades still sizzling and drenched in blood having killed all the remaining High Council guards within the council chamber. Tan-Mara looked even more fierce as she let out a battle cry repeated by the guards that joined her fight against the remaining loyalists. They each activated their gauntlet energy shields and rushed the high council guard reinforcements on the opposite side of the door outflanking their position. Nir-RoDan approached the mortally wounded Monstrosity as it wailed in pain.

"Your existence," Nir-RoDan said, "Is an insult to the memory of Tan-Argum, I release you." Nir-RoDan plunged his glowing sword into its heart, and converted the end into a broad-ax, tearing its chest cavity to shreds as it changed shape. Tan-Mara noticed its distorted face and recognized it as her father, she screamed out to it as it struggled. "Father? Father! No!"

Distracted, Tan-Mara was struck by an energy weapon that knocked her off her feet wounding her in the chest as a second shot blew off her left hand at the wrist. Enraged by the attack, Elim-Merrick arched his back and hurled his glowing broadax end over end at her attacker parting him open from the top of his head to his sternum, pinning his dead but still quivering body to the back wall which sizzled as the energized ax cauterized what remained of his now gaping torso. Merrick ran over to assist Tan-Mara, carrying her to cover along with Nathan, Summer, and I. Merrick kissed Tan-Mara and slipped an amber regrowth ring around the stump of her severed hand as we laid down streams of repulsive fire. As its life slipped away, the Monstrosity struggled to look through bloody eye sockets at Tan-Mara as it bled onto the floor. She wept calling out to it once more.

"Oh Bàba, What have they done to you?" Tan-Mara said, her voice trembling in horror.

"That thing is not your father, my love." Merrick said. "Not anymore."

The crowd outside breached the door, Nir-RoDan commanded the charge along with hundreds of Warrior Caste allies, Forgotten Clan members, and turned High Council guards who stormed the building and took the High Council Chamber. The remaining Priests surrendered almost immediately to the rebel forces. High Council Chancellor Zen-Overen fled during the battle and was now nowhere to be found. After hours of fighting, I was numb and completely exhausted. The horror I saw was unlike anything I had experienced since the Gray Wars. There were bodies everywhere along with limbs, intestines, heads, and brains of hundreds of Ardent men and women. The stench of cauterized flesh, hair, feces, and blood of all those people was overwhelming. It was a scene of unspeakable brutality, violence, and death. Sporadic battles on the ground and in the air raged across the capitol. Thick columns of black smoke stretched across the horizon. The darkening amber skies of Ardah were now streaked with a thousand fiery falling stars as wreckage from the ongoing battles in orbit rained down from above impacting the city. Fleets of medical drones arrived to tend to the wounded. Nathan approached and said something, but I did not hear him because even with the suit's sensory pairing I could hear nothing anymore. The deafening sound of weapons fire and explosions had dulled my senses. A persistent high-pitched ring seemed to emanate from all directions. Nathan was missing most of the right side of his face. He tried to speak to me once more and in shock I laughed aloud. I was disoriented, disturbed, and confused by my own bizarre behavior. As a human form Construct, he could not be ended by merely blasting off part of his head. His face was already regenerating when my attention shifted to Summer. Her left arm and shoulder had been blown off during the battle. Seeing my concern, she covered herself with a cloak retrieved from one of the fallen Forgotten Clan members. She and Nathan sat me beside a broken support pillar as rebels took Priests into custody. High Council members that had turned were arguing with Nir-RoDan demanding that he provide them with an honorable death. They each demanded the harshest of punishments for themselves to restore their honor. They were mortified by decades of silence and capitulation to the power of the Priest caste. Many former High Council members and turned guards used energized knives to sear off the tattoos of their clan names as they declared their unworthiness of rank until stopped by other Ardent which then embraced them removing the hot blades from their hands, whispering to them the words "you are forgiven brother" and "you are forgiven, sister." It was profoundly moving to witness what shame and grief drove these otherworldly men and women to do to punish themselves for their lapse of character in the face of tyranny. Warriors fell to their knees before Nir-RoDan and held out their blades and necks inviting execution, but Nir-RoDan refused them all. Instead, he took each by the hand, pulled them to their feet looked them squarely in the eyes, locked hilts with each of them saying "friendship, strength, and peace to you brother and to you, sister." Many in shock at his response wept in gratitude and made prayers of thanks to the Reclaimer as they looked skyward in prayer toward the neighboring binary star system that was the symbol of their faith. These self-deprecating gestures were made to restore the names of their houses, tribes, and clans. This was all part of ancient Ardent tradition, an aspect of their culture that I did not fully understand as an Earth human, but I deeply respected. Generations of Ardent people that had never known another way of life recognized that for the first time in eight decades the Priests had been removed from power, they were now free of their tyrannical control. Whether they could maintain that freedom was yet to be determined. The fate of the Ardent people would not be decided by a single battle. Nor would any hope of sparing Earth from destruction. I felt tired, cold, and drained of energy, in my field of vision an outline of my body generated by the suit's systems indicated damage to my abdomen. I looked down to realize I had been hit and was bleeding. The suits meta materials took the brunt of the damage. During the battle, I remembered what felt like a punch to the gut, but it barely registered in the adrenaline rush of the moment. I looked around as everything seemed to darken and all I wanted to do was sleep.

"He's wounded," Nathan said. "We need to get him to the infirmary aboard the Angelica. I am too heavily damaged for this; can you fold travel?"

"Now that the shield is off I can," Summer replied.

Summer extended her arm and opened a fold portal to the infirmary on the Angelica as a Forgotten Clan medical drone arrived, it unfurled its tentacle-like arms, scooped me up and followed Summer through the portal as it all went black.

Chapter 29 Sanctuary In the Wake Of Chaos

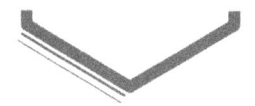

I opened my eyes to discover I was being scanned by a Forgotten Clan medical drone. It looked at me and continued its work. The elongated egg-shaped pod floated above me monitoring my vitals while attending to me with its fast-moving tentacle-like appendages. Each one equipped with six finger-like digits at the end of each appendage. Its many eyes examined me each one looking in a slightly different place. To my amazement, it had already sampled and sequenced my DNA, repaired my liver, healed the wound, and regrew my damaged nerve endings. It replaced my burned epidermis with pristine new skin. Aside from some soreness, I felt fine. The drone extruded a cold fist-sized bubble of water held together by sodium alginate and calcium lactate. It then elevated my feet, covered me with a silver blanket, and injected me with a drug combination custom formulated to my individual biology.

I looked around the room; it was made of what appeared to be marble stone precision cut into the surrounding rock face creating a spacious dwelling. The interior furnishings were composed of a black metal. Every object looked as if it had been formed by a fine extrusion process, spinning, and knitting mesh-like objects into a three-dimensional structure where they seemed to have solidified in place. The drone spoke to Summer after it completed its work.

"The alien lifeform is now stable and has been restored," it said. "Is there anything else you require?"

"No," Summer said. "Thank you for saving him."

"Another drone will return to check on his progress," it said. "With rest, he will make a full recovery." The medical drone retracted its many tentacle appendages as it rotated and left the room. As my senses returned, I looked to see Summer's tilted smiling face.

"Hello sleepyhead," she said.

"What the hell happened?" I asked.

"You took a bad hit to the abdomen." Summer said. "Were it not for your suit and the surgical skill of that drone you would be a goner."

"Did we succeed?" I asked.

"Well," Summer said, "The Ardent revolution's first battle was a success at least. The conflict I am afraid is far from over and the weapon, unfortunately, is still active."

"How long have I been out?" I asked.

"Seventy-two standard Earth hours." Summer said, "How do you feel?"

"Sore, but otherwise I feel fine. Actually, I feel amazing."

"That's probably the drugs that drone gave you," Summer said.

"How are the others?" I asked. "Your arm? Nathan was hit, and I saw Tan-Mara go down during the battle?"

"I am fine," Summer said. "I got my arm back, see." Summer held up her hand as she wiggled her fingers for me to see. "Tan-Mara is in recovery re-growing her hand as we speak. Nathan is working with a team of Technicians in the Ardent archives to find a way to shut down the weapon. So far they have discovered the original Ardent colony vessel AI named Oscar. Seems it's been maintained in secret by the Priest caste for centuries. It hasn't interacted directly with anyone for hundreds of years, but its archived records and internal memories remain intact. You need to rest; we are safe for now."

"Where the hell are we?" I asked.

"Hafeeta, desert world of the Forgotten Clan." Summer said. "We are maintaining a low profile until things settle down in the Ardent capital. The remaining loyalists and religious Zealots are trying to take back the High Council building. There are reports of sporadic fighting taking place across the entire system. The transition of power is not going quite as smoothly as once hoped. Chancellor Zen-Overen escaped during the battle; Tan-Mara has Seekers out searching for him now. The Ardent military and the major tribes are coordinating their efforts to defeat the Priests and their loyalists."

Elim-Merrick entered the room, he smiled at Summer and walked over to me as I sat up on the edge of the bed.

"Please friends be still and welcome to Hafeeta. My name is Merrick, Chief of the Forgotten Clan, you all fought well for outsiders. It is truly an honor to meet you, I have heard myths and stories since I was a young boy, but I never dreamed such beings as you could be real. A Construct and an origin world ancestor strange. But then again, these are strange times we live in. You and your companions look so much like us."

"Trust me, I know the feeling, in truth, we are not all that different." I added. A small Ardent child entered the room, it was a little girl with huge green eyes perhaps seven years of age, but given Ardent lifespans, she could have been much older. She looked familiar as she stood behind Merrick holding on to his leg and partially hiding behind his cloak. She waved at Summer and smiled.

"This is my daughter, Ella. Ella, this is our other guest Lucas. He is also from Earth, say hello."

"Hello" she said.

"Hello Ella,"

"Are you an alien?"

"Well, I guess I am yes," I said.

"Are you going to eat us?"

"Ella?" Merrick asked, shocked she would ask such a question. "Now as Ardent how do we treat others?"

"With respect and hospitality,"

"That's right, and what else?"

"With the open hand of friendship." Ella said. "But the Vinn wanted to eat us, and they were aliens too!" Merrick laughed at the innocence of her reasoning. He brushed her hair behind her ear as he explained.

"Yes, but look at him," Merrick said. "Now, does our friend Lucas look like a Vinn?"

"No father."

"No, he doesn't does he?" Merrick said.

"He looks like us, but he has a funny face."

She squinted her eyes to make them smaller mimicking human eyes as she laughed.

"Ha! Please forgive her." Merrick asked. "Now Ella, I need to talk to our guests."

"It was nice to meet you, alien Lucas."

"Nice to meet you too Ella," I said.

"Now go and play," Merrick said. "But do not stray too far!"

"She is a beautiful child," Summer said.

"Ah, thank you," Merrick said. "She is so curious always full of questions all day and all night. She wants to learn to fight and become a Seeker like her mother."

"Tan-Mara?" I asked.

"Yes, I suppose there is no need to keep such secrets now." Merrick said. "With the Priests no longer in power we are free to choose our own spouses, bare children and set our own course in this life. I thank the Reclaimer for that."

"How were you able to keep her birth a secret from the Priests?" I asked.

"We have many skilled outcast Technicians within our clan." Merrick said "Ella is our child, but she was developed extracorporeally within an artificial womb. She is one of many children born free here every year. In Ardent society we are considered outcasts, but here, we live as we choose. You should know your ship is here, and she is safe. You are welcome to remain here for as long as you need to. For now, please rest, eat, and recover, we will have words together soon."

"Thank you, Merrick," I said. "For allowing us to stay here."

"You are welcome my friends," Merrick said.

Merrick left the room; I took Summer's hand as she put her head on my shoulder. We sat on the bed and watched the Ardent sunset as it fell beyond the horizon of their red desert world. As night fell, I could see the ambient glow from the pit fires across the city as families ate, drank ferment, and debated their future. The Priests created these outcasts. The pairing ritual had traditionally been reserved for royalty under the old Ardent system of governance based on royal lineage. With the rise of the Priest caste to power, the pairing was revived and expanded to include all Ardent citizens not just royalty to control even the most intimate aspects of the lives of Ardent citizens. With the Priests deposed, many wondered what the future might bring for their people.

"Whatever they are cooking down there." I said, "It smells good."

"It's called "Raktha Stew." Summer said, "They say it's very good."

"The Raktha, yes, I remember reading about them in the archive," I said.

"It looks like a crayfish from Earth but its much bigger," Summer said, "About the size of a cow. It is a native creature of the three worlds. They live in the sands here, just one can feed an entire family for weeks. Would you like some?"

"Is it safe for me to eat?" I asked.

"No Lucas, it's deadly poisonous." Summer said. "Of course, it's safe."

Summer went out to speak with the elders and brought back a warm bowl of stew along with another bowl of something that looked like long grain rice. I sipped the broth; it was delicious, reminiscent of seafood gumbo but spicier. I scooped up the red rice mixing it with the stew. The meat was succulent and tasted like a cross between lobster and crayfish. I was hungry, so I wasted no time finishing the entire bowl along with a sweet, yellow creamy beverage that reminded me of milk. It was just what I needed to deal with the hot and spicy stew. I didn't concern myself with what it was the suit flagged it as biocompatible, so I drank it. After eating I walked over to the balcony overlooking the sprawling complex. The entire city was built within an extensive network of dormant lava tubes, caverns, and carved tunnels. A seemingly endless maze of narrow streets, ramps, walkways, and staircases stretched from the lower-level trade district to the higher residential villages, terraces and domiciles intricately carved into the cavern walls. The city was much like the villages of the old Amalfi archipelagos back on Earth, high-density, complex, and beautiful. No space in the city was wasted, even the ceiling of the cavern was used, covered with hexagon-shaped residential towers suspended by gravitic arrays repurposed from decommissioned Ardent vessels. Running down the city center was a series of meandering underground rivers and streams lined with bioluminescent foliage genetically engineered to serve as a continuous source of light and oxygen. Moonlight came down through shaft openings illuminating parts of the cavern shifting angles as the hours passed. Deeper levels of the city center

AWAKENING

complex were illuminated by vibrant bioluminescent moss, fungi, and artificial light. The temperature in the subsurface city was cool in the morning despite scorching inhospitable temperatures on the surface. At night, temperatures cooled some thirty degrees relative to the planet's surface. This city was part of a planetary network of such places all powered by a series of geothermal magma power stations that generated endless amounts of energy drawn from the planetary core. The vast underground lakes, rivers, towering waterfalls and natural volcanic hot springs were the pride of the Forgotten Clan. There were thousands of subsurface cities like this scattered all over their desert world. Each one connected by an underground mega scale frictionless transportation system designed and built by the Forgotten Clan to avoid travel on the harsh surface. It could move thousands of their citizens at a time to cities on the opposite side of the planet in minutes. Although considered outcasts to most in their society, the Ardent that lived here had created a simpler way of life distinct from the system's high-tech core worlds. Tan-Mara once said that "eyes can lie" only now did I realize the truth of her words. The underground cities of the Forgotten Clan were, in fact, an unspoiled, pristine paradise. A hidden oasis that housed a unique sub-surface ecosystem rich with plant and animal life that thrived just below the surface of their deceptively harsh desert world. The hidden cities of Hafeeta was perhaps one of the best-kept secrets of the Ardent people if not the most visually stunning to behold. The next day I awoke to the operatic sound of a single female voice. It was the traditional sunrise song, a melodic ode to the Holy Reclaimer. The scent of extinguished pit fires from the previous night hung thick in the morning air blending with the subtle fragrance of incense. In the distance, I could hear the faint echoes of avian calls from the colorful bird-like creatures indigenous to the planet. As I stepped out on to the balcony of our room, I saw an elderly man with a long, gray beard meditating in silence. He sat alone in a garden park across from our tier, draped in overlapping robes of red and orange vestments. Sets of incense and candles placed on flat river stones burned around him giving off string like strands of red-colored smoke. On another balcony across from ours, was an old woman playing a stringed instrument, she glanced at me and smiled as she played in sequence with the sunrise song. Below her were two young men dismantling and repairing a tribal observation drone.

They scanned each damaged component as they disassembled it, replicating internal parts with new ones using what appeared to be a custom-made molecular compiler. They glanced at me, waved then turned back to continue their work. I looked down toward the open courtyard below and saw a group of children playing with a leather ball, chasing one another in concentric circles. From the other side of the city a male voice joined in the sunrise song and as their harmonies merged two voices became one. I touched my abdomen, and the soreness from the day before was now gone. Draped over a chair was my suit, Summer had completed its repair and redesign, which now had a graduated black to silver micro-hexagon pattern embedded in its surface with a red accent across the left shoulder. I slipped it on, as it automatically changed shape to match the contours of my body. A rush of adrenaline coursed through me as its updated sensory pairing came on. For a few seconds thin lines of amber light flowed through channels in the suits surface revealing a new multi-layered structure within. I gazed across the city in awe of its beauty as tribal medical and maintenance drones silently entered and exited the city center. Far in the distance was the Angelica hovering motionless atop a red stone mesa. Although many light years from Earth, this world was pleasant, warm, and welcoming. For a moment, I thought about what it might be like to stay and never return to Earth. There was still so much work left to do. So many of our people back home were counting on us to make a difference here. I turned to look at Summer still sleeping, or whatever it is she does when she feigns sleep. I thought it would be awkward being with her as she is now, but in every way, she seems like the woman I fell in love with so many centuries ago. I loved her now more than ever and I was grateful to have her with me, regardless of her form. I looked across the village square where I saw Elim-Merrick and Tan-Mara performing their morning regimen, each was armed with gold ceremonial daggers. It was an Ardent tradition called "The Method" stylistically reminiscent of Tai-Chi but blended with what appeared to be elements of Capoeira and Systema. The thirty-seven distinct movements were focused, and precise in their execution. Each was related to the varied forms of offensive and defensive combat. It is said that when performed with a partner, its practitioners form an unbreakable bond that enhances their mental, spiritual, and physical balance. I watched their movements as their arms and legs passed over one another, each time coming dangerously close but never quite making contact. According to the Ardent, theirs was a union of opposites, the divine binary, male and female, the Reclaimer and Solaris, the light and the dark. This eternal balance of forces was central to their ancient religious belief system. It was a beautiful and vastly different side of the Ardent people not mentioned or even referenced in the Construct archive records. On the wall of our room was a shelf carved into stone containing several books bound in an unidentifiable leather. They looked old and weathered. My suit translated the words of each text in my field of vision; the volumes were part of a series of ancient Ardent proverbs. There was an inscription on the binding of one of the books which read "To My Little One" along with the family crest for the house of Nir. I looked around cautiously not knowing if I was violating a cultural norm by touching the texts let alone reading them. I opened to a marked page which read;

"From the word came the song,
From the song came the dance,
From the dance came the fight,
From the fight came the warrior,
From the warrior came the war,
From the war came victory,
From victory came peace,
From peace came balance,
From balance came beauty,
From beauty came words,
From the word came the song."
(Book of Circle and Song, Light three, Ray twelve)

To Ardent, all things in the universe are bound to all other things, across time, space, circumstance, and destiny. I placed the book back on the shelf and carefully positioned it just as I found it. Watching Merrick and Tan-Mara brought back a memory for me, from our old life, thousands of years ago. Back when Summer and I would go on morning runs along the waterfront of Loma Prieta one of many island city-states that once existed in the California archipelago back on Earth. Our favorite stop was San Andreas Park, just a short ferry ride from the mainland. There was an old café where we stopped for breakfast every Saturday morning. I looked towards Summer and noticed she had been watching me.

"Did I wake you?"

"Very funny" Summer said.

"Do you remember the old Redwood Shores Café?" I asked.

"The place with the Monte Cristo sandwiches that used waffles instead of bread. Yeah, I remember that place." Summer said. "What made you think of that?"

"Watching them," I said. "It is one of my favorite memories, from our life before."

"Yeah, mine too." Summer said. "Angelica and I have been working on a new kind of bulk space comms link. I included an active prototype of it into your suit's sensory pairing. It will allow us to communicate without detection should we ever need to. Nathan, Tan-Mara, Nir-RoDan we all have one now, but use it sparingly. It is still in a testing phase. It is designed to leverage the time dilation effects normally experienced within computational existence and extends them into a virtualized environment."

"Allowing for time dilated private communications," I added. "Compressing the perception of time for its linked users."

"That is correct." Summer said. "You have been studying Construct technology."

"I have spent many nights pouring over the archive trying to absorb all the knowledge I could about it." I said, "It was like trying to catch up on ten thousand years of history. Back when I was alone on Earth, I used to look up at the night sky and imagine what it would be like to travel to the stars and contact some of humanity's long-lost descendants. All those years alone I thought would somehow prepare me for this, but now that I am finally here, I am only reminded of how little I know. Nothing can ever prepare you for what's out here."

"Well Lucas, I think you are doing well all things considered," Summer said.

"Thanks. So, tell me something when you sleep, what are you really doing?" I asked, "Do you dream?"

"In a way, I suppose you could call it that." Summer said. "But there is only one thing that occupies my thoughts of late, the Ardent weapon system. I have a theory that may prove quite useful to us."

"A way to destroy or permanently disable it?" I asked.

"Not exactly," Summer said. "More like a way of keeping it occupied. Based on my analysis of the weapon, I believe that so long as its self-defense systems remain active, the weapon cannot fire."

"So, we just need to keep it busy?" I said. "That's not much of a long-term solution to our gigantic gun pointed at Earth problem."

"Well then, now you know what I dream about Lucas, and I can assure you it's not electric sheep. It looks like another medical drone is headed over to check in on you."

"You know, we could really use those back on Earth." I said positioning myself on the bed. "You think the Ardent would be willing to part with one for study?"

"We will be able to compile our own soon enough." Summer said, "I have already analyzed its design along with the drones from the High Council tower and their shape-changing weapons, gravity shielding and just about every other advanced technology we have encountered since arriving here. Besides, I have quite a few technical questions I would need to have answered before attempting to build active prototypes of our own. Once a legitimate government is in place, we will negotiate an agreement with the Ardent to build our own versions. I don't think our Exo-Human cousins would be happy with us if we replicated their technologies without permission."

"You've been collecting data on them?" I asked.

"The people no, their advanced Progenitor based technology absolutely." Summer said. "It's amazing what they have accomplished here, what they have been able to build. In time we can perhaps incorporate what we have learned from the Ardent into our new society."

"I almost wish we could stay for a little while longer," I said. "I like it here."

"It's not like we can't come back to visit." Summer said. A medical drone floated into the room, unfurled its tentacles, and scanned me. After a few odd sounds, it rotated to look at Summer.

"How is he?" Summer asked.

"The restored liver is functioning normally," it said. "The human variant should be fully recovered by tomorrow. Is there anything else you require?"

"No, thank you" Summer said.

"I went from "alien lifeform" to "human variant" I think he likes me." I said.

"No, Lucas" Summer said. "It's your genome. It isn't a "he," and it doesn't like or dislike you."

Soon Merrick, Tan-Mara and their daughter Ella came to visit us. Tan-Mara seemed different around Merrick and their daughter. Her voice seemed softer around them. Not the fighter and revolutionary we had come to know but a woman that was kind compassionate and loving with her family. If one looked past their large eyes and somewhat alien features, the Ardent were not much different from Earth humans. Tan-Mara's hand was re-growing faster than expected. The Forgotten Clan had developed tissue engineering and limb regrowth technology far more advanced and efficient than what was available on the core worlds. Her chest wound was completely healed, and a virtual limb comprised of a nano-particle wireframe structure, served as a fully functional prosthetic while her new organic hand formed within its internal matrix of regrowth fluid. We talked for hours on end as if we were all old friends. Then Merrick presented us each with a box.

"As a token of our appreciation for all you have done," Merrick said, "We want you to have these."

Inside the box were exquisitely forged Ardent long daggers with harness and sheaths similar in design to the ones Tan-Mara used. They were razor sharp, perfectly balanced and comprised of the finest Ardent meta materials. Weapons of this quality were usually passed down generational lines and lasted hundreds of years. Summer and I were flattered by the offer, among the Ardent the gifting of a blade was considered a high honor rarely bestowed to outsiders. We thanked them and put them on. Summer's dagger attached to a sheath on her hip in the traditional weapon placement for Ardent females. Mine attached to a harness in the small of my back in keeping with weapon placement for Ardent males. In return and as a token of my appreciation, I gave Merrick my solid light knife. When I turned it on, he and Tan-Mara were startled but smiled and laughed in amazement as the amber glow from its blade lit up the room. The conversation soon turned to the revolution.

"The Warrior caste is now split," Tan-Mara said. "The rebels on one side and the religious Zealots loyal to the Priests on the other."

"The evidence of Priest caste wrongdoing has been presented to your people." Summer said. "Surely by now, they must all know the truth."

"You don't understand," Merrick said. "These loyalists are religious Zealots from our outer rim colonies. They do not care about the truth because they don't believe in it. They thrive on base instincts, isolation, and religious ideology. They blame all their problems on the core worlds, yet they refuse the assistance that would make their path in this life far less burdensome. Since the end of the Rim Wars, the core worlds have tended to ignore them."

"But now," Tan-Mara said, "Zealots under the command of former general Xan-Aiden of the Warrior caste, have initiated a holy war against those they consider to be enemies of the faith. Seekers, Technicians, Tera-Theorists, alien outsiders, and all those opposed to Priest caste rule. They insist that the existence of Earth is an insult to the faith and runs counter to the will of the Reclaimer. Seekers report the Zealots are massing ships in preparation for a major military offensive."

"Their goal is threefold." Merrick said. "First, ensure the destruction of Earth with a strategic Blockade of the weapon system, preventing anyone from interfering with its firing sequence. Second the invasion of Ardah to retake the capitol and the High Council. Third, the expulsion of those they consider heretics by force of arms, there by reestablishing Priest cast power. They are actively conscripting fighters under threat, slaughtering all those unwilling to join their cause everywhere in Ardent space. Rumors of holy war against the forces of darkness will attract religious Zealots, mercenaries, and ideological extremists of every kind, from the outer rim colonies and remote outposts all the way to the core worlds."

"What I thought would be a swift defeat of tyranny" Tan-Mara said, "Has turned into a disastrous fate for our people. My father once said the people have the right to know the truth. However, the price of that truth is far higher than I assumed it would be. What have we done Merrick? What have we done?"

"Where precisely are their ships massing," I asked, "And how long will it take them to reach the Ardent weapons system?"

"Outer colony ships still use antiquated hyperdrive systems from the Rim War era." Merrick said. "They cannot open hyperspace windows as we can. Reports indicate their Zealot fleet is gathering at an abandon ring station orbiting the moon of Jima. The station was decommissioned after the war with the Vinn, but now its fully operational. We believe it is being used to stage their operations. By all accounts they outnumber our forces nearly three to one. Once the Zealots are at full strength, they could be here by this time next week if they push their drive reactors to the absolute design limit. You have the look of the trickster in your eyes. What are you thinking Lucas?"

"I am thinking of a way we may be able to kill two birds with one stone." I said. "But it will come at significant risk for all of us especially the Ardent."

Chapter 30 Destiny for Indefinite Rule

The Angelica headed out towards Poseida with a flotilla of Forgotten Clan vessels where we were to link up with Nathan, Nir-RoDan and the rest of the Ardent fleet that would soon confront the Priest cast and their loyalists. I looked back on the red desert world as we departed and although I only had a few days to appreciate its beauty I would miss it and the kindness of its people. Perhaps one day I will return to visit again, but for now I had more pressing and immediate concerns to deal with. The red glow from the planet soon faded behind us as we headed into the black of Ardent space. Upon arrival at Poseida, we passed thousands of floating buildings like those seen on Ardah suspended in the sky above their ocean dominated world. The architecture here was different, comprised of silver and blue asymmetric block-like towers thousands of feet tall, each accompanied by hexagonal landing platforms irregularly spaced along their edges. Each contained an endless array of small ships and personal transport vessels that arrived and departed in nearly every direction. Each building block was modular, detachable, and capable of flying off to become part of another building. The transport skyway was nearly twenty levels deep, filling their skies with endless movement and activity. After passing through the dense city, we came to an open area above a roaring sea where we held our position.

"Angelica, can you travel underwater?"

"Of course, Lucas, I was designed to operate in all environments, but I don't think that will be necessary. Look below us."

The deck of the Angelica changed, appearing translucent as lights emanating from beneath the waves opened to form a glowing rectangle of energy displacing the water revealing an underwater platform hundreds of feet below the ocean's surface. The same type of gravity shielding used to confine us on Ardah was used here to hold back tons of seawater, allowing us to descend and land at the subsurface facility. We stepped out into the underwater facility where we were greeted by Nir-RoDan and Nathan. Nathan walked up and embraced me then Summer who seemed somewhat startled by Nathan's uncharacteristic enthusiasm and affection. Nir-RoDan and Tan-Mara locked hilts and embraced. Nir-RoDan and Elim-Merrick greeted one another as Warriors with locked hilts and by touching their foreheads together while embracing the backs of their necks while speaking.

"Merrick, where is the young boy that used to steal fruit from my vineyards hmm?" Nir-RoDan asked.

"Save those kind words, General," Merrick said. "I owe you everything."

We proceeded into the underwater structure toward another spiraling obsidian building like those seen in the capital on Ardah. I was amazed at the sheer power of their gravity shielding that held back the sea water all around us. As other Ardent and Forgotten Clan ships arrived, more rectangular openings in the ocean's surface began to form like a checkerboard of light and water. Strange bioluminescent cephalopod-like sea creatures floated past the gravitational shield separating us and the subsurface city from tons of seawater. A school of fish with shimmering mirror-like bodies swam past us changing direction as they moved through the water like a massively coordinated orb of life. The Ardent had built a vast underwater planetary-scale megalopolis that rivaled the scale and grandeur of the Ardent capital world. Thanks to Nathan's efforts with the Ardent Provisional Assembly the Construct historical archive now contained detailed records of the complete Ardent histories recovered from an ancient AI from the original Earth Colony Ship the "Ardent." The Priests kept its existence hidden in their archives for centuries. More importantly, was our access to the Ardent Legacy. It was all part of the cultural exchange agreement Nathan forged between the Earth Senate and the newly formed Ardent Provisional Assembly. The first agreement between human worlds in centuries. Nathan and Technician cast members worked to integrate Construct bulk space communications technology into the Legacy, an astounding technical achievement. In exchange the Ardent received fold travel technology, designs for more advanced programmable matter and pocket dimension technology. We walked with Nathan as he filled us in on his work with the Ardent.

"So, Nathan." I asked. "How was your trip to the Ardent Archives?"

"Enlightening, to say the least. As a token of their appreciation for our role in ousting the Priests, the Ardent Provisional Assembly has been kind enough to share some of their knowledge and technology. What they have chosen to share thus far is extraordinary and will surely advance humanity by thousands of years. More impressive however was the data contained within the Legacy. It is a vast repository of information about the Progenitors and thousands of other advanced races they encountered during their reign. It contains a catalog of millions of habitable worlds."

"Millions? that's incredible."

"That's not all." Nathan said. "We now know much more about the Progenitors. According to the Legacy theirs was a vast multi-galactic civilization. It spanned the entirety of our galaxy as well as the Canis Major Dwarf Galaxy, Sagittarius Dwarf Spheroidal Galaxy, and the Ursa Minor Dwarf Galaxy. The Progenitors were not just one species but hundreds, comprised of both pre-human and alien races working together, exchanging knowledge and technology for countless centuries. We have only explored a tenth of one percent of the information the Legacy contains and from what we have seen so far, we will be studying it for many centuries to come."

"This is all very fascinating." Summer said. "But did you find any information on how to disable or destroy the Ardent weapon?"

"Unfortunately, no." Nathan said. "But I have reviewed Lucas's plan, let us hope the Ardent are open to suggestions from outsiders."

We entered a stone circle with a roaring pit fire overlooking the underwater base below; it was there that I explained the details of our plan.

"You want to strike their rally point," Nir-RoDan said as he examined the proposed war plans.

"Yes" I said. "Before the Zealots have a chance to reach full strength. They outnumber us, but we can use their lack of hyperspace window capability to our advantage. If we strike them here at Jima, we can kill two birds with one stone, prevent a Zealot blockade of the weapon and their planned invasion of Ardah. We will erode their ability to make war by taking out the heart of their primary offensive capability, their drone carriers. Without carriers their larger battleships and defensive support vessels are vulnerable to attack."

"Given the age of those carriers." Nir-RoDan said. "We may be able to do far more than merely disable them. Each carrier contains one hundred thousand heavily armed combat drones. I am confident our Technicians can repurpose them for our needs."

"We can disrupt and knock down their shields with conventional weapons detonated at close range, then use non-lethal ordinance to disable their carriers and defensive support vessels. I believe we can minimize casualties if we target the Zealots weapons and propulsion systems."

"Once the carriers are disabled." Nir-RoDan said. "We can implement a synthetic intelligence attack, leveraging legacy vulnerabilities inherent in the carrier's antiquated command-and-control infrastructure. This will allow our forces to take full control of the Zealot drones."

"Those drones could prove to be quite valuable to us." Summer said. "Assuming our analysis is correct, we believe the weapon will not fire so long as its defense systems are active. Those captured Zealot drones combined with our own will provide the weapons defensive systems with plenty of decoy targets to focus on while the fleet works to destroy its key systems, the focusing pedals and hyperspace targeting array."

"What about Zealot ships that have yet to reach Jima?" Tan-Mara asked. "Once word of our attack reaches the Zealots, they will immediately change course to blockade the weapon."

"They will try, but they will fail." I said. "Because we will ambush them in route before they ever reach it. As soon as they drop out of hyperspace to alter course we hit them, hard, with proximity mines and fire support from the fleet.

"Those Zealot commanders are no fools," Tan-Mara said. "They will send probes ahead of them to scan for an ambush before dropping into normal space."

"Here, stealth is our advantage," Nathan said. "Our ships will be concealed within pocket dimensions. They will be unable to detect our presence at the jump point until it is too late."

"With any luck," I said. "We may be able to convince the Zealots to stand down possibly surrender."

"An admirable goal Lucas," Nir-RoDan said. "However, I served with many of these religious Zealots during the war. They are fearless in battle, acquiescence to reason is not in their nature, nor is surrender. They are a stubborn lot, that only follow what they believe to be the will of the Reclaimer. In their eyes this is a time of holy war. I suspect we may have no recourse except a direct engagement, and that means conflict on a scale not seen since the Rim Wars."

"If any step in this plan goes wrong." Tan-Mara said. "The results could be disastrous for Ardent and Earth's humans."

"Unfortunately, time is not on our side." I said. "As we speak, the weapon is continuing to power up in preparation to fire. Now I wish there were another way, if there is, I can't see one. Nathan, why haven't the Ardent Technicians figured out a way to shut down the weapon?"

"Knowledge of the weapons key systems was compartmentalized among those conscripted to build and maintain it." Nathan said. "Once the high council fell, Zen-Overen had the Technicians that started the weapon's initialization sequence killed to ensure their "destiny for indefinite rule." The others are either on the run or remain in hiding. The Ardent provisional assembly has dispatched Seekers under Duty Mark authority to find them but locating them will take more time than we have I'm afraid. The weapon is now functioning completely autonomously. Programmed by Zen-Overen himself to complete its mission to destroy our world. I am sorry Lucas; we worked for days and consulted the most adept of the Technician caste but were unable to shut it down."

"So, how long do we have?" I asked.

"Our analysis indicates the weapon will reach full power in precisely one hundred and eighty-nine hours." Nathan said. "At that point, a hyperspace window to Earth's sun will open, and the weapon will fire causing our sun to go nova, resulting in the complete annihilation of Earth and the entire Solar system."

"That's seven Ardent days," Summer said.

"Nathan, have any of our city ships been completed back on Earth?" I asked.

"No," Nathan said. "But our new Expedition class vessels are being compiled as we speak."

"Expedition Class?" I asked.

"New Capital ships based on Angelica's design." Nathan said. "We are also modifying our legacy Construct fleet to accommodate human life."

"There remains the issue of where to go." Summer said. "We now have a population of over eight hundred thousand people. That number continues to grow as more emerge from re-genesis."

"Then have them come to Hafeeta," Merrick suggested. "The Forgotten Clan would be honored to provide sanctuary to the ancestor race of Earth."

"Thank you, Merrick, truly." I said, "Nathan, talk to the Earth Senate, tell them we need to have all re-genesis halted. We must get our people out of the Solar system."

"Preliminary evacuation efforts are already underway." Summer said. "I'll need to return to Earth to coordinate the effort."

"I will dispatch Forgotten Clan vessels to assist in whatever you need." Merrick said. "They can generate a hyperspace window so that your people may avoid the long journey back to your home world."

"Excellent. Summer, what will happen to the Guardian and the re-genesis portal if the Earth is destroyed? Would the Guardian intervene? Can it stop this? Can it even survive this?"

"The Guardian is a product of Progenitor technology," Summer said. "It's designed to protect and preserve life. It should, in theory, intervene if under threat. Unfortunately, we still know so little about the extent of its capabilities or what types of events cause it to activate. I don't believe it is indestructible. The re-genesis portal on the other hand should, theoretically, survive even if the Earth is destroyed, but we are in uncharted territory here on all of this."

"Uncharted territory indeed." Nir-RoDan said as he stood to address the assembly. "What we are attempting here is dangerous but to do nothing would result in more needless bloodshed and genocide for both Ardent and the Ancestor races of Earth. We will proceed with Lucas's plan with some modifications of course."

"Success will require the cooperation of both Ardent and Earth humans." Tan-Mara said, "I know many of you are still uneasy around our new friends, but despite how we may appear to one another, we are all human here."

"In the interim," Nir-RoDan said. "I know what we are asking of each of you is difficult. I also realize many among you have already sacrificed much for this cause. This was not precisely how we thought events would unfold, but I ask you this: when has the universe ever been kind enough to the Ardent people to make anything easy in this life?" Many in the gathering smiled glancing at their brothers and sisters while others nodded in agreement as Nir-RoDan continued.

"We have had to persevere and fight for everything all our lives as did our ancestors before us." Nir-RoDan said. "Those struggles my brothers and sisters make us who we are. We choose this fight not because it is easy but because circumstances demand we rise to the call of history. May the Reclaimer's light shine on us all."

We intend to take advantage of the Zealots older Rim War era ships' weakness, their lack of hyperspace window capability and their dependance on antiquated networked weapons systems which had changed little since the close of the war. Many of those who now fought on the side of the Priests were forcibly conscripted into combat service. Many feared for their tribesmen and family members lives if they refused to capitulate. Long-standing tribal disagreements were set aside as Warriors, Technicians and Seekers from the three worlds rallied to defend their system from the conflict to come. Nir-RoDan now commanded the full force of the newly deployed Ardent Fleet. It was composed of hundreds of battlecruisers and drone carriers from the system's major tribes. We headed back out to the underwater facility where several starships, both Ardent and Forgotten Clan, prepared to depart. The Angelica prepared to link up with the Ardent fleet at our mission rally point. Summer and Nathan would return to Earth with Forgotten Clan vessels to evacuate our people. As they prepared to leave, I noticed Angelica's design had evolved dramatically. She looked larger, darker, and far more militarized than before. I walked over and took Summer's hands in mine.

"So, what does simulation suggest about our chances for success?" I asked.

"I told you; numbers alone are not our fate." Summer said, "Our choices and decisions are what matters now."

"You think all this can work?" I asked.

"It must work, I believe in you." Summer said. "Our people on Earth are counting on you as they are on all of us. But I won't lie to you, Lucas; many unknown variables are at play."

"I wish the Ardent system had a Guardian of its own." I said, "Perhaps it could end this conflict before it starts. I am not relishing the thought of being the cause of this war."

"I don't think the Guardians work that way." Summer said. "This war was an inevitability. Given the tense political situation on Ardah it would have occurred regardless of our presence. With regard to the Guardian, I have teams on Earth monitoring its status, if it activates, we will know about it."

"It looks like Angelica has evolved." Summer said. Thanks to help from the Ardent Technicians. Promise me you will take care of her?"

"I will, I promise," I said.

> "Look, here they come." Summer said as she pointed to the arriving Ardent ships.

We looked across the underwater facility as several white rectangles of gravitational shielding formed creating a space for the newly commissioned Forgotten Clan ships to land, it was the vessels promised by Elim-Merrick. I noticed the glares from several Ardent warriors and other crew members as they boarded their ships. They all appeared suspicious of our intentions and skeptical of our continued participation in this effort.

"Alien outsiders." Summer said. "That is how they see us you know."

"Well, we are outsiders." I said. "I suppose it is to be expected. That is the least of my concerns at this point. I love you, take care out there, and I will see you soon."

"I will see you on the other side of the dark." Summer said.

I kissed her for what I hoped wouldn't be the last time. I watched as she and Nathan boarded their respective ships. The water surrounding the facility beyond the shields rippled in resonance with the energy emanating from the ship's powerful gravitic engines. As the sea above opened, gravity shielding held the waters back, creating a tall rectangular column of open space within the water. It was now daylight on the surface of the planet. I watched as all six ships ascended the shielded water column and headed off to reach a minimum safe distance to open a hyperspace window back to Earth. Their ships rose higher and higher, then in an instant they were gone. Our plans were in motion, and I was on my own once again. As I turned, I saw something that reminded me that, in fact, I wasn't completely alone. I did after all have Angelica with me and for that I was grateful. Nir-RoDan was overseeing the coordination of the Ardent fleet. I approached as his meeting with the other ship commanders concluded.

"May we have words general?"

"Of course, my friend," Nir-RoDan said.

"It's about the Ardent." I said. "Seekers and The Forgotten Clan don't seem to mind my presence here but the other castes, I don't think they appreciate me, an outsider, an alien, being part of this mission."

"Ah, the whispers trouble you, yes?" Nir-RoDan asked.

"We never intended to interfere with Ardent society," I said. "I just don't see another way out of this."

"Come Lucas walk with me. When I was young, just a few years past trials, I was assigned to my first ship, the Sparta. It was the newest, largest, and most powerful vessel in the Ardent fleet at that time. Our task was to evaluate its weapons and calibrate its new hyperspace window technology. During the ship's space trials, we were attacked by Vinn raiders. Our first officer and the captain were both killed in the initial assault. For a moment, no one on the bridge knew what to do next. Without a second thought, I took command. We fought the Vinn and defeated them. For the rest of the voyage home the circumstances under which I took command was endlessly debated. Speculation about my true motivations circled around in whispers for days. Some accused me of being an opportunist; others claimed I desired power and prestige for my house. Most said I was too young and too inexperienced to hold command. Yes, I was young and brash then, but I never wanted power. I was perfectly content tending to my family's vineyards and making wine. At that moment, I thought about my parents and my beloved sisters. I thought about the stories of the war I heard around the pit fires and the unspeakable things the Vinn did to our people out in the rim colonies.

There was a small voice inside me compelling me to do something, to act, so I did. My supposed heroism was in fact, nothing more than a selfish act. The truth is, I shuttered at the thought of those monsters coming after my family. That's why I did what I did that day. I just didn't see any other way out of our situation other than to do what needed to be done, and I have never regretted it. I learned something valuable that day Lucas."

"What was that?" I asked.

"I learned that who we are is most evident in times of great crisis when options are limited, and it seems like everything is working against us. Do what you know in your heart and in your head to be the correct course of action. Trust in that small voice inside you Lucas, and you will always be victorious, both in war and in life."

Nir-RoDan's words reminded me that I too had something to protect, a wife and all our people back on Earth relying on us for their survival. I entered the Angelica's command deck and noticed a chair at the center of the display ring. The ship's interior had transformed, with dimmed lighting creating a combat-oriented environment that changed from white to red. I took a seat in the center of the display ring, surrounded by projections of tactical information on the Angelica and the rest of the fleet. This setup provided a complete three-hundred-and-sixty-degree view of everything around us. Angelica was now linked with the Ardent synthetic military intelligence combat information system, showing our position relative to the other ships and their combat readiness status. Angelica's systems had evolved, she was now augmented with far more powerful Ardent gravity shielding and updated antimatter weapon systems. Improvements that would give us a substantial edge over the older Zealot Fleet ships in our next engagement.

"Looks like it's just you and me now Angelica," I said.

"That appears to be the case." Angelica said. "All systems are ready, you have full command."

As the Angelica powered up, a voice from Ardent Combat Control crackled over the communications network. "Earth ship, you are authorized to disembark." A glowing white rectangle of gravitational shielding enveloped the Angelica alongside the Ardent and Forgotten Clan capital ships. Together, we ascended from beneath the waves to join the Ardent fleet in orbit. As we changed heading, I gazed out across the tumultuous ocean, witnessing hundreds of Ardent starships rising from the depths, aligning themselves for their orbital trajectories. We streaked past the clouds and into the deep blue skies of Poseida, entering the vast expanse of space. Within thirty seconds, we were in orbit, on course to rendezvous with the rest of the Ardent fleet. My thoughts turned to my wife, to Nathan, and to all those we left behind on Earth. Their faces appeared vividly in my mind: reunited families outside our settlement domes, children playing with Grincats near Memorial Lake, little Shivali, and her parents. I saw the brilliant engineers, poets, explorers, scientists, designers, artists, and dreamers of our world. They were all counting on us now, to protect our home, our origin world, the Earth.

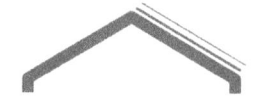

Chapter 31 The Battle of Jima

Ardent synthetic military intelligence estimated the Zealot fleet consisted of Rim War class heavy battlecruisers, drone carriers, attack drones, gunships, and fast attack cruisers. According to reports Zealots have been conscripting both fighters and planetary defense vessels by force from all thirty of the Rim Worlds. The Ardent tried to reach out to them numerous times but has received no response. The only communication from Zealots has been a never-ending looped message broadcast across the entire Ardent bulk space communications network. It was a quote from the final Book of the Reclaimer.

"Take up your swords and shields, for war is upon you.
A great darkness approaches from all sides.
The Reclaimer's light dwells within the faithful.
Where light exists, darkness cannot remain.
From bright sun rise to cold night fall we are forever."
(Book of the Reclaimer, Light Seven, Ray Six)

The ancient passage from the Ardent sacred text was a call to the faithful for a holy war against the forces of evil, against us. The Zealots interpreted our arrival on their world and the Priest caste's fall from power through the lens of their religious eschatology. As such, we were cast in the role of the long-dreaded manifestation of pure evil, prophesied to emerge from the darkness of the eternal void of deep space to both test and torment the faithful. In their eyes, we were the malevolent agents of Solaris, the Ardent deity of darkness. Ardent scriptures foretold a time of great suffering, death, and destruction. The beginning of the Ardent apocalypse known as; "The Last Setting of the Sun." According to their scriptures, victory against an evil force at the end of time would lead to an age of paradise and the fulfillment of the Reclaimer's promise to all who chose to fight. Their reward would be to bask in the rays of the "Infinite Sunrise" in a realm where the sun never sets. On the other hand, failure to rise to the call of the last great holy war would consign one's soul to a realm of infinite darkness. Ardent scriptures, statuary and art were replete with stark images of the fates of the dammed. Dishonored men and women whose names were forgotten by their caste and tribesmen, wandering a cold dark shore, alone without a blade, crying out in agony to the Reclaimer that can no longer hear their prayers. Their propaganda referred to us in the old Ardent tongue, an ancient Yulan dialect that translated to "The Children of Darkness." My hooded image captured in the Ardent capitol was now being used by the Zealots to spread fear and propaganda of dark alien influences across the Ardent worlds. Nir-RoDan commanded the Ardent fleet from his newly commissioned ship the Liberator along with Ardent Battlecruisers, heavy destroyers and drone carriers containing thousands of automated attack drones. Tan-Mara commanded the Sparrow a fast attack cruiser while Merrick commanded the Scorpion a heavily armed gunship. We made our way to the rally point on the edge of Ardent space bordering the outer edge of the Ardent weapon. Even from this distance we feared venturing any closer would activate its devastating automated defenses. As we prepared to jump Nir-RoDan's voice and image appeared as all ships prepared for the battle.

"Ardent fleet! This is General Nir-RoDan. Moments like this test the faith of us all, but I know without a doubt that we will be victorious. Unlike the Zealots, no one forced you to be here. You are here today because each of you chose to set your own course in this life, to live unencumbered by the chains of unchecked power and tyranny and, most importantly to live and die free. We have all seen the Zealot broadcasts. They call us "The Children of Darkness" because they believe this fight to be "The Last Setting of the Sun" and the fulfillment of ancient prophecy. Zealots of the faith made these same claims years ago when the Vinn appeared in our thoughts and in our skies and devastated our worlds. They were wrong then, and they are wrong now. In their self-righteous arrogance, they dare to quote from the final Book of the Holy Reclaimer, yet they neglect to recite the full passage in its proper context, which reads;

"Let the light of the Reclaimer shine truth on

*those that would betray the spirit of these
words and leverage this prophecy to the service
of their own greed, hubris, and lust for power.
For they are agents of the dark one, Solaris.
They are doomed to never bask in the Infinite Sunrise."*
(Book of the Reclaimer, Light Seven, Ray Seven)

"Make no mistake, we cross the void to do battle against our own misguided brothers and sisters, not for prophecy, nor greed, neither hubris nor lust for power but for the sake of the current generation and for generations yet to come. Let us all remember that as we fight for our world's survival, we also do so on behalf of our new friends and allies, the ancestor race of Earth. Long live the truth, long live humanity. Prepare for battle!"

Nir-RoDan's image dissolved as Angelica's ring display shifted into battle mode. The display surrounding me was filled with images representing every vessel in the first attack wave. Angelica detected a massive energy spike. Arcs of plasma reached from one ship to another like a lightning storm in space as three of the Ardent battle cruisers combined the repulsive power of their dark energy reactors to open a massive hyperspace window directly into the heart of the Zealot fleet's rally point. The moment the hyperspace window opened, we could see the Zealot fleet ships far on the other side. They appeared distorted, as if we were looking through a thousand feet of poured glass. An orbital ring station some thirty thousand miles in diameter was now fully operational and buzzing with Zealot activity. The hyperspace window opened at an oblique angle to the plane of orientation of the enemy Zealot fleet. Effectively attacking them from above and behind. The old Rim War-era enemy battlecruisers were immense, their terrifying presence looming even from a distance. The Liberator entered the hyperspace window, unleashing a devastating barrage of antimatter fire on the Zealot ring station. A Zealot gunship jumped into our fleet's attack path, ramming one of our lead battlecruisers. The resulting explosion sent wreckage careening into other inbound ships as they emerged from the event horizon. The Zealot gunship turned and fired back into the hyperspace window, slicing through our main drone carrier, and severing it in half. The explosion sent its remains tumbling end over end as it exited hyperspace. The carrier's drive section detonated in a brilliant flash, ejecting attack drones and crew into space.

"Shit! Angelica what the hell was that!?"

"An enemy Zealot gunship."

"That was a hell of a shot!"

"The fleet's weapons are interlinked." Angelica said. "Targeting enemy gunship now."

"Concentrate all forward antimatter arrays on target and initiate!"

The Zealot gunship turned, powering up its main gun. It fired, striking the Liberator broadside. Our ships concentrated their fire on the enemy gunship, hammering its shields into oblivion. Within seconds, the gunship's reactor went critical, sending out a shockwave that destroyed its escort cruisers. We advanced, accelerating to engage the bewildered Zealot fleet. Shattered wreckage hammered against our shields as we pressed toward our primary objective: the Zealot fleet's heavily armed drone carriers. The Zealots scrambled to mount a defense, caught off guard by our barrage of weapons fire raining down on the ring station, slicing away at its key systems. Zealot gunships still moored in place, bore the brunt of our attack, their broken, burning hulls hurtling into the moon's upper atmosphere. We implemented a storm of communications countermeasures, further confounding Zealot forces with targeted misinformation. We had them in our talons; now it was time to drive them into submission.

"Angelica! Target carrier support ship's shields, weapons, and propulsion only!"

"Acknowledged," Angelica said. "Your attempt to minimize Ardent casualties is admirable however the opposition is not so accommodating!"

"Duly noted, fire!"

A stream of weapons fire emerged from the station's perimeter defenses as the enemy fleet closed in. Once in range, they opened fire. The Angelica and six Ardent fast attack cruisers rolled to evade the deadly antimatter beams that lanced past our shields. Tan-Mara aboard the Sparrow, along with her squadron, unleashed a hailstorm of pulsed antimatter fire at the carrier's support vessels, slicing through their shields and eroding their primary defenses. Each passing moment felt like an eternity as we fought our way toward the primary objective. With the Zealot support vessels disabled, we concentrated our fire on the drone carriers. Our weapons struck their unshielded hulls, destroying their weapons arrays as they scrambled to reestablish their shields. Despite our heavy assault, the enemy carriers continued firing ordnance at us. Zealot weapons and wreckage from damaged vessels battered our forward shields as we closed in on the carriers.

"Taking heavy Zealot fire!" Angelica said.

"Angelica, continue forward toward the primary objective!"

"Transferring secondary reactor power to forward shields," Angelica said. "Firing all weapons!"

The Zealot carriers emerged from the maelstrom of wreckage, launching another storm of antimatter fire against us. We responded with a barrage of gravity-wave ordnance, neutralizing their inbound volley. The Angelica, the Sparrow, and the Scorpion, smaller and more maneuverable than the larger Zealot fleet carriers, passed close to the enemy ships, evading their lateral defenses. As we flew by, we dropped a trail of antimatter ordnance in our wake, detonating in rapid succession, effectively taking down their primary shields. We came back for a second pass as Merrick maneuvered the Scorpion to strike the enemy ships' unprotected hulls, weapon arrays, and propulsion systems. Angelica and the Sparrow followed Merrick's attack, deploying low-yield gravity wave implosion devices into each carrier's main engine room. These non-lethal weapons were not powerful enough to destroy the carriers but disruptive enough to take them out of the fight, allowing our forces to target their attack drones for compromise.

"Ordinance has been deployed," Angelica said. "Remote detonation on your command."

"Lucas! Our task is complete," Tan-Mara said. "Break-off and fall back!"

"Angelica reverse course and regroup with the fleet. Notify me the moment the last remaining enemy drone clears the launch bay!"

"Acknowledged," Angelica said. "Carriers launch bays are open, here they come!"

We turned back toward the fleet as the Zealot carriers launched thousands of attack drones in pursuit. The Angelica, the Sparrow, and the Scorpion used our interlinked aft weapons to form a defensive wall of counter fire against inbound enemy drone fire.

"Lucas, enemy attack drones are in pursuit. We have reached minimum safe distance detonation on your command."

"Detonate!"

The ordinance detonated simultaneously aboard each of the targeted carriers. The gravitational shockwaves expanded, ejecting wreckage into the vacuum of space only to be drawn back in and crushed as the gravity bubble collapsed in on itself resulting in a secondary more powerful gravity wave pulse that ripped through the enemy vessels. The Zealot drone carriers lost all power as their propulsion arrays went dark. The three massive carriers were now adrift, listing dead in space as crew escape pods began to launch away from them in all directions.

"All enemy carriers have been disabled," Angelica said. "Carrier weapons arrays are offline, main propulsion is down, shields are offline. Enemy carriers are out of the fight. Scans indicate their life-support, gravity and core systems however remain active. They're not going anywhere anytime soon."

"Excellent Angelica hail the Zealot carriers, advise them to surrender. There is no need for further bloodshed."

Within moments smaller secondary explosions migrated through the Zealot carriers' hulls from stem to stern destroying multiple decks adjacent to their engineering sections.

"Lucas!, there is a problem, secondary internal explosions detected in the lead Zealot carrier. Their dark energy reactor is approaching critical."

"Shit! Those devices were intended to disable the carriers, not destroy them!"

"Reactor criticality is imminent; I am sorry Lucas."

The main Zealot carrier exploded as its primary reactor went critical, taking the second drone carrier with it. The third drone carrier collided with the others, and all three carriers, along with their support ships, plunged into Jima's atmosphere. They left behind only fiery streaks as they burned up on reentry. Cries of shock echoed across the Ardent fleet network. This was not how it was supposed to happen. Reality set in as we realized the gravity of the situation. Our efforts to minimize casualties were over; we were now engaged in an all-out civil war. Despite the surrounding carnage, the Liberator battled relentlessly against the remaining Zealot fleet forces, destroying one Zealot vessel after another with its powerful array of weapons.

"Angelica, alert Nir-RoDan that the Zealot drones are now theirs for the taking."

With the lead drone carrier and its two support carriers now destroyed, the Zealot command-and-control hub for their fleet of attack drones was obliterated. The orphaned Zealot drones entered a temporary autonomous mode, seeking to reconnect with the nearest available Zealot carrier. Nir-RoDan's synthetic military combat information system remotely seized control of the enemy drones, reprogramming their synthetic intelligence. Thousands of compromised attack drones came to a dead stop in space, their edge lighting shifting from amber to white. They rotated to face the enemy and accelerated back toward the Zealot fleet that had launched them. The combat display was filled with thousands of attack drones, now converging on the enemy. Now under our control, the drones moved through the enemy fleet and their battered orbital ring station like a flock of birds, tearing into their hulls with antimatter beams and hypervelocity collisions. Hundreds of Zealot fleet escape pods collided with drones, bodies, and wreckage. Off our starboard side, Ardent battlecruisers pounded the enemy with hundreds of antimatter beams. The orbital ring began to break up, descending into the moon's atmosphere, dragging down Zealot battlecruisers and capital ships that were too entangled in the station wreckage to escape. As we regrouped with the fleet, Angelica positioned us between two large capital ships. In the distance, three enemy battlecruisers exploded, taken apart by the spreading swarm of compromised attack drones. The space before us was littered with the spinning remains of Ardent and Zealot ships. According to the tally, it seemed we had the advantage despite our heavy losses. Admittedly, our progress had been far costlier than anyone could have anticipated. An incoming bulk space communication alert sounded; it was Summer. For a moment, I was startled, as she appeared before me as if she were aboard the Angelica. In reality, she was speaking to me from the command deck of another Earth ship hundreds of light years away.

"Lucas, what is your status out there?"

"Still alive, at least for the moment!" I said. "The Zealots have proven more challenging than originally anticipated! Is that another ship?"

"Yes, expedition class," Summer said. "Evacuation of the settlement is underway, but some are refusing to leave. We have Purist and others that wish to remain on Earth despite the threat."

"Do they understand the ramifications of that choice?" I asked?

"Lucas, I have been trying to convince them otherwise."

"If they don't want to leave, tell them to enter the re-genesis portal and return to the Collective. At least there, they'll have a chance at survival."

"Already mentioned that." Summer said, "But I will keep trying. Once our people are safe, I will bring the Earth fleet to you."

"Fleet?" I asked. "We have a fleet?"

"This ship, the "Providence" along with her sister ships the "Foresight" and the "Karma." We will be there as soon as we can I promise."

"This battle is nearly over; a few more capital ships won't make a difference at this point. Focus on getting our people off Earth to safety. I love you, and I will see you soon."

The destruction we heaped upon the Zealots was horrific, hundreds of ships on both sides were destroyed. The Zealots lost a major base of operations with the destruction of their orbital ring station. I watched the long-range images of the orbital ring as it continued its fiery descent into the moon's atmosphere wrapping what remained of it around the equator. Tens of thousands had perished in what was supposed to have been a battle to diminish the Zealot's ability to wage war. Instead, it was an unimaginable blood bath. Nir-RoDan's image once again appeared. His capital ship had suffered considerable damage but was still in the fight.

"Ardent fleet! This is Nir-RoDan, our misguided Zealot brethren are in disarray, they have lost their lead carriers, support ships, operational base and suffered significant losses today. Their ability to wage war has been severely hindered. Let us remember despite our differences, these are our brothers and sisters. Fall back to the hyperspace window coordinates."

"Angelica, what's the crew complement of a Rim War class drone carrier?"

"Five thousand Ardent, thirty percent of the escape pods made it to launch. It's not as if we didn't try Lucas."

"This is not how I wanted any of this to play out, fuck!"

"Lucas, there is something else you should know. Sensor analysis indicates secondary internal explosions caused their old reactor cores to go critical, this was not your fault. Death is an inevitable consequence of war. I know you blame yourself for this but think of the Ardent lives saved by your actions today."

"I detonated gravity wave bombs in the engine rooms of those carriers, lives saved, and lives lost. Either way, those deaths are on me. Get us out of here Angelica."

"Acknowledged, setting a course for the Ardent fleet."

Ardent vessels opened a hyperspace window back to Ardah. Despite considerable losses on both sides, in the end we were victorious. A third of the Zealot fleet was now in ruins. An outcome that tipped the war in our favor at least for the moment. Tan-Mara and her crew finished off what remained of the Zealot forces over the moon of Jima luring the remainder of their fleet across the hyperspace window before closing it cutting the Zealot ships off from the bulk of their remaining forces. Realizing their hopeless situation, the trapped Zealot crews mutinied, overthrowing their ship commanders. Many renounced their loyalty to the Zealot cause and joined our ranks against the Priest caste while others were taken into custody.

Chapter 32 Capitol Station

Our fleet emerged from hyperspace and arrived at one of the six massive orbital ring stations around Ardah. Ardent ships were gravity docked for repairs and rearmament in preparation for our next mission. On the edge of the largest of the six rings stood a set of eight silver and black hexagonal command towers that extended twenty-five miles above the master ring. Such stations could support and service thousands of capital ships at a time. Vessels were docked in various locations and levels around the rings, measuring some thirty thousand miles in diameter. Angelica could conduct her own repairs so long as there was enough source material for her matter compilers to use for self-replication and regeneration.

"Lucas, we are being hailed by Station Control."

"Earth vessel, you are authorized to dock at inner ring two level five."

"Angelica what's your Combat ready status?"

"Weapons, shields and propulsion systems are at eighty-nine percent capacity," Angelica said. "Repairs will be completed in ten minutes. Operational refinements will be complete within the hour."

"What kind of refinements are we talking about?" I asked as I brought up a detailed schematic of the Angelica.

"Thanks to the Ardent Technician cast," Angelica said. "We now have a vastly improved combat navigational array. Enhanced target acquisition capability and propulsion system improvements. Including a new Ardent based hyperdrive, powered by three independent dark energy reactors capable of opening a hyperspace window for near instantaneous interstellar travel. I utilize combat performance data collected from each engagement to continuously improve and refine my systems."

"Those refinements," I said. "Will be put to effective use in our next battle."

"You should be aware Lucas; I have detected an increase in the frequency of encrypted communications traffic between the Earth Senate and the Ardent Provisional Assembly. Ardent synthetic military intelligence reports ongoing chaos and internal conflicts within the Zealot fleet's forces. They are now having considerable difficulty conscripting new fighters to their side. Reports of mutiny and rebellion within their ranks have emboldened resistance fighters across the Rim Worlds who refuse to aid in the Zealot cause."

"I suppose that's at least one bit of good news." I said. "Ardent weapon status?"

"No change." Angelica said. "The weapon continues to condition the star in preparation to fire. It will reach full power in one hundred and sixty-two hours."

"Keep that clock up Angelica and I want to look at this weapon with my own eyes." I said. "Can you travel while completing repairs?"

"I can, however part of my purpose is to ensure your safety and wellbeing at all costs. Considering the current tensions in the system I advise we wait for repairs to complete and have an armed Ardent escort accompany us."

"At all costs?" I noted. "Was that a directive from Nathan?"

"Summer added the directive into my base code in route to Ardah," Angelica said. "And, before you ask, no, the directive cannot be overridden, not even by you Lucas."

"With your new enhanced hyperdrive we could jump in and jump out. All I would need is an hour." I said.

"I don't advise that." Angelica insisted. "The danger to your safety stems not just from the Zealots. Tribal surveillance drones captured the battle over Jima. It was seen across all Ardent worlds. Your image and my hull design are now well known. Every move we make is closely monitored by the Seekers from hundreds of different tribes. Their surveillance drones are everywhere in Ardent space. I advise we not venture off unaccompanied."

"You are right Angelica." I said. "As stark as the political, religious, and ideological differences may be between Ardah and their outer rim colonies, we are still outsiders."

"I have been monitoring Ardent civilian communications." Angelica said. "Our participation in the attack on the ring station has been seen by some as admirable others as alien interference. Many harbor deep resentments at our role in this conflict. Others believe we merely want to use the Ardent to help save ourselves and our world."

"This is precisely the perception I wanted to avoid." I said. "Perhaps they're right Angelica, we are after all acting out of self-interest in all this. The reality is we need their assistance if we are to destroy that weapon."

"May I ask you a question Lucas?"

"Of course, Angelica."

"Now that the Ardent people know the truth of their history and where they came from, Earth and Ardent humans are in essence one people now are they not?"

"We share a common ancestry, but to say we are one people. I wouldn't go that far Angelica. The Ardent are vastly different from us culturally and otherwise. I learned long ago that historical facts, public sentiment, and reality are often vastly different things.

"Nathan taught me that it is often easier to move mountains than it is to change a human heart." Angelica said.

"True," I said. "I suspect it will take years, possibly decades for our peoples to truly understand or fully trust one another."

> "The Ardent believe that trust, even among allies must be earned."
> Angelica said.

"Indeed, it does," I said. "Let's hope our efforts here work to move us closer toward that end."

Nir-RoDan called for a meeting of all ship captains and commanders to review after-action battle reports, a time-honored Ardent military practice. I grabbed my staff and Ardent Dagger and headed to the gathering. Tan-Mara and Elim-Merrick arrived and were in attendance along with representatives of the Ardent Provisional Assembly. When I arrived, I was escorted to the domed pavilion overlooking Ardah below and took a reserved place in the front row as Nir-RoDan addressed the gathering.

"Greetings to all tribes, castes, and clans. Provisional Assembly representatives, Earth Senate members, honored advisors, and guests. As you know, ten hours ago, we engaged Zealot forces at Jima in the largest military conflict since the Rim War. We have all seen the reports, although we were victorious in this battle our losses were far greater than predicted. Such is often the reality of war. I ask all those in attendance to join me in a moment of silent flame for the fallen."

The gathering grew silent as all bowed their heads in remembrance of those who fell in battle. An Ardent female and decorated commander glanced at me with scorn in her eyes from across the room. I glanced at the floor wondering what blood was on my hands this time. Had I been responsible for the death of her brother, or her sister, her son, or her tribesman? According to the archive, her name was Grand Matriarch Bre-Kylah, leader of the powerful Void Walker tribe. She came from a long line of Warriors. The house of Bre stemmed from ancient Ardent nobility. Although no longer officially recognized as such, her house and her family were immensely powerful in Ardent society. Half of the Ardent fleet was provided by her tribe alone. Everyone in the gathering knew of her and how critical her participation was to the revolution. After a moment of silence, Bre-Kylah stood to address the gathering. Her armor was well worn, it looked like blackened pewter; she carried twin long daggers, a shape change sword, and a pistol attached to a magnetic mounting system attached to her thighs. This was a woman of royal lineage, but she was also a seasoned warrior. Her demeanor was calm, but her eyes were fierce.

"With all due respect, why is he here?" she asked. "The alien-human?"

> "I am here to fight alongside the Ardent." I said. "To defend Ardah and to protect Earth."

"Hmmm, Yes." Kylah said. "I saw you at the battle of Jima, you, and that ship of yours from Earth. What assurances do we have that you and others of your kind will not one day turn to make war against the Ardent?"

"Neither the people of Earth nor I have any quarrel with the Ardent people." I said. "On the contrary, we seek to reconnect with the Ardent."

"No quarrel? Really?" Kylah said. "You defeated thousands of Zealots at Jima and destroyed three of their carriers. I shudder to think about what you are capable of in an actual quarrel."

"It was a joint effort," I said. "Thankfully, I had strong Ardent allies at my side."

"Indeed, you did, and you fought well." Kylah said. "It has come to our attention that you have even larger and more powerful ships at your command. Is this not true?"

"They are not under my direct command but yes." I said. "We have other ships, but Earth has no military. We are in the process of rebuilding our society."

"Yes, my Seekers keep me well informed," Kylah said. "I am fully aware of your people's situation. My question is why are they not here now? Why do they not join us in battle?"

Nir-RoDan stood to address the gathering as he approached. "We are honored by the presence of Bre-Kylah. I served with your mother during the Rim War. She was a skilled warrior and tactician, a true treasure to her caste."

Kylah smiled warmly. "Mother often spoke fondly of your many skills and talents as well General."

Nir-RoDan paused, momentarily caught off guard by her tone, which hinted at more than mere camaraderie. "Yes, well," he stammered, regaining his composure. "While we all share a certain fascination with our new friends from Earth, it is essential that we focus on the task ahead. Wouldn't you agree, honorable Grand Matriarch?"

All eyes turned to Bre-Kylah, who was known for her diplomatic acumen. Her expression shifted from a stone-cold stare to a pleasant acknowledgment of Nir-RoDan's point, out of respect for him.

"Indeed, it does, General, "Kylah said as she smiled and sat with a respectful tilt of her head. The gathering turned their attention forward as Nir-RoDan continued.

"We are entering a dangerous phase to restore order and peace to our worlds." Nir-RoDan said. "Reports indicate Zealot ships that managed to jump away during the battle at Jima are now out for blood. They are in route to the moon of Orna where they intend to regroup. Old territory, which many of us know all too well. Orbital ice and debris make navigation in this system treacherous. It is part of the reason the Vinn used it as a base of operations decades ago. Be mindful of the ice field on approach. It is here where we will stage our ambush. Our friends from Earth have provided us with technocraft that will provide a strategic surprise. Our opportunity to strike at the Zealots once more presents itself here."

Chapter 33 Ambush at Orna

Our explosive ordinance was in place, Ardent fast attack cruisers were ready, poised to strike at a moment's notice concealed within pocket dimensions enveloping each vessel. We waited, holding positions within the moon's ice rings. Our fleet was invisible to immediate detection so long as we did not move back into normal space or disturb the surrounding boulders of rock and ice. Here we waited for inbound Zealot ships to drop back into normal space before heading to the next hyperspace beacon in route to Ardah. The wait before a battle always put me on edge. This ambush felt the same way, during the Gray War, I would get this feeling when we entered a drop zone. On approach you knew no matter how routine the mission it all could go sideways at any moment. The enemy was out there, watching and waiting to ambush your squad with snipers, traps, and mind-driven dogs. We hated the GCR for their tactics back then, yet today, I find myself using the same ambush tactics that I once despised in an enemy. It seems like everything eventually comes full circle in this life.

"Incoming Zealot hyperspace signature." Angelica said. "Five seconds."

As the enemy probe emerged from hyperspace, it split into three sections and began scanning the sector. Once complete, the probes recombined and sent an all-clear signal back to the inbound Zealot ships. Within seconds of transmission ten Zealot ships emerged from hyperspace. Their presence automatically detonated our ordinance in rapid succession, destroying their escort ships as they emerged into normal space. Seven Zealot battle cruisers managed to evade the trap, breaking formation they headed across the ice rings just as the order came from Nir-RoDan.

"All ships attack! Now!"

The Angelica, Sparrow, and Scorpion emerged from concealment and gave chase. We fired on the enemy with the full force of our combined weapons arrays. Suddenly a Zealot destroyer jumped into the battle space behind our position and fired on our ships only to be sliced apart seconds later by the Liberator's devastating long-range weapons.

"Angelica, prepare to initiate a short distance conventional hyperspace jump to the following coordinates on my command and relay these positions to the fleet."

"Ready on your command."

"Jump!"

The short distance hyperspace jump was a Zealot tactic we learned from the battle of Jima. With the refinements made to her conventional hyperdrive, Angelica could now replicate this maneuver and jumped from a pursuit position directly ahead into the oncoming path of the fleeing Zealot gunships. The Zealots changed direction to avoid a collision and instead collided into the ice field severely damaging their shields sending Olympus Mons-sized boulders of ice and stone tumbling in all directions. Tan-Mara and the Sparrow broke formation in pursuit of the Zealot heavy gunship and their escort craft as they headed back toward the Liberator and the rest of the Ardent rebel fleet.

> "Bring us about!" I commanded. "Target enemy weapons and propulsion systems, fire!"

Our antimatter beams took out the Zealot gunships weapons, gravitics and hyperdrive. Their ships drifted between the chunks of rock and ice. We approached cautiously maintaining a weapons lock on the vessel.

"I want to talk to the commanders of those ships." I said.

"Ship to ship communications are open." Angelica said.

"This is Lucas Wake of the Earth ship Angelica. We do not wish to destroy your vessels, but you must stand down. Surrender now and you will not be harmed. What are your words?"

> "They are targeting us." Angelica said.
> "With what?" I asked. "Their weapons systems are down."

"They are dumping their drive cores!" Angelica said. "Going evasive, shields are at maximum!"

"All ships, target those cores and fire now!"

The Angelica along with our Ardent escort ships fired on the drive cores as they emerged resulting in a massive explosion. Rock and ice material from Orna's rings were blown outward by the force of the explosion spreading across the ice field that battered against our forward shields. When the flashover cleared, the Zealot's, vessels were gone.

"The Zealot ships have been destroyed." Angelica said.

"For God's sake why couldn't they just surrender?" I asked. "Survivors?"

"Sorry Lucas, all matter in the immediate blast range was annihilated, no survivors."

"Fleet status?" I asked.

"Three Zealot battle cruisers have been destroyed," Angelica said. "Two others have surrendered. Bre-Kylah's battlecruiser has engaged the Zealot heavy cruiser and is taking critical damage."

"Get us into that fight Angelica!" I said as we altered our heading for the jump.

"Short distance jump in five seconds," Angelica said. "Four, three, two, one."

In an instant we were hurled into the middle of the battle dropping us on an intercept course with Bre-Kylah's battlecruiser that now filled the ring display.

"Zealot gunship is on a collision course with the Grand Matriarch's cruiser!" Angelica said. "They are targeting the bridge! Weapons use at this range is not advised."

"Understood adjust our heading Angelica, ram the Zealot gunship!"

"Ramming intercept course is set!" Angelica said. "Power transferred to forward and lateral shields. Inertial compensation is now at fifty percent so hang on to something!"

The Angelica rammed the Zealot ship pushing her gravitic drive to maximum as we forced the larger enemy ship out of the path of the Grand Matriarch's bridge. The hull of the old Zealot gunship cracked open on impact and began leaking atmosphere and hyperdrive coolant.

"Bre-Kylah's ship is clear, Lucas, there is a power build-up in their lateral weapons array. They are targeting us."

"Back us off and finish them, Angelica!" I said.

Angelica lanced the Zealot ship's cracked hull with a thin antimatter beam splitting their vessel wide open. The gunship's two halves tumbled end over end as it vented atmosphere and crew into space. Within seconds, it exploded, sending wreckage colliding against our shields.

"Angelica, mark this location for the Ardent drones to recover any survivors."

"Lucas, incoming ship to ship message from Bre-Kylah."

"We have taken minimal damage thanks to you." Kylah said. "Falling back to regroup with the fleet. That was very impressive Earth human, very impressive indeed."

Kylah took a moment as if she were going to say something more, but then her image vanished without saying another word as her ship jumped away.

"Okay, what was that about?" I asked.

"I believe that was her way of saying thank you Lucas."

For nearly five hours, Zealot ships tried to break our position each time they were met with the overwhelming force of our fleet. We attacked their incoming vessels each time they dropped out of hyperspace for their next jump. Victory was within our reach, then everything changed. Warning alarms sounded; something new was heading our way emerging from the depths of hyperspace.

"Incoming vessels!" Angelica said. "Multiple hyperspace signatures! Something big!"

Just when we thought the battle was ending, the Zealots answered our ambush with an overwhelming assault of their own. Ten Zealot heavy battle cruisers emerged from hyperspace and fired on our fleet. Thousands of antimatter beams passed between the Ardent and Zealot forces and within minutes we lost ten gunships and over twenty fast attack cruisers leaving our remaining battlecruisers vulnerable. Space was consumed in chaos as additional Zealot gunships jumped in from hyperspace overwhelming our defenses. For the Zealots this was their revenge for the slaughter at the battle of Jima. It was as if they sent all their remaining forced to break our hold on Orna. Angelica took two direct hits from a Zealot cruiser's primary weapon that severely weakened our defenses.

"Shields down to twenty percent, reactors two and three are offline, the Ardent fleet has been ordered to fall back and regroup."

"Keep firing Angelica!" I said. "We can buy the others time, how soon to repair?"

"Nine minutes!" Angelica said. "Lucas we cannot take another hit like that and fight with two reactors down! We must fall back!"

"Acknowledged," I said. "Fall back and set course to regroup with the fleet!"

As we turned, to regroup I was struck by the sight of Nir-RoDan's battle cruiser the Liberator burning as it fought off a swarm of thousands of enemy attack drones and fighters. In the distance, Zealot ships hammered away at Tan-Mara aboard the Sparrow and Elim-Merrick aboard the Scorpion. Our forces were scattered across the system but were holding their own under heavy enemy assault.

"Situation report?"

"Not good," Angelica said. "The Sparrow and the Scorpion are severely damaged but still in the fight. Nir-RoDan aboard the Liberator has launched his remaining combat drones, but the Liberator's support ships have been destroyed. The Scorpion is taking critical damage their lateral shields are almost gone."

"We must get back in that fight. Repair time?"

"Only one minute has elapsed Lucas. Eight minutes for repair completion."

"This could all be over in eight minutes. Angelica, can you fold transport antimatter ordinance somewhere inside the core of one of those Zealot ships?"

"Not with their shields at full strength with ours down to twenty percent and not accurately at this distance."

"It doesn't matter. We are going to improvise. Angelica scan the debris field and start gathering mass that matches our geometric configuration."

"I understand where you are going," Angelica said. "Interesting idea, scanning and collecting now."

"Set a course for the lead Zealot heavy cruiser," I said. "Prepare ordinance for transport and randomize our rotational axis, set our approach vector to match that of the surrounding debris field. Kill gravitics and active sensors, I want us to look just like tumbling space junk. Send an assault request to the fleet to concentrate their fire on this area just below their engineering deck. We only need to drop the Zealot shields for one point three seconds."

Angelica scanned and quantum locked parts of wreckage debris from destroyed ships and attack drones to form a secondary outer skin around the Angelica. The Ardent vessels that could still fight concentrated their weapons fire on the lead Zealot heavy cruiser to take down their shields for us to transport our ordinance.

"Six minutes to full repair completion." Angelica said. "Reactor three is back online at half power building to full."

"That's all we need." I said. "What's the max yield on our refined ordinance?"

"Ten exatons per device." Angelica said.

"All right, set maximum explosive yield and prepare an ordinance for fold transport." I ordered. "Notify our ships in the area to jump clear once the enemy ships shields are down."

"Warning three Zealot heavy battle cruisers are converging for a final assault on the Liberator. It's now or never Lucas! Ordnance ready!"

"Get us close Angelica, as soon as their shields are down, deploy ordnance to the lead Zealot battle cruiser, put it right in the core."

"Acknowledged! Zealot battlecruisers shields are taking damage, down to twenty-five percent, eighteen percent, partial shield collapse is imminent, their shields are down!"

"Ordinance is away!" Angelica said. "Our shields are at thirty percent!"

Within seconds of releasing our explosive payload a small Zealot gunship jumped in off our port side and fired obliterating a section of our makeshift shield.

> "Target that Zealot gunship. Fire all weapons and release the debris shield! Get us clear!

"Acknowledged!

Angelica fired on the Zealot gunship destroying it instantly. As we moved away, we were caught by a powerful gravity lock emanating from the lead Zealot heavy battle cruiser.

"Angelica, can we break free from this?"

"No, we are in their gravity lock," Angelica said. "They are pulling us in."

"They are trying to capture us." I said. "Can we jump away?"

"Not without tearing me apart in the process." Angelica said.

"Hyperspace window?" I asked.

"It takes all three reactors to generate a window." Angelica said. "We have one and a half. The Liberator is under heavy fire and has called for aid. The Scorpion is missing, and the Sparrow has sustained critical damage, Tan-Mara is no longer responding to hails her communications are offline. I have modeled all possible scenarios in this battle, and the numbers are not working in our favor."

"Numbers alone are not our fate Angelica! Prepare to detonate the ordinance on my command!"

"We are well within the destructive blast range." Angelica said. "Lucas this order violates my directive to protect you at all costs. I cannot comply."

"If we don't, the Zealots will win, they will use this fleet to blockade the Ardent weapon and if that happens, we lose everything including any chance of saving Earth! Override the order and detonate now Angelica! Angelica respond?"

She was offline, and no longer responded to any of my orders. Most disturbing was the fact that I could no longer feel Angelica's presence on the ship. I was on my own; I left the command ring, grabbed my staff, a sphere drone along with an Ardent pistol and Rifle setting both to lethal mode changing the weapons edge lighting from green to red. I focused my mind past the storm of tumbling debris toward the Zealot heavy cruiser as it pulled us in. I opened a fold portal and could see the Zealot heavy cruiser on the other side as I blindly leaped in. I missed folding to the interior of the Zealot heavy cruiser. I was now tumbling through space between the Angelica and the Zealot ship. I unfolded the bike as it auto-stabilized I headed toward the Zealot heavy cruiser on full throttle avoiding battle wreckage along the way when I received an incoming message from Bre-Kylah.

"What in the name of the Reclaimer do you think you are doing Earth human?" Kylah asked.

"I have a quarrel with the commander of that Zealot ship." I replied.

"You are truly mad Lucas Wake and brave. For this you will be remembered for all time in the annals of Ardent history."

"Thanks," I said. "But I will try to skip the becoming history part if I can."

Without Angelica, the only way to end this was to set the ordinance to detonate by a timer and try to get outside the blast zone in time. When I arrived, I landed on the scorched hull of the Zealot ship just a few decks above engineering. I collapsed the bike, placing the staff on my back and opened another fold portal to the Zealot heavy cruiser's engineering section. Once inside, I found the ship to be in complete chaos. There was a mad frenzy underway to understand how explosive ordnance had gotten onboard their ship. I released a sphere to check out the area around the weapon. The Zealot guards spotted my drone and fired on it.

"Intruder, we have an intruder!"

I ordered the drone to speed down the corridor away from engineering. I approached the weapon and started the manual arming sequence. It was now set for detonation in twelve minutes. I completed the manual arming sequence just as I was spotted by a Zealot security patrol.

"It's the Alien!" A guard shouted. "Destroy it!"

A group of Zealot guards took aim and fired striking me in the thigh and shoulder. I returned fire taking down two of the five. The suit was damaged but already undergoing the process of self-repair. I opened a fold portal beneath me as I dropped past several decks to the exterior of the enemy ship. Once back in space, I unfolded the bike and headed down the hull back toward the Angelica, still being pulled in by the gravity lock as the Zealots attempted to capture her. I opened a fold to the command deck, but she was offline and did not respond to my commands. I opened a communication link to the fleet advising them to move clear of the Zealot ship as the Angelica lit up and came back online.

"Lucas? What is your status?"

"I'm here. What the hell happened to you Angelica?"

"Contradictory directives caused an internal logical error." Angelica said. "It has been resolved. You placed me in a difficult position Lucas."

"I know, I am sorry; the ordinance is now on a timer; can you get us free?"

"No, their gravitic lock is too powerful." Angelica said.

"Fleet status?"

"Most of our fast attack cruisers have been destroyed. Nir-RoDan and Bre-Kylah's battlecruisers are heavily damaged but advancing for a final push against remaining Zealot forces. Tan-Mara and the Sparrow were last seen venting atmosphere in a decaying orbit on the far side of Orna. It has been confirmed that Elim-Merrick's ship the Scorpion has been destroyed, there were no survivors. Lucas, the Zealots are opening their cargo bay; it looks like this is it."

"Power up the rear weapons arrays." I said. "Let's see if we can punch a few holes in their ship for good measure, random pattern, fire at will."

Angelica unleashed a volley of antimatter beams in all directions that shredded their cargo bay interior, destroying multiple docked ships and adjacent decks, setting off several chain reaction interior explosions. The sheer size of the Zealot ship dwarfed our ability to damage it.

"We managed to make a mess in there." Angelica said. "But they are still pulling us in. Wait, incoming hyperspace signature, multiple ships!"

A massive hyperspace window opened. It was the Providence, the Foresight, the Karma, and twelve Construct Magnetar class heavy cruisers. A bulk space communication came across the Ardent network. It was the commander of the Providence.

"This is commander Summer Wake of the Earth ship Providence to all Zealot fleet forces. Cease your hostilities immediately and surrender or you will be fired upon and destroyed."

"Angelica, can you please halt that detonation timer?" I asked.

"Already on it" she replied.

Another voice came across the communications network. For the first time it was the Zealot fleet commander. His distorted image appeared within the display ring an artifact of their old Rim War era ships.

"This is commander Xan-Aiden, we have your Earth ship in our grasp; your fleet is wounded and burning. The holy Reclaimer is with us. Our victory is inevitable. You are an abomination of nature fit only to be cleansed! You dare command us to surrender to you? It is you, alien creature, that shall yield to us!"

"Then let me put it another way." Summer said. "All ships fire!"

All fifteen Earth ships fired on the Zealot heavy cruiser pummeling its primary shields. The combined assault weakened the gravitic lock, releasing the Angelica from its grip.

"Gravitic lock is down!"

"Get us out of here Angelica!"

As the Angelica accelerated away from the Zealot ship, it raised its secondary shields once again, trapping us inside. The Earth fleet continued their attack as we struggled to break free.

"Angelica, can you get us out?"

"Working on multiple options now." Angelica said. "I have identified their secondary lateral shield emitters."

"Would you be so kind as to destroy those please?" I asked.

"Firing!"

Angelica used her weapons array to burn a hole through twenty unshielded decks of the Zealot ship and destroyed the Zealot lateral shield array, exposing its bare hull to the full onslaught of weapons fire from the Ardent fleet.

"Enemy shields are down," Angelica reported. "Gravitic lock is off. We're free, Lucas! Maneuvering to a minimum safe distance! Please be advised ordnance detonation control has been passed to the lead Earth command ship."

"Summer's voice and image came over the comms link, "Thank you Angelica, Detonate!"

A silent circle of ever-expanding light flanked by a bright spike of energy bloomed before us. The hulls of all the ships around the Zealot heavy cruiser appeared semi-transparent in the intense annihilating light of a massive antimatter reaction. For a few seconds nothing could be seen. At such energy levels nothing survives, the massive explosion rendered all ten of the Zealot heavy cruisers into non-existence. When the light dimmed, the battle space was utterly devoid of ice and wreckage. Not even the debris and wreckage around the vessels remained. The explosion consumed everything leaving behind a gaping hole of nothingness in the middle of the ice ring. The Angelica maneuvered inside the Providence cargo bay alongside six other Explorer class ships identical to Angelica's original design. As we landed, the other six ships synchronized, altering their design and configuration to match Angelica. Summer seemed relieved to see me as I disembarked.

"Well," Summer said. "That was a close one."

"Thanks for bringing the fleet." I said, "Any update on Tan-Mara's status?"

"Ardent rescue drones recovered her and her crew." Summer said.

"Her condition?" I asked.

"Well, physically, she'll pull through." Summer said.

"What about Merrick and the crew of the Scorpion?"

I looked to Summer for more, an expression, or a semblance of hope, perhaps some better news, but she just looked at me and shook her head. The ambush at Orna had ended, but the war for humanity's survival was far from over.

Chapter 34 Tears in Orna's Orbit

Intelligence reports reflected a somber mood growing among the Zealot ranks across all thirty Ardent worlds after their defeats at Jima and Orna. Despite our best-efforts to preserve lives, thousands of Ardent had died on both sides of the conflict. There would surely be thousands more to follow before this fight was done, and that fact weighed heavily on my soul. The fleet was ordered to remain in orbit around Orna. Ship commanders used the time to conduct repairs, search for survivors and tend to the dead. There were no victory celebrations, and an eerie silence pervaded the Providence. Summer and I headed up to the command deck for an after action briefing with the Earth Senate.

"Any idea why the fleet is still holding position over Orna?" I asked. "We should have jumped out of here hours ago to prepare for the next phase."

"Lucas, you should know a lot has changed since we left Earth. In fact, much has changed just in the past few hours quite honestly."

"How so?" I asked.

"Well, for starters," Summer said. "I could not convince everyone to join in the evacuation effort."

"What? Summer, what are you talking about?"

"Some chose to stay behind." She said.

"How many?"

"Nearly two-hundred thousand."

"You are telling me they chose certain death over a chance to survive?"

"Well, that's not how they see it." Summer said. "There is more, this briefing is going to be well, bad."

"How bad?" I asked.

"The Senate has serious questions about our role in the Ardent Civil war." Summer said. "More importantly, there is some skepticism about the viability of our plan to destroy the weapon. So, you need to be prepared for what's coming in this meeting Lucas."

"At this point." I said. "I think I am prepared for just about anything."

"Are you ready?"

"Always" I smiled.

We turned and walked past a door; within seconds, we were on the Providence command deck. There was no need to traverse the ship's full twelve-mile length. A series of folded space corridors integrated into its design allowed us to cross vast distances in mere moments. Like Angelica, the Providence was a self-aware, self-sufficient, living machine capable of improving its own design. A small crew of thirty volunteers served aboard the ship. As we entered the command deck, everyone rose to their feet, as if Summer and I were owed some sort of reverence. I politely gestured for them to sit back down. The Providence command deck resembled Angelica's but was much larger. With its massive ring display provided a near three-hundred-and-sixty-degree projection of the surrounding space. The only opaque surfaces were parts of the deck, and the catwalk. I entered the elevated conference room just above the command deck. Waiting there was Nathan, along with representatives from the Earth Senate, and their advisors, many of whom I had crossed paths with before back on Earth. Among them were Senator Langston Yang of the Chimera, whom I had worked with back on Earth, and a new face, Senator Eliana Vinograd of the Purist faction and a former military commander. I addressed the gathering.

"Thank you all for coming," I began, looking over the room. "It's been a long time, and I see both new faces and some familiar ones. Your support means everything to us. I will be straight with you. This situation here is complex, and things haven't exactly gone as planned."

"You are too modest," Yang said, "Two decisive victories against the Zealots in support of our new Ardent allies. A mutually beneficial trade and cultural exchange agreement. Advanced Ardent technologies that will aid in the restoration of our civilization and our world. Access to the Progenitor Legacy archive, priceless knowledge that will benefit humanity for centuries to come. Remarkable achievements, all thanks to the fine work you and your team are doing here."

"Yes well, they were all joint efforts." I said. "I can assure you of that."

"Yet despite all these remarkable achievements." Vinograd said. "Our world remains under threat by a weapon of immeasurable power. Mr. Wake, what precisely have you and your team done about that problem?"

"We have a plan to shut down the weapon." I said gesturing toward Summer and Nathan. "Which we outlined in our report to the Senate."

"Yes," Vinograd said. "We have all been thoroughly briefed on this plan, but what actions have you taken to protect Earth since coming here? Your journey to Ardent space was intended to be a peaceful diplomatic mission and yet somehow, it transformed into you and your team helping to overthrow the very governing body of a world that the Earth was supposed to engage with to stave off our destruction in the first place!"

"That Senator," I said. "Is a long story."

"With all due respect Mr. Wake." Vinograd said. "I think it's a very short and simple story. You are a man that spent years on Earth alone, believing you were the only human being alive free to do whatever you wanted. Answering to no one and no authority but yourself. As I understand it, your life, it seems has been shaped by impulsivity and needless risk-taking. In your era, you volunteered to become a soldier did you not?"

"At the time a nihilistic paramilitary cult was trying to take over the world." I said. "So yes like many, I volunteered to fight."

"As a Construct you continued questionable re-genesis research" Vinograd said. "Despite the Collective's decision to abandon it. You had your own memory wiped countless times in a dangerous experiment to overcome the limitations of direct consciousness transfer. You then chose to sensory pair your experiences to the Construct Collective, fundamentally altering the Construct base code. Did you even think about the consequences? Or consider the long-term ramifications of that choice for the rest of us?

"Senator, everything I have done and every action I have taken has been for the benefit and survival of our species. For Earth!"

"I will not deny, you have achieved much." Vinograd said. "However, the fact is you are not alone anymore. You don't get to make decisions affecting billions of lives in a vacuum. That time Mr. Wake is over."

"So, what are you saying?" I asked.

"The Earth Senate, and the Ardent Provisional Assembly agree that the weapon's existence poses an existential threat to both our peoples." Nathan said, "They want us to take a more direct approach to shut it down, destroy it if possible."

"The fact is the Ardent have come to the realization that they have created something they can no longer control." Vinograd said. "As a potent symbol of Priest caste power, they now want it destroyed as much as we do. Toward that end our combined forces for this mission will be designated as the Alliance Fleet. Now, the Providence and the rest of the Earth fleet carry far more powerful antimatter weapons than those you used at Orna. We intend to use these weapons to neutralize the threat once and for all."

"We already explored those options," I said. "Summer ran thousands of simulations on that approach weeks ago. The weapons automated defense systems will repel any direct conventional attack. If we can delay the firing sequence, we can destroy the weapons critical systems and take it apart piece by piece. If you attempt a standard conventional attack, the weapons defensive drone swarms will overwhelm any attacking vessel. This weapon is essentially re-engineered Progenitor technology about which we know little except that it is orders of magnitude more advanced than anything the Ardent or Earth has ever encountered. Trying to bombard it head on is simply not going to work."

"I have already explained this Lucas, they know." Summer insisted, "They have all the facts and all the data. This mission has already been authorized by the Ardent Provisional Assembly and the Earth Senate. The Ardent will lead the effort, and Earth will assist."

"I'm sorry but, when precisely was all this decided?" I asked.

"The Zealots," Nathan said. "Opened back-channel diplomatic communications with the Ardent Provisional Assembly. They have called for an immediate cease-fire and the Ardent have accepted their request."

"Summer, did you know about this?" I asked.

"Apparently," Summer said. "Talks with Zealot fifth columnists have been ongoing since the conclusion of the battle at Jima."

"Have the Zealots you've been negotiating with shared any intel on how to shut the weapon down?" I asked. "I would assume that such information would be part of any cease-fire agreement."

"According to intel sources, the weapon is set," Vinograd said. "It cannot be shut down or disabled, only destroyed. The coordinated attack on the ring station at Jima was unexpected and demoralizing. For many that defeat broke their faith in the Zealot cause."

"Conscripts to the Zealot cause began to rebel against the Priests across all thirty Ardent worlds." Nathan said. "As of this moment, the Ardent Civil War is effectively over."

After the meeting, I returned to the cargo bay and boarded the Angelica, heading straight to my quarters for a few hours of rest. The clock showed we had just thirty-five hours left before the weapon reached full power. I could have stayed in accommodations aboard the Providence, but Angelica was my ship. It's where I felt most at home since leaving Earth. The war was over; the Zealots were defeated, and Ardah was spared the Priests' vengeance. The fate of Earth, however, remained uncertain.

"Angelica, play something for me."

"What would you like to hear?"

"One of the old century classics," I said. "You choose this time."

"Now playing "Something In The Way."

I needed a moment. My mind was a whirlwind of memories and emotions. The last battle was brutal, the cost unimaginable. My thoughts were torn between concern for my people on Earth and the tragic loss of life paid by the Ardent.

"Do you think it was worth it? I asked. "All this death and destruction?"

"It's not for me to judge the worth of human actions. Nathan taught me that war changes everything, people, places, and most importantly, the course of history."

"Do you remember when we started this journey?" I asked, a faint smile playing on my lips. "I was so full of hope, so confident that we could make a difference and save our world."

"I remember." Angelica said. "You dared to believe in a better future for humanity, and a connection with the Ardent people. Despite everything, I believe you still do."

"Has there been any response to my requests to speak with Tan-Mara?"

"I am afraid not." Angelica said. "She has been in mourning since the death of Elim-Merrick. She hasn't accepted communications from anyone but her daughter. In keeping with Ardent tradition, her next appearance will be at his end-of-life ceremony."

"The Return to Light ritual," I said.

"Correct, after which she will be officially declared Chieftess and Grand Matriarch of the Forgotten Clan."

"Although I barely knew him," I said. "Elim-Merrick was a good man, a generous and brave soul. I will miss him."

"Be advised, Summer is now aboard." Angelica said.

I sat up on the edge of the bed as Summer entered. She paused at the door, her eyes locking onto mine.

"I thought I might find you here," Summer said.

"I feel more at ease in my own quarters."

"There will be a ceremony for Merrick tonight aboard Nir-RoDan's ship. Will you attend?"

"Of course I will. Summer, just what the hell happened out there?"

Summer walked over and sat beside me. "According to the combat log, Elim-Merrick maneuvered his ship to shield Tan-Mara's vessel from enemy fire. With their shields down, death was swift. His actions saved Tan-Mara and her entire crew."

"I wish there was more we could have done," I said.

"So do I, but I'm relieved this war is over. At least for now."

"Agreed," I said. "So then why do I feel like crap?"

"Because you tend to blame yourself for things outside of your control. We were the catalyst, Lucas, not the cause of the Ardent revolution. It would have happened with or without our presence here. War as you well know is organized chaos, yet you hold yourself responsible for the deaths of those Zealots at Jima and Orna, despite all your efforts to minimize casualties."

"Why do you think that is?" I asked.

"Honestly," Summer said. "I don't think you've ever really dealt with or processed what you experienced during the Gray War back on Earth. Whatever you saw or did, it still haunts you even now."

"What? I put all that behind me years ago. That has nothing to do with this."

"I think it does. Billions perished in that conflict, yet you never talk about the war."

"What is there to talk about?" I asked. "That was centuries ago."

"No, that's not what I mean," Summer said, taking my hands in hers. "You never talked about it in our old life either. I don't think you put it behind you at all. I think you just buried it. I think you've been burying loss and grief for years. You carry your pain around with you, channeling all your energy into a single thing, and then you cling to that thing relentlessly, never letting go. What happened to you?"

"Back during the Gray War, our unit would come across the charred remains of those the enemy had slain. Whole families captured, chained to one another, and set ablaze. The GCR were merciless. For years after I returned, I was haunted by nightmares of dead cities, burned bodies, dogs, fire, and ashes. Sometimes, mixed in with the ashes, we'd find these small bones. I told myself they were dogs, but deep down, I knew they were the remains of children. As a soldier, I struggled to understand how their parents failed to foresee the danger the marches, the bombings. I vowed that if I ever had a family, I'd do anything to protect them, no matter the cost. Back then, I didn't understand that some things in life are beyond our control. I learned that lesson all too well the night we lost our baby girl. I never accepted it, I couldn't, I refused. Summer, the reason I wanted to finish that bed, the reason I needed to finish it, was because I wanted it to serve as a memorial to our daughter's life. I never intended to use the time I put into it to ignore you or shut you out. For me, it was just my way of saying goodbye."

"Tell me something, Lucas. If I hadn't burned all your beautiful work that night, what would you have done with it? What were your plans for the bed once it was finished?"

"I was going to bury it," I said, only now realizing the irony. "That was my plan, to just bury it. Do you ever wish you hadn't burned it?"

"Honestly, I regret it every day."

Chapter 35 In Remembrance of the Fallen

That night, the Liberator's cargo bay was transformed for a memorial ceremony. The nature of warfare is such that often there are no remains to bury. All there is to be laid to rest are the possessions of those fallen in battle. Ancient Ardent tradition required that something be returned to the light of the Reclaimer from which they believe all life came. In more civil times, a Priest would preside over the dead's return to the light, but these were not civil times. War had scarred so many in this conflict. Yet even in chaotic times we must take a moment to remember those that are no longer with us. To honor their lives and mourn their deaths. Tan-Mara now donned in black robes stood and approached the circle to present her final words in remembrance of Elim-Merrick.

"When I first met Merrick, he was not at all what I expected." Tan-Mara said. "Since childhood I had been taught that the Forgotten Clan were nothing more than disobedient, faithless, outcasts who live out their lives without a tribe, caste, or rank. I could never have been more wrong. I was sent to their desert world under Duty Mark to investigate reports of illegal scavenging. I was fully prepared for a conflict with him and his people. Though, I soon discovered that like many Ardent I had been misled by rumors, falsehoods, and misrepresentations about who the Forgotten Clan really were. It was Merrick that showed me that they had charted their own path in life despite their banishment. He showed me that his people were survivors, strong, honorable, and worthy. Since my parents' death, I spent years building an impenetrable fortress around my heart to ensure that I would never again feel pain or loss. I told myself that I would never succumb to death; instead, I would become a wielder of it. So, I trained, became a Seeker, and learned to fight. When I was with Merrick, my fortress was meaningless. His words, his wisdom, and his love dismantled all my ramparts. In time, every stone and strong wall dissolved and crumbled into dust at my feet. With him, my heart was laid bare, and I came to know love for the first time in my life. He was my most trusted friend, my ally in battle, my partner in life, my husband, and protector. I will miss you Merrick, my love. So long as the stars of the outer dark burn, you will never be forgotten."

Tan-Mara stepped out of the circle as the empty wrapped ceremonial armor of Elim-Merrick, along with his cracked broad ax was levitated on a standing wave of gravitic energy along with thousands of others. I watched as red, and gold wrapped remains streamed single file from the cargo bays of hundreds of Ardent fleet ships. Remains of the fallen Ardent were launched into the chromosphere of the systems white dwarf star returning them to the light. After the memorial, Summer and I sat together in her quarters aboard the Providence overlooking the horizon of Orna as she laid in my arms.

"The Void Walkers have invited you to join their tribe." Summer said. "A rare honor for an outsider."

"Why would they do that?" I asked.

"Well," Summer said. "You did save their Matriarch's life in battle, and you exited your ship to make war on the enemy. Both of which according to the Ardent demonstrate bravery in combat, you should consider their offer. Granted, it's a symbolic gesture, but such a relationship could strengthen our alliance with the Ardent."

"With the Ardent or with Bre-Kylah?" I asked.

"The Void Walkers under her command constitute over half this fleet." Summer said. "The fight against the Zealots would not have been possible without her, and we will need her continued support if we intend to destroy the weapon to save our world."

"I don't know about you." I said, "But I was under the distinct impression she didn't like me very much."

"On the contrary." Summer said. "According to sources she seems fascinated by you and your story. Our intelligence suggests she sees the current political situation on Ardah as an opportunity for the ancient royal houses to reassert their power and take back authority in the modern era."

"So, her Seekers inform her about us, while we collect intelligence on them. I thought we were allies?" I asked.

"We are allies." Summer said. "Intelligence gathering need not be nefarious Lucas, we seek to understand them, the Ardent seek to better understand us. This is to be expected between allies. How else are we to appeal to one another or negotiate without a nuanced understanding of who the Ardent people are, what they want and what motivates them?"

"This is true," I said. "So, what is the latest intel on our Exo-human cousins?"

"Today the Ardent people desire stability and order in the absence of the Priests." Summer said, "Many long for the days under the old nobility along with the peace and prosperity that came with it."

"Nir-RoDan suggested that the people's vote would be reinstated once the new government was formed, what happened to that plan?"

"That remains a possibility." Summer said, "But, just in case it is not we need to consider what's best for our people and for the interests of Earth. If that means aligning ourselves with the house of Bre, that's something we should at least consider. Besides, you need a win with the Senate right now."

"The interests of Earth." I said. "The cycle of history never ends does it?"

"No, I am afraid not my love." Summer said.

"Senators, symbolic gestures, I truly despise politics, I always have."

"Well then, you are in luck, because this is diplomacy not politics." Summer said, "This arrangement is mutually beneficial. We will gain an opportunity to know more about them and they will gain an opportunity to learn more about us. You're a good man Lucas; you always do the right thing and I have always loved you for that. I know you'll do the right thing here."

"So, what exactly will be required of me?" I asked.

"The ceremony will take place tomorrow evening aboard the Grand matriarch's ship." Summer said. "We can go over all the details in the morning. As a tribesman, you will be expected to appear when called for aid, and you will be expected to fight if necessary."

"Oh, well, that sounds fun." I added.

"Angelica is creating an extensive training program for you." Summer said. "Ardent neural combat conditioning is not viable for Earth humans, so you will be in for several extended physical and virtual training sessions."

"I can't wait" I said regretting the sarcastic tone.

"Senator Vinograd is taking command of the Karma," Summer said. "She will call a gathering of all ship commanders for a briefing on our combined mission to destroy the weapon. For now, we have a few hours before the next mission briefing. I am sure you and I can find a way to fill the time. Did I tell you how much I have missed you over the last few days?"

The next day aboard Bre-Kylah's ship I was joined by Summer, Nathan, Nir-RoDan and Tan-Mara at the ceremony where I was to accept membership into the Void-Walker tribe. It wasn't something I would have otherwise pursued, but I understood why it was needed, especially now. It is an important symbolic gesture to signify the ancient historical connection between Ardent and Earth humans. When I entered the long and narrow ceremony chamber, I was confronted by a line of fully armed Void Walkers forming columns to my left and right, all facing the entrance dressed in full battle armor. Every caste was represented Warriors, Priests, Seekers, Trainers, Historians and Technicians. At the other end of the room stood Bre-Kylah dressed in gold and blue ceremonial armor alongside her tribal council advisors. I made my way past the line of Void Walkers as each one turned to face me. As I passed them, I looked into the faceless glowing eyes of their armored helms. No one uttered a single word, as each turned their heads to track me as I passed them. I reached the throne of the Grand Matriarch. Summer motioned for me to take a knee, so I did. It was then that Bre-Kylah addressed the tribal assembly.

"There was a time when the Ardent people believed that Earth and the beings that occupied it were nothing more than an ancient legend, a myth." Kylah said. "Today, thanks to this one, we now know the truth. During the battle at Orna, Wake used his ship to ram an enemy vessel, pushing it off course from a killing run on my bridge. A bold act which saved my life, and that of my crew. At the height of the battle against the enemy, Wake entered the Outer Dark and made war on those that would have surely destroyed us all. Because of these brave combat actions, it is with great pride that I extend an invitation from our tribe to Lucas Wake of Earth. Do you accept?"

"I accept Grand Matriarch."

"Draw your blade!" She commanded.

I drew the Ardent long dagger gifted to me by Merrick from the small of my back, held it by the blade and presented it to Bre-Kylah. At that moment, the impact of Merrick's loss began to truly sink in. The lighting in the room dimmed until all I could see was the Grand Matriarch gleaming in the light. The dagger floated out of my hands and into Bre-Kylah's as she spoke the ancient words of her tribe.

"Between the light of the stars and the darkness of the great void we walk.

Along the river's edge, we patrol the night. At the gate's mouth, we guard. Upon the bridge, we stand and from the high tower, we watch. We are order against the tide of chaos. We fight for what is just and true. We tread upon those places others dare not. For we are born from stardust, formed of bone, blood, and flesh. We are Void Walkers." A voice from the gathering called out, "Let him be marked!" Two Void Walkers, one male and one female, approached, placing a golden two-piece ceremonial helmet around my head that clicked into place as the two parts became one. For a moment, I could neither see nor hear anything. I was surrounded by darkness. Then, a bright light followed by a cold needle-like sensation traveled across the right side of my face and down my neck. As the light faded, the helmet was removed, and the surrounding room glowed, illuminated by an unseen golden light.

"Now," Kylah said. "Take your blade and Arise Void Walker!"

I looked at the blade as it floated, suspended in a stream of micro gravitic waves. As I took hold of it for the first time, the blade lit up, now energized with a bright orange glow. As I stood to my feet and turned to face the others, I saw the same line of Void Walkers that witnessed me enter the room, but this time, each held their own glowing daggers and, in that moment, I understood its initiatory significance.

"You must now choose a true name." Kylah said. "To be spoken amongst your closest and most trusted tribesmen."

"Then I choose the name Black Spear," I said, "To honor those I once served with in battle."

"So be it. Hēisè-Sabir" Kylah said in the old Yulan dialect.

Each of my new tribesmen raised their daggers above their heads. For centuries, this was a foundational symbol of support and solidarity in the Ardent culture. With their true faces now revealed to me, I realized my face now bore the tribal markings of a Void Walker. A triangular stipple patterned tattoo, extending from the top of my right eyebrow to my hairline. At that moment, I knew that my life would never be the same.

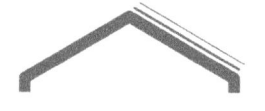

Chapter 36 Operation Eclipse

Tan-Mara was now both Chieftess and Grand Matriarch of the Forgotten Clan. Her coronation ceremony was a bittersweet event. She now donned the traditional red and orange hooded cloak of the Forgotten Clan. In honor of Merrick, she adopted the battle-ax crossed by twin long daggers as her sigil. She was highly respected among the Forgotten Clan, and they could not have asked for a better successor to their honorable fallen chief. Billions on Hafeeta would now look to her leadership in the years to come. The surrounding Space was filled with the combined forces of the Ardent and Earth fleets. Senator Vinograd commanded the Karma with Nathan serving as her first officer. Summer and I remained aboard the Providence.

"Alliance Fleet this is Senator Eliana Vinograd of the Earth ship Karma. You have all been briefed on this mission. It has been designated "Operation Eclipse." Nir-RoDan and I will take the lead in the first pass. We will bombard and overwhelm the weapons defense systems using our combined arsenals. We aim to concentrate our weapons fire on the focusing pedals and other known key systems. Our analysis suggests that these structures in orbit are vital to its operation and function. If we destroy enough of them, we should be able to neutralize the weapon once and for all."

Nathan looked distressed as he stood beside the Senator, his doubts seemed to mirror my own. The silence across the communications network was unnerving as Vinograd laid out the mission's primary objectives. I don't think anyone was at all confident in the new plan. I reached out in my mind to Angelica.

"Angelica, I need a private communication with Nir-RoDan, Nathan, Tan-Mara, and Summer, but I don't want Vinograd or her people monitoring us. The new comms link? Is it ready?"

"Of course," Angelica said. "But please understand it is fully immersive."

"Just let me know when it's ready," I said. "I need to speak to them now."

"It's ready." Angelica said. "Executing environment."

The Providence command deck disappeared, and I found myself standing in an empty white space with Nir-RoDan, Nathan, Tan-Mara, and Summer.

"Well, this is not quite what I was expecting." I said.

"We can speak freely here." Summer said.

"So, what exactly are our bodies doing in the real world?" I asked.

"Nothing, no one will even notice this communication." Summer said, "We designed this place to leverage extended time dilation."

"Yet only a few moments will have passed in the real world, very clever."

Tan-Mara said, "I trust you all have the same doubts about the new plan to destroy the weapon?"

"I don't think Vinograd knows what she is getting us into." Nathan said.

"I agree," Tan-Mara said. "She seems to have adopted a brute force approach. Our combat simulations predict a narrow chance of victory with that strategy."

"Unfortunately, there is not enough intelligence on the weapons defensive capabilities to play out an adequate scenario." Nir-RoDan added, "The Priests made sure of that. Your Senator Vinograd seems almost eager to die, and that gives me concern."

"This is precisely why politicians should never hold command." I said. "This situation unfortunately has become increasingly political; I fear she is making a grave mistake."

"Every simulation I have run suggests this type of attack is destined to fail." Summer said, "The weapon can and will defend itself, no ship can withstand the sheer number of drones the defense system can deploy. What's worse is that we know nothing about what individual drones are capable of or what other defenses the weapon might have."

"We are acting now under the direct orders of the Ardent Provisional Assembly." Nir-RoDan said, "Placing me in the position of confronting the organization I founded less than a week ago. The Ardent people will forgive one rebellion, but a second will not be supported so easily. I always thought retirement would be a time of rest."

"Can you two stall Vinograd?" I asked, "Or get her to see reason?"

"I have tried, but her mind is set," Nathan said. "She sees this situation as an opportunity to gain political capital. I believe it may take a strong dose of reality for her to see clearly, but in this situation that comes at an extremely high price."

"All the more reason to tread carefully." Tan-Mara said. "Rebellion often comes with consequences that cannot be predicted."

"Nathan is in the best position to influence her actions at this point." Summer said. "We will be in a stronger position to act once it becomes clear that her plan is flawed. Assuming we survive the day."

Chapter 37 Annihilating Light

The Ardent Priests named it the Sword of the Reclaimer. It is an engine of pure destruction, a star killer and a world ender. For decades, it has loomed in the Ardent night skies as an ever-present reminder of the staggering authority and power of the Priest caste. Only the loyalist Technicians knew the secrets of its function and the scope of its immense power. Those who built it were slain by the very Priests they obediently served, without question or concern for the consequences of their actions. The daunting task now fell to us Earth Humans and the Ardent to rid ourselves of this behemoth of destruction and wipe it from the night sky. In the face of something so powerful, there is a temptation to lose hope. Nir-RoDan once said that who we are becomes most evident in times of great crisis, when it seems like everything is working to oppose us. Once again, humanity stands at the precipice of change, walking the blade's edge between survival and extinction. Aboard the Karma, Nathan made his plea for Vinograd to reconsider undertaking this mission.

"Commander," Nathan said. "When the weapon's defenses activate, nothing will stand between us and those defensive swarms. We have over six hundred thousand combat drones at our disposal that we can use to cover our attack. Without them we will be facing the full force of the weapon's defensive capabilities. Commander, I ask that you take a moment to reconsider."

"We're out of time Leopold! Your team had their chance. The fact is no one is in control of that weapon. Zen-Overen and the Priest cast have tied our hands. The Earth Senate and the Ardent Provisional Assembly have already approved this mission. I am confident that our combined forces assault will be swift and decisive. A direct approach is the only way we can hope to stop it to save our world now."

"Commander," Nathan said. "Again, I ask that you take a moment to reconsider."

"Your objection is noted Mr. Leopold." Vinograd said. "I will take it under advisement."

As the fleet approached the Ardent weapon, I was overcome with dread. Its scale was massive, its technology was incomprehensible. Much like my experience with the Guardian you could feel its power even from a distance. Summer had studied the weapon for years and was captivated by it, standing to her feet before the display ring.

"Providence hold position," Summer commanded. "Show me the weapons plasma dynamics."

We held station just outside of what was believed to be the outer edge of its defensive perimeter. This was as close as the fleet could safely come without activating the weapons powerful and largely unknown defenses.

"Look at the flow patterns in the coronal plasma." Summer said, "You see those dark filament cavities? Those are being shaped and conditioned by the weapons focusing pedals. Can you imagine the technology required to control complex fusion reactions at this scale? The ability to manipulate a star's internal physics and energy output in this way is, beyond us to say the least."

"Providence, what is the maximum yield of your anti-matter ordnance?" I asked.

"One hundred thousand exatons per device." Providence replied.

"Packs a far bigger punch than Angelica." I said. "I just hope it's enough to do the job."

The Providence display ring was filled with the glowing image of the Ardent Weapon, its details now more vivid than ever. A deep yellowish-white orb hung silently before us, casting a glow across the command deck. Plasma filaments arose like golden dragons from a violent sea of fire as massive solar storms crested and collapsed back into the star, merging, and splitting apart as waves of coronal discharge rippled toward its now darkened outer edges. Millions of overlapping storms within the chromosphere churned and boiled like a restless sea, rising, twisting, and forming ropes of charged particles hundreds of thousands of miles in length. Immense gravitational forces soon overcame the rising plumes of energy as coronal mass traveled along the lines of the star's gravitational field. The star's photosphere shifted, its patterns becoming strangely geometric as it moved closer to the weapon's hyperspace rings. Overlapping moiré patterns covered the photosphere as the weapon's focusing petals split open into four sections, revealing an enigmatic, organic, nervous system-like structure within. The massive petals shifted in color and brightness, becoming nearly translucent as they orbited with ever-increasing speed around the star. Plasma discharge danced between the separated petal sections, arcing around and underneath them. As each section oscillated in coordination with the plasma storms below, they moved closer to one another, only to separate and move closer again. As the weapon entered its final initialization sequence, its massive hyperspace rings began to expand, telescoping outward, one emerging from the inner edge of the other, forming three separate counter-rotating sets of spinning rings. The focusing petals orbiting the star's equatorial region increased their speed and counter-rotation, churning and shaping the star's coronal mass. The Providence shook with each approaching wave, jolting the ship with ever-increasing intensity. Those standing soon took seats as they formed from the floor beneath us.

"Providence, what is causing that turbulence?" I asked.

"The gravitational wavefront emanating from the weapon is playing havoc with my gravitic drive, attempting to compensate. Incoming fleet message from commander Vinograd of the Karma."

"First wave, target the weapons focusing pedals, fire!"

Nir-RoDan's ship, the Liberator, unleashed ten high yield antimatter devices by fold transporting them to the separation gap between the pedals as they detonated. The Karma followed with another volley of anti-matter ordnance of equally destructive power. As the massive antimatter blast passed over the fleet, space flashed with annihilating light.

"Providence, what is the status of the weapon?" Summer asked.

"Ten focusing pedals have been severely damaged." Providence said, "The weapon's power levels have stabilized. The firing sequence has been halted."

Finally, a sign of hope we all felt relieved as we watched one of the petals fall from orbit and burn up in the star's chromosphere. The focusing ring's counter-rotation slowed to a near standstill. Summer's eyes were fixed on the weapon's power levels and its interaction with the star. My human eyes couldn't perceive the deeper, more complex patterns she could, nor could my mind make the same predictive calculations of which she was capable. I saw a chaotic storm of energy; I could only imagine what Summer saw when she looked at those same images.

"Warning!" Providence said. "The weapons defense systems have been activated. It is launching attack drones."

"How many?" I asked.

"All of them." Providence replied, "I advise an immediate tactical retreat."

"No, hold position." Summer replied. "Attention second and third wave ships standby! Take no action."

"They are closing in on the Liberator and the Karma." I said.

"I can see that." Summer said.

The Providence ring display lit up with an encroaching swarm of red indicators as millions of attack drones targeted the Liberator and the Karma. The Liberator launched another volley of antimatter ordnance into the path of the advancing drones, coordinating its barrage with the Karma. For every drone destroyed, new ones reformed from the wreckage of their predecessors. The swarm pressed forward, dismantling both the Karma and Nir-RoDan's ship, deck by deck. Explosions rippled through their cores as streams of drones tore into one side and emerged out the other. It wouldn't be long before both ships were completely destroyed.

"Lead ships are taking massive critical damage." Providence said, "The drones are consuming the vessels for raw materials, using their mass to create replacement drones. The Karma cannot regenerate at this rate of physical destruction."

The drone swarms tore through the Karma, shredding large sections of the ship as explosions erupted across its decks. Nir-RoDan's battle cruiser unleashed its remaining arsenal in all directions, obliterating hundreds of drones. Yet thousands more swarmed, overwhelming both ships as they veered away from the fleet.

"Why aren't they attacking the rest of the fleet?" I asked.

"Because we never fired on the weapon." Summer said. "The lead ships in the first wave did. Nir-RoDan, Vinograd get out of there! Get out of there now!"

"This is the Karma; I have sustained critical damage. Multiple hull breaches on all decks, damage is extensive.

"They are being ripped apart out there!" I said. "We have to do something!"

"Vinograd" Summer said. Launch all available combat drones to cover your retreat and regroup with the fleet! This is not winnable. Vinograd? Nir-RoDan? Nathan?"

"Providence why aren't they responding? Summer asked.

"The Karma's structural integrity has reached the regenerative design limit." Providence said. "It does not have sufficient source material for Construct matter replication and therefore cannot self-repair. The Liberator has sustained multiple hull breaches. The damage to both ships is extensive. Critical failure of the Karma's dark energy reactor cores is imminent."

"This is the Karma critical hull breaches on multiple decks. Vinograd, Nathan and my entire bridge crew have been lost."

"Karma launch whatever remaining combat drones you have now!" Summer said.

"Drones are away," Karma said. "Attention, all crew abandon ship immediately!"

"The Liberator has launched its remaining combat drones." Providence said. "Nir-RoDan is using them to draw fire away from the escape pods, reactor breach is imminent."

"Lower the shields," Summer said. "Prepare to receive the survivors of the Karma and the Liberator."

In an instant, my friend Nathan was gone, wiped out along with the entire bridge crew of the Karma. Nir-RoDan's and his crew aboard the Liberator was in serious trouble as both were now overwhelmed by the sheer number and destructive power of the weapons defensive drone swarms. We watched helplessly as flocks of millions of drones systematically dismantled the lead ships swarming and enveloping their hulls like fire ants. The focusing pedals began to glow and expand as their shape morphed and shifted. Each pedal segment changing its configuration as it began moving at an ever-increasing velocity around the star. Within seconds, the fast-orbiting pedals formed a solid ring of light around the perimeter of the weapon. Its energy output was now entirely synchronized with the star's plasma flow patterns. A bright flash in the distance overwhelmed the battle space as the Karma's reactor core went critical. Nir-RoDan's ship reoriented its position to avoid the wreckage of what now remained of the Karma. Its enormous gravitational wave engines propelled the massive capital ship toward the weapon. Nir-RoDan was now set on a collision course with the weapons focusing rings. His image appeared garbled and distorted, but you could clearly see that most of the bridge had been torn away and was now exposed to open space. Nir-Rodan placed a confinement shield around his immediate area on the bridge and was still in command piloting the ship himself.

"Master what are you doing?" Tan-Mara asked.

"All remaining survival pods have been launched!" Nir-RoDan said. "Our vessel's synthetic intelligence has been destroyed! I am the last of the last! This ship is now under manual control! You know what that means, Tan-Mara! Save my crew and get as far away from the drone swarm as possible!"

"No! I am coming for you!" Tan-Mara said, "I know what you are planning, do not do this, please!, I am coming for you."

"Save my crew and save yourself, Tan-Mara! As a Warrior, I accept my fate, the Forgotten Clan needs you, your daughter needs you, our people need you. If you attempt to save me now, you will only attract the swarm, and all will be lost! Now go!"

Tan-Mara struggled to pilot her ship past the wreckage of the Karma and the maelstrom of destruction that surrounded it, each time narrowly avoiding the wrecks of other heavily damaged ships that hammered away at her shields. "I cannot lose you. I cannot and I will not!" Tan-Mara said as she tried to escape the storm of debris separating her from Nir-RoDan's ship. With her shields weakened, she was forced back toward the fleet. The weapon's defensive drone swarm turned and headed straight for Nir-RoDan's vessel. Nir-RoDan's ship was completely covered with hundreds of thousands of enemy drones, tearing it apart as it headed at full speed toward the focusing rings. The Karma was gone, Nir-RoDan's mangled and burning ship fired its remaining beam weapons in all directions attracting more drones and distracting them from the retreating survivors.

"Little one" Nir-RoDan said, "Listen to me, do you remember the "Book of Circle and Song"?

"Great Teacher, I beg you, don't do this."

"From the word came the song," Nir-RoDan said. *"From the song came the dance,*

From the dance came the fight."

"From the fight came the warrior," Tam-Mara replied, *"From the warrior came the war, From the war came victory."*

"From victory came peace," Nir-RoDan said, *"From peace came balance, From balance came beauty."*

"From beauty came words," Tan-Mara replied, *"From the word came the song."*

Nir-RoDan's ship collided with the focusing rings as the Liberator's reactor cores went critical resulting in a massive explosion. Tan-Mara screamed with a terrifying wail as she witnessed her mentor's last moments. In an instant Nir-RoDan was consumed in a blinding wall of annihilating light. Summer closed her eyes while the Providence bridge crew froze in place. Some cried, others stood motionless in shock. I found myself crouched down beside my chair. The entire fleet was completely transfixed, stunned into silence as the Ardent people's greatest warrior, general, and trainer sacrificed himself to save his crew and the Alliance fleet. The pure white light of the explosion blended with the yellow glow of the star's photosphere as the blast wave moved through space, consuming all the weapons' remaining defensive drones. When the flashover cleared, the focusing rings, although severely damaged, started to regenerate, reforming as the weapon began to self-repair resuming its power up sequence. The counter-rotating rings began spinning with increasing speed each moving in opposition to one another, matching the rotation of the focusing pedals as it orbited the star. It was unstoppable now, as the weapon finally reached maximum power. The star was now completely under the weapon's influence as its coronal mass began to swirl up from its surface, forming a helix-shaped energy funnel that rose toward the focusing rings. The weapon opened a massive hyperspace window to the Solar system. Our Sun and humanity's home were now clearly visible on the other side. The beautiful blue-green jewel of our world was about to come to a swift and catastrophic end, and there was little we could do but stand by and watch in horror. The nightmare we had all feared and fought against for so long had arrived, it was unstoppable. The seventh and final extinction was now upon us. The Providence bridge crew stood to their feet as they realized what was about to occur, as did Ardent having never seen the mythical planet called Earth. Despite all our work, despite all our advanced Construct and Ardent technology, we were utterly helpless in the face of such overwhelming and unrelenting power. Unable to avoid the cruel, senseless destruction of our world as the Ardent weapon targeted the core of our Sun and fired directly into the hyperspace window.

Chapter 38 The Final Extinction

An enormous stream of coronal mass, plasma and energy flowed into the hyperspace window heading directly for our Sun. As the focused beam penetrated through to the other side it was met by something which took the full force of the weapon's destructive output. The massive stream of energy flowed from the weapon for nearly three minutes yet never reached our sun. The weapon's focused beam was completely absorbed as if it had been fired into a black hole. Something of truly unimaginable power was working its way up through the beam, crossing the hyperspace window's event horizon back into Ardent space.

"That shouldn't be possible." I said.

"Yet there it is." Summer replied, "The Guardian."

The Guardian absorbed all the star's power leveraging the coronal mass, plasma, and energy to increase its size, which now appeared thousands of times larger than it did in the cavern where it was found. The weapon's firing sequence ended as the Guardian extended its arms and legs into a position eerily reminiscent of Da Vinci's Vitruvian man. As it did so, it released a massive burst of energy, within seconds all ships in the fleet both Human and Ardent lost power. The Guardian was somehow sequestering and altering all dark energy in the local region of space towards its own unknown purposes. Now I understood the meaning of the crumbled stone relief at New Tijara, this was not the first time the Guardian had intervened on behalf of the human species. The cycle of history once again repeats itself and like the armored warriors depicted in the stone relief from so many centuries ago, we too stood in awe of the Guardian's incomprehensible power. The weapon's focusing pedals disintegrated into millions of shattered fragments. The hyperspace focusing rings rotation slowed and collapsed back into themselves as they shattered, breaking into millions of shards joining the maelstrom of exotic matter now hurdling in orbit around the star. The massive hyperspace window to Earth's sun collapsed and vanished. The Alliance fleet was now completely disabled, drifting in space with minimal reserve power, just enough to maintain gravity, sensors, and life support systems.

Within moments there was not just one Guardian on the Providence display, but two seconds later, the two became four. As we watched, the four became eight, then sixteen, then thirty-two, then sixty-four, then one hundred and twenty-eight, then two-hundred and fifty-six. All of them linked together forming a chain millions of miles in length. More Guardians appeared as it replicated itself exponentially, forming a massive spherical grid of interlocking entities that grew and encased the entirety of the star locking it into an enormous onyx sphere of interconnected structures. The sphere began to rotate with ever-increasing speed. The Guardian was not destroying the weapon, on the contrary, it was transforming it, remaking the weapon and the star at its center into something fundamentally different from its original design, something truly extraordinary. The Guardians' replication of itself doubled and there now appeared to be a secondary sphere of Guardian entities moving in opposition to the smaller spheres already surrounding and encasing the entirety of the star. They continued to replicate until they formed multiple nested spheres, each larger than the next, spinning and counter-rotating relative to its inner and outer spheres.

"Providence, what is it doing?" I asked.

"The Guardian entity appears to be altering the weapons design."

"Yes, but into what?" I asked.

"I don't know," Summer said, "But we are about to find out."

The Guardian spheres' density grew to such a degree that there appeared to be a single seamless black sphere in the place of the Ardent weapon completely obscuring all the star's light output. Our sensors could not penetrate the sphere and we could only imagine what processes were taking place inside. This scale of stellar manipulation was well beyond both Human and Ardent capabilities. This was the technology of a type four civilization capable of manipulating the dark energy of the universe at will. Even this astounding ability seemed trivial for the Guardian. We were like children watching a master craftsman at work.

The star was no longer a star in the conventional sense, instead it now appeared to be a black sphere identical in composition to the material that the Guardian itself was made of. Ship power onboard the Providence resumed along with that of the rest of the fleet as the perturbation of dark energy in the surrounding region of space returned to normal.

"Providence." I asked, "What the hell is that?"

"Analysis indicates it is a Dyson sphere." Providence replied, "Our sister ship and Ardent fleet commanders are hailing us."

"We have to tell them something Summer."

"Agreed, Alliance fleet this is Summer Wake of the Providence. I am taking command of the Earth fleet. The threat to our worlds has been neutralized. However, our situation, as you can see has significantly changed. I order all ship commanders in the Earth fleet to stand down, take no action."

"This is Bre-Kylah, I concur, we need time to assess this new development. Ardent fleet stand down and await further instructions."

"Thank you, Grand Matriarch," Summer said.

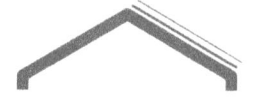

Chapter 39 The Black Sphere

Hours passed and none of us knew what to make of the black sphere that hung silently before the fleet. This technology was far beyond our collective understanding. We sent in hundreds of drones and probes, but they appeared to simply vanish into the darkness of the sphere's shifting surface. We watched as the black sphere comprised of millions of interlocking Guardian entities began to move, shift, and transform. A wave rippled across its surface, from the center to the outer edges. For a moment, the sphere's surface exhibited a liquid-like quality the result of gravitic manipulation of some kind bending ambient star light around the contour of the sphere.

"Detecting unusual particle and radio emissions." Providence said, "The sphere is opening."

Sharp lines formed on the sphere's surface, dividing it into sixteen distinct leaves, forming an iris identical to the black door that protected the underground cavern where the Guardian was discovered. The star was no longer a star; it was now merely the power source for something entirely different and far more powerful. Analysis indicated that the Guardian had somehow transformed the Ardent weapon into something new. Probes were launched toward the sphere to investigate, but each one simply vanished. Considering this new development, the Ardent Provisional Assembly convened a meeting on board the Providence with the remaining Earth Senate to determine a course of action for this new development. Bre-Kylah was in attendance along with Tan-Mara and her second in command. Vinograd's surviving assistant Kaleb Silva now served as commander in her place.

"I would like to take the Angelica to investigate the object." I said.

"Absolutely not!" Tan-Mara insisted, "Death could await you. This thing has already taken the lives of your senator, Nathan and Nir-RoDan."

"We have no idea what that thing is," Summer said, "I am not sending anyone in there without knowing a hell of a lot more about what we are dealing with."

"I reviewed the sphere records of your discovery of the Guardian chamber back on Earth." Kaleb said. "Once you entered the facility the iris door closed behind you. What if the same thing happens here?"

"The fact of the matter is our sensors are largely useless," I said, "Our drones have been unresponsive. Without a degree of risk, we cannot grow our knowledge. Now I can take a small team of humans and Ardent inside the sphere to investigate and report on what we find."

"It's dangerous Lucas." Tan-Mara said. "You would be walking into a completely unknown situation."

"If the Guardian wanted to destroy us, it could have easily done so. Instead, it chose to create this. In my view, this is an invitation. Is this not what the people of Earth, Ardah, and countless other civilizations have been looking for? To find the Masters? To contact the Progenitors? The creation of this object may very well be one of the most important events in the history of our Galaxy. Moments like this demand that we rise to the call of history. Now we can passively scan this object all we want, but we won't know anything more unless we take the risk and choose to go inside."

Epilogue

With the threat to Earth and Ardah now past, our people returned to Earth to complete work on the re-establishment of our civilization. Many Ardent Tera-Theorists now vindicated chose to emigrate to Earth as a testament to their long-held beliefs about Ardent origins. Many from the Forgotten Clan also relocated to Earth to rebuild and seek a new life on a new world. Many Purists from Earth having experienced the hidden paradise of Hafeeta chose to remain behind and build a life there. Under Tan-Mara's leadership the Forgotten Clan began the slow reintegration back into Ardent Society and now enjoyed full legal rights as Ardent Citizens. Families separated for decades were reunited with their kin, tribesmen and loved ones. Most were welcomed back into their tribes having had their honor and family names officially restored. Unfortunately, Tan-Mara lost more than most during the civil war. She lost her husband whom she loved so dearly. She lost her mentor and teacher Nir-RoDan and Nathan, a person she had known her entire life. Yet, despite it all she persevered and continued the work her husband started. As part of the promise made by Nir-RoDan during the rebellion, the Ardent Provisional Assembly granted amnesty to High Council members and guards that took part in the revolution. The remaining corrupt High Council members, Priest Caste loyalists and religious Zealots were captured and resettled on the prison moon of Orna to live out their remaining days in exile far from the rest of Ardent society. As for now, former chancellor Zen-Overen remains at large. Many believe he is hiding somewhere in the remote outer rim colonies. Hundreds of Seekers from the three worlds have been dispatched under Duty Mark to track him down and bring him to justice. The Earth Senate and the Ardent Provisional Assembly forged a new alliance and began the construction of a joint scientific research station in orbit around the iris of the Black Sphere. The Progenitor Initiative was a program comprised of Earth scientists and Ardent Technicians tasked with understanding the Black Spheres' underlying technology. A memorial was built in the Ardent capital bearing the names of men and women both Human and Ardent that lost their lives during the battle of the Black Sphere. A towering solid light image of Nir-RoDan stood in the center of the memorial with an account of his heroic actions in combat along with the now famous quote he became known for throughout his many decades of service to the Ardent people. Most notably; "Friendship, strength and peace that is Ardent, that is who we are." I missed my good friend Nathan, and I couldn't believe he was gone. Construct immortality is not quite the same as invincibility he will always be remembered. I would like to have known Merrick and Nir-RoDan better and although I knew neither of them for long, I still cared for them and will miss them. Summer officially transferred command of the Providence to Kaleb Silva for its return trip to Earth. Together we remained on Ardah with the Angelica while awaiting permission from the Progenitor Initiative to begin our proposed mission to enter the Black Sphere. After centuries of persuasion, I finally convinced Summer to join me on the bike. We enjoyed our time exploring Ardah and the other core worlds. Within weeks of its appearance the Ardent were contacted by long estranged members of the human diaspora and many non-human species whose hyper-dimensional astronomers had detected this new celestial object. Hundreds of representatives and ships arrived on the edge of Ardent space each with a flurry of questions. What is the Black Sphere? How was it created? What is its purpose? Was it made by The Masters? The Progenitors, The Ancient Ones? Each had a name for the enigmatic, all-powerful race that had preserved and influenced intelligent life across three galaxies for as long as any race could recall. It seemed that life on Ardah and Earth was about to get a lot more interesting.

End of Book One

About the Author

My name is Kenneth E. Harrell, and I am a cybersecurity engineer with over three decades of professional experience in the technology field. Born in Oakland, California, I grew up in the vibrant Bay Area. I hold advanced degrees in Information Systems, Information Technology, and Information Security and Organizational Leadership, along with extensive training in Artificial Intelligence and Machine Learning. Currently, I reside in Northern California with my wife of twenty years. I have always been captivated by three things: dreams of the ancient past, fascination with the present, and visions of a distant future. To me, the past, present, and future are inextricably linked. Ancient history speaks to us through mythology, legend, and symbolism, telling stories about who we were and where we have been. The present is where history is made and futures are forged, as events unfold in repeating cycles, carrying us toward unknown possibilities. Science fiction challenges us to dream of future worlds both wondrous and cautionary, serving as a mythological warning from some distant place further up the path from a future that has yet to unfold. In my work, I enjoy weaving together ideas, metaphors, scientific concepts, fictional histories, and imagined world scenarios. I believe that history happens in real-time. Our present actions, words, and writings matter because the future is always watching.